The Truth Serum

My Lady's Potions, Book 2

Katherine Lyons

ARE YOU SIGNED UP FOR DRAGONBLADE'S BLOG?

You'll get the latest news and information on exclusive giveaways, exclusive excerpts, coming releases, sales, free books, cover reveals and more.

Check out our complete list of authors, too!

No spam, no junk. That's a promise!

Sign Up Here

www.dragonbladepublishing.com

Dearest Reader;

Thank you for your support of a small press. At Dragonblade Publishing, we strive to bring you the highest quality Historical Romance from some of the best authors in the business. Without your support, there is no 'us', so we sincerely hope you adore these stories and find some new favorite authors along the way.

Happy Reading!

CEO, Dragonblade Publishing

Additional Dragonblade books by
Author Katherine Lyons

My Lady's Potions Series
The Love Potion (Book 1)
The Truth Serum (Book 2)
The Beauty Serum (Book 3)

Rogues Gambit Series
Rules for a Fake Fiancé (Book 1)
Rules for a Bastard Lord (Book 2)
Rules for a Wicked Wager (Book 3)

Prologue

Cornwall, 1795

"BUT WHAT ARE you going to do?"

Lord Nathanial, third son of Earl of Killeagh, looked up into the sky to contemplate the question. He wasn't going to answer Becca's question out loud. He was a man of action, he told himself. He was going to kiss her.

Today.

He'd been thinking about it for weeks now, planning for just this moment. It was a beautiful summer afternoon, they were down by the creek supposedly studying Paul's letters to the Thessalonians after the parish children had been called home by their mother. Which left them blissfully alone.

Now was his moment, and yet he couldn't quite do it. First, he needed to inch closer. He shifted off the rock to settle on the blanket beside her. It was an awkward motion, and he was sure she knew what he was about. After all, she shot him a playful look under her bonnet. But then she repeated her question, this time with more force.

"Seriously, Nate. If you won't go into the clergy—"

"Ugh," he groaned, cutting her off. "You know I'd be a disaster there." He couldn't sit still through a Sunday service. How was he going to live the life of a priest? The most exciting thing they got to do was drink wine. He could do that without getting frocked.

"The military then—"

He kicked at a rock and watched it splash into the stream.

"There isn't enough money to buy two commissions. Simon's older, he's planned for this forever, and—"

"Your grandmother wants you baptizing all the parish babies."

He rolled his eyes. His grandmother had lots of ideas about his future, none of which interested him. Fortunately, the only person who listened to her was the vicar, and Nate had been fobbing that man off for years.

"Maybe I want to spend my days reading books with you."

Her expression softened. "Wouldn't that be wonderful?"

The only thing better would be kissing her. A lot.

"What does your father think?"

That school was expensive. That his mother spent too much money in London. That the farmers weren't working hard enough, which was a lie. Whenever Nate wasn't "studying with the vicar" (his own lie so he could spend time with Becca), he was helping with the crops or the pigs or repairing someone's roof—endless tasks for their tenants in the hopes that it would turn the family's finances around.

It hadn't so far, but maybe this would be the year that everything worked out.

And with that thought in mind, he turned his attention back to the beautiful Lady Rebecca. Auburn hair, blue eyes, and one dimple on her left cheek. She thought her nose too big and her hair too curly beneath her demure bonnet, but all he'd thought about for the last month was kissing her full lips and touching her sweet curves.

She was nothing like he'd been taught to expect. Thanks to the feud between their families, he'd expected her to be a shriveled prune with hoary skin and a devil's tail. She'd been taught to expect the same of him.

But the vicar was a reforming sort. He thought a feud between the two reigning families was an invitation to the devil. So he'd conspired to get the earl's youngest son (Nate) and the viscount's youngest daughter (Becca) into a friendship.

That had been three summers ago. Becca's family had been told she was teaching the village children their letters. Nate's family had been informed that he must study the Bible in preparation for the clergy. Then the two children had discovered that their activities occurred in the same location, and the vicar had been lax in his supervision. He'd even given them their first novel to read, as long as they read a chapter of the Bible for every chapter in the book.

This was their fourth summer together, and Nate was determined to end the feud for good. He was going to kiss her. He was thinking about marrying her. But first, he had to see if she was amenable.

"Nate!" Becca said, her voice light despite her frown. "You're seventeen. What are you going to do when you graduate?"

"Become a pirate," he quipped. "I'm going to sail the seven seas, gather booty, and rescue stolen princesses." So saying, he grabbed her ever-present stitching and pulled it from her hands.

"I don't know that there are very many stolen princesses to rescue." Her brows were arched, her expression coy, but he knew her moods as well as his own. He knew she was as tired of mending clothing as he was of Paul's letters to the Thessalonians.

"I'll find one," he said as he drew closer to her. "Maybe one with golden locks and rosy cheeks. Someone who is sick to death of tending to the poor. Someone who wants a life of adventure."

She tilted her head, her eyes sparkling. "Adventure, you say? That doesn't sound at all proper."

"Which is why you like it."

"No," she said as she lifted her chin. "That's why *you* like it. I'm a proper girl."

"Liar," he accused, as he drew closer.

"Never," she countered, but she didn't draw away.

He could smell the lemon scent on her hair, but it was the sweet catch of her breath that drew him. Her cheeks flushed rose and her lips parted.

"Becca," he whispered. "If I were a pirate, I'd whisk you away from here."

She leaned toward him. "Where would we go?"

"To my ship, where I would clothe you in pearls."

"Pearls? That's hardly clothing."

"It would be for you. Just pearls. Nothing else." He stroked a finger up the side of her arm, watching the goosebumps trail in his wake.

"Pearls are very impractical."

"That's why I like them."

"What if I don't like pearls? What if I prefer silk?"

He frowned. "Since when don't you like pearls?"

"Since when do I love silk?"

"Always! You called it the most heavenly fabric in existence. Ever since your mother brought a bolt back from London."

She stared at him. "You remember that?"

Of course he did. He remembered everything about her. "It's hard to forget," he drawled. "You went on and on and on—"

"I did not!" she cried. She made to hit him on the shoulder, but she missed because he had seen the movement coming. Indeed, he'd known she would do it, and so he caught her hand and then rolled away from her.

She went with him because he was pulling her forward. And when she lost her balance, he spread his arms wide so she would land on his chest.

"Oh my," she whispered. "I believe I have been caught by a wicked pirate."

His expression grew serious. "Have you? Have you truly?"

He caressed her cheek, then pulled her bonnet ribbons apart. She tugged it off her head. Her hair spilled down, rich and luxurious, but his gaze remained locked on hers.

"I don't know," she said. "Are you a wicked pirate?"

"Absolutely." He threaded his fingers through her hair and drew her down to his mouth. It was a fumbling kind of kiss. Too much pressure, then too little, then a slow maneuvering between them both. He let her settle, and she let him tease her lips with his tongue.

They soon got the hang of it, and he had never been happier. Never, until the next afternoon by the creek. Or the next morning behind the vicarage. Or any of a million stolen moments they spent debating his future while pretending to study theology.

Unlike him, her path was set. She was the daughter of a wealthy viscount who would marry a titled gentleman and have a pack of fat, happy babies. She might express interest in plants and medicine, but her destiny was as a wife and mother.

His future, however, was murky, wholly dependent upon if his family could find the money to send him to university. And of course, what would he study there, when he'd much rather be out sailing the high seas or training with a bayonet? Mostly, he wanted to be with her because she asked him questions no one else asked.

Was it fair for the magistrate to take away Farmer John's pig just because he'd stolen it from Farmer Tom? John had raised it like a family member for two years. Didn't two years of care and feeding count for anything?

Who was the guilty party when a lame veteran stole to feed his family?

Was it safe to use heavy sauces when the meat has gone off? Especially if one could not afford better food?

And why did he always answer her with kisses rather than admit he had no answer?

Because he loved the taste of her lips. Because she gasped when he touched her breasts, and he adored the dazed look in her eyes when he showed her how to feel good.

And because one day, he would marry her and end the ridiculous feud between their two families. She was an heiress. Her dowry property was large and on the coast. It would sustain them both, especially since he had skill in managing crops and tenants. And where better to learn about piracy than from there?

So he kissed her whenever he could. He stroked her breasts whenever she allowed it. And because he was a gentleman, he held back from the rest. Though he whispered to her about it. He told her, in great detail, the things that married couples did. He'd learned them from his older brothers, and he planned to discover them all with her.

And she was willing.

Until the day they were caught.

That was the day that the vicar lost his position. It was also the same day Rebecca's father had a heart attack and died.

And the very next day, Nate was sent for "special education" with the Foreign Office.

Chapter One

London, 1815

LADY REBECCA TUCKED away her novel and dismounted from the travelling carriage, breathing deeply of the London air despite the coal dust that hung everywhere. She was out of the carriage and away from her mother—for a moment—and that was cause for relief. As was the idea that she would be able to get a new book soon. Indeed, she couldn't wait to get to the lending library. But first—

"Don't just stand there!" her mother called. "Help me out!"

Rebecca sighed. First, she had to get her mother settled in their London home. She smiled, reminding herself that she was moments away from locking herself in her room to read. She just had to get through this final bit.

"Here you go, Mama," she said as she extended her hand. A footman stood by her side, his own gloved hand outstretched. Together, they got the Countess of Estril safely onto the street outside their Mayfair townhouse.

"Where is Fletcher? He was supposed to meet us here."

"I'm sure he'll show up soon," Rebecca lied. She wasn't sure of any such thing, but her mother liked to believe everyone was at her beck and call. And sometimes she was right.

Like now, when Fletcher appeared at the front door and then condescended to come greet them halfway down the walk. His expression was pulled into his habitual smile, one that never reached his eyes and often missed his tone.

"Welcome," he said as he pressed a kiss to her cheek.

"Hello Fletch—"

"Mama!" he cried with all semblance of enthusiasm. "How can it be that after all those hours of travel, you look as if you are freshly stepped from the boudoir?"

"Oh stop with those Frenchie terms," Mama chided. "We're at war with them, you know."

"Have we ever stopped?" her brother quipped.

"All the more reason to call it my bedchamber."

"Absolutely not!" her brother said, his brows arching. "You shall never hear me refer to such a location that way, as it pertains to my beautiful mother. Come inside. I've made sure the tea is ready."

Their mother dimpled prettily and allowed Fletcher to escort her into the house. Rebecca was left to watch the baggage to make sure it was adequately unloaded and sent to the right rooms. Normally this would be the job of the butler, but he seemed to be occupied elsewhere. Didn't matter. She knew how to direct servants. Just because their London home was Fletcher's primary establishment, that didn't mean she was unprepared. And truthfully, she relished the moments away from her mother.

"Rebecca! Quit dawdling and come here. Fletcher has things to tell you."

"Coming Mama," she replied, feeling a twinge of guilt because she had been lingering. "Are you feeling chilled?" she asked as she entered the house. "Shall I fetch your shawl?"

"Chilled?" her mother said, rolling her eyes. "It's perfectly warm in here. Now come listen to what Fletcher has to tell you."

Rebecca dutifully crossed into the parlor to face her second brother. How handsome he was, she realized, as he stood right where the sun would turn his hair to burnished gold. But his face was sour, and his words likely moreso. She didn't know what had happened to the sweet boy he'd been. As an adult, Fletcher was a pompous ass. Nevertheless, he was her second older brother, and she was unmarried. Custom dictated that she must listen to him, and she did. She just didn't always obey.

Rebecca faced him, gave him the tiniest bit of her attention, and began thinking about something else entirely. She'd already realized that her best friends from school were away this Season, but maybe some of their younger sisters were around.

"Yes, Fle—"

"I've done a great deal to arrange your visit to London. I've told all the right people that you're here. I know Mama would like to rest this evening and I haven't the time to squire you about today anyway, but it's time to get serious about marriage."

She bristled at the statement but didn't interrupt. It only caused more delays. Besides, he was right. She was much older than most girls in their come-out, and though she'd been to London on and off for the last five years, she'd never caught a husband. And now, at twenty-seven years old, she was technically on the shelf, but she still had hopes. Fortunately, she'd sent her measurements ahead, and several gowns should be waiting for her upstairs.

"I should be happy to accompany you tomorrow," she said, hoping it was true.

"Good. I've primed the pump with several gentlemen, and thanks to your dowry, you should take with one of them. But you must follow my directions."

Follow his directions? "Fletch, I'm perfectly capable of selecting my own husband—"

Her brother dropped down to one knee before her, his expression kind even if his words were not. "I don't want to hurt you, but it's time for plain speaking, don't you think?" He turned on that last bit, his brow arched at their mother.

Right on cue, Mama sighed and nodded. "He's right, dear. You've had five Seasons to find a husband."

"Interrupted Seasons, late start Seasons," Rebecca reminded them, but Fletcher squeezed her hands to silence her.

"And you've always gone for the wrong kind of gentleman. *Always*."

She winced. Always her family returned to her indiscretion

when she was sixteen. They had good reason to. What she'd done was foolish and had had dire consequences. But why did one mistake when she was a teenager have to color her entire life?

"That was ten years ago," she said. "I'm a grown woman now."

"Of course you are," he soothed, "but you've led a sheltered life. You don't know London the way I do, and you certainly don't understand men. Add in your very large dowry, and every blackguard in England will be trying to seduce you."

"I know—"

"I won't let you fall for another rake or scoundrel."

She hadn't fallen for anyone. She'd never had the chance. As soon as she showed a partiality to anyone, she'd been whisked away back to Cornwall because Mama fell ill or something had to be managed there. Bad timing or ill luck didn't matter. She'd ended up aging another year with no appropriate suitor. Even this Season was already underway because Fletcher had said he couldn't find the time to escort her until now.

"I'll be careful," she said. "I'm not so gullible—"

He sighed and truly looked apologetic as he began listing off all the gentlemen she'd shown some partiality toward. "Do you recall Mr. O'Brien? Debtor's prison right now. How about that Van Der Berg gentleman? He was drummed out of society for scandalous activities. Then there was Lord Cholmondeley. At least he had a title, but what a rake! My dear, you fell for them all and if we hadn't gotten you back home, you'd be miserable right now, married to a wretch, and fat with his babe."

She looked away. She truly had enjoyed the company of those gentlemen. If they were now exposed as fortune hunters, then she really didn't know how to judge London company. And that thought ate at her confidence.

"I won't mention the men back home," he added with a repulsed shudder.

"There haven't been any," she snapped. Except for Nate, but that had been ten years ago.

"Nevertheless, you must see my point. You don't know anyone in London or how to judge their true intentions."

That wasn't exactly true. Her friends from school might not be here, but there were girls she'd met during other Seasons. Most were married with children now, but she planned to visit as many as she could. "I've been writing to several of my friends," she said. "If you would give me the schedule, I—"

"Yes, yes, of course I'll tell you the schedule. Every morning over breakfast, I'll tell you where you're going and who you'll meet. I've got it all planned, so you needn't worry about anything."

"I'm not worried—" she said.

"Good. Because I'm running for our seat in the House of Commons. There's a lot to do with managing that, meeting the right people, and greasing the right palms."

She winced. She didn't like to think that her government ran on bribes, but according to Fletcher, everyone everywhere wanted a bribe and only a fool would ignore that.

"Oh don't worry," Mama said as she beamed at Fletcher. "Henry will support you. You're very well thought of back home. You'll get the votes."

Henry was her oldest brother and the current viscount. He held his place in the House of Lords by virtue of being born first. Fletcher, on the other hand, had to make his political bones in the House of Commons, and that required the county to vote him in. And not everyone back home loved him.

Fletcher smiled. "You see me with the eyes of love, Mama. But in order for this family to prosper, we must all pitch in. And that means Rebecca cannot make a bad marriage."

"I don't intend to," she said, some of her pique showing through.

"And you won't," Fletcher returned, "I'll make sure of it. Henry has given me total control over the selection."

Unfortunately, that was true. Her oldest brother despised London, hated the social rounds, and wanted nothing more than to live in the country with his books. He knew as little as possible about the peerage and would follow Fletcher's advice in such things.

Nevertheless, she'd had to draw clear lines with both brothers over the years, and this was the clearest, darkest line she could imagine.

"You're not picking my husband," she said, her voice firm.

He sighed, the sound coming from deep inside him. "You want a husband, don't you? You don't want to molder away as a spinster, do you?"

"No," she admitted. "I don't, but—"

"Then you must let me guide you or you'll end with a fortune hunter or worse." His expression softened as he gave her a tender smile. "I will get you what you want. I promise."

"I'm twenty-seven. I know my own mind."

"Your mind killed our father," he shot back.

And there it was. The one thing she could never outgrow, outrun, or forget. Finding her and Nate half naked together had so shocked her father that he'd had a heart attack and died. From that moment on, nothing was the same. Suddenly burdened with the title, Henry had retreated into books and management, rarely to be seen beyond the borders of their estate. Fletcher had turned controlling, as if only he could manage things without disaster. Any deviation from his plans brought out his vicious temper.

Mama was the least changed. She'd relied on her husband for most things before. She now relied on her sons. And Rebecca was relegated to the one who had made the mistake, the one who had destroyed their family with her misjudgment. And the hell of it was...perhaps they were right. If what Fletcher had just said was true, then she truly did have terrible taste in men.

Before she could say anything more, the mantle clock chimed the hour. Fletcher looked up with a grimace.

"Damnation, I'm late." He pushed to his feet and pressed a quick kiss to their mother's cheek. "Mama, do get some rest. The Season will be taxing for you, I know. And Rebecca..." He patted her arm. "I hate that I have to disillusion you this way. I truly do, but never fear. I'm looking out for you. I'll see you married to someone worthy of our family."

Rebecca matched his movements, standing up to face him squarely. Or as squarely as she could, given that she was several inches shorter than he. "Fletcher, I know you mean well, but—"

She saw anger flash across his features, and she tensed. After their father had died, he'd had violent outbursts, but as far as she knew, he hadn't thrown anything or hit anyone in years. Still, the memory of his rage remained stark in her mind, so she offered him a conciliatory smile.

"Fletcher, I surely will listen to your advice." That's the most she could promise.

"I will take care of you," he said, the tightness in his jaw abruptly fading. "But of course, your wishes will be consulted throughout the process."

"Do you swear it?"

"Of course!" He pressed a hand to his heart. "Really, Becs, you wound me. And after all the trouble I'm going to on your behalf. I want you to have a lovely Season. I want you to marry well. You'll be such a beautiful bride." He grabbed her hands and drew them up to his mouth. "You'll love the gentleman I've selected. I'm sure of it."

Gentleman? Singular? "Who is he?"

"You'll meet him tomorrow night." He grinned. "I won't spoil the surprise."

Of course not. Fletcher did love the dramatic. "What if I don't like him?" she pressed.

"Then I'll find another one for you somewhere. Someone worthy of you."

"Thank y—"

"But you must understand that the field is shrinking. There aren't many gentlemen interested in an old wife."

"I'm not—"

"I've got it all arranged!" he said with excitement as he

pressed a kiss to her cheek. "It's going to be a whirlwind Season."

"A whirlwind?" her mother gasped. "Oh, I hope my health is strong enough for it."

"Well, that's why I'm here," he said. "Brothers are perfectly acceptable escorts." And with that, he whooshed out the door.

Rebecca watched him leave, her hands twisting together as the feel of his dry kiss lingered on her cheek. She didn't want to rely on her brother. She didn't want to rely on anyone, but he did have a point. She didn't know the members of the peerage, and it was hard to judge a man's character during a dance.

Who else could she rely on to give her good information?

She had no answer to that for a very long time. Indeed, it wasn't until late that night when she was talking with her maid that the girl offered up an alternative suggestion. It was a bad one, of course, but such was the nature of gossip and whispers.

"A truth serum?" she said as she stared at Missy. "You must be joking."

"Am not! It's been the talk of the *ton*."

Missy and a couple other servants had arrived in London three days ago. She'd been in charge of seeing that Rebecca's gowns were well made. And in that time, Missy had sought out all the London gossip.

"But whyever do you think that would work?" Rebecca pressed.

"Because that same apothecary gave the Duke of Harle a love potion. A couple dabs here and there, and poof! Miss Kynthea Petrelli is engaged to a duke! Their wedding is in a few weeks, just after the end of the Season."

"Because of a love potion? But if he knows—"

"Doesn't matter! He's besotted with her. It's the talk—"

"Of the *ton*. Yes, you've said. But that doesn't mean any-thing."

Missy sat down across from her mistress, her expression earnest.

"I heard your brother. We all did. You're an heiress, and all them London gents only want your money."

"Not every man is a fortune hunter."

"But how are you going to know the difference?" She patted Rebecca's knee. "Just tell me the word, and I'll pop over and get you the serum. You can drop it a gent's wine with no one the wiser. Then just ask him. Do you want me or my money?" Missy winked. "He'll answer with the truth and then you'll know."

"I can't go dosing a gentleman without his knowledge."

"Course you can. Just pour a good measure into a man's drink, wait twenty minutes, and then he'll tell you whatever you want to know."

"That's silly," Rebecca pronounced.

"Maybe," her maid returned. "And maybe not. How are you going to know if you don't try it?"

A truth serum? Rebecca shook her head. "I don't know..." she said.

"It's only a few quid," Missy said as she set Rebecca's purse in her hand. "What harm could it do?"

Plenty. She knew enough about medicines and supposed cures to realize that not all of them were harmless. What worked for one person might be poison to another. But for the most part, magic elixirs were a waste of money. Their only danger was in how much coin was spent to buy it.

"It's a waste of money," Rebecca said.

Missy grinned. She knew Rebecca too well. "You want to try it, don't you?"

No. Well, maybe. She was interested in medicines, and the idea of a serum that would force a gentleman to tell her the truth? Well that was intriguing on so many levels.

"Can you find out what it's made of? How to administer it, and who should take it?"

"Course I can," Missy answered as she pocketed the pound notes from Rebecca.

"I won't use it," Rebecca said. "Not until I know a great deal more about it."

"Course you won't. But if a gentleman presses you before you're sure, you'll have it to hand." Then her maid paused. "But it's a magic spell, you see. So you won't know as much as you like."

There was no magic spell. Of that she was certain. In her last few years studying medicine with the widow Chenoweth, she'd learned that potions had no need for special words beyond blessings. The "magic" so to speak, was in the ingredients.

"Don't you fret," Missy continued. "I'll get it and set it in your reticule. You never know when it might come in handy."

Chapter Two

"Nate? Are you up for a visitor?"

"Yes!" Nate's answer popped out before he'd even focused on his surroundings. He'd been one week recuperating in Ras's ducal household, and he was nearly out of his mind with boredom. Ras had been his closest friend all through school and they'd remained so despite their difference in status. Ras was a wealthy duke, Nate an impoverished third son, but their friendship was stronger than ever. That was good. Nate's cracked ribs and broken feet were very bad. But worst of all was the boredom.

There were only so many salacious novels he could read before he was chomping at the bit to get out and do some swashbuckling himself.

"Come in, come in!" he called as he twisted to smile at whomever had entered. He grinned at Ras, but then his expression fell. Behind him stood Lord Benedict, Nate's supervisor at the Foreign Office. The one man who never came just for a social call because Nate was a spy and Lord Benedict was a spymaster.

Sadly, there was little Nate could do for the war effort while lying flat on his back and staring at the ceiling.

Nevertheless, the visit was welcome. "Lord Benedict! So happy to see you."

The gangly man greeted him warmly. Then there was the requisite set of pleasantries while Ras remained in the room. No one could know exactly what Nate did for the Foreign Office.

Being a spy meant he had to keep his most private thoughts from everyone, including his best friend.

And so the conversation remained superficial as long as Ras was there. Yes, Nate was healing from his injuries. Damned thieves were everywhere, and he was lucky to have survived. Lord Benedict was healthy, his work at the Foreign Office kept him busy, but he was thinking about finding a wife someday soon.

That was it for the bulk of the conversation. At least until Ras excused himself, claiming a correspondence he needed to write. Ras gave them both a cheerful goodbye, and left, shutting the door behind him.

Which was when the real conversation began. In Spanish.

Lord Benedict started first, as was appropriate in a superior officer. Even among unofficial, unsalaried spies, there was a superior and a small amount of protocol.

"Tell me everything about your attack again. From the beginning. Leave nothing out."

Nate obeyed, speaking slowly as he pulled up his Spanish, knowing that he'd be switching to Russian soon, then Greek, or maybe Latin whenever the mood struck. They'd even speak in French if Lord Benedict chose. It was because he was always afraid of being overheard, and this diminished the risk.

At least it wasn't boring.

"I went to the docks because it was time. The Blanket's ship had come in the night before, and I usually visit the taverns until we meet up."

The Blanket was an Italian sailor who sometimes carried news from other informants. Sometimes letters, but more often messages about the war against Napoleon. As always, it was difficult to assess the truth of any one message, but so far, the man had proved his worth.

"You found him," said Benedict in Russian. "Where?"

"The Painful Seadog," Nate answered, switching languages. He was better with Russian, so he spoke more quickly. "He was already there. I sat by the fire."

"What did he say?"

"Black Betties were recovered from seven dead Frogs." His tone was grave as he spoke. The betties were rifles—good ones— only made in England. The Frogs were French army, which meant that somehow Napoleon had gotten a hold of the English weapons.

But how? He had no answer. Luckily, Lord Benedict wasn't one to leap ahead.

"Anything else?"

Nate shook his head.

"Then what?"

"Nothing. He left. I waited. Drank my fill as I thought about it."

"You should have come straight to me," Benedict said, his gaze travelling down the coverlet. Nate's body was a bulge underneath thin linens, but they both knew he'd nearly died.

"I had nothing to tell you. Those rifles could have come from our own dead. It meant nothing." Or at least nothing concrete.

Of course, Benedict understood what Nate hadn't said. "But you lingered. You think it means something."

"I think everything means something." Nate sighed. "Plus, I've heard things."

Lord Benedict arched a brow, and Nate struggled to find the right words. The man wanted to hear every vague supposition, every whispered possibility. If someone, somewhere, didn't seem exactly honest, then Benedict wanted a report on it.

None of this would hold up in a court of law. Hell, none of it was anything more than guesses and gut feelings, but Nate felt sure that someone in London was shipping English rifles to Napoleon.

And that had to be stopped.

"Someone is running guns here? In London?" Lord Benedict was quick. He'd also switched to Greek which was not Nate's strong suit. He answered in English.

"I don't know."

"But you waited at the docks. You didn't come straight to me."

"I wandered. I loitered. I watched." He sighed. "I was clubbed from behind and they stole my boots.

"Did you black out?"

"No. I pretended to be unconscious. There were five of them. I'm good, but not that good." Not after getting clubbed. His head had been reeling as he stumbled before getting knocked again. That time he'd just collapsed, only half on purpose. He'd thought it best to fake being out cold and wait for his head to clear. But that had cost him his boots and the few coins he had on him. And several kicks to the ribs as he realized they meant to beat him to death.

Then it had been an effort of discipline to remain still, as if he were still unconscious. He'd had to wait until a couple of them got tired. And then one of them had slammed his heel down straight on Nate's right foot. The shock of having his toes crushed had him abruptly howling, which set his attackers back a step. It was only for a second, but Nate took the chance and bolted straight for the Thames.

Thank God he could crawl quickly. Better yet, he was a good swimmer, even with broken bones. But damn, it had been a near thing. If the water hadn't been so cold, he might not have made it. But the bracing shock of the water focused him enough.

Meanwhile, Benedict looked steadily at him. "That was too big a risk on so little information."

"It's how all my information comes. By wandering and making friends."

"Those weren't friends."

True enough. He wasn't sure if he'd been careless or wandered into something truly nefarious. He'd been too busy trying to survive to figure much else out. And then, once he'd swam far enough away, he still had to limp his way across London back to his rooms.

It had been one hell of a night.

Benedict studied him in silence, obviously calculating something in his massive brain. The man played the movement of nations the way card sharks played idiot boys. But that didn't mean he understood how Nate's information was acquired. Benedict's strengths were in using knowledge to England's benefit.

Nate's job was to get the information to him in the first place.

Fortunately, Benedict understood who was better at what. He rocked back in his chair and leveled Nate with a hard stare.

"What do you want to do now?"

"I need to get back out there. I have friends. If someone is shipping Black Betties through the London docks, I'll find 'em." Part of his training as a young man had been to work as a London waterman, manning the little boats that ran back and forth between the London "stairs" and the ships too big to settle on the shore.

It had taken some time for those rough men to accept him as one of their own, but once included, he had lifelong friends. And not a one of them would support gun running to the French.

Naturally, Lord Benedict saw the obvious problem. "How are you going to do that with your feet cut to hell?"

Good question. "They're getting better," he said as he flexed his toes. They moved with minimal pain, but the bones in his right foot would take much longer to heal. He could manage a limping kind of walk, but he couldn't run. He might never run again.

Benedict came to the same conclusion. "Don't go anywhere until you're healed. You're no good to me dead."

That last was spoken in a coarse French that was equal parts curse and admonition. Nate understood it, but he doubted he could comply. This was what he could do for his country—lurk in shadows and listen to gossip. He hadn't expected to grow up into such a patriotic soul, but over the years, he'd seen the damage that war did to ordinary folk. Not just the people of France and

Spain, though that was horrifying enough, but the English boys lost on the battlefield.

He vowed young to do what he could to end the war. It turned out that his greatest skill was in being a jolly good fellow. People assumed he was completely harmless as they chattered around the docks, in taverns, and in the ballrooms. Everyone knew something, and Nate had good ears, a good memory, and several good aliases.

But he couldn't hear anything while laid up in Ras's ducal mansion.

"I'll find a way," Nate promised.

"You'll work as I tell you to," Benedict said. "This is no time to go rogue."

Benedict always said that because Benedict believed in structure, even among spy organizations. Especially among spies. Otherwise, there was no safety anywhere for the men under his command.

Nate knew that was a dangerous illusion. He functioned as he always had, a lone figure wandering places he shouldn't go in the hope of finding answers. His success was a product of luck and diligence. It was what he could do for England. Though, in his honest moments, he knew that excitement was his real motivator.

"Be careful," Benedict whispered in English. "I don't want to lose you."

Was there anguish in his tone? Desperation? Or simple anxiety as his gaze hopped to the clock on the mantlepiece.

"I need to leave," Benedict said as he switched into bastardized Portuguese. "Do you trust your host?"

"Ras? With my life."

"You're sure." It wasn't a question.

"I'd bring him into the work if he weren't about to get married."

"Hmmm," Benedict said. "And do you trust his fiancée?"

Nate's nod came slower this time. He didn't have the benefit of years of friendship with Kynthea, but everything he'd learned about her said she was exactly as she appeared: a poor relation who was abruptly, suddenly, in absolute love with a duke.

What he wouldn't give for Rebecca to look at him the way Kynthea gazed as Ras. She'd done that once, but that had been long ago.

He sighed. Inactivity was turning him maudlin. He couldn't even write in his journal right now. Thoughts kept running chaotically through his brain, thanks to the fever. That was gone now, but he still hadn't picked up a pencil. He hadn't the will.

He mustered a smile as Lord Benedict rose to his feet. The man didn't say anything more beyond his customary good-byes, but the look he gave Nate was something else. It was long and full of worry. But then he'd often looked that way when considering Nate.

After all, he knew more than anyone else about what Nate had been doing for the last ten years. He and Lord Benedict had grown up together in the spy service, though the man was his senior in age and the service.

Benedict's final words were, "Don't be stupid. And don't talk." Which for Benedict was the same thing.

"Go on wit ye," Nate drawled, pulling out his best no man's accent. Neither Cornish nor Cockney, he centered it as a general low-brow London accent. It usually served his purpose and was enough to make Benedict wince at the coarse tones. The man hated pretending to be anything less polished than what he was, a future earl with a very bright future in diplomacy.

So the man shot Nate a long-suffering stare before taking his leave. Less than five minutes later, the door opened again, this time by Ras. The duke's gaze was somber as he stood in the doorway with his arms crossed. He looked like he was about to discipline a recalcitrant boy.

Nate was having none of it. "Leave off, Ras. And fetch me some fresh water. I need to clean my wounds."

"Water's there," Ras said as he gestured to the pitcher set to the side of the table. Then he appeared to make a decision. He entered the room and shut the door firmly behind him.

"Interesting conversation you had there. I counted five different languages, plus English."

Nate's gaze abruptly sharpened. "You were listening at the door?"

"I was." He didn't sound the least apologetic, but he did grab the water pitcher and filled a basin before dropping a clean cloth into it. "Not at first," he added. "But when I overheard Russian, I was intrigued."

"Did you understand it?"

"Not a word. Don't speak it. But I did wonder what Lord Castlereagh's right-hand man was doing visiting you. When did you two become friends?"

Nate waved a hand in a casual gesture. "Oh, we met when I first came to London after…" After he and Rebecca had blown up both their lives. "After I left school."

"Was he here then?" Ras clearly was thinking about the man's age. "Wouldn't he have been in school?"

"Sometimes. Sometimes not."

"And you were here sometimes, sometimes not." It was an echo of what Nate always said about his early training. He did this and that. Went here and there. Met some people, kissed a few girls, killed a few villains.

He never said that last part out loud, but clearly Ras guessed that his wastrel life was a bit more complicated than it appeared.

"I see," Ras said.

No, he really didn't. But he knew more than nearly everyone else outside of the Foreign Office.

Ras waited a bit, no doubt hoping that Nate would break down and share more information. He wouldn't, but Ras always tried. In the end, he sighed.

"Keep your secrets," he said. "I came in here to talk about Fletcher."

Nate winced. Rebecca's brother was a problem. Always. He

was the man who constantly stood between Nate and Rebecca. He was the one who blamed his father's death on their tendre. He was the one who had intercepted Nate's gossip columns to add extra damaging paragraphs, attacking Kynthea under the guise of Nate's alias, Mr. Pickleherring. Why? He'd said it was to discredit Nate in Ras's eyes.

As if that wasn't convoluted. No sane man could understand.

Which, of course, was the point. He wasn't exactly sure Fletcher was sane.

"I think he's been following me," Nate said. In fact, Nate had a feeling that Fletcher had set the ruffians on him in the first place. He didn't want to think that the man hated him that much, but he couldn't discount the possibility. Which was a much better scenario than the one where Fletcher was a French spy. None of which made logical sense, but that was the whole problem. Fletcher didn't make sense.

Ras leaned forward. "Did Fletcher attack you? At the docks?"

"It was five men who wanted money and my boots. I have no idea what Fletcher wants."

Ras frowned, clearly thinking hard, but he didn't pursue the topic. "I've spoken with the newspaper. Mr. Pickleherring's gossip column is gone for good."

Nate sighed. That had been one of his few reliable sources of income. "Another columnist will take up the mantle."

"But it won't be you."

"It wasn't me anyway. Not toward the end."

Ras didn't comment as he wrung out the washcloth and handed it to Nate. Except Nate couldn't reach his feet without straining his ribs. After two painful attempts, he gave up with a grunt.

"See?" Ras taunted. "You need help." He took the cloth, lifted the linen off Nate's feet, and began unwrapping the bandages. Once that was done, he began washing Nate's abused feet.

Fortunately, the wounds he'd acquired while trying to walk home with broken toes, appeared to be healing nicely. But before he could comment, Ras shot him a hard look.

"So what do you think Fletcher saw that night? Why was he there? Why is he following you?"

Nate winced as he glared up at the ceiling. He hated lying here helpless, staring at the ceiling while someone else tried to help him. Especially since there wasn't anything his friend could do.

"It's not your problem."

"I've had Kynthea invite Lady Rebecca over for tea."

Nate jolted. "What?"

"You heard me. Look, I don't know what you've been doing all these years, but I'm beginning to guess. Let me help you."

"By bringing Rebecca here?" Right downstairs, when he couldn't walk without a crutch. Damn it, it would be torture to have her so close and not be able to talk to her!

"She'll naturally want to see how you're faring, won't she? We can arrange a sick room visit. You could ask her about Fletcher."

Fletcher would be the last thing on his mind when he was talking to her. God, he'd longed for just such an opportunity. Ever since her father had caught them doing so much more than kissing.

"Will she tell you why Fletcher seems intent on destroying you?" Ras pressed. "Should I talk to her instead?"

"No!" Nate struggled onto his elbows. "I need to talk to her. It needs to be me."

Ras finished cleaning one foot and went on to the other. "I'll see what can be done to arrange it, but it'll only work if she comes alone."

True, but the odds were strong that she'd be alone. "Her mother prefers to hold court rather than go out visiting."

"What if Fletcher escorts her?"

Nate grinned. "Then I'll happily have a talk with him." He might not be able to stand without pain, but he sure as hell could tolerate a little discomfort if he could give Fletcher the drubbing the man surely deserved. The man had stood by and gleefully watched while Nate was nearly beaten to death. Nate needed to know exactly why the man would do that. Did he just enjoy watching brutality? Or was there something more?

Ras shot him a hard look. "We're trying to quiet the situation, not exacerbate it." He pursed his lips. "If Fletcher comes, I'll talk to him. I hate giving him the satisfaction of thinking we're friends, but—"

"Don't try to play him. He's not stupid."

"No, but he does have an ego. I can play to that." Nate didn't like involving his friend in any of this, but Ras was right. They needed to know why Fletcher was following him. It seemed remarkably coincidental that Fletcher had been there just as Nate was investigating gun running, but the two things could be completely unrelated. Either way, Ras wasn't trained in this type of investigation.

"Don't interfere. I'll can figure out what Fletcher's issue is with me, then I'll do what needs to be done."

Ras sighed. "That's what I'm afraid of."

Chapter Three

L̲ADY REBECCA DIDN'T know the duke's fiancée except by reputation. So when the invitation came for tea, she wasn't sure what to do. Naturally, she was incredibly curious, given that gossip said the woman had caught a duke by love potion. Since the truth serum was currently burning a hole in her reticule, she was desperate to quiz the woman. But she also couldn't bring up the topic with someone she'd just met.

She was still staring at the invite when Fletcher intruded upon her morning salon. Like her, he was a ridiculously early riser, and so she had no escape from his intrusive presence.

"What's that you got there?" he asked as he peered over her shoulder.

She didn't bother trying to hide it. He would badger her about it until she gave in. He was nosy that way.

"An invitation to tea."

"With whom?"

She didn't want to answer. There were some names that were anathema in their house. The duke's fiancée wasn't on that list—yet—but the duke himself had sparked several outbursts over the years.

"Come, come," Fletcher chided. "You cannot go without my approval anyway, so you must tell me."

"Fletcher, I am a full adult who has been managing my correspondence and mother's for years without your—"

"Sweet heaven, Becca, why must everything be an argument

between us? I swear you have been in a foul mood since you turned twelve. I'm only trying to help. You don't know anyone in London, and an invitation to tea is never just tea. Especially since I've started my campaign for the House of Commons. Can you not simply trust me?"

Rebecca bit her lip. Had she really been surly since she was twelve? Maybe. Her mother had certainly said as much.

"I'm sorry, Fletcher. And of course I don't want to hurt your campaign."

"Good, good," he said, patting her shoulder. "I'm glad we understand one another. Is that the duke's stationery?"

Well, there was no stopping disclosure now. "It's from his fiancée, Miss Petrelli. She's inviting me to tea."

To her shock, he brightened immediately. "Excellent! I shall be happy to escort you."

"You can't." She traced her fingers over the words. "This is a ladies' tea. It would be horribly rude to—"

"Nonsense," he said as he lifted the invitation from her fingers. "Gentlemen come to these things all the time as escorts and friends of the family. Besides, I have things to discuss with her."

She twisted to face him directly. "Whatever do you have to say to Miss Petrelli?"

"Just that her fiancé and I are the best of friends. And if you women truly don't want me there, I can wander off with Ras. Hopefully outside, where everyone will see."

So that was his true goal. He wanted to be seen in the duke's company.

"I don't like being used in this way," she said. "If you want to speak to his grace—"

Fletcher set the invitation down with more force than necessary. "You are fighting me again. You don't know the rules, Rebecca. You don't know London."

"I've been here for five Seasons already! And I know that a women's tea is not a place for men."

He regarded her solemnly, his expression sad. "Very well," he said softly. "I can see that you don't understand. I am running for a seat in the House of Commons. The duke's support could make the difference, but he has been caught up with his new fiancée. Understandable, of course, but this gives me the perfect reason to be seen in a friendship setting with the man. Indeed, that was probably the reason for the invitation in the first place. Why else would you get invited to tea with a woman you've never met?"

She had no answer to that. Indeed, she'd wondered that exact thing a few moments ago.

"This is politics, sister dear. Men use their wives and their sisters to have an excuse to be seen together. Do you understand now why I must be there?"

When he put it that way, it sounded plausible. And she certainly didn't want to hinder his run for the House of Commons.

"If you're sure," she said.

"Of course I am," he said as he pressed a kiss to her temple. "Trust me. I have it all in hand. Be sure to wear something nice."

"Yes, Fletcher." He always liked it when she said that.

He waited again, then patted her head as if she were a dog before sauntering away. She watched in growing frustration. Fletcher always liked to be in control of things. Ever since Father died, his need to control every aspect of life had bordered on obsessive. Rebecca guessed it was his reaction to grief. He needed to feel safe and so he made everyone dance to his tune.

At home, she would either laugh it off when he became encroaching or, if possible, pretend to agree before doing exactly as she wanted anyway. But that was where she knew everyone and could accurately judge his claims. Did he need to be involved when purchasing a new horse for him? Absolutely. Did he need to be there directing her selections? No.

Better yet, she had allies at home. The servants were her servants, and they knew to agree to his demands and then run whatever request through her. But she was in London now, the place he spent the bulk of his time. The servants here were loyal to him, and she had little control. Plus he had made a big show of excitement when they'd first arrived. He'd been truly helpful getting her to a good modiste and making sure everyone knew she was ready to join the Season. There were a stack of invitations waiting for her when she first set foot in the house. And more came every day.

She couldn't have managed half as well without him. So it was only logical that she let him guide her now. It was only that he patted her head at the end that truly bothered her. And if she cut up stiff at such gestures, then she was the one being silly. What difference did it make if that was the way he expressed his love? Maybe she'd mention later that such things were insulting.

But she already knew she wouldn't. Fletcher's moods were unpredictable, and it made no sense to risk that on something as silly as a pat on the head.

In any event, she needed to respond to the tea invitation. And really, Fletcher was right. She was looking forward to meeting the duke's fiancée. From what little she'd heard, Miss Petrelli sounded very interesting or very silly.

Imagine using a love potion to catch a duke. But it had worked!

REBECCA AND FLETCHER set off for the London residence of the Duke of Harle at precisely twenty minutes before the appointed hour. Fletcher had been very specific about the time, and Rebecca had met it easily. She was never the one who delayed a departure. That was their mother's particular foible.

She was even in a genial mood as they climbed into the carriage, but then Fletcher handed her a list of discussion topics. A written list! She'd been conversing in polite society since she was seven. She didn't need his guidance, but then he pointed out one significant item.

Love Potion

"You must find out if she believes in that nonsense."

She'd been fidgeting with her reticule, the one that carried the truth serum. But at his words, her head shot up.

"Why do you want to know about that? Especially if you think it's nonsense."

Her brother rolled his eyes. "Because if Ras is marrying a ninny, I want to know."

"I wouldn't think it's your business either way."

"That only shows how provincial you are. The Duke of Harle is one of the foremost leaders of the country. If he is set to marry a ninny, it is everyone's business." Then he got a sly grin. "And if she is an idiot, then we must work to get you in Ras's company as much as possible."

"Why?"

"So you can marry him, instead!" He leaned forward, his eyes dancing. "Shall I teach you? Listen, Ras isn't a fool. If Miss Petrelli is, then he will soon tire of her. We must delay their wedding, and you must show him that you're clever."

He smiled indulgently at her, and she was human enough to warm at his words. Fletcher's compliments were rare things.

"Thank you, but I can't chase after an affianced man." Or any man, for that matter. "And you said you'd selected someone else."

"Of course there are other options. I've got them at the ready, but can you honestly think of anyone better than a duke? If he will have you, then you must say yes!"

She smiled wanly at her brother. He couldn't possibly think that the duke would take one look at her and drop his affianced bride. Especially with her sitting in the room!

"Fletcher, this is a ladies' tea."

"No buts. Learn what you can about her and most especially about that potion. If she believes in that, then she can be manipulated."

"You should talk to the duke directly. You don't need me to—"

"If he's going to marry you, then you must be involved! Rebecca, this is why you haven't taken in previous Seasons. You don't think strategically. But never fear, I shall show you the way." He patted her knee fondly. "I fear moldering in the country has dulled your wits."

He wasn't the only one to think that. As much as she loved her life back home, many of her days did indeed feel dull. Certainly, she found ways to fill her time, but she often longed for more. Something that occupied her mind. Or perhaps *someone*. All of her friends were wed, and many already had their first child. She'd begun to feel like a forgotten piece of clothing stuck at the back of a wardrobe. She couldn't wait to be pulled out and worn, so to speak, so that she could finally be used as a woman was meant to be used.

She wanted a husband and children. She hoped for some activity that was more fulfilling than making sure her mama's tea was at the right temperature. And she was desperate for more intellectual stimulation than being told that warts could be cured by washing one's feet under the light of the full moon.

But in order to do that, she had to find a husband. And one that was not the engaged Duke of Harle!

"This is my first meeting with Miss Petrelli," she said. "I'll do what I can, but some women are not amenable to talking about the way they caught a fiancé."

"Good," Fletcher said. "And one more thing. If Ras isn't there, I'll endeavor to leave you women alone. Privacy should encourage intimacy. Perhaps I'll visit Lord Nathanial. He's staying there, recuperating from his latest drunken orgy."

Rebecca jolted. She had years of practice learning to control her expression, but the sound of Nate's name on Fletcher's lips never failed to pull a cringing reaction out of her. He knew that, of course, so his gaze was steady on her face, watching her every reaction. But try as she might, she couldn't suppress her next words.

"He's there?" He'd be within several feet of her. So close she could speak to him if she wanted. If Fletcher didn't interfere. And if... "Did you say drunken orgy?" She wasn't even supposed to know what that meant, but she did. She was well-read in many things that were not typical fare for young women.

"Yes, apparently it devolved into a brawl and..." Fletcher shrugged. "Well, the details don't matter. He'll tell you he was accosted by thieves or some such thing. It's a convenient lie."

She swallowed. She didn't want to know more about the man she'd once thought was the love of her life. Except that was a lie. She did want to know. Desperately.

"Why is he there?" To the place they were going to. Right now!

"Ras has a soft heart for old friends despite how very hideously they've grown up. I mean to tell him so. Associating with that roue will only destroy him."

Rebecca frowned. "I doubt the duke has to worry about losing status."

Her brother sighed. "*Everyone* worries about losing status. And every man has a soft spot. You must be careful not to tread heavily upon it. The duke's blindness is in his love for that cretin, so you must not speak ill of him."

"Of Lord Nathanial?" How her throat closed up when she spoke his name. Even now, ten years later, too many emotions crowded her whenever she thought of him. She'd best keep the man firmly shoved into the back corner of her mind.

"Yes. Him." The word was heavy with hatred. "Don't say a word against him to the duke, but you can encourage Miss Petrelli to voice whatever objections she may have. And be sure to tell me her confidences. I'll give Ras the information in a way that he will hear. Do you understand?"

Rebecca nodded, though she kept her lips buttoned. She understood what he wanted. He didn't understand that she had no intention of betraying anyone's confidences, much less the future Duchess of Harle's.

Thankfully, she didn't have to hold her tongue for long. Their carriage arrived at the ducal residence. Fletcher took a moment to inspect her from head to toe, nod his satisfaction at her appearance, and then smile reassuringly at her.

"This is a delicate situation with a great deal of potential," he whispered before the door opened. "I am relying upon you."

Rebecca descended from the carriage first, her gaze already jumping to the house. Miss Petrelli must have been watching for them because the butler had already swung open the door and the lady was just stepping out. That gave Rebecca a few moments to assess the woman as she began the walk up the path.

Brown hair, sweet smile, and a composed way of moving. That made sense, given the amount of gossip surrounding her. Rebecca knew from experience that gossip tended to dampen any person's enthusiasm. But she also seemed genuinely warm as she held out her hands in greeting.

"Lady Rebecca, I'm so pleased you could visit."

"It is my pleasure," Rebecca answered. "Though, I must be honest, your invitation surprised me."

"I shall be happy to explain…" Miss Petrelli's voice faded as her gaze went over Rebecca's shoulder to where Fletcher descended from the carriage. All warmth bled from her expression as her chin lifted, and her jaw tightened.

Clearly oblivious to the reaction, her brother gave an expansive greeting. "Miss Petrelli!" he exclaimed as he walked up the path. "What a pleasure to see you this day."

"Lord Fletcher." Miss Petrelli's tone was icy cold. "I am surprised to see you here for a lady's tea."

"But I am my sister's escort—"

"You are not welcome, my lord," she interrupted. "Why you think I would welcome a man who wrote such horrible lies about me is beyond my comprehension. I was prepared to extend friendship to your sister, but you, sir—"

"Lies!" Fletcher cried. "Whatever have I done to offend you? Miss Petrelli, we barely know one another."

Rebecca looked between the two. And then, to her horror,

she saw people slow down as they promenaded on this exclusive street. Good God, they were creating a scene!

"Perhaps we should go inside," she offered. "We can discuss things more comfortably—"

"I name you Mr. Pickleherring," Miss Petrilli said firmly. "And your column was vicious and filled with lies."

Fletcher gaped at the woman. It was a good expression, but Fletcher was her brother. She'd seen him in every phase of deception, and she knew that this reaction wasn't genuine. Indeed, she was sure it was for their audience's benefit. Especially when he began to chuckle.

"Miss Petrelli, you are confused. Whyever would I stoop to writing a gossip column?"

It was a good question, but Miss Petrelli wasn't swayed. Her arms were crossed now, and she appeared on the verge of saying something else. Except at that moment, the duke appeared a step behind his fiancée.

"You admitted to it, Fletch," he said, his voice firm.

Fletcher threw up his hands. "Have you gone mad, Ras? Good God, whatever would I gain by tarnishing Miss Petrilli's reputation? I don't even know her!" His voice softened. "We have been friends for so long, Ras. Honestly, I don't understand this animosity."

Becca looked at her brother, seeing in him the picture of a wounded friend. He was so earnest in his statement that she did indeed begin to question the duke's sanity.

"My brother doesn't write gossip columns," she said quietly. "He has expressed disdain for those who read such things." Indeed, he thought the novels she read to be pablum for weak minds.

"Quite correct," Fletcher agreed. Then he stepped forward to bow low before Miss Petrelli. "My dear, pray forgive me for any sleight I may have perpetrated upon your person. I most sincerely apologize. I would never want to hurt you or Ras. You must believe me."

"I don't," Miss Petrelli said, her words thankfully muted. But her tone and her face were very clear.

"Then why invite me to tea?" Rebecca pressed. All of this seemed very strange. "Especially if you believe such a terrible thing of my brother?"

"Not to mention," her brother added, "that you've obviously gotten the better of Mr. Pickleherring. You are engaged, are you not? To a duke."

Miss Petrelli said nothing. Indeed, what could she say in the face of Fletcher sounding so reasonable? In the end, she turned to her fiancé. "It is your house, Ras. What do you want?"

The man sighed audibly. "I think Fletch and I will go for a stroll. Pray enjoy your ladies' tea."

There was a long silent exchange between the engaged couple. A quiet message that only the two understood. But in the end, Miss Petrelli stepped backward into the house.

"Pray come in, Lady Rebecca," she said. "I have just purchased a new tea that I am anxious to try. I wonder what you will think of it." It was a polite compromise, and Rebecca accepted the gesture.

"I look forward to tasting it," she said as she followed the woman inside. Even better, she was quietly pleased that her brother remained outside. Distantly, she noted the duke's tightly controlled expression and her brother's gleeful smile, and she had to admit, Fletcher had handled the situation masterfully.

She had no idea what the disagreement was, but she knew enough about society to see that her brother had come out the winner in this instance. Everyone would assume now that it had been Miss Petrelli's mistake. After all, the duke was walking about in public with Fletcher, so clearly the problem wasn't between the men.

Which naturally led her to be a bit suspicious of the woman. Miss Petrelli was either more naïve than Rebecca about the workings of society—something that was hard to imagine—or she was indeed simple-minded. Imagine accusing Fletcher of writing a gossip column! Whatever would he gain by it? And whatever would he say? It was clear to Rebecca from their earlier conversation that he knew very little about Miss Petrelli.

The whole situation was very bizarre. But maybe a few private moments with the lady would make everything clear. Especially as she had every intention of forcing an explanation.

Chapter Four

Rebecca followed Miss Petrelli to a back parlor, steeling herself to demand some answers—in the nicest possible way. But first they had to get through the pleasantries.

They each took a seat while the tea was served. Then they discussed the décor and if Miss Petrelli would change it once she became duchess. The tea cakes were delightful. The conversation easy. All in all, the lady seemed warm and completely rational. Beyond her obvious distaste of Fletcher, of course.

It took some time, but eventually the servants withdrew. Then Miss Petrelli exhaled in relief. "Well, now that they're gone, we can finally talk."

"They" obviously referred to the servants. Rebecca felt a twinge of amusement. "Are you not used to having a full complement of staff?" Personally, she hated having Fletcher's servants staring at her all the time.

"Good heavens no. I was the staff for my parents. And my aunt and uncle didn't need as many as a duke. I fear my future. I've never managed this many all at once. They're everywhere."

"I'm sure you'll do fine."

The lady chuckled. "I'm sure Ras's housekeeper will do fine. I merely follow her lead."

Rebecca suspected the lady was being modest, but what did she know about a ducal household? Perhaps that was the way of things in London. Either way, she had no reason to object. And in the silence, Miss Petrelli folded her hands and finally addressed the issue.

"I'm in a bit of a quandary, Lady Rebecca, and I have absolutely no skill at subterfuge."

Becca quietly set her teacup down. "How may I help?"

"It has to do with your brother. There seems to be some longstanding animosity between Lord Fletcher and my fiancé's best friend. Normally I wouldn't interfere. Honestly, men's relationships can be as confusing as a flock of wild birds fighting over a favorite tree. But the argument seems to have spilled over to me."

"I don't know anything about Fletcher's friends."

"Do you know why he hates Lord Nathaniel?"

Ah. Rebecca looked down at her hands, grateful she had thought to set down her tea. But without the cup in her hands, she was left to twist her fingers together in awkward shame.

"It's a long, ugly story, Your Grace."

"Oh! Don't call me that yet! I'm Kynthea. And I shall call you Rebecca, if I may?"

"Of course."

There was a moment's awkward silence, and then Rebecca took a deep breath. Might as well get it out in the open. Then she could find out why Kynthea thought so ill of Fletcher.

"Our two families have had long standing animosity going back several generations. Someone poisoned the water between our two lands, we don't know who. Everyone claims it was the other family, and as far as I am concerned, it should have been forgotten years ago. My family has control of the water, and we have prospered because of it. If anyone should be upset, it should be Lord Nathaniel's family."

"And they aren't?"

"Oh, they are. For as long as I can remember, we've called each other ugly names, accused everyone of cheating, pillaging, murdering." She shook her head. "I honestly don't know what's true. I don't think anybody does."

"But they believe it?"

"Everyone in our respective families believes it."

"But you don't?"

"No. I haven't since…" She shrugged. "Since I was fourteen."

"What happened then?"

"I met Lord Nathinal. We used to spend summers together in secret."

Miss Petrelli's eyes widened. "Really?"

"The vicar thought the feud was ridiculous, and he was right. So he lied to our parents and found excuses for Nate and me to be together."

"That sounds incredibly risky."

"Not as much as it sounds. We weren't the Montagues and the Capulets." And they certainly weren't Romeo and Juliet, though the consequences had been equally tragic. "My grandfather wasn't as entrenched. And neither was Nate's mother. So the vicar helped me see that Nate was just a teenage boy. Nothing like a monster. It opened the door for our friendship."

"The vicar's gambit succeeded."

Rebecca shook her head. "It did not. And he lost his appointment because of it." Because of what she and Nate had done, and the hideous consequence of their discovery.

"Oh dear."

Rebecca shifted her weight on the chair. She couldn't seem to get comfortable, and she shouldn't confess to this stranger what she had done with Nate. Guilt ate at her even as her anger simmered that she still suffered for something she had done when she was sixteen. It was a confusing mix of emotions that tied her insides into knots whenever she thought of it.

And in that silence, a male voice spoke. It was deeper than she remembered, but she knew who it was. After all, she'd spent the last ten years both hoping and fearing to speak with him again.

"It was my fault," said Nate.

She looked up and there he was. Nate was taller than she remembered, and his face appeared leaner, as if anything childish in his body had been removed by a hard chisel. He walked slowly, his gaze never wavering from her. She matched his gaze, memorizing every curve of his face, every minute shift in his expression.

He'd grown into his height, she realized, her awareness expanding beyond his face. His shoulders had broadened, and the muscles stood out on his wiry frame. No fat, she realized. None. Had he not had a sweet in ten years? But he wasn't hallowed out in starvation or in the wasted way of a drunkard. He seemed healthy, though his jaw was gripped tight.

Was he angry? In pain?

"Becca," he finally said, "how are you?"

She swallowed, her insides shifting like wax under pressure. She'd forgotten how she responded to his voice. And no one else called her Becca. Two syllables that held such earnestness. As if he truly wanted to know how she fared and would wait patiently for her answer, no matter how long it took to frame the words.

When she was fourteen, it had taken her forever to say anything to him. By the time she was sixteen, he knew everything about her.

And now? She felt like she was fourteen again, her voice caught thick in her throat.

He took a step closer, and she saw him wince. His next step was more awkward than the last, and she knew he was hurt. Once, she'd thought she would know his pain from a world away. Now she could see it from across a room. See it but not feel it.

"Sit down," she chided. "You're hurt."

"It's nothing."

"It's enough that you've been recuperating here for the last week."

He shrugged. "Did Fletcher tell you that?" There was no accusation in his tone, but she still bristled.

"What I know is irrelevant. What have you hurt? How is it healing?"

His brows rose, a teasing glint in his eyes. "Always so practical. I was attacked by thieves. They took my boots, broke some bones, and I had to walk across London to get home."

He spoke as if an attack like that had been of no consequence, but she knew better. She knew that when he tucked his chin, he was making light of something very dangerous. His eyes could hold steady, his hands casual in their dismissal, but that chin of his would move tight as if he braced against a leash.

The image made no sense, but it had always been true with him.

First things first. "What are your injuries?"

"Did you become a doctor?" he asked, fondness in his gaze. "I remember your fascination with medicines."

"I had many silly dreams," she said and even she winced at the strident note in her voice.

"I never thought them silly," he said.

She felt her body twist. It wasn't a natural position. It was a reflection of her split desires. Part of her ached to reach him again. That part remembered how he never made light of her thoughts, even if he teased her for her worries. What did she care what others thought? he would ask. With him, she laughed out loud, spun circles in the fields, and let him touch parts of her body that ached to be free. With him, she'd *lived*.

The other part remembered that all actions had consequences. And her freedom had cost her father his life. Worse, her entire family had never been the same afterwards. Henry had locked himself away on the estate. Mama had turned even more helpless than before. And Fletcher had become so controlling that she no longer really liked her brother.

Which meant that as much as she yearned to speak with Nate again, she also despised him for his part in how her family had fallen apart. And that contradiction made her feel ill.

"Becca?"

Oh, how she loved the way he spoke her name.

"I am not a doctor," she said firmly. Indeed, her throat nearly closed down on the word. "But I have learned a few things. Are your feet cut?" That would explain the way he limped. "Are the wounds festering?"

"You are going to tell me to slather them with honey."

She nodded.

"I have made a mess of the duke's linens, but your poultice recipe has served me well. And the doctor said I could not do much about the broken bones, but give them time."

She nodded. That much was true. "Still, you must wash regularly and watch for the first signs of infection. Be rough enough on the new skin to push out any pus, but not so rough as to damage healing. It's painful, but necess—"

"I know. I am." His voice warmed her. His eyes seemed to hold her. And damn if his very presence didn't turn her into a twisting mass of conflicting feelings.

What did he want from her? Why was he here?

She looked away, too confused by her own reaction to hold his gaze. So she turned her attention to the other occupant in the room.

"My apologies, Your Grace. This must seem very odd to you."

"Call me Kynthea," the lady reminded her gently. "And I find this very interesting. To answer your question, Lord Nate's injuries included cracked ribs, several broken toes, and cuts all over. The worst of the black eye has faded, but you can still see the shadow of it if he were to sit in the sunlight."

"Kynthea," Nate growled. "I can answer for myself."

"Except you did not." She leveled a hard gaze at him. "Lord Fletcher targeted me because of you. I have yet to understand why." Her gaze shifted to Rebecca. "I meant to have a quiet conversation with you, but it appears that the men must intrude upon us, no matter what we want."

Rebecca completely understood that irritation. And because she did, she chose to explain what she could. "Like everyone else in my family, Fletcher blames Lord Nate for everything ill that has happened. Bad crops. A sickened pig. And the death of my father who discovered us one afternoon in a hayloft." She swallowed. "In that, at least, I am equally complicit and equally damned."

"No, Becca. It was—"

"I will take responsibility for my part in this," she snapped. "My father's heart was weak. It is a family trait. But the shock of the discovery…" She bit her lip, remembering. She'd been half dressed when her father burst in on them. And as she shot to her feet, he'd clutched his chest and collapsed.

Her screams had brought everyone running. The vicar, nearby farmers, the ladies who cleaned the church. But it had been too late. There was nothing to be done when a man's heart stopped, though she and Nate both tried. She'd read that hanging a man upside down could restart the heart. So under her direction, Nate had lifted her father up by his legs, trying to get him to breathe again.

It didn't work. And Fletcher had used that attempt to claim that Nate had tried to break her father's neck.

"My father died that day."

"Oh my God," whispered Kynthea. "I'm so sorry."

"I tried to talk to you afterwards," Nate said. "I saw you at the funeral—"

She shuddered. She'd seen him there. Of course, she had. But at the time, she'd been too steeped in guilt and pain to do anything about it.

"So many times," he continued. "I have tried to speak with you. I've written letters—"

Her head shot up. "You didn't send them! Please, no!" What a disaster that would have been.

He shook his head. "I knew they'd never reach you. But I wrote them because I had to. I had to tell you how sorry I was—I am—for everything."

She didn't write to him. She knew better. After their relationship had been exposed, her family took great pleasure in pawing through everything she owned, everything she did. Flether was the most zealous at it, but everyone else had looked at her private things. Indeed, her mother continued to search her room on a regular basis. And the dark accusation in their eyes remained to this day.

"The rift between our family continues," she said, as she looked to Nate for confirmation.

He nodded, his expression grim.

Then she turned back to Kynthea. "But I cannot imagine why Fletcher would involve you in our family's idiocy. I don't believe it."

"So you still think the feud is idiocy?" Nate asked.

"Don't you?"

"I do," he agreed. "But my family was furious I wasn't able to go back to school."

He hadn't? She hadn't known. "Why not?"

His gaze grew sober. "Fletcher swore he would kill me if he ever saw me again. Even if I was willing to risk it, my parents weren't."

She shook her head. Her brother was hot tempered, but… "He didn't mean it," she said. But even as she spoke the words, she wondered. Fletcher had been furious back then. And sneaky. What kind of mischief could he have created at a boarding school? She didn't want to think about it.

"I'm sorry," she said. "I didn't know." She'd felt so guilty back then. She'd spent most of her time hiding from everyone. Her only respite was when she'd disappeared to study herbs with Mrs. Chenoweth, the local witch woman. She couldn't wait to head back to school in the fall and prove to everyone that she was a reformed girl.

And that was exactly what she'd done for the last ten years. She'd worked with the new vicar, she'd waited on her mother hand and foot, and she'd acted in every way as a proper English girl.

Looking back, she couldn't believe ten years had passed like that. Even when she'd made it to London for her debut, she'd dressed demurely, kept her head down, and pleased everyone as best she could.

Meanwhile, the future duchess was still trying to understand the history. "What was the original sin? Between your two families?"

Nate shrugged. "We don't know. Our second summer together, we decided to find out. We searched family journals, and the vicar even looked into the legal records."

She twisted her fingers into her gown. "All we know is that my family got the water. His owns the forest. The stream between our lands may have been poisoned, but we don't know how."

Nate took up the tale. "Our land has not been as profitable as theirs, but that's because my grandfather was an idiot."

Her expression softened. "According to Mrs. Chenoweth, both families came to her grandmother to buy curses. She took their money then performed ritual blessings for both sides."

Nate's expression softened. "That sounds like her."

Becca agreed. Theirs was a stubborn community. From mother to daughter, from father to son, no one could change anybody else's mind. Except for the two of them. Except for a vicar who tried to find a way out for both families.

"Becca," Nate said, his voice soft. "I think of you often. I would still marry you if you would have me."

It took a moment for his words to make sense to her. And when they did, his meaning left her reeling. Good God, the man hadn't changed from the feckless wild teenager he'd been so many years ago. Reckless! Passionate! And...

And so heartbreakingly earnest, for all that he was spouting idiocy.

She closed her eyes against the yearning that swept through her. She wanted to say yes in the way one wanted to return to childhood innocence. Wouldn't that be fun? Fall into the romantic tale of lovers lost. Heal the breach between the Montagues and Capulets. Take away the taint of being a wanton woman by marrying the man who had touched her body so wonderfully when she was sixteen.

"You haven't changed a bit," she said.

"That doesn't sound like a complement."

It wasn't.

"I have changed," she retorted. "And if you refuse to grow after what we happened, after ten years of whatever it is you have been doing, then you are as stupid as our ancestors. Change, Nate. Mature. And do not ever speak to me of marriage."

He abruptly leaned forward, his expression shocked. "Becca, I've waited all this time just to apologize to you. I've wanted to do the honorable thing from the very beginning—"

She cut him off with a wave of her hand. She didn't want to hear any more from him. She's spent the last ten years trying to get past what had happened that day. Ten years trying to forgive herself, working to fashion a life from the ashes. She would not allow him to draw him back into that quagmire where she'd been a confused and grieving sixteen-year-old. That girl had been a disaster. She was a woman now, and she refused to feel that nightmare again.

But that meant she had to get out of here. She couldn't look at Nate and stay calm. So whatever it took, she had to find an excuse to leave.

"Miss Petrelli," she said, "I do not think you wished to speak directly to me. I think you planned this intrusion."

The lady stiffened. "I did not. I intended to bring you upstairs if you wished to speak to him. I would never have done this to you without warning."

She believed it, and that gave her a measure of forgiveness to the lady. "Nate always does as he wants. And nary a thought to the consequences."

"That's not true!" Nate exclaimed.

She didn't even look at him. Her words were still for Miss Petrelli. "I don't know why this Pickleherring targeted you, but I also don't believe you are fully innocent." She gathered her gloves and reticule with shaking hands. So many feelings churned inside her. She didn't want to latch on anger, but it was the only one that kept her from breaking down in tears. "So much meddling," she said, her voice tight. "Gossip columns, secret assignations." She shot Nate a glare. "I want nothing of this subterfuge. Good afternoon, Miss Petrelli. Lord Nathaniel. I doubt we will speak again."

And with that, she turned and walked steadily out of the parlor. Unfortunately, the moment she made to the front foyer, she realized she had a problem.

Fletcher was nowhere in sight. Neither was her carriage. Which meant she was trapped here. Which meant Nate would not let her have the last word. Damn it! Why wouldn't people leave her alone so she could manage her life as she saw fit? Everyone had to interfere.

Sure enough, Nate hobbled to her side before she could storm out into the afternoon sun.

Chapter Five

R AS WATCHED THE women go inside then pasted on a tight smile as he turned to Fletcher. He was fully aware that he'd just given the man a "win." Just being seen publicly with Fletcher gave everyone the impression that he sided with Fletcher against Kynthea in that very public altercation.

Nothing could be further from the truth, but he needed Fletcher to think they were friends if he intended to get to the bottom of the man's accusations against Nate. He'd accused Nate of everything from petty secrets to destroying Fletcher's family, not to mention driving a wedge between Fletcher and Ras. That, at least, wasn't true. Fletcher himself had destroyed their friendship by obsessing on Nate's supposed perfidy their last year in school. Nate had disappeared, Fletcher's father had died, and when the boy returned to school, all he could talk about was how Nate had killed his family.

He'd been grieving, obviously, but there was only so much hatred and venom Ras could take. He'd iced out Fletcher, and for that he felt some guilt. Had he, inadvertently, added to Fletcher's madness? If so, then perhaps this walk would make some amends. But in the meantime, he wanted to know—exactly—what Fletcher had discovered about Nate's activities.

Thankfully, Kynthea understood the situation and had agreed to the public slight. It was one of the reasons he loved her. She saw the bigger picture, could be counted on to make sacrifices if necessary, and—best of all—no longer cared what the *ton* thought of her.

She loved him and so had promised to support his machinations in this matter. After all, Nate had become Kynthea's friend first. Ras had realized what a treasure she was long afterwards.

"It's a lovely day for a stroll," Fletcher said, his expression genuinely happy.

Ras eyed the myriad people walking ever so slowly by them. Fletcher would want to parade their renewed friendship in front of the entire *ton*, but Ras had little interest in being so public.

"Let's go to my stable. I want to check on the salve that Lady Zoe sent. She says…" He frowned. Kynthea's cousin Zoe was brilliant when it came to horses, but listening to her talk about them was like getting a lecture in Greek. He couldn't understand anything beyond the first few words. "She said it'll make them spry. Or something like that."

Fletcher chuckled. "You really did make the right choice in refusing to marry her. The two of you have nothing in common."

They had a love of Kynthea in common, but that was about it. "Lady Zoe is very happy where she is. And very determined to win her bet against Prinny."

The man made a delicate shudder. "No way to win in that situation. Stupid to win a bet against a royal and well, she's not a girl who will lose gracefully."

Ras shot Fletcher a sidelong glance. The man was perceptive. That was exactly Ras's fear when he'd proposed the arrangement with Lady Zoe. Either way, that was a problem for another day.

"Fletcher," he said as they rounded the corner into the alleyway. "You must know that I have not forgiven you for maligning my fiancée."

The man huffed out a breath. "Honestly, Ras, I have no idea what you're talking about."

"You told me so to my face."

"We haven't spoken in an age!"

Ras turned to face the man, studying his baffled expression. If he didn't know better, he'd believe Fletcher's every word. There was such sincerity in the man's tone, such earnest passion that he led Ras to doubt himself. But Ras did remember. And now he wondered how far Fletcher would take his lies.

"The day I brought Nate to my house," Ras said. "You were outside his building. You told me what you'd done."

"Yes!" Fletcher huffed. "I was trying to find out if he lived. You must know that he's involved in…" He shook his head. "Unsavory things. He was at the docks. I told you that."

"And what were you doing at the docks?"

He folded his arms. "Investigating! Don't you know that there are smugglers everywhere? Right under our noses! Things that are supposed to be English are going other places. They're going *French* places."

"What things?"

Fletcher made a disgusted noise. "That's what I was trying to find out." He continued walking toward the stable doors. "England has always had smugglers. Cornwall was built upon it, for God's sake. But it's a bold man who manages it right here in London."

Was there admiration in the man's tone?

"You think Nate is smuggling something to Napoleon?"

Fletcher shrugged. "He's always been one to play both sides. He'll pretend to be your friend as long as it's to his advantage. But the minute he doesn't need you…" Fletcher made a stabbing motion with his fist. "He's ruthless. He killed my father."

That didn't sound like Nate at all. Though again, Fletcher said it with such conviction that Ras had to reconsider certain things.

"Nate didn't kill your father, Fletcher. He had a heart attack."

"Brought on because of him! Good God, Ras, why can't you see him clearly? Do you know what he does with his time?"

No, he didn't. And that was where there was some truth to Fletcher's ravings. Nate had always been mysterious about his activities, brushing off questions with vague sayings like, "Oh, this and that. Here and there." Several times he claimed to have spent some months in a certain lady's arms, without ever naming the woman.

It could be true. Or it could all be lies. Ras had never pushed him for specifics, and Nate—even in his cups—had never told.

"You're thinking of it, aren't you?" Fletcher asked. "What do you really know of the man? Where does he go? How does he make his money?"

"Why are you so obsessed with him?"

Fletcher didn't answer at first. He wandered into the stable, looking at the horses there. It was Ras's private stable, housing his horses and vehicles in a modest display. A stableboy ran out to greet him and Ras waved him away. He didn't intend to ride.

"It's not bad business," Fletcher finally said once the boy was out of earshot.

"What?"

"Some people—smart people—have always profited from war." He held up his hand. "Don't get me wrong. Napoleon is a monster and all that. I'm sure we'll defeat him eventually. But there is money to be made. If one is willing. And desperate."

"And you think Nate is doing that." The very idea made Ras's stomach rebel. Not only because he couldn't believe it of Nate, but also because the idea of profiting while men were dying made him physically ill.

Not so Fletcher. The man's eyes practically gleamed.

"I think *someone* is doing that," he said slowly. "I was investigating when I saw Lord Nathaniel skulking around the docks."

"That's what you were doing? Investigating?"

He pressed a hand to his heart. "I am a patriot. I don't know what Lord Nathaniel is." He lifted his chin. "And you don't either."

Ras didn't argue. For all that Fletcher was sowing doubt, Ras knew he would trust Nate long before he trusted Fletcher. He busied himself with looking at his horses. Lady Zoe had sent a long list of instructions, and he was curious to see if there had been any change. Meanwhile, he kept his tone casual.

"What, exactly, did you see Nate do?"

"Exactly? Nothing. I saw the thieves tearing off his boots. He howled when they stomped on his foot, then he crawled away like a cockroach and fell into the Thames."

Ras looked up, alarmed. "You didn't stop them?"

"What could I do? I thought he was dead."

"But you came back to his home."

Fletcher nodded. "Certainly. I had to tell somebody, didn't I? That he was dead."

"But he wasn't."

"You found him." Fletcher's expression turned sour. "Is he recovering?"

"He's getting better." Ras stepped into the stall of his favorite mare, running his hands over the creature's fetlock. Had the swelling gone down? Was she healthier? He had no idea.

"What has Nate said?"

"That he was having a pint with old friends." He looked at Fletcher. "Back when we were kids, after he didn't return to school, he spent some time on a merchant vessel. Made friends with the captain and they still get together when he's in port."

Fletcher scoffed. "And you believe him?"

"No reason not to."

The man snorted. "You're too gullible. Believe me, the man is up to no good."

They were going in circles here to no point. Fletcher just wanted to lambast Nate while Ras was determined to learn details. "Did you find any evidence of smuggling? Or were you just watching Nate?"

Fletcher shot him an annoyed look. "I found something. Maybe."

"What?"

"This isn't the place to discuss it. Meet me at my club—"

"No." Ras straightened up next to the mare. "This is more private than—"

"I told you!" Fletcher retorted. "I don't object to the profit. If a man finds himself short of funds—and I've experienced that here and there when Henry gets prickly with my allowance—then that man gets desperate to find a solution. If he's smart, he knows how to make coin. And if the worst happens and that Corsican wins, then you've got a way to make sure your family survives."

Ras arched a brow. "By making up to Napoleon?"

Fletcher held the stall door open for him to step out. "He's a monster, but sometimes monsters win. The families that survive take the long view."

Or the traitorous view. "Did you find evidence of smuggling?"

"I know something," Fletcher hedged. "I don't know all."

"Tell me—"

"You picked the better lady when you selected Miss Petrelli over Lady Zoe, but are you sure of her loyalties? She seems awfully fond of Lord Nathaniel. Sure, you've fallen head over heels for a woman. We're all stupid now and then. But you wouldn't be the first man to reconsider while waiting for the banns to be called."

The first banns would be called next week and each successive week until they married in a month's time. He had absolutely no intention of calling off the wedding. He was more in love with Kynthea every day. But Fletcher was hinting at something, and Ras wanted to know what that was.

"You want me to throw over Kynthea? Why?"

"If she's a traitor to the crown, you have to throw her over—"

"What the devil are you talking about? Kynthea's no traitor and I'll call you out if you say such a thing again!"

Fletcher abruptly backed up a step, his hands raised in surrender. But even as he appeared apologetic, his slanderous words continued.

"Of course, she isn't. Of course not! But what if Nathaniel is? What if he's right now tempting her with easy money. She doesn't have any, you know, and a woman likes to come into a marriage with something to offer her husband. Perhaps she just wants to buy you a bridal gift. Where is she going to get the money but—"

"Stop it." There was only so much Ras could take, even in the name of getting information out of Fletcher. "I will hear no more of this. Do not ever speak of Kynthea again, to me or anyone else."

Fletcher bowed his head. "Of course, of course. I am only looking out for you. You're a duke and so many people will lie straight to your face." He put on a winning smile. "Fortunately, I don't have to worry about that with my sister. You don't know her well because she's been with my mother at home. But she's here now. A good woman. Beautiful, refined, and knows when to listen to wiser people."

That was not how Nate described Lady Rebecca.

"I'm sure she's a fine woman," he said, merely because polite responses had been drilled into him from the cradle.

Fletcher smiled. "You haven't seen her in a while. We should head back and let you do the pretty with her."

Ras looked at the man, seeing that he was all smiles and what appeared to be genuine warmth. And it was because Fletcher was so good at that—at seeming to be genuine—that Ras gave an honest answer.

"I will not throw over Kynthea."

"Of course not! You're too honorable a man to do that. But if Nate is leading her astray—"

"Suggest that again—to anyone—and I will destroy you."

Was there a flash of annoyance in the man's eyes? It was hard to tell. Whatever emotions flitted through Fletcher, they were quickly gone. The man's eyes softened, his expression grew fond.

"Of course, Ras. I would never hurt someone you love. But it's good having someone look out for you, isn't it? Just like I used to?"

They started walking back toward the house as Fletcher reminisced about the things they'd done when Ras had first gone to Eton. Fletcher was older by a year and had taken the young, future duke under his wing. Everyone had known who he was. They'd either wanted to cozy up or skewer him, depending upon their nature, and Fletcher had been a welcome bulwark against all that confusing attention. It was thanks to Fletcher that he'd survived his first year. And thanks to him that he'd passed Greek, because he was bollocks at ancient languages.

But then Ras's father had died, and Fletcher couldn't seem to handle the emotions that blew like storms through the boy he'd been. Nate had, though. They'd been roommates at the time, and Nate had stood by him through every raging moment.

And that was just the beginning of the things that had cemented their friendship.

Still, there had been good times with Fletcher, especially that first year. And in the walk back to the house, Fletcher brought up the best ones. Which meant Ras was smiling when they made it back onto the street, and chuckling when they entered his home.

Then they both saw the disaster in his front foyer.

Chapter Six

NO, NO, NO! After a decade of dreaming about reuniting with Becca, Nate couldn't let her run away from him! He shot to his feet, cursing the pain that burst through his consciousness with every step.

"Becca! Becca, please!" he called as he rushed after her. It wasn't fast enough, damn it, but she slowed in the foyer. He wanted to believe it was for him, but he saw her peering out the door for her carriage.

Thank heaven it was nowhere to be seen. He had a few seconds yet before she fled.

"Becca, please just talk to me."

She whipped around to face him. "My name is Lady Rebecca!"

He winced. She wanted to be on a formal basis with him. She wanted to put barriers between them when he wanted…everything from her. Just as he wanted to give her everything he had.

Well, "everything" included polite respect.

He dipped his head. "Yes, of course, Lady Rebecca. My apologies." God, the formal words tore at his throat, but if this was all he could have of her, then he would take it. With gratitude.

"Lord Nathaniel," she said through gritted teeth. "Please remove your hand from my person."

He looked down, a little startled that he had grabbed her elbow to keep her close. He wasn't gripping her tightly. Last thing he wanted to do was give her bruises. And yet, it still took a conscious effort of will to open his hand.

"I apologize," he said. "I've done this badly. I've been thinking of this for ten years and have stored up so much I want to say. Please, can we not speak as we used to? Like old friends who…" He swallowed as he searched for the right words. "Who care about each other."

Her expression shifted through a myriad of emotions. He saw pain and fear. He thought there might be a softness in her, but it was quickly suppressed along with everything else. By the time she spoke, her words were coolly formal.

"Lord Nathaniel, we do not know one another. The… the child you once knew is long gone. The woman who stands before you is a stranger."

"Then let us speak as strangers meeting as if for the—"

"No!"

The word burst out of her in pain and fury. And God, how that hurt. In the past ten years, he'd imagined their reunion a thousand different ways, but not once had he thought she would refuse all communication. That she would reject him so soundly.

He swallowed down the pain and pushed through a single raw question.

"Why not?"

"I beg your pardon?"

"If everything that… if we are to ignore everything that happened when we were younger, then why—as adults—can we not speak? I am as aristocratic as you. We travel in the same circles. I am a man in search of a wife, and you are a woman in search of a husband. I have no debts nor noxious habits. And my best friend—the Duke of Harle—appears to be friends with your brother. Therefore, why am I so objectionable to you?"

He could see her jaw work, tightening and releasing. More telling still, her hands twisted in their reticule. "Fletcher says—"

"Do not parrot your brother's words to me," he said, his voice cold. "You and I both know that he is not objective. Tell me from your own experience how I disgust you."

She looked away. "It is not disgust."

"Isn't it?" he pressed, his voice softening. "Your hands are pressed tight into your belly. How do you feel?"

"Nauseous."

He reached up, wishing to touch her. Aching to caress her cheek and somehow soothe her. But he held back. "How can I fix this?" he whispered. It was the one question that had reverberated through his thoughts for ten years. How could he repair the damage between them? How could he prevent her father's death, find her again in a hayloft or a ballroom, and let her know how much she meant to him?

"Some things cannot be fixed," she said. "You know that."

He did. And yet he wanted to try. He stroked his thumb across her cheek, catching the tear that hovered at the edge of her lashes. She blinked at the gesture, as if surprised that she was crying. He wasn't. He knew that her emotions were often close to the surface, and that she hated that about herself. Her family ridiculed any emotional display.

He pulled his thumb back and kissed the wetness there.

"Don't hold back your feelings from me," he said.

He saw her jaw firm and then she struck, giving him a fast, whipping slap across his cheek, hard enough that his head twisted to the side, and loud enough that the sound echoed in the room. And it was painful enough that he automatically readied himself for a life or death fight.

Then he strangled the thought. He wasn't being chased by Napoleon's men. He wasn't being beaten by five thugs. He was safe in a ducal household. And she was no match for him physically.

Emotionally, however, she could slay him. Indeed, she just had.

"I never meant to hurt you," he said. Then he gave her a wan smile. "Do you want to hit me again?"

She didn't. Indeed, she appeared to be shocked and appalled

by her own behavior.

"Curl your hand into a fist. Leave your thumb outside. And punch through the knuckle of your index finger. That will save the rest of your hand."

"I'm sorry," she whispered. "So sorry."

If there was more, she didn't get to voice it. Neither did she get to hit him again as her brother burst through the front door, followed quickly by Ras.

"Get your hands off my sister!" Fletcher bellowed.

Nate immediately lifted his hands, showing that they were nowhere near his sister. He also stepped protectively between Fletcher and Becca. "Your sister is fine."

"You keep her name out of your filthy mouth!"

It was part of his own personal perversion that those words conjured a very pleasing image. But he knew better than to say it. "Fletcher, your sister is well able to protect herself."

"Thank God!" Fletcher responded as tried to grab Becca. He couldn't reach, but he could glare at the red mark on Nate's face. "I hope she hurt you," he hissed. "Come along Rebecca. I should never have trusted that this reprobate would remain decently upstairs."

"Fletcher—"

"Don't say anything now. It will only further upset you." He turned to Ras. "You see now, don't you? You see the insult he is? He is a damage to yourself and all decent people."

Ras didn't answer. His gaze was dark and troubled, especially when it landed hard on the stinging handprint on Nate's face.

"It's not what it seems—" Nate began.

Ras interrupted. "Lady Rebecca, are you all right?"

"Yes," she said as she stepped around Nate to go to her brother's side, but Miss Petrelli held out a hand. He hadn't even noticed her there, but she had been close by. No doubt ready to interfere if she were needed.

"Lady Rebecca," she said. "This is not at all what I planned, and I most sincerely apologize. I hope you will consider speaking with me again. At my cousin's house. Away from…" She gestured to everyone. "Whatever this was."

Fletcher didn't give his sister a chance to respond. "We have no desire to speak with you again, Miss Petrelli. Indeed, I sincerely hope—"

"Have a care, Fletch," Ras rumbled as he crossed to his fiancée's side.

Fletcher visibly swallowed his next word. Then he lifted his chin. "Good day to you all." The words were hurled as an insult. Then he glanced at his sister. "Come along," he commanded.

Becca did as she was bid. She didn't look back. She didn't pause to throw him a glance. She didn't twist just enough so he was in her peripheral vision. If it were possible for a woman's back to throw up blinders, she would have done it all around her.

And he, as usual, watched her go, unable to talk to her, unable to make up for the blunders of the day or of the last decade. God, what a mess.

Then, to make it worse, when the door finally closed behind them, Ras dropped his hands onto his hips and glared straight at Nate.

"What the hell were you thinking? You were supposed to stay upstairs! Let her ask to see you! Let her choose, instead of being forced into a confrontation."

He swallowed. "I couldn't wait."

"Then you're a bloody idiot."

Obviously. But there was another concern. "Did you learn anything? What does Fletcher think?"

Ras shook his head. "That you're smuggling something to France."

"What?"

"That's what he thinks."

"But why?" Nate fought to keep all his whirling thoughts from his tone. "Was he following me or investigating smuggling?"

Ras frowned. "I'm not sure. He seemed to be saying both."

"What does he know about the smuggling?"

Ras's gaze sharpened. "He didn't elaborate. Why? What do you know about it?"

He threw up his hands in disgust. "Nothing!" That was the damned problem. And now he had to investigate Fletcher. It was possible the man had stumbled upon important information, or maybe, the man was making up idiocy just to make himself look important. That happened more times than not.

Either way, he needed to know the truth.

Meanwhile, Ras took Nate's arm and gently forced him toward the stairs. Good idea because Nate's feet were burning.

"I don't what to think," Ras was saying. "Fletcher could be deluded or a very skilled liar."

"Or both," Nate said, his tone dry. Meanwhile, he had to pause on the steps to let his feet rest a moment. God, it felt like his stockings were soaked with blood, all inside his shoes. Which meant he'd have to buy new ones, and damn it, that was an expense he didn't want to manage right now. Spying for the government was not as lucrative as he would have liked.

But first things first. "Think back," Nate said in an undertone. "Tell me the entire conversation word for word."

KYNTHEA WATCHED THE men go, her hands on her hips as she quietly shook her head. Ras had asked her if she was all right. She reassured him that she was fine but then lost his attention as he focused on the drama in front of them.

That was all well and good, but he'd forgotten to ask her if she'd learned anything. He was deep in his whispered conversation with Nate as they headed upstairs, no doubt to assess how much damage the foolish man had done to his feet.

"Send up hot water, cloths, and more of that honey unguent, if you please," she directed the butler.

"Yes, Miss Petrelli. Right away."

"Thank you. And…" She sighed. "Try to keep the gossip to the minimum. We don't know what all that was about, and speculation only makes us appear foolish."

The man dipped his chin. "I quite agree."

Of course he did. He was a ducal butler and had likely seen a great deal in his life. In the meantime, she had her own investigation to begin. The men might not have learned anything from Lady Rebecca, but Kynthea was not as blind. Kynthea had seen several abused women in her time. There weren't any bruises on Lady Rebecca's body, but the woman was trapped nonetheless. Whether or not the lady wanted to run to Lord Nathaniel was her own business. That was a choice for when she was free.

Escape, however, was an option she needed to be offered now. And Kynthea knew just how to begin the process.

Chapter Seven

R EBECCA CLIMBED INTO the carriage behind her brother, her hand still stinging from slapping Nate. Whatever had possessed her to do that? All he'd done was take the tear off her cheek. A tear she hadn't even realized she'd shed.

That hardly merited a slap, and yet she'd felt such a rush of raw fury that she'd lashed out.

And what had he done in response? He hadn't fought back or even grabbed her wrist. And he'd had every right to contain her, but he hadn't even been angry.

Do you want to hit me again?

Yes! No! God, what was wrong with her?

She settled on the squabs beside Fletcher and closed her eyes. Lord, she hadn't felt this emotional in years. In ten years, to be exact. Ten minutes with Nate and she was slapping people. Or rather, him.

"Tell me everything that happened. Exactly."

She sighed. Fletcher would demand a recounting. "We talked, we had tea. Lord Nathaniel proposed."

"He what?"

She arched a brow at him.

"Well? What did you say?"

She snorted. "You saw the result."

"You slapped him? Excellent. He just wants your dowry. Imagine the audacity of thinking that you would still be vulnerable to him. Good God, he is a fool. I suppose he's too lazy or too stupid to try to seduce other heiresses."

"I think he's trying to make up for the earlier disaster. Marriage would erase some sins."

"Will it bring our father back to life?"

Rebecca sighed. "No, of course not."

"Exactly. I'm pleased that you handled it. I would have had to call him out if I were there. That would be awkward."

She jolted. A duel? "Fletcher, you wouldn't!"

"Of course not. There are easier, less public ways to kill a man."

"Fletcher! Good God—"

"I'm joking. Calm down." He flashed her an indulgent smile. "In any event, I'm pleased you put him in his place."

She wasn't exactly sure what she'd done, but she didn't express that to her brother. Meanwhile, he folded his gloves in his lap and turned to her.

"Now tell me about Miss Petrelli. Any oddities there? Did you press on that love potion nonsense?"

"I didn't get the chance."

Fletcher grunted in disgust. "I told you most specifically—"

"It was an odd situation from the beginning. I don't know what game you're playing but leave me out of it."

"Game!" her brother huffed. "This is the game of living. It's the game of finding a husband who will bring advantage to yourself and our family. And I am going to great lengths to see that you do it well."

"Perhaps you should go to less effort, then," she shot back. "Fletcher, I did not ask for your escort today. Nor did I need it."

"Be thankful that I was there. I was able to plant some seeds with Ras. I don't suppose Miss Petrelli is silly enough to be tempted away from a duke, is she?"

"No," Rebecca said, the word hard and cold.

"And Ras seemed determined in his choice as well. Very well. You'll have to marry the baron then. He's your next best option."

"Baron?" She gaped at him. "What baron?"

Fletcher waved a hand at her. "Baron Courbis. You'll meet him tomorrow night. Wear something low-cut. He likes breasts."

"Fletcher!"

"I've already primed him in your direction. Let him touch you a bit, tell him how handsome he is, and he should be amenable. Needs a mother for his daughter. You can be wed as soon as the banns are called."

"You're joking."

"Oh, don't cut up stiff. We all know that your breasts have been out for everyone to see. He doesn't know though, so keep that to yourself."

"Fletcher!" She glared at him, but he was completely impervious to her fury. And damn him for bringing that up whenever he got out of line. It had been her father and the vicar who had seen her. And Nate, of course. But that was ten years ago!

"Fine," he said, as if he were giving her great boon. "Let him touch them but no more. They're large enough to be tempting, thank God. Then go all maidenly shy. He'd be down on one knee in ten minutes."

She shook her head at her brother. "No one will be touching my breasts, and I shall not accept any proposal so soon!"

Fletcher looked at her then, really looked. His expression shifted to rueful even as he patted her knee. "You're overwrought. Of course you are, seeing that blackguard again after all this time."

That was the first correct thing he'd said all day. Unfortunately, it wasn't the least bit relevant. "I want to have a full Season this time," she said. "Give me time to see who's about before I make my choice. You can understand that, can't you?"

Fletcher squeezed her knee, his affection for her obvious. "Of course I can. It's only that I'm so busy. It's hard to find time for all this."

"You don't have to escort me—"

"But I do. Mama can't handle all the parties, as much as she wants to. How long before she gets another migraine?"

A day. Maybe two. The London air did not agree with her.

"And I have already looked at the crop of men for you. I know who is suitable and who is not."

"Then give me a list. Write down their names, and I shall make pains to meet every one."

His smile softened and she remembered the boy he'd been before their father died. Open. Funny. And if not exactly considerate—what boy was—but at least he'd never needed to manage every aspect of her life. And her future.

"You must trust me," he said gently. "I've given this a great deal of thought. And you're not at an age where you can afford to be picky."

And who's fault was that? His and her mother's, both. For the last five years, there'd been one problem after another. She'd come into town for a few weeks and then be pulled back home because Mother grew tired or Fletcher had other things to do than ferry her around. She'd barely get comfortable before she'd have to leave again. And any gentlemen she'd liked had disappeared from her life the moment she left London.

But sulking about the past was a child's game. She had to focus on the present.

"Tell me about this Baron Courbis. What's he like?"

"Oh, you'll adore him!" Fletcher enthused. "I've spent a great deal of time cultivating him. He's smart, rich, and willing to give some his considerable fortune to helping my campaign. Mother already approves of his suit."

She shot him a skeptical look. "Has she really approved or has she just left the matter in your capable hands?" Those last words were a mimicry of how Mama would have phrased it.

"Don't cut up stiff just because Mama trusts me," Fletcher said, a teasing note in his voice. "Oh, and the baron has a daughter. She's cute as a button with big brown eyes and so in need a mother."

A pang hit her. The idea of a motherless child did tug at her heart. But becoming a child's mother wasn't as easy as saying 'I do'.

"How old is she? What happened to her mother?"

"I don't know. Four maybe five? The baron's wife died in childbirth with the second child."

"How awful."

"She'd adore you. I'm sure of it."

She sighed. "Fletcher," she began, but he cut her off.

"Oh good God. I'm trying every way I can to help you, and you just don't appreciate it."

Now he was the one getting overwrought. "Of course, I appreciate—"

"But you're always complaining. You won't even give the baron a chance. He's perfect for you."

She gritted her teeth. She'd been conditioned from birth to stop arguing the minute someone took that tone. The words, "You don't appreciate all I've done for you," had been spoken in their home from her earliest memory. It was what her mother said whenever she became overwhelmed. Henry grumbled similar things, though never to her. And here was Fletcher voicing the same sentiment. The only one who hadn't used the phrase was their father. He'd had no patience for anyone who needed appreciation.

But Father was dead and gone, and Rebecca had learned that there was no changing her family's mind once that phrase was used. For whatever reason, Fletcher was determined that she like this Baron Courbis. And so she would give him a chance. But she made no promises on marriage.

"I look forward to meeting the baron."

Fletcher was not mollified.

"You will be kind to Baron Courbis tomorrow night. You will wear a gown that emphasizes your full assets." He flicked a glance at her breasts. "And if he proposes, you will accept."

"And if I don't?"

"Then you will go home where you can marry the bootblack, for you will be of no more use to anyone."

It wasn't an idle threat. For all that mother loved London

during the Season, she hadn't the stamina to stay more than a few weeks. She was prone to illness, the London air was terrible on her lungs, and someone was always slighting her, or so she claimed. If Fletcher turned irritable, if he refused to escort them, her mother would grow petulant. It wouldn't be long before Rebecca was shipped back home to wait hand and foot on her mother—again. And where—Fletcher was right—the only possible husband was far below her social status.

She wouldn't care if any of them were remotely interesting. But she was well-read, intelligent on several medicinal topics, and wanted a man who loved her and all her foibles. Those men were non-existent back home. So she had to do what she could to stay in London.

If that meant temporarily appeasing her brother, then so be it.

So it was time to use her own well-used phrase, the one she pulled out whenever someone in her family grew stubborn.

"Of course, Fletcher. You're right."

It was a lie. It was always a lie, but she'd learned that the appearance of giving in was usually enough. It kept the peace while she went ahead and did what she wanted. And if there were consequences for the lie, she would face them later. But right now, she couldn't risk Fletcher's ire. Besides, maybe the baron was perfect for her. She would wait and see.

"And I will wear something appealing," she added. Then a defiant part of her pushed back because she hated being such a docile creature. "I will also meet other gentlemen there. That is the point of a ball, is it not? To meet eligible bachelors?"

Her brother flashed her a superior look. "Meet whomever you like but recall that I know better than you what they want and what are their peccadillos. You will trust me when I tell you that a gentleman is unacceptable."

She had no answer to that. She knew from her work with Mrs. Chenoweth that some men had vices that were not shown to an innocent virgin. And though she wanted to believe she had some discernment when it came to the nature of men, her family obviously did not.

So she would have to walk a fine line while she was in London. But surely there was a man somewhere who would satisfy both herself and her family.

"Don't pout," Fletcher said, though if anyone were pouting it was him. "You'll like the baron."

"And what does he give you?" she asked, her voice carefully modulated to seem calm.

"What?"

"I am to help the family with my choice of bridegroom, yes?"

"Yes."

"So what does the baron bring to our family?"

"Money." Fletcher smiled. "He is richer than Croesus, and he will fund my bid for a seat in the House of Commons."

"But we have plenty of money."

"You have your dower property. Henry has the income that goes to the title. I have nothing." He said that last part with an indignant sniff.

Fletcher had a generous allowance, according to Henry. But prices were different in London, as she had cause to discover when she saw the bill for her gowns. Perhaps Fletcher was more pinched than she knew. Especially since he paid for the London staff out of his own funds.

"What does the baron offer me?"

"Money, a doting husband, and the children you've always said you wanted."

"He can't be doting yet. He hasn't even met me."

"I have faith in your powers of persuasion."

He meant in the power of her breasts. She arched a brow, and he finally relented.

"He is handsome, rich, and will treat you well. What more could you want?"

Nate's face flashed through her mind. Not just his face, but the way he looked at her when he said, *I never meant to hurt you. Do you want to hit me again?*

It made no sense. It wasn't even a flattering picture of him. But she thought about it nonetheless. Nate didn't react with violence, he took responsibility for his mistakes, and he asked her what she wanted to do next. Even if it was hit him.

What man did that? Would Baron Courbis do the same?

"You'll like him," Fletcher promised. "He's very charming."

And, strangely enough, it turned out that Fletcher was right. Two nights later, she met a very handsome, very delightful Baron Courbis. He said all the right things, laughed at all the right times, and smiled in a way that set many hearts to fluttering, not just her own. But his attention was fixed unnaturally on her.

It was a heady thing from so handsome a man. From any man!

If it weren't for Fletcher's smirk—visible from across the room—she might indeed be tempted to walk into the shadows with the man. But it had been ten years since she'd entertained so foolish an idea.

She settled for talking with him as much as a ball allowed. And promised to walk with him in Hyde Park on the next day. And perhaps a theater visit with him after that. If he still pleased her by next week, then she would consider something more permanent.

Indeed, he was so perfect that she began to question her own sanity. Could this man really be exactly what she wanted? Honestly, he seemed too good to be true. If only there were a way to quickly determine if everything he said to her was a lie. After all, anyone could keep up a front during the few hours of a ball.

And that was when she remembered the Truth Serum still tucked in her reticule. It was ridiculous. But what other choice did she have?

Chapter Eight

REBECCA ENTERED THE ballroom behind her brother and mother. They greeted their hosts with general politeness and then wandered away as was their usual pattern. Her brother would set their mother down with the dowagers, then he would head straight for the nearest group of political gentlemen, usually near the footman who served liquor. Neither would glance back at her. They assumed she would find her own group of friends.

In a smaller setting, she would have no problem. She knew how to make small talk with strangers. But this was a ballroom stuffed with people, and she had entered the Season late. The young girls had all made their clutch of friends. And her older schoolmates were not in town this year for a variety of reasons, but primarily because the married ones were increasing.

Just about everyone she called a friend was married.

"Oh sweet angel, I have been waiting an age for you to arrive!"

She smiled as Baron Courbis sauntered up to her. He was a broad man with exquisite taste in clothes. His hazel eyes sparkled when he saw the flowers pinned to her bodice.

"I knew the lilac would be perfect on you." He took a deep breath. "Smells heavenly when it mixes so sweetly with you."

She felt her cheeks flush. He'd worn a lilac waistcoat to match the flowers he'd sent, and when he bowed to kiss her hand, his gaze travelled lovingly over the flowers she'd pinned to her gown and then slid down to linger on her cleavage. Fletcher had ordered all her gowns altered to emphasize her bosom. She thought it just on the edge of vulgar, but there was no denying the male attention she received. Whether because of her breasts or her dowry, she'd already been labelled a success.

Of course, out of all the gentlemen who stepped forward to scribble their name on her dance card, none was as attentive as the baron. He never left her side as she slowly walked the perimeter of the ballroom. She was looking for some of her old friends while he entertained her with constant expressions of his devotion.

"Did you find any entertaining books at the lending library? I recall that you were specifically looking for a tome on medicinal plants."

It was uncanny how well he remembered her plans.

"Sadly, I didn't find anything useful. At least nothing I haven't read before. Though I did find some fun things."

"A few novels of romance and derring-do?" His brows rows suggestively.

"Maybe." She did have a weakness for those silly tales. Who didn't want to read about love and adventure? "Oh, hello Mr. Moltzer, Mr. Bremen." She curtsied politely to the gentlemen, then offered her dance card at the appropriate time.

The baron stood by, looking on like a disapproving uncle. Once the niceties were completed, he took her arm and continued to escort her around the room. "You know," he said as they moved past the lemonade, "I was at a bookseller's yesterday and saw something you might like. Have you read, William Withering's *Account of the Foxglove and Some of its Medical Uses*?"

She turned to stare at him. "No, I have not, but I have heard of it. Please tell me the name of the bookseller. I shall get a copy immediately."

"Oh dear, I'm afraid he can no longer help you," the baron said with teasing smile. "His last copy was purchased this morning."

She sighed. "Well, perhaps he can find me—"

"By me, my dear. I bought it off him, sent it round as I was leaving to come here. It's probably waiting in your bedroom now." He leaned forward and tapped her nose. "Promise me you won't stay up all night reading it."

She blinked. "I shall promise you no such thing!" And though she knew it was improper for her to accept such a precious gift from a man not related to her, she couldn't bring herself to refuse it. But she could attempt to be proper. "Pray let me repay you. That book was probably very expensive."

"You are worth it, my dear. And if I have my way, I shall be buying you many more books in the years to come."

She flushed and looked away. He was always saying things like that, declaring his interest for all to hear. It would be delightful in a man who had known her for years, but their acquaintance was barely a week old.

"I have embarrassed you," he said, his voice filled with contrition. "Janet used to tell me that my passions overwhelmed people. That I should moderate my public desires. It is only that when I see something I desperately want, I cannot stop myself."

Janet was his first wife, tragically gone of childbed fever. "How was your daughter this morning? Has she recovered from her cough?"

"Nanny says she is nearly recovered. But of course, what she really needs is a new mother. And perhaps a brother." At this, he slid his hand down her arm to grasp her fingers through their gloves. The fabric muted his touch, but she felt his meaning like a heavy cloak. He was clearly anxious to find a new wife, and he'd obviously selected her.

But why? Why her?

Just about any woman in the room would leap at the chance to marry him. He was handsome, rich, and not disgustingly old. At thirty-nine, he wasn't young, rash, or foolish either. She should be falling over herself at his attention.

Instead, she felt a bit smothered. And ungrateful. He was giving her wonderful gifts, showering her with more attention than she'd ever received. Better yet, he'd encouraged her to talk about her interests (medicines) and her fears (biting insects). They'd even discussed her teenage disaster with Nate, and he had seemed to understand. Teenagers are so impetuous, he'd said, and relayed a tale of his own adolescence.

He'd been trapped by a scheming barmaid and discovered by her horrible mother. He'd barely escaped marrying the shrew which, he claimed, was very similar to her own tale. An innocent teenager faced disaster because of someone else's duplicity.

But Nate hadn't been duplicitous or scheming, and so she'd explained. But the baron waved away her comment with casual dismissal. "You were innocent. He was not." Then he'd taken her hand and kissed it. "I forgive you," he'd said.

And the next morning—during Fletcher's regular grilling of her activities—her brother had crowed about how generous the baron was being about her indiscretion. No other gentleman, he claimed, would be so understanding.

That was likely true. So why wasn't she falling at the baron's feet? Why wasn't she blushing with delight every time he whispered that he wanted to deepen their relationship? She wanted to get married. She wanted children, and he already had a four-year-old girl desperate for a mother. She'd met little Edith on their walk in Hyde Park. The girl had been sweet as she'd walked alongside her nurse.

He was everything a woman could desire in a husband: attentive, understanding, and rich. But she just wasn't sure. Or perhaps she didn't trust herself to know what she wanted.

"Why?" she abruptly blurted.

The baron stopped their slow circuit of the ballroom. "Why what?"

Oh! Goodness, she hadn't meant to be so blunt. But now she'd said it, so she might as well explain. "You've been so attentive, Baron Courbis. Wonderful and amazing." So many adjectives could apply. "But why me? You could have anyone."

He chuckled and patted her hand. "So modest. Beauty, intelligence, and modesty. What more could a man want?"

That didn't seem like a real answer, and she gently removed her hand from his. "Your first wife was correct. You're overwhelming sometimes."

"But surely that's not a problem. She understood that it came from a place of love."

"Of course," she said as she resumed walking. He matched her pace, his words earnest.

"Do you wish me to declare myself? I will. I have! I shall go down on one knee now—"

"No!" Her cry was too loud and nearby people turned to look at her. She felt her cheeks heat as she quickly moved further down the room. "No," she repeated. "I've just gotten to London. I been here barely a week. I cannot make such a decision so quickly."

He firmly picked up her arm and placed it on his. She could have resisted, but that would be churlish.

"I know my mind," he said in an undertone. "What can I do to convince you that we are perfect for one another? Tell me, and it shall be done."

Who wouldn't be overcome by such a statement? By such a declaration! She couldn't think of a thing that would satisfy her questions. Especially since they'd had some version of this conversation at least three times already. Why do you want me? Because you're beautiful or intelligent. This was the first time he'd added "modest," but that was hardly convincing.

She needed a way to get him to answer honestly. But how…

She bit her lip, the bottle in her reticule suddenly burned into her awareness. Indeed, she'd tried to forget it several times this week, but her maid insisted she keep it with her at all times. And the dratted woman kept adding it to her tiny purse.

Just how far was the baron willing to go? Just how much silliness would he accept from her in the name of honesty? Especially since their entire future hung in the balance?

"I should like a private conversation with you," she began.

"Done."

"But, um, only after…well, it's silly, of course."

"I adore silly."

Really? He'd disparaged the way his daughter had pretended to be a walking flower. Rebecca had thought it sweet and funny.

"It's a silly thing my maid wants me to try."

He turned to face her. "Sounds intriguing."

"It's a truth serum. You'd drink it a half hour or so before—"

"What? Truly?"

She shrugged. "Well, I should like to know if it works. And I should like to have a private conversation with you."

"Do you have it with you?"

She blinked. "Uh, well, yes. But it doesn't—"

"Give it to me. I shall take it now. The dancing is about to begin. That should be enough time, yes?"

"I, um, I suppose so."

"And then after the set is done, we can take a walk in the gardens. No wait, that won't be private enough, will it?"

Given the size of the ball, it wouldn't be very private. Everyone would want to wander during the pause between sets.

"I know. There's a window into the library. I'll make sure it's open, then we can stroll outside before ducking in there."

She frowned. "You sound like you've done this before."

"Taken a truth serum? Of course not. But every gentleman knows how to be secretive when a lady's honor is at stake."

She stared at him, completely overwhelmed. Again. The man did nothing by halves. "Baron, surely this is not the right—"

"Come, come. It's time to be a little daring, don't you think? Give me the potion."

What could she do? He was insistent upon it now. She opened her reticule and pulled out the small bottle. It was made of heavy clay with a cork stopper. It could contain anything from simple water to poison, but he clearly trusted her. He pulled out the cork and sniffed.

"There's lemon in there, I think." He looked at her. "Do you know the recipe for this?"

"No. It came from an apothecary. But you shouldn't—"

Too late. He'd already tipped the full bottle into his mouth and swallowed.

Chapter Nine

NATE DIDN'T WANT to go to tonight's ball. And he sure as hell didn't want to go dancing. His feet were healing but still hurt whenever he put pressure on the right foot. But he needed to speak to his contact during the Joguet ball, and he couldn't use his typical disguise of a footman or delivery person. Any servant would be expected to work, and the best he could do was recline in an elegant lounge.

So he had to attend the ball as himself, and he had to convince Ras to let him go alone. The two of them together drew too much attention. Everyone tracked a duke's movements, especially one newly engaged. And then there was all the love potion stuff, which made him especially interesting. If Nate entered with him, everyone who couldn't get close to Ras would sidle up to him.

That was hurdle one. The second was getting enough coin to handle all the logistics. Hackney there and back, new stockings and shoes, because he'd bled all over his, and the bribe. All information had to be paid for one way or another. In time and attention if nothing else. But his contact in the Joguet household needed cold, hard coin. And Nate was sadly lacking in that.

Fortunately, he'd been able to borrow some of Ras's clothing to cover the basics, including a fresh cravat. And he'd won a couple pounds playing cards with Ras last night, so that covered the hackney. But the bribe?

That was going to take finesse.

Ras walked in as Nate was dressing.

"What are you doing?" the man asked as he leaned against the doorframe.

"I can't sit around any longer. The boredom is killing me." At least he'd managed to write a little, but he was accustomed to being a great deal more active.

"Your feet will be permanently damaged if you don't give those bones time to heal."

It was a real risk but so was letting Napoleon win the continent. "I don't intend to dance. Just…" He waved a negligent hand in the air. "You know."

"No, I don't."

Damn it, Ras was getting prickly demanding answers. It was a lot easier five years ago when he could distract the man with women or liquor. Fortunately, he had a ready excuse. "Cards, you cretin. I need to win some money. My tailor bill is due."

"I'll pay your tailor. You stay here and get better."

"No." And at his friend's sudden sharp look, Nate flashed him a cheeky grin. "But I will borrow a cravat, if you please." He pointed at a pair of stockings resting on the coverlet. "I've already stolen these from you, so you can add those to my bill."

Ras folded his arms. "Your feet are a mess. The bones have barely had time to mend, you still run the risk of infection, and if the fever strikes, you could die. Why are you risking your life?"

"Don't be dramatic. It's just a ball, with pretty ladies who will ooh and ahh over me as I regale them with a tale of my terrible attack. They'll fall over themselves to pamper me."

"Hmmm."

Nate matched Ras's tight expression, slowly exaggerating it until the duke snorted at the comical display. "Very well. What ball?"

"I'll take a hackney."

"The devil you will. I'll go with you just to make sure—"

"No, Ras. You suck up all the air when you arrive. Not a single pretty girl will look my way when you are there."

"I'm engaged."

"Nevertheless."

Ras stepped further into the room, shutting the door quietly behind him. "You are my closest friend, and yet I know nothing about how you spend the bulk of your time."

"Sitting on my arse, staring at the ceiling! Ras, don't make more of this—"

"I'm trying to help you!"

Nate had several ready answers to that. He could laugh it off without giving any details. It was what he'd always done with Ras, but that technique was wearing thin. Ras wouldn't tolerate it any longer. Which meant he had to give a cutting remark. He had to push his dearest friend away, thereby beginning the end of their association. It was what he'd done with so many others over the last ten years.

One after another had realized their friendship had been built on sand. The moment they pushed to know more was the moment he had to grow cruel and shove them away. That was how this game was played.

But he couldn't do it with Ras. Just like he'd never been able to stop dreaming about Becca. They were embedded deep in his childhood, which made them tethers to his true identity. He wasn't a footman slipping through the Joguet's kitchen. He wasn't a Portuguese sailor burning through his pay after smuggling supplies to the English soldiers. And he definitely wasn't a feckless aristocrat with nothing but time on his hands, though he spent a great deal of effort to appear so.

He was Ras's friend. And Becca's lover. And the man who risked everything in service to his country when his country couldn't even admit he was anything but a half-drunk hanger-on.

"Don't make me do this, Ras," he said. "Please."

He'd already lost Becca. That disastrous tea a week ago had shown him that. He couldn't lose Ras as well. It would destroy him.

"You can trust me," his friend said.

"I do." Two words that meant the world to him. He trusted Ras as much as he could trust anyone. But the only reason he could function as a spy, the only way he could slip in and out of the shadows as he did, was if no one saw anything but the feckless, irreverent ne'er-do-well that he presented to the world.

And that included Ras.

Because one exception here and another exception there was how people got exposed. Or played. Or killed. And that didn't even factor in all the English boys who would get killed if men like him failed.

So he looked at his very last friend and flashed an irreverent smile. "Come on. Lend me a cravat and let me go play with some pretty girls. You've got Kynthea. Let me—"

"Will Lady Rebecca be at this ball?"

He winced. He couldn't hear her name without flinching in memory. He'd really botched that reunion.

"I don't know."

"And if she is?"

"I'll call for a glass of brandy and devote myself to charming the nearest blonde." His lips curled. "I've always had a fondness for blondes."

"No, you haven't."

Truth. Becca had curly brown hair. And the prettiest blue eyes.

"Ras…" he began but then didn't know what to say. He'd run out of convenient lies, and he hadn't the wits to craft another.

The duke waited, his expression somber, and then he sighed. "I'll get you a cravat that will match your droopy green eyes."

"And fifty pounds, if you please."

Ras jolted. "What?"

"I suppose I could make do with forty." Then he glared at his friend. "And my eyes don't droop!"

He thought for a moment that Ras would cut up stiff. Indeed, he waited with his gut clenched tight and his breath suspended. He couldn't bear it if…

"God, you are an intolerable burden."

The words were spoken as such phrases often were. It was a throw-away line. A grumble. It meant nothing, unless it meant everything.

So when Nate didn't chuckle, Ras's expression abruptly softened.

"You're not a burden," he said gently. "Well, you can be, but not in the way you think. Damn it, man, I want to help!"

"Damn it, man, you are!" Then he pointed. "Stockings! Honey ointment! Safe lodging!" Then he grinned. "Fifty pounds."

"Forty. And a cravat."

"And a partridge in a pear tree," he sang.

In the end, Ras brought him fifty pounds, a cravat, and use of the ducal carriage. Normally he would refuse, but since he was going to the ball as himself, there was no reason to refuse the conveyance. And if his eyes were moist when he accepted the pound notes, then that must have been because he'd shoved his broken feet into his shoes.

He hoped Ras knew how much of a lifeline he was to Nate. Just as he fervently hoped that tonight's excursion would be worth the effort.

Then he gingerly walked down the stairs before directing the ducal carriage to Madame and Monsieur Joguet's ball. The two were French emigres, loud and proud royalists, and connected enough to London society to host an annual ball. But they wouldn't be the first French emigres to harbor split loyalties.

The Joguets' ball was an obvious place to go, in order to ascertain the couple's potential as rifle smugglers. They had money, connections, and an interesting one-upmanship relationship. Husband and wife made sport of finding interesting ways to make coin. While all of society disdained those who worked for a living, the Joguets were open about their ventures. At least some of them.

Even if the Joguets weren't the ones smuggling guns, they might know who was.

Either way, it was a good place to start. And Nate already had someone on the inside. Still, he quietly hoped he was on a fool's errand. He liked Madame Joguet. She was funny and sweet. She was also a great deal more intelligent than she let on.

Which, of course, made her a strong possibility.

He arrived after the first set had begun. He waited at the top of the staircase, surveying the crush. He immediately noted the cluster of the crowd, all the various possible suspects, Madame and Mons...

Becca.

Damn. The last thing he wanted was to be distracted by her, and yet, his gaze followed her no matter what he told himself. He needed to start chatting people up. He needed to find his contact. She was Madame's maid and was undoubtably here somewhere. And he needed to sit down because his feet hurt like the devil.

Instead, he descended the steps and wandered to the edge of the dancing so that Becca would see him. He had to know if a week apart had softened her attitude toward him.

He waited, watching her too intently when he was supposed to be a devil-may-care nob. But then he was rewarded. She turned in the movement of the dance. He lifted his hand as if to wave to her. And she stiffened to the point of nearly stumbling.

He held his breath as she recovered. Her partner helped in this, and the peacock grimaced at having to support her for that split second's change. Nate watched as her cheeks darkened in embarrassment. And then...

She pointedly caught his gaze before sharply turning her back on him. Ouch! A cut direct, only marginally disguised by the movements of the dance.

Becca was still angry then. He deserved it, of course, so he let his chin dip in acceptance—not that she could see it—and turned to find a chair. He needed to rest his feet.

He made his way to the dowagers. They always had the best gossip. Sadly, they were much more interested in the tale of his attack than in sharing any interesting tidbits. He regaled them with a fictional account of what had happened. He pretended it was one ruffian plus a small boy who caught him unawares. He bemoaned the loss of his boots and laughed at any suggestion that he had been by the docks. Apparently, Fletcher had already spread that rumor. He reassured everyone that he had been at a less than reputable gambling den and got exactly what he deserved.

It was gratifying to see his version of events quickly make the rounds. Soon, just as he predicted, he was surrounded by lovely girls enchanted by his tale. It was during this gratifying bit of attention that he realized two things.

The first was that Becca was watching him. He caught her several times as she glanced his way, but that was because he couldn't stop searching for her. That gave him hope for some kind of reconciliation, though she remained stubbornly on the opposite side of the ballroom. At least, she wasn't indifferent to him.

The second, much more alarming realization was that something was wrong with Baron Courbis.

The man was a lecher, albeit a wealthy one. Nate had no quarrel with any man indulging his proclivities, assuming he had the coin to pay for it and the lady was willing. Like everyone, he thought the baroness's death was a tragedy, but at least she didn't have to suffer having Courbis humiliate her at every turn. The man was not subtle about his entanglements.

But the one thing that could be definitely said about Baron Courbis was that he was an excellent dancer. He moved with grace, loved being the center of attention, and never, ever appeared in public at disadvantage. Whereas Nate played a ne'er-do-well for the *ton,* Baron Courbis displayed excellence, at least in all the ways of polite society.

Until tonight, that is.

Tonight, he danced like a man with no rhythm and leaden feet.

He wasn't obviously drunk or ill, but his debonair smile

looked more like rictus. His brows were drawn down in concentration, and he was sweating—profusely. But just as Nate readied himself to investigate the situation further, his opportunity arrived.

He looked up at the dias where Madame Joguet sat and saw a stern-faced maid appear, carrying a wrap for her mistress. In keeping with French styles, Madame's gown was nearly diaphanous, but since she wasn't prone to vigorous dancing, she always called for a wrap sometime during the first set.

And that was his cue.

"Well, well," he said to his crowd of admirers, "I have spilled my tale for all your ears, and now I must go say my proper hello to our hosts." He turned to the matron nearest him. "Unless, of course, you want to tell me something salacious." He waggled his eyebrows. "Something like what your son-in-law has been doing with your daughter's plump little dowry." He leaned forward. "Did he take your advice?" It was a serious question. The boy thought he could make a fortune in the Exchange, but he hadn't the wit to do it properly.

"You might as well go," the dowager said, "because I shan't say a word." But there was a smirk on her face that told him she'd managed to guide her son-in-law into repairing their canals instead. A much better investment, and one Nate had recommended.

He kissed her hand by way of good-bye and then maneuvered gingerly to his feet. He was halfway to the dais when the musicians ended the first set. There was the usual bit of commotion as the dancers made their final bows and curtsies before everyone separated and began a great milling about. That was the problem with a crush, everyone got in everyone else's way.

And who was making the biggest fuss? Baron Courbis as he blundered his way to Becca's side. He made a show of bowing with overlarge movements and then holding up his arm as if he were demanding her attention. And she took it.

In fact, she took his arm and began walking with purpose.

Nate frowned. What the hell was Becca doing, accepting the arm of an obviously inebriated gentleman? Except the baron wasn't exactly stumbling drunk. But something was clearly wrong. Surely Nate wasn't the only one who could see that.

And where the hell was Fletcher? Becca couldn't have come here alone.

Nate grimaced, seeing his hostess fretting. Madame Joguet wasn't the most patient of women. She'd seen him now and was gesturing him over. And Becca had made it clear that he needn't be concerned about her. She wanted nothing to do with him.

His duty to his country demanded that he continue with his plans. There was no reason to jeopardize a smooth transfer of information just because Becca might be in trouble.

And yet, damn it! She and the baron were going out the French doors into the back gardens. Out where anything might happen.

He turned to follow but then saw Madame Joguet's brows narrow. Oh hell. The lady wasn't his contact, per se, but he couldn't get access to the maid without a friendship with Madame. At least not easily. Which meant his path was clear.

Country came first. Even before Becca. He turned his back on the French doors and headed up the dais.

Chapter Ten

REBECCA SAW NATE arrive. She wasn't surprised that he arrived late and then stood at the doorway, like a king surveying his kingdom. It wasn't that he appeared confident or even dominant. He wasn't that kind of king. Instead, he held himself as if fondly amused by everything he saw. Everyone here was his subject whom he loved and had pledged his life to protect. So perhaps not a king, but a knight errant, aware of all he risked and for whom.

It tugged at her romantic heart. She'd never been impressed by power, and she daily endured the petty exercise of it while she served her mother and brothers. So she had special fondness for the souls who worked, who served, and who did so out of love not obligation.

If only Nate served something other than his own amusement. If that were true, then she'd tumble straight back into love with him. But he *was* working for his own amusement, and so she had to communicate clearly that she was uninterested in furthering their acquaintance.

She gave him the cut direct, softening it by using the movements of the dance to turn away from him. Mentally, she gave her back to what he represented: privilege without responsibility. She knew he didn't have the wealth that her family did, but he'd been educated. His family had some money and even more connections. He could have become anything he wanted—a barrister, a politician in the House of Commons, a scholar. Any of the many respectable professions available to younger sons.

Instead of using his brain to do something worthwhile, he'd become a social fribble, a lazy, self-indulgent waste. So she cut him—socially—but inside, she ached. It hurt to see him so small.

Then she pushed him out of her mind. She was on a husband hunt and addressed herself to that task. She smiled, she danced, and she tried to learn more about her partners than their taste in attire and favorite hobby. And she waited for one to fire her imagination, if not her heart.

The dancing ended without anyone sparking her interest. So when the baron made his way to her, she happily took his arm. She could tell, if others could not, that he wasn't steady on his feet. The truth serum was affecting him, and she was interested to see what answers he would give to her questions.

"I am ready for your inquisition!" the baron rasped into her ear.

She smiled and allowed him to escort her. There were too many people around to begin her inquisition, so she remained silent as they passed through the ballroom to the back garden. She was startled as he took deep breaths, not just outside in the fetid London air, but inside as they passed through the various perfumes and body odors that occurred during any crush.

"Do you smell that?" he asked. "So many scents. So strong!" His head kept swiveling as he picked up one scent after another. Then they stepped outside, and he flinched. "Coal dust. We need a good wind to blow it all way. Plus rain. The rain will clear it up."

"For a time," she agreed, though wishing for a strong spring storm wasn't a typical thought. "Sir, now that we're outside—"

"The wind," he said as he lifted his face to the sky. "Where is the wind?" He looked at her. "Let me have your fan."

He didn't wait for her to offer it to him but took hold of the delicate wood and pulled it up toward his face. Unfortunately, it was still attached to her wrist. He didn't seem to care as he flicked it open to wave in front of his face. So she was left standing there with her arm extended while people looked at them in amusement.

"Balls, that feels good," he said as he closed his eyes and stretched his chin into the wind he created. "Aren't you feeling the heat?"

Obviously, this was a side effect of the serum, so she smiled and gestured to a back corner of the garden. "I believe there is a better breeze over there. Shall we—ouch!"

The baron was jerking her arm this way and that, trying to free the fan from her wrist.

"Blasted thing," he grumbled.

"If you would let me—"

Crack!

To her shock, he broke the fan, then cursed it before throwing it aside. Then he stripped off his gloves, tossing them aside as well while she tugged at the ribbon on her wrist. It took her a moment to pull it off because he'd jerked the ribbon so tight, but she finally accomplished it. And when she looked up, he'd wandered away from her, deeper into the shadows.

"Do you see the lights here? Such colors? It's like they're dancing." He was waving his hands in front of his face. "Do you think they're fairies?"

"Baron?" she asked. "Perhaps you ought to sit down."

"Sit down?" He turned to her, and true to her fear, he wobbled on his feet. But then he steadied himself with a hand on the nearest tree trunk, and his eyes widened in surprise. "Do you feel that?" he asked as he ran his hand up and down the bark. "That's incredible! Come, come!"

He grabbed her wrist and bodily dragged her forward. She started to resist, but he insisted, and she had no desire to create a larger scene. They had already attracted the attention of another strolling pair. More would wander near soon. Better to simply give in and let him press her hand to the tree trunk, then rub it up and down the bark.

It was a London plane tree with smooth and coarse patches,

depending on where the bark had flaked off. He seemed particularly fascinated by a nub, running her fingers over and around the peak.

"Do you feel it?" he asked. "Like a nipple only better. Firmer. Makes me want to suck on it."

"What?" she gasped.

"And your glove," he said. "My God, it feels so soft." He drew her hand up to his cheek while his fingers stroked her glove all the way up to her elbow.

"Baron, please. Let's sit down. I have an important question to ask you."

"Take it off!" he demanded, as he began to tug and her glove. "I have to see if it's different. Your glove or your skin. Good God, that feels so good." He was rubbing his face on her glove, using his larger size to muscle her into moving where he wanted her.

This was getting alarming, and she tried to twist away. "Baron, please. We were going to have a discussion," she said, trying to return to a normal conversation with him.

It didn't work. He pushed her against the tree trunk, then set his attention to pulling off her glove. She allowed it only because the more he focused on her glove, the more she could maneuver her body out from between him and the tree.

"Certainly," she said, her voice tight as she unbuttoned the clasp on her glove. "Here, let me help you." Once unfastened, she pulled away, letting him keep hold of her glove.

He tugged it off her, then rubbed his cheek against it. "So soft," he murmured. Then he started tugging at his cravat. "I feel so hot," he said as he let her glove drift to the ground.

"Baron. Please, I think you should sit—"

"Oh, do shut up!" he snapped. "Always talking. Never listening." He stopped with his cravat and glared at her. "Fletcher never said you'd talk so much!"

"What?"

Once his cravat was off, he began stripping out of his coat. "You have the breasts of a goddess," he said, "but damn your mouth!"

"What?"

"Questions, conversations. Just like Melanie. Only good when it's stuffed with my cock."

Melanie was his first wife, the woman he'd claimed he'd adored. The woman he had praised as a sweet goddess who had gifted him with her heart.

Rebecca took a step back. "Do tell me more about Melanie, please. Did you love her?"

"Love her?" he scoffed. "Such tiny tits. Couldn't believe she could nurse a baby." He grinned at her. "Nothing like yours."

She fought the urge to cover her breasts with her arms. "Is that why you want to marry me? Because of my breasts?" She was shaking as he looked at her. He was a big man who could easily overpower her, but she stood her ground.

"So tight," he murmured as he pulled off his waistcoat. Good lord, the man was stripping right in front of her!

She backed away another step.

"Don't go," he said, his eyes gleaming in the moonlight. Then he closed them as he threw aside his waistcoat. "There's so much I want to say but nobody listens!"

Really? Well, she was all ears now.

Except, as a proper girl, she ought to take this chance to run back to the ballroom. He was a large and unpredictable man. But she hadn't given him the truth serum to turn tail when it finally took effect.

So she stood her ground, in part because of a sense of responsibility. After all, she'd dosed him. She couldn't abandon him in a dark garden without anyone to care for him. What if he collapsed?

Mentally, she catalogued the serum's effects. The baron was overheating, and his skin seemed sensitized to the breeze. As she watched, he stripped out of his shirt and lifted his chest to the sky. Then he raised his arms, his hands clenched into fists.

"I feel so powerful!" he exclaimed.

Oh dear. That was loud enough to attract many people. The first couple who had followed them had wandered away in their own pursuits. But there were others around. Which meant she had little time to ask her most important question.

"Baron, why do you want to marry me?"

"I am a god among men!" he exclaimed as he thrust his hands to the sky.

"Yes, of course you are," she said. How else could she respond?

In truth, the whole display was rather cute. He kept moving, flexing his muscles, arching in a way that emphasized his size. His legs were planted wide, and his head was thrown back which exposed his chest to the moonlight. It was clear he adored his own body, and she found herself smiling.

He was like a little boy who had leapt upon the tallest rock and was declaring to one and all that he was king.

He looked at her. "You will worship me!"

She chuckled. "Wouldn't that be fun?" she quipped. "But about my question," she began. She had little hope that he would answer, but she had to try.

"No questions!" he cried. "Kneel!" Then, to her shock, he ran his hand down his cock before dropping his hands onto his hips and thrusting his groin forward. "Worship!"

She gaped at him. He could not have just done that. But then, she knew enough little boys to know how proud they were of their cocks. But rather than argue with him, she did what she did with all little boys who were being inappropriate.

She folded her arms, arched her brow, and smiled at him, even though her tone was stern. "That's wonderful, Baron. You are a good boy. Now let's put on your shirt and we'll find you a cherry tart, hmm?" At least she thought there were tarts planned for the supper buffet.

She picked up his shirt and held it out for him. She was smiling the whole time, cajoling him into obeying as she would any child. But he wasn't a child. And the moment she stepped close, the entire situation changed.

His face contorted as he knocked her hand aside. She gasped, but that was all the reaction she managed as he grabbed her hair and hauled her forward.

"I own you!" he declared.

Chapter Eleven

ATE KEPT THE French doors in his peripheral vision as he climbed the dais. He needed to pay attention to his chat with his hostess Madame Joguet. She hated boring conversations and valued him because he was entertaining. But he couldn't stop himself from watching for Becca's return from her stroll. He knew it wasn't his business, but damn it, he couldn't concentrate on Madame until he was sure Becca was safe. And it was too hard to split his attention between Madame, her maid Heidi Frid, and both open exits to the back garden.

Fortunately, he was skilled in juggling social situations. He kept his expression warm as he greeted his hostess. His gaze flicked to Frid who was once again adjusting the wrap for her mistress's cold shoulders.

The fabric was twitched this way and that by the woman's right hand. That was the signal that the stern-faced woman had information she wanted to discuss. And that, of course, was the reason Nate was here when he'd much rather be reading in bed with his feet raised. Or outside making sure Becca was safe.

"Lord Nathaniel!" Madame Joguet cried. "I have heard such a tale of your attack. Are you recovered?"

He shrugged. "Not enough to dance, I'm afraid. Otherwise, I would whisk you onto the floor."

"I think even you could not manage that," she said as she squeezed her swollen knee. More than a year ago, the lady had fallen badly on winter ice, and her knee had never recovered.

Indeed, that was how Nate and her maid had first met: at an apothecary shop that made healing salves for joints.

He leaned forward and kissed her cheek in the French way of greeting. "Perhaps an adjustment to your salve is in order. Shall I take Frid back to the apothecary shop to discuss it?"

Madame trilled a coquettish laugh. "Don't be silly. Frid has other things to occupy her time, and there are some things that one must accept."

He shook his head. "You are too young to live in pain. Come!" he said. "I insist. Besides, I need to visit them anyway for my ribs." He pressed a hand to his side and winced in pain. It was an exaggerated movement, but not by much. It hadn't been nearly long enough to heal his bones.

"Oh, you poor boy," she said as she patted a stool next to her. "Sit. Tell me the tale in detail. Everyone is talking about it."

"Everyone is saying nonsense," he countered, refusing to move to the stool. It would set his back to the French doors and he'd lose his ability to see Becca, if she returned. "My tale is simple. I was winning at the tables. And drinking heavily." He gave her a guilty shrug. "Of course, I would be robbed on the way home."

"So you were not skulking around the docks? Peering into places that you should not be?"

He rocked back on his heels—a painful move that served to sharpen his wits. "Minx!" he said. "Whatever have you heard?"

"Darling, do you think that I don't know about French champagne? And I know you enjoy the brandy." Both of which were smuggled goods. Goods he knew she brought in to England. But did she sell English guns out to the French?

"I do," he said. But he did not value the drink above the war effort. "And I have a very big appetite. Can you help me gain…satisfaction?" He glanced to where her husband was enjoying a lively discussion with an infamous widow. "Or shall I apply to Monsieur—"

"You shall speak to me!" she snapped. There was little love

between Madame and her husband, but they had a common mutual interest: that of finding income in England and not being beheaded in France. That resulted in a kind of gamesmanship between the two of them, each seeking to find security in England in the crassest way possible. Resale of smuggled goods was Madame's favorite pastime. Monsieur relied on bedding wealthy women for the jewels they gave him. He was known to be an exceptional lover.

But had Madame resorted to selling rifles to France? And would she, since she hated Napoleon almost as much as she hated poverty?

"Who told you I was at the docks?" he pressed. "The brutes who attacked me smelled of fish, to be sure, but I was outside a gaming hell that I shall never frequent again."

"Really," Madame drawled. "Could Frid have been mistaken?"

He looked back at the dour woman. He knew for a fact that she could appear very pretty when she wanted to but chose this sour look when serving her mistress. "Frid, what did you see?"

"A man beaten and stripped of his shoes—"

"That was me all right—"

"One who survived by diving into the Thames."

Oh! She had been there. Just how many people had been watching as he was nearly killed?

"That sounds like a very dashing escape," he drawled.

"That's why I thought immediately of you," Madame said. She squeezed his arm. "Now sit down. Ease off your feet, and tell me everything—"

Nate wanted to do it. Besides the pain in his feet, he'd been angling for months to learn more about Madame's smuggling network. This was the most open she'd been about her activities, and exactly the opportunity he'd been looking for.

But he couldn't stop thinking about Becca outside with the baron. They hadn't come back in. That wasn't unusual, of course. The musicians would be out for another twenty minutes. Many couples took the entire time to stroll outside.

But he didn't like it. And Fletcher was nowhere to be seen. Good God, didn't the man comprehend what was involved in the word "chaperone?"

"Nathaniel?" Madame said, a pout in her voice. "I begin to believe you think of another woman!"

"I do," he said as his gaze slid to Frid. "Do you trust your handmaiden?"

Madame didn't even look behind her at her maid. "She is paid well and knows the penalty for disappointing me."

That sounded ominous. Especially since Frid was already betraying her by whispering secrets to Nate. "Then perhaps…" he said as he pressed a kiss into Madame's palm, "I shall speak with her."

"Her!" she gasped.

"After I do what I do best," he said with a suggestive waggle of his brows.

Moving a footstool around, he settled too close to her legs for propriety. It was also a good position to block the view of what he was doing from most of the ballroom and yet still have a sideways view of the French doors.

And then, while he grinned mischievously at Madame, he began a technique that Becca had taught him to reduce swelling. A series of squeezes on the leg, beginning high up and then slowly travelling downward, though still squeezing in an upward motion. It wasn't sexual, though it could certainly be made so. This would move the body's fluids up the leg, reducing the swelling in her knee.

And Madame's eyes fluttered closed as she enjoyed the pressure.

"You have such marvelous hands," she murmured.

"I shall meet Frid at the apothecary," he said, his tone firm. "We shall get you a new salve and I shall—"

"You will bring it to me." She opened her eyes. "Then you will teach Frid how to do this."

He nodded in agreement. The woman was not lascivious, thank God, though he knew that many would assume so if he were seen going in and out of her chamber. It didn't matter to him so long as Monsieur didn't come after him with a weapon. And besides, it perfectly complimented his image as a ne'er-do-well.

"Then I shall meet Frid at the apothecary shop at…"

"Thursday, my lord. Nine of the clock," the woman said.

He stifled a sigh. That would feel especially early, but he had to fit into her schedule.

"And then," Madame said with a smile, "you shall come to me."

He pursed his lips in a kiss, though his face was far from hers. He had to finish the series of squeezes before he could leave her, but he resented every moment that prevented him from checking on Becca. And, damn it, he needed to press his hostess for more information. He'd been working on Madame for months, trying to earn her trust enough to let him in on her smuggling network. He knew she smuggled goods in to England. That was probably what Frid had been doing when she'd seen him beaten. But did Madame smuggle guns out?

"This knee must prevent you from carrying all that brandy," he murmured so quietly that Madame's eyes narrowed in on his mouth. She was reading his lips because she could not have clearly heard everything he said. "Mayhaps," he said clearly, "I can help."

She shook her head. "Mayhaps, I don't need you."

"Alas," he sighed. "I am struck down." She would not let him into her smuggling operations yet, but he was making progress. And a good spy knew when to push and when to be patient.

The lady chuckled as he finished the last of the squeezes. He'd rushed the sequence, but something was happening outside. He saw several people glance out there before oh-so-casually strolling out.

"I must go," he said as he straightened to his full height. "Frid, a word, please. I must know exactly how you have been using the salve. Details are important."

"Of course—"

"Damn, it's too noisy in here," he interrupted. "Come outside." He patted his pocket. "I need to make notes to give to the apothecary."

The maid waited until her mistress agreed and then followed a half step behind Nate. It wouldn't be appropriate for the woman to walk by his side. But that also made it impossible for him to have a whispered conversation with her.

There were far too many people between him and the French doors. Rather than wade through them, he motioned to the back of the ballroom. If he remembered the layout of this house correctly, there should be a servants' hallway just over…

"This way, my lord. Madame has paper and quill through there."

"A pencil will do," he quipped as he ducked into the back hall. But the moment he was through the doorway, he looked to the maid. "Heidi, does she export?"

The woman frowned, clearly not understanding.

"Buy goods, sell them in France?"

"Oh!" Frid kept her voice low. "No, but Monsieur might. He brags to her that he will make more money than her soon."

"Soon? Not now?"

The maid shook her head. "No, not now."

He wanted to ask more. Indeed, Lord Benedict would be furious if he knew that Nate had given up this chance. But the need to find Becca was eating at rational thought. And he'd just found the servants' door to the back garden.

"Tomorrow," he whispered. "Full details." Then he rushed out the back.

There was quite the crush of bodies here. Not so tight as he couldn't get through, but whatever was happening had drawn a great deal of attention. He had to skirt the wall, slipping behind some of the trees to get past. He constantly scanned for Becca's face or—more likely—the baron. Given Becca's petite stature, the baron would be easier to spot.

But he didn't see either of them. Fortunately, he didn't need to. He could hear them.

"I am a god among men!"

That didn't sound right. Well, the words were fine. Baron Courbis had an ego that befitted the words, but he was usually smart enough not to bellow it out loud.

"Yes, of course you are!" Becca said.

She sounded amused, and that immediately set his teeth on edge. She clearly had no idea that the baron had a vicious temper. He may be amusing right now, but that could change in a heartbeat.

Nate eased forward only to realize that Becca wasn't the only one amused. Clusters of people stood around chuckling at the display—whatever it was—while they left Becca to handle the obviously unstable Baron.

He just had to slip around this last tree to see…

Well, hell. He did not expect that. The man was naked from the waist up, his clothing scattered onto nearby bushes and rocks. And Becca stood in front of him, her hands on her hips as she tried to reason with a crazy man.

"You will worship me!" the baron commanded.

"Wouldn't that be fun?" she answered. "But about my question…"

"No questions!" he cried. "Kneel! Worship!"

This was getting out of hand fast. And none of the onlookers seemed inclined to interfere. It was just a show for them, and Becca had no understanding of the danger. Worse, Nate wasn't at an angle to interfere, not to mention that he wasn't exactly in fighting form.

Then Becca proved just how naïve she was as she treated the inebriated baron just as she would a stubborn child.

"That's wonderful, Baron. You are a good boy. Now let's put on your shirt and we'll find you a cherry tart, hmm?"

Oh bloody hell. No man liked being talked to as if he were a child, and the baron was pricklier than most. Nate guessed he was a second or so away from becoming violent. But how could he stop it from his position? There were people between him and the scene, and…

Wait a moment. He knew that shadow ahead of him. He knew the size and shape of the person skulking in the shadows just ahead. It was Fletcher! And he was watching!

Nate didn't waste time. Any so-called chaperone who stood around while a man disrobed in front of his sister deserved what was coming.

He moved quickly, alarm flooding him when he heard the baron's bellow.

"I own you!" That was quickly followed with an alarmed scream from Becca.

Nate couldn't see what had happened. He was too busy ramming his shoulder straight into Fletcher's back. The man surged forward. Indeed, he had no choice. And he landed exactly where Nate had aimed.

Right on top of the baron. Except that in his flailing, Fletcher also hit Becca. All three went down in a tumble of limbs.

That wasn't exactly what Nate had planned, but either way, he was prepared. He quickly stepped forward and gathered Becca into his arms. God, it was good to touch her again. And then he bodily pulled her out of the pile.

Unfortunately, that made everything worse.

Chapter Twelve

REBECCA HADN'T ANY breath to scream when a heavy weight landed on her. Had the baron toppled? Was it something else? She hadn't the time to process it as strong arms grabbed hold of her.

Thank God! Someone was helping her escape this terrible pile. She latched onto whomever's arms, using his strength—she thought it was a man—to twist and kick her way free. But there was a complication. The baron still had her hair gripped hard in his fist.

"Damn it, let go!" she cried.

"Get off me!" bellowed someone else.

Fletcher? Was he the newcomer to this scene? Whomever it was, he was equally anxious to escape. And the sounds he made confirmed his identity. She would recognize Fletcher's gasps of outrage anywhere. And the telltale sound of her gown ripping.

What a disaster!

But she couldn't deal with her dress until the baron released his grip on her hair.

Then she saw a gloved hand reached around her to grip the baron's hand, forcing it downward at the wrist until his fist opened. He released her hair!

Fantastic. She'd managed to get her feet under her and so was able to pull her head back, though she lost several strands of hair in the process. Either way, she could stand tall and deal with this social disaster. Assuming, of course, her dress was partially intact.

Meanwhile, Fletcher also gained his feet and was spouting the usual outrage.

She heard, "How dare you!" Then "I cannot believe…" something she didn't understand. And the ever annoying, "I demand an explanation!"

She ignored Fletcher, her attention split in two different directions. The first was on the baron, who had flopped onto his back, chest exposed to the moon. He was roaring like a stuck bear. Except he didn't seem unhappy. He sounded like he was enjoying the sound. And who wouldn't prefer such a thing over Fletcher's indignation?

The other part of her attention—the larger part—centered on the man behind her. The one who had pulled her from the pile and had forced the baron to release her. She felt the strength in his body as he cradled her, the heat from his chest on her back, and the angry huff of air as Fletcher pointed at him.

"You!" Fletcher hissed. "What have you done?"

He'd saved her from something a great deal worse than a torn dress. And *he* was Lord Nathaniel. His hands were larger than she remembered, and his body had more heft than when they were teenagers. But there was no change in the way he surrounded her, near enough to support her without restraining her.

He was the only man who'd ever made her feel protected without making her feel caged. And she turned to smile up at him in thanks.

"Are you all right?" Nate asked her.

"Yes," she said in the pause between roars as the baron drew breath.

"Your dress—"

"Not so bad." Not so great either. The skirt had ripped at the seam right under her bodice, so now there was a gaping hole that revealed her shift underneath her left breast. She grabbed the loose fabric and did her best to tuck it underneath the ribbon, but it was useless. She would have to stand there and hold it up.

Meanwhile Fletcher was being Fletcher. "Get your hands off of her!" he cried as he tried to grab hold of her arm. He would have caught her too if Nathaniel hadn't blocked her brother.

Meanwhile, the baron had stopped roaring. Instead, he lay on the ground chuckling to himself.

"Stop it, Fletcher," she said, her voice weary. "I'm fine."

"Yes," the baron said as he pushed himself into a seated position on the ground. "It's good, Fletcher. She will make me an excellent wife. Just as you promised."

"Of course she will!" Fletcher huffed. "And this would have been done in the proper way if Lord Nathaniel hadn't embarrassed himself and everyone—"

"Enough Fletcher," she said, fully irritated by the entire situation. Of everyone here, Nate was the least guilty. She, of course, was the most culpable, given that she'd dosed the baron with the truth serum.

"Be quiet!" her brother growled. "I'm trying to recover the situation for you."

The baren let his head drop back as he if appreciating the breeze on his half naked body. "There is no recovery," he said. "We will be married as soon as the banns are read." Then he turned to grin at her. "I am excited by the thought."

She folded her arms. "My brother cannot give away my hand without my consent—"

"What a happy situation!" Fletcher cried over her. He leaned down to help the baron gain his feet. "Especially since you have clearly been celebrating a bit too soon. But there are people here, Baron. Best put your shirt on."

"Bah," the man said as he gained his feet. "She likes the sight of me."

"She does not," Rebecca corrected, but it didn't penetrate the baron's self-absorption.

"Feel this soil," the baron said as he grabbed a fistful of it and squeezed. "Good English dirt. Gritty. Smelly."

The man was still enthralled by feeling things. As if smelling dirt was a fine thing to do in the middle of a ball.

"Never fear," Fletcher continued, his voice growing louder. "I shall have the marriage contract drawn up tomorrow. This is a happy day!"

"Stop it!" Rebecca said. "I'll not—"

"Look around you. You're ruined!" her brother snarled in an undertone. "Take your medicine and be happy that your reputation can be saved by marriage."

"Not to—"

"If a marriage is needed," Nate said, his voice dominating everyone. "Then let me extend my hand as I ask for yours, Lady Rebecca."

There was a moment's stunned silence as Nate's words seemed to echo in the air. Even Rebecca, who remembered how Nate was prone to sweeping statements, was shocked by his words.

But then she recovered.

"I'm not marrying anyone!" she cried. "Not because of..." She cut off her words. She couldn't confess to using a truth serum. "The baron overindulged this evening. That is all. Now, Fletcher, I should like to go home. Let the others recover as they see fit."

She felt a great deal of guilt at saying that. Shouldn't someone stay with the baron to make sure there were no other ill effects? He seemed healthy enough sitting there and looking up at the stars through the leaves, but one never knew with medicines. Though, of everyone, he seemed the most serene as he slowly turned to her.

"You mean that, don't you?" he said, sounding shocked. "You don't want to marry me?"

"Don't listen to her," Fletcher snapped as he brushed dirt off his jacket. "She doesn't know what she's talking about."

The baron shifted, leaning back against a tree truck. "Say it again," he said to Rebecca.

"I do not love you," she said, knowing it was true. "Do you

love me?"

He gaped at her. "Good God, no! It's your land I want." Then his gaze turned soft as he looked at her bodice. "And those magnificent breasts."

Well, that was plain speaking. She hadn't thought her dower property all that valuable. It was pretty, of course, situated right on the Cornish coast. But she realized now that it likely abutted the baron's property. And perhaps any land was valuable.

Meanwhile, her brother decided that was enough plain speaking. "Baron, we will discuss this matter in the morning." Then he grabbed her arm as if to drag her away.

"And what of my proposal?" Nate challenged. His tone was light, but his hand was still gently clasped about her elbow. Then he drew her hand to his mouth and lightly pressed a kiss to her wrist. "Shall I get down on one knee?"

"Don't you dare!" she muttered, knowing full well that he would. And indeed, there he went, dropping down before her.

"I am quite sincere," he said and the hell of it was that he probably thought that the truth. The man was ridiculous, and yet, her heart lurched to see him down on one knee before her. If only he'd lived up to the promise of what he'd been as a teenager.

How she'd dreamed of their future together. Him, as a re-spected leader. Her, with their children about them. In her mind's eye, she'd given him all sorts of different careers. Banker, barrister, advisor to the king. Never once had she seen him as a man who lived off of gossip gleaned during other people's parties.

It hurt to see him so small. Worse, he was making fun of something so serious. Marriage. Love. He played at them, and she turned her head away from the sight.

"*I* will pick my husband," she said her tone loud. "And I do not choose either of you."

She wanted to stomp off in a huff. She did not enjoy such spectacles. But before she could leave, she had to manage the baron. She couldn't leave him like that, sitting in the dirt and looking shocked that she didn't want him. It was the effects of the serum, and she couldn't abandon him until it had worn off.

But she couldn't stay either. That would be tantamount to accepting his proposal.

Damn it. Whyever had she even mentioned that silly serum?

She looked around her. There was no one here whom she trusted to keep the secret of what she'd done. No one except Nate. He might be a society fribble, but he'd proved his loyalty to her. He'd never betray her.

So he was her only option.

Shaking off Fletcher's hand, she turned back to Nate who was still on one knee. "Oh get up," she huffed. He came up easily. The man had always been nimble. And then she leaned forward to hurriedly whisper in his ear.

"I gave the baron a truth serum. Please watch him until he's better."

Shock flared across his expression. "What?" Then his gaze ticked to the baron and back, showing he understood what she'd said.

"Please," she whispered. "There is no one else."

He stared at her, then his gaze flicked not to the baron but to the shrubbery where a maid hovered in the shadows. Is that what had brought him out here? An assignation with a maid?

"Nevermind," she huffed, but he cut her off.

"I'll help," he said in an undertone as he brushed dirt off his pants. Then he straightened, his gaze heavy as he arched a brow.

It was a particular look, one he'd perfected when they were young. And it told her that their conversation wasn't done. Indeed, when they were kids, that look meant he would sneak to her bedroom in the dead of night. She never let him in. Well, except for once and that was only because it was raining. Usually he would hang from the ivy by her window as they talked. Or kissed.

Fortunately, there was no ivy by her London window. There would be no dead of the night whispers or anything else. And that made her sad. But everyone had to grow up sometime, and she no longer risked her reputation on midnight rendezvous.

Instead, she looked back at the baron. He was now inspecting his hands, moving them through the air as if he were running them through water. "The air is different," he murmured.

"I'll see he gets home safely," Nate said, his voice gentle.

"Thank you."

Nate bowed before her in a courtly move reminiscent of an earlier age. It was a silly gesture, but one that made her smile. And if she hadn't felt so guilty about the whole debacle, she might have laughed. But as it was, she could only feel gratitude toward him. He was doing her a kindness when not an hour before, she'd given him the cut direct.

"Are you quite finished?" Fletcher drawled, fury vibrating in his voice.

"Yes, brother," she murmured as she moved to his side. She had to find a way to mollify the man before he started taking out his irritation on her. Or anyone else who happened to be in his way. She didn't much care if he screamed at her. It was how she kept the peace, and it was a small price to pay for doing what she wanted. Let him bellow after the fact. But she didn't want him harping at the servants. He'd done that at home when he was angry, and she'd always had to find ways to make amends.

Sometimes, she wondered if it was worth it. Why did she give his moods free reign over her life? The answer was that she didn't. Not at home. But this was London where she wanted to remain for the rest of the Season. That required his charity, and so she would allow him to rant at her. She was of age, so he couldn't force her to marry anyone she didn't choose.

They walked smartly back to the carriage, neither saying a word. That held until they were both inside the vehicle. Then he began his tirade.

Fletcher was thorough in voicing his disgust of her. She had no sense, according to him, and frankly, given what had happened, she couldn't disagree. Her brother knew nothing about the serum, but she did. And she was disappointed in herself.

She should not have dosed the baron. He'd taken it willingly, but obviously, neither of them had guessed at the effects. Good God, she never would have dreamed that the stuff was that effective!

Meanwhile, Fletcher continued his tirade, adding in pressure for her to accept the baron's suit. He really wanted her to marry the man. She told him explicitly that she would never agree to that. If nothing else, the truth serum had revealed his brutish side. No man had ever tried to haul her around by her hair, and now that she was sitting safe in the carriage, that memory surfaced stronger than any other.

The baron had been brutish and cruel. She shuddered to think what might have happened if they'd been alone. Certainly, he hadn't been in his right mind. She might be able to excuse his behavior because of that. But she would never get past it.

He had hurt her. And he'd revealed that he only wanted her dowry property and her breasts. There was no way she'd marry the man.

Nevertheless, she let Fletcher blather on. It was what Fletcher always did. He lectured, he threatened, and when they were children, he would strike her. But that ended after Henry taught her how to fight back. Indeed, Henry had often protected her from her brother's rages. Her father, when he'd been alive, had also kept Fletcher's tirades in check, but after his death, everyone hid in their own private places. That left Fletcher to do as he wanted. And sometimes what he wanted was sneaky and cruel.

There was never any proof. A dog who disliked him disappeared. A farmer who had cursed him found his pig pen open and his pigs gone. A barmaid who refused his advances was attacked from behind and beaten. None of these things were ever tied to him, but Rebecca wondered.

The best practice was to let Fletcher blather on, appear to agree, and then do whatever she wanted once they were apart. Back in Cornwall, that had been easy. Here, it would be a great deal harder, but she would find a way.

She sought her bed as soon as they entered the house. Fletcher wouldn't stay long, she knew. He was never in bed before two or three and it wasn't even midnight now. So she waved him good night and headed for the peace of her bedroom. He let her go, his expression tight with annoyance.

She made it into her bedroom and quickly undressed. As soon as she could, she dismissed her maid and exhaled in relief, relishing the quiet. And though she was ready for bed, she settled into her window seat to read. A light wrap pooled in her lap, and a pillow cushioned her backside. And though it was hard to see by the light of the candelabra, she gloried in the peace of the moment. And the excitement in her book.

Until the moment someone tapped on her window.

Nate.

Chapter Thirteen

NATE CURSED AS he secured his rope on Becca's rooftop. It had been touch and go getting up here. This was an elite neighborhood, so the rooftops were spaced further apart, which meant that he'd had to jump a large span before he could land safely up here. "Safe" meaning he didn't plummet to his death, but his feet were an aching, throbbing mess. Not to mention his ribs.

A few years ago, he'd run ratlines in a storm without thinking. Today, he felt every year of his life as if it had been a decade. Nevertheless, he'd take ten times the pain if it meant he could talk to Becca without interference.

God, he prayed tonight would finally be his moment.

He tied off his rope and carefully climbed down. He'd left his shoes on, even though he was more secure on ropes barefoot. The calluses on his feet were fading. He needed the dubious protection of the leather. And his right toes were wrapped and braced with pieces of wood to prevent the bones from re-breaking. So he secured himself as best he could and wondered what had happened to the devil-may-care boy he'd once been. Right now, he was a knot of anxiety.

Nevertheless, he descended to her window, taking a long moment to watch her reading there. Her hair was down, gathered to the side in a mahogany cascade of silk that would smell like summer. Or at least it used to. Her head was bowed, but he still saw the curve of her shoulder half hidden by her worn cotton shift. No silk for her. She was a simple cotton girl.

Then she smiled as she turned a page, and his breath caught at the sheer beauty of her. Pleasure in a book. Sweetly innocent. And so damned sensual that he was rock hard just looking.

He tried to see the book but couldn't manage it. Still, he guessed it was a scandalous tome of adventure, read only at night. During the day, she pulled out scientific inquiries or treatises on household management. But night was when Becca let her real self shine, if only in the pages of a book.

God, how he wanted to touch her.

He tapped the window instead and her head shot up, her blue eyes jumping to meet his.

He waved and tried to look dashing. Then he tried not to be disappointed when her expression shifted to chagrin. At least that was what he labelled it in his mind. It could just have easily been "annoyance" or "anger." He countered by putting his hands together in a prayer position and mouthing, "Please, please." Unfortunately, that loosened his grip on the rope, and he slipped.

He didn't go far. The hemp was tight around his good foot and shin, but the burn as he slid ripped his pants. Worse, the act of stopping tore at his hands. He should have worn gloves. That would be his usual practice, but he had so few left, he'd thought he could go without them.

It was fear of his death that had her springing to the window. She jerked it open with a hard pull, then leaned out and reached for his shirt. He let her, wanting the comfort of her grip even though it would not stop a fall.

"Are you mad?" she cried.

Quite possibly.

"Let me in, Becca. Please, I want to talk."

"I will not!" she said, her tone prim.

"I'm not going to accost you," he grumbled. "But this is harder than it looks. I'm not a teenager anymore, and there's hard cobblestone beneath me, not soft grass."

"You shouldn't be here!"

He held his tongue, reminding himself that he wasn't the only one who had changed in the last decade. She was different. He couldn't prattle nonsense and expect her to give in. But he didn't really know the woman she'd become. He didn't know how to persuade her to talk to him.

"Five minutes. Please. I just want to see that you're all right."

She lifted her hands. "I'm fine! I was fine before! I'm—"

"Are you going to marry him?"

She frowned. "Who? The baron?"

"Has anyone else offered for you?"

"Besides you? No."

"Then yes, the baron."

"No."

That was a relief. "But Fletcher—"

"I know," she said with a sigh. "I'm not sure how to manage him. He's gotten worse."

How sweet that they could still understand each other in abbreviated sentences. Even so, there was a lot unspoken here, and he wanted details. Just exactly how had Fletcher gotten worse? Was she in danger?

"Let me in, Becca. My ribs are killing me."

Her gaze dropped to his torso as she quickly backed up. At least she was still tenderhearted. She hated for anyone to be in pain, him included. She helped him inside, and within moments, he set his feet lightly on her floor before sliding the rest of the way inside.

Relief.

The scent of her was everywhere. He smiled as he inhaled deeply.

"Can you breathe?" she pressed. "Without pain? And your feet—how bad are they?"

He smiled. It was good to see she cared. "I'm better now that I'm here."

"No, you're not! You're being very bad."

His lips quirked as he looked at her. She sounded like his old matron at Eton, but she was far lovelier.

"You used to like me when I was bad," he teased.

She crossed her arms, and he couldn't help but appreciate the way her bosom plumped. "Stop looking at me like that! I'm not sixteen anymore. I'm not going to swoon just because you're being scandalous."

"You never swooned."

"I never…" She abruptly cut off her words, her lips pressed tight.

"What?" he pressed. "Don't hold back. You know I hate that."

She dropped back into her chair with a heavy sigh. "I never stood up to you either. I never stopped you—" She glared at him. "I never stopped *us* from being insanely daring. I look back on that girl, and I think, what a fool she was." She lifted her chin. "So I didn't swoon, but I might as well have."

There wasn't another chair in the room, so he pulled out the footstool and sat upon it. That put her at a higher eye level than him, but he liked looking up at her.

"I remember you very differently," he said quietly. "You stopped me from so much idiocy. If it weren't for you, I would have tried swinging from tree to tree like a monkey."

"You would have fallen to your death."

Maybe. "Probably just broken a leg." Though he'd seen a sailor fall from the lowest spar once. It was a small height, one that he'd often jumped. But there'd been water on the deck, the man had hit his head, and the result had been gruesome. And fatal.

"You also kept me from stealing chickens to release in church," he continued. "From blowing peas at people through a blow gun, and baking sawdust into tarts."

"You stopped yourself with the tarts," she corrected.

Had he? "Oh yes! Too much work to make something I couldn't eat."

"No." She relaxed back in her chair as she chided him. "You couldn't manage the oven. Burned everything into an ugly mess."

Oh yes. "Cook made me clean all the pots as punishment."

He chuckled at the memory as did she. It was a softening of her attitude, and he touched her bare foot at the sound. He had to touch her somewhere, and this was the most polite thing he could do from down here.

Still she stiffened. "Nate—"

"You stopped me from doing so many things," he said, trying to distract her from his touch. "Many, many stupid things."

"And we still did so much." She bit her lip, her gaze skittering away in shame.

"Yes. We read books, taught the village children their letters, and fought over economics."

She snorted. "You encouraged me to read things that no girl should learn," she said. "Just so I could argue with you."

He shook his head. Didn't she remember? "You read them because I had to study them in school. You kept asking me what I had learned, what did I think." As if he wanted to remember any part of his education during the summer months. But she had been interested, and so for her, he'd looked back at his textbooks. He'd remembered them enough to teach her. "The only reason I know anything now is because of you."

She frowned as if trying to reconcile what he said with her own memories. "I did want to know," she said softly.

That was why he'd worked hard to learn things he could teach her. Her mind was always active, always seeking something more than what her family allowed. It was a damn shame that women weren't educated better. If she'd been given a decent education, she'd be an Oxford don by now.

Instead, she was waiting hand and foot on her mother while trying to avoid Fletcher's insanity.

"Why haven't you married before now?" he asked.

Her brows shot up. "What a question!"

"You're attractive, titled, and an heiress. You should have taken in your first Season."

"I couldn't go to London until after we were out of mourning. That was a blessing, I think. I was so young then."

He'd spent that time learning how to sail on the Thames as a waterman. And then he was sailing back and forth to Spain, learning too much about war, and trailing after Sir Benedict so he could ferry messages to the Foreign Office.

"I wasn't in London during your come-out. What happened then?"

She shook her head. "I don't know. There was attention, of course." Her expression softened. "There was a boy I really liked, but then he lost interest."

"Who?" The word came out harder than he intended, but he was jealous. He didn't want her to have that expression for anyone but him.

"Jonas Gaynesford. He ended up marrying my friend Eunice. They're very happy now."

She didn't sound particularly upset. "Did you ever ask him what happened?"

"Goodness, no. That would be rude. But of course, Mama says it's always the same thing."

"The same what?"

She shot him a heavy look. "My purity is in question," she said.

His mouth dropped open. "We never… I didn't…"

"No one believes me. I even have a letter from my doctor, but still…"

"You got a doctor's letter?" Good God, what had she endured just to get that? And the necessity of it shocked him.

"I did. Doesn't seem to matter."

"But that's ridiculous!" he said. "Even if it were true, there are enough gentlemen who would overlook such things. Men who want your dowry, if nothing else."

She jerked her foot out of his hand as she glared at him. "What makes you think I would want such a man?"

"I didn't mean it like that."

"I don't care how you meant it! It's an impertinent question.

I'm not married because I'm not. You've no right to question me that way."

"Keep your voice down," he said softly. "Your mother's asleep, but even she will rouse if you yell at me."

She opened her mouth to argue but then frowned. "How do you know my mother's asleep?"

Because he'd checked. "Same way I know Fletcher's gone, and most of the servants as well. For a prestigious London home, there are very few servants who reside here."

She shrugged. "It is Fletcher's primary residence. He loves a large staff during the day, but then they all go away at night."

That surprised him. Fletcher seemed like a man who enjoyed all levels of ostentation, including a large number of servants available day or night. Curious, but Nate hadn't come here to discuss her brother.

"And you're correct," he added, forcing the conversation back to her. "I have no right to question your choices." Then he arched a brow. "And just to be clear, I'm not questioning them. I want to learn what you've been doing these years. I once thought I knew everything about you. Now, you're like a different woman."

"I *am* a different woman."

"So let me get to know her."

She looked at him, her expression softening. He wanted to believe it was yearning, but he didn't know for sure. Once he knew her every expression. Now, he hesitated to even guess.

"After..." She shifted her position, pulling her feet back until they were primly covered by her nightrail and a blanket. "After we were discovered and Father passed, you disappeared."

"I was sent away. Fletcher threatened to kill me. My parents feared he would follow through at school." He watched her carefully for her reaction. Would she dismiss her brother's rantings? Or did she credit them as serious?

She did neither.

"I was in such a fog of guilt and grief." She looked down at her hands. "I didn't come out for a long time."

"I'm so sorry Becca. About everything."

"I am, too." Then she caught his eye. "I don't blame you any more than I blame myself."

At least he shared in her guilt. Whereas in his mind, he'd been older and the man. He should have taken better care, but prudence wasn't something he'd learned until he'd been in a war.

"What did you do?" he pressed. "What made the grief ease?"

"Time. And a sickness came to the village. Everyone's help was needed, including my own."

He frowned. "Did you get sick?"

"Yes, but nothing like some of the others. I started working with Mrs. Chenoweth and…" She shrugged. "I stopped feeling sorry for myself."

"I wish I could have been there. I would have helped."

She arched a brow at him. "You'd clean up, change diapers, feed the livestock?"

He'd done all of that and more in his life, but much of it came after he'd left her. "I have done my share of farming," he reminded her.

She frowned then nodded. "I guess you have."

"How can you not remember these things?" He was a little insulted that he had to remind her.

"I don't know." She leaned forward. "I suppose I have heard over and over that you never did anything good in your life. You or your family."

"You know that's not true!" At least she'd *known* it once upon a time.

"I do. I did. I just…" Her gaze grew abstract. "I'm an idiot. I knew it wasn't true. But they kept telling me things."

"They?" he prompted. "They who?"

Her gaze tightened back on him. "Fletcher and Mama. Henry doesn't say much at all. He's too busy managing the estate, and he was never one to socialize. He's gone months without saying a single word to me or Mama."

Her oldest brother Henry could easily be characterized as a

hermit. A blind, deaf, and dumb one, unless you talked to him about soil. Then he transformed into a genius who had no patience for anyone else's ignorance.

But that genius had made the family incredibly wealthy, so Nate had no reason to disparage the man. The same couldn't be said for the rest of her family.

"You said Fletcher is getting worse. What do you mean by that?" Was she in any danger?

"He's protective to a ridiculous degree. I can't go anywhere or do anything without him. He tells me what social events I can attend, and the few times he's not with me, he demands to know who I talked to, and about what." She shuddered. "He was never like that at home, but he's different in London. And I'm getting tired of it."

"That's not protective, that's possessive. He doesn't own you. You've reached your majority."

She nodded. "Mama says that's the surest sign I'm a spinster and that I must resign myself to living exactly as I have been for the rest of my life." She looked at her hands. "I take care of her. I manage the house for Henry. I help the vicar with the children. And Mrs. Chenoweth is getting old now. I help her a lot."

That would be a full life for many women, but clearly not for her. She'd always wanted to travel, to experience new things. No wait, that was him. He'd always wanted to wander until he'd spent ten years travelling for the Foreign Office. She'd always wanted to learn useful things. How to manage a burn, what was the best mash for pigs. If the clouds looked one way, did that foretell rain or wind?

"Why does Fletcher want you to marry the baron?"

She snorted. "Fletcher wants a seat in the House of Commons. Your brother has the one for our borough. He's hoping to get the one in the baron's borough."

"And you marrying the man will assure that?"

"Fletcher thinks so."

It was possible. "Is that what you learned with that truth

serum?"

He watched as her cheeks pinked, but she didn't shy away from what she'd done. "No. I already knew that. I wanted to find out what the baron got from this deal."

"Besides you as his wife and mother for his child? Besides your dowry?"

She nodded. "I wanted to know if he had feelings for me." She looked away from him then, her gaze going out the window to the night sky. "I shouldn't have done it, but Fletcher is pressuring me, and I didn't know what else to do." She looked back at him. "Is he all right?"

"He's fine. It took an hour or more to wear off—"

"That long!"

"I stayed with him until he seemed rational. He refuses to believe he beat his naked chest between sets. Called me a damned liar."

She blew out a slow breath. "Did you take him home?"

"Yes." He scanned her from head to toe again. "Are you sure he didn't hurt you? He's very strong." It had taken Nate plus two footmen to force him into a carriage. But once there, the man decided to relax and stare into the darkness. Talked about beautiful lights in front of his eyes, and the glory of breasts. All breasts, not just Becca's. And Nate spent the entire ride telling himself it was wrong to punch the man.

"He didn't hurt me," she said. Then she touched a hand to the side of her head. "He surprised me, is all."

"He grabbed you by the hair. He could have—"

"He didn't," she rushed to say. "I'm fine." But the hurried way she spoke told him she'd thought about what might have happened. What was underneath the baron's normally urbane manner.

"He has a temper, Becca. A bad one."

She swallowed. "So it would seem."

Good. She'd figured that out on her own. She'd never been stupid. Except, of course, with him.

"And what will you do if Fletcher keeps pushing you?"

She sighed and plucked at the blanket. "I already told him I wouldn't marry the baron."

"And?"

"He lectured me."

"And when you still won't? What will happen?"

"I don't know. He might send me home." She stared down at her hands. "He's never been so determined before. At home, I could always delay things until he was gone. I could pretend and—"

"And make him think he'd gotten his way?"

She nodded.

"You're afraid of him," he guessed.

"I'm afraid of being sent home. I'm useful there, but it's not what I want for the rest of my life."

"But Fletcher's never been so adamant before," Nate pressed. "Never this determined?"

"He's my brother. He's trying to protect me." She said the words like a litany. As if she were trying to convince herself, and he hated it. He hated that the girl he'd known had become this shadow of herself, whispering lies as reassurance.

Damn it, he needed her to listen. "Your brothers have never protected you. It's been you taking care of them. From the beginning, it's always been you." Her father had been the one in charge of the family, but when he died, it had all fallen on her. Especially since her mother was useless.

She glared at him. "They're busy men with a great deal of things to do. And I can take care of myself."

He leaned forward, squeezing her knees as he tried to impress his next words on her. "That's right. You can. You don't need them to tell you who to marry or what to do."

"I'm not going to marry the baron! I don't know what else you want me to say."

He didn't know either. Or rather, he knew—he wanted her to say she would marry him—but knew that wasn't possible. At the moment, his hope was that they could be friends.

"You have so much to offer a man," he said softly. "You are so much more than your dowry. Do not settle for anyone who doesn't see that. You'd be better off alone."

She snorted. "Spoken like a man who hasn't been controlled by others his whole life. Without Henry's say-so, I can't have my dowry. Without Fletcher's escort, I can't meet eligible gentlemen. If Mama says she needs me, I am not allowed to leave the house. I am not better off alone," she said. "I am better off married to a good man."

He looked at where he touched her. She had set her hands upon his to emphasize her point, and now he flipped his hands over so they were palm to palm. How he wanted to touch so much more of her. If only she'd—

"And you, Lord Nathanial, who are so free… What have you done with your freedom since leaving home ten years ago?"

He winced. He knew what lies he had to say. What he always said. *Oh, this and that. I've been here and there. All in a good day's fun, eh?* But he already knew how she would react to that. She'd see the words for the empty platitudes they were, and she'd never open up to him again. Not if that was all he gave her in return.

But what could he say? Not that he'd been working for the war effort since the day he left their borough. Not that he spoke five different languages plus a dead one. That he'd travelled enough to see that people could be awful to one another, and that he missed the comfort of home. And that he couldn't be honest with his friends, and that made him so achingly lonely that he would climb into her bedroom in the middle of the night just so he could talk so someone who remembered the boy he'd been. Who remembered and didn't call him a scapegrace.

Except, of course, now she would. Because he couldn't tell her.

"Nate?"

"I have done nothing of note. Nothing as worthy as caring for my family even when they're awful. Nothing as intelligent as learning how to dose sick children. Nothing..." Nothing that he could tell her.

"So it's true. You've just wandered about. Ten years of indulging yourself?"

He laughed. "There has been little indulgence. That I can swear to."

"Because you had no money?"

Because he was working in secret for the Crown. And the Crown didn't pay very well.

"Because you weren't there to keep me on the straight and narrow."

He'd thought it was a romantic line. He'd thought that she would melt at those words. She would have ten years ago. Instead, she looked like she wanted to slap him.

"Don't you dare," she growled.

He reared back. "What?"

"Don't make me into your salvation, you lazy ass. You're a grown man! Either grow up or don't, but don't make me the reason for either of it."

He held her gaze, saw the ferocity in her reaction, and felt ashamed. She was a woman restricted on all sides, and here he was, trying to tease her by suggesting he needed her as well. He did need her, but not to make him responsible. Not to make him a man.

He needed her because she knew him best of all. She remembered the boy he'd been, and she'd had a hand in shaping his moral core. That wasn't a casual statement. They'd discussed all manner of philosophical things. Things like who was responsible for the poor who had no food? What was justified when a man was caught beating his child? Who owned a woman? Was it herself or her guardian?

These were practical questions for her. She worked much closer with the vicar than he ever had—helping with the sick and tending the poor. He'd avoided such things in favor of fixing fences and watering crops. But together, they'd discussed the politics of it. Because she liked thinking through systems. Systems in a house to make cooking more efficient. Systems in the parish to see that the right people got help. And systems in the country or the world.

But, of course, systems had to be based on fairness, and that was what they argued. What was a fair wage? Who got to decide? When was a woman a full adult? When was a man? They'd discussed that ad nauseum until he discovered he could kiss her into acquiescence.

And here he was pretending that those discussions meant nothing, that he hadn't thought about them while walking through war-torn Spain, or that he'd never disobeyed orders when they were unnecessarily cruel. Fortunately, he'd gotten away with his actions. He was, after all, a secret part of the war effort. And Sir Benedict had a rebellious streak as well.

But all that virtue, such as it was, could be traced back to her and the things they'd discussed. Except he couldn't tell her that, without explaining everything. So he was left staring at her as he searched for something to say.

He needed some way to tell her his true heart without any details. And that was an impossible task.

He sighed. "I'm not what you think." It was the best he could manage.

"Then what are you?"

He didn't know how to answer that. At least not until his gaze landed on the book she'd set on the windowsill. Just as he'd guessed, it was a raucous novel filled with silly situations and a moronic heroine. He'd read every word. As had every literate woman in London who had the time to spare.

That was his answer.

He looked up at her. "Does Fletcher allow you to go to the lending library alone?"

Her eyes widened. "Yes. I have to take my maid, of course, but she doesn't care what I read." Then she stiffened. "Are you going to say that's not an appropriate book?"

"What? No!" Indeed, the idea that he would, was pretty funny.

"Meet me at the Minerva library tomorrow. Say, two o'clock?"

"That's visiting hours. Fletcher will be angry if I'm not here to entertain guests. And it's Mama's favorite time of the day." And when he frowned at her, she shrugged. "Mama likes me to see that everyone's needs are attended during her salon."

"You mean she treats you like a servant, waiting on everyone while she holds court."

Far from being insulted, Becca gently chided him. "I am her daughter and the one looking for a husband. It is appropriate for me to be there."

Present, but she shouldn't have to wait on everyone. Still, he held his tongue on that regard. He knew better than to wade into complicated mother-daughter relationships. Besides, they were figuring out when he could see her again.

"When can you get to Minerva's?"

"Thursday. Nine o'clock?"

He groaned. That was when he was supposed to be meeting Frid at the apothecary shop. "Why so early?" he asked.

"Fletcher will still be asleep at nine. I hope."

Nate sighed and dropped his forehead onto her knees. "Only for you, my dear. Only for you."

"For me what?" she asked, her voice tart.

"Meet me there at ten. That's when it opens." He should be done with Frid by then. "I'll show you what I've been doing."

"What?"

"I'll show you," he repeated. At least some of what he'd done. The light stuff. The silly stuff. The only way his sanity had survived some of the places he'd been. He lifted his head and put on his most winning expression. "Please?"

Then he waited while she studied him. Lord, the woman could drag out a decision, looking at it from all angles before she committed. But in the end, she nodded.

"At ten."

"Good."

And then he kissed her. Because he never wasted time on deliberation, even when he should.

Chapter Fourteen

GOOD LORD, HOW could she have forgotten? No one but Nate kissed like this. Enthusiasm and care. She could feel the hunger in him, the desperate need, but also the way he held himself back for her sake. He touched her face softly, a barely-there caress while his lips moved over hers. Then his tongue pushed forward, only to pull back. Forward and back, penetrating a little bit more each time.

She sank into the experience. How could she not? He'd given her her first real kiss, her first sensual touch, her first in so many things. But with ten years of time between this time and the last, she wanted to know how he had changed. How she had changed. And how much was exactly the same.

Arousal. Pure, sweet, hungry need for touch. She'd suppressed it over the years, but now it hit her harder than before. It said, *This*. This is what she needed. This is what had been missing from her life for ten bleak years. No one touched her anymore, not even her maid who always had a layer of clothing between her fingers and Rebecca's body.

His fingers skimmed along her jaw and down her neck. How sensitive he made her. Suddenly she was aware of not just his fingers but the weight of the blanket over her knees, the rough texture of her nightrail, and the heated press of his arm against hers.

His tongue probed against her mouth, and she stretched to meet him. Tongue to tongue, she'd never had to think about such things when she was sixteen. She'd just kissed. But now she doubted herself. She shouldn't be doing this. She shouldn't have let him into her bedroom.

She had such bad judgement.

And yet, those thoughts were soon buried beneath the sensations—*his* sensations. His scent, now mixed with Bay Rum and London coal dust. Different, and yet undeniably him. His caress, so gentle, even as he seemed to tremble with need. And his sigh as he forced himself back.

That she remembered so clearly. Every time he pulled back, it was as if he had to force himself away from her. How many times had she heard that sigh from him when they were kids? When he stopped what he was doing, only to hover on the precipice of starting again. Could he pull himself away or steal another kiss, another touch?

She answered the question for him. When he began to draw back, she lurched forward. She grabbed his arm and drew him to her. She fused her lips to his, she thrust her tongue in his mouth, and she did everything possible to keep him with her.

She didn't say the words. *Don't stop!* echoed in her mind and her body.

She didn't need to say them because he knew what she wanted. He'd always known. And when she grabbed his hand and set it to her breast, he cupped her as he always had. Reverence and strength. He never hurt her, but the way he shaped her set her body on fire.

How had she gone ten years without feeling this?

Don't stop!

He pulled back from their kisses. His breath was ragged. Hers was non-existent. Not with him brushing her nightrail aside. Not with his fingers on her flesh as he bared her shoulder and then her breast.

Her head dropped back, her body trembling beneath the onslaught of sensation.

His hand cupped her naked breast, his fingers pulling at her nipple. And then she felt his mouth on her chest. A kiss. A lave with his tongue.

Don't stop!

She arched into his hold. And when his tongue coiled about her taut nipple, a sob of relief rasped through her constricted throat.

He paused, lifting his head to look at her. Her eyes flew open, and their gazes met.

Don't stop!

"Becca?"

Don't stop!

"Are you crying?"

What?

She swallowed as she pressed a hand to her cheeks, wiping away the wetness there.

"No," she gasped. Then steadier. "No. Of course not."

He gently withdrew from her body.

No!

He reset her nightgown and fastened buttons that she hadn't bothered with.

Don't stop!

"Becca," he whispered. "I'm sorry. I shouldn't have done that."

Part of her wanted to leave the fault with him. Let him take the blame. But she'd never been one to hide from her own mistakes. "My fault," she whispered.

"No." His tone was decisive. "There is no fault. We kissed. I'm sure you've kissed dozens of men by now. It's something that happens between men and women. But we've stopped now. No harm done."

No harm done? How could she say that? Ten years of suppressing those memories, ten years of forgetting those needs—all gone now. She remembered. Her body remembered. How could she ever forget again, while her heart still beat hard and fast? When her skin still felt on fire and her breasts...oh how they ached for him.

No harm done? She'd never be able to forget again! How could she go back to her sterile life now? How could she pass another day, another week, another life without his touch?

Damn it! He'd made her *remember!* And that made her mad.

"Get out, Nate," she said, the words coming out harder than she intended.

"Becca—"

"Go! Before I scream and bring the whole house running."

His eyes hardened. "Never make idle threats."

"I'm not." Except, of course, she was. She'd never do that to him.

And damn it, he knew it. He reached out to caress her cheek again. Her skin tingled in anticipation, but he never connected. He held himself back and she nearly cried at his restraint.

"It always seems to go wrong with us," he whispered. "I don't know why."

"Because I'm an idiot." Because she let him. And he was a man to take what was offered.

No wait. That was a lie. In all their time together—now and at sixteen—he was the one who'd always stopped. Not her. Not ever. Always him.

"You never used to say that," he whispered. "You never used to think that!"

What?

"You've called me an idiot, rightly so. You've pointed out so many wrong things in the world and called them idiotic. But you never turned it on yourself."

"Teenagers always think they're smarter than they are."

"But you are smart. You're brilliant."

She swallowed, tears flooding her eyes. She'd forgotten that too, the way he looked at her in shock and surprise whenever she said something smart. But that was only at the beginning, when the vicar had first put them together. It hadn't taken long before he accepted her intelligence. Though, truth be told, she'd always tried to surprise him. She loved the way his eyes widened and then he'd give her this big grin and call her brilliant.

He liked that she was smart. But he didn't like what she was doing now, when she looked down at her hands and felt ashamed. "You always muddle my head."

"That's fair," he said. "You always muddle mine."

She didn't know what to say to that. Her emotions were running hither thither. Anger, fear, lust, shame. What were the seven deadly sins? Was she experiencing all of them at once?

"Say you'll come on Thursday. Promise me you'll be there," he said.

She nodded. "I promise."

"Good." Then he hesitated and she wondered if he would kiss her one more time.

Please.

He did not. He pulled back and headed toward the window. He made quick work of opening it before grabbing the rope that still dangled outside, but she could see that his movements were rough. He limped and his ribs obviously ached.

"How long since your attack?"

He glanced back at her. "A couple weeks. Why?"

"Not enough time to heal broken ribs."

"This?" he chuckled. "This is nothing. I've suffered worse, I promise you."

She narrowed her eyes. More important, she pushed to her feet, wrapping the blanket around her as she moved. "Don't lie to me, Nate. After everything, I cannot abide it."

"After what everything?" he asked.

She shook her head, refusing to answer, mostly because she didn't know what she meant. After the last decade of grief and self-doubt? After finally waking up from a decade of numbness?

"Nate!" she huffed. "Don't lie. How bad are your ribs?"

His expression softened. "I really have had worse," he said gently. "But only once and that was..." He grimaced. "That was bad. This..." He gestured to his ribs. "They ache. My feet are swollen, and every step reminds me that I just want to lie down."

"Nate! You shouldn't—"

"Yes, I should have." His voice was emphatic. "I've wanted to talk with you for ten years. Nothing was going to stop me tonight. Certainly not a few bruises."

"But they're more than bruises," she said.

"I'll be careful. But don't expect me to do much standing. The lending library is a place to sit and put one's feet up."

She snorted. "You sound like you've been there before when I know you haven't. You probably don't even know where it is."

He rattled off the address while flashing her a cheeky grin. "Thursday morning, Becca. Don't be late."

As if she was the one who was ever late.

He pressed his fingers to his lips and blew her a rakish kiss. Then he gripped the rope and swung himself out, just as if he were a pirate. She rushed to the window, afraid to see if he'd fallen, but of course he hadn't.

Actually, she couldn't find him anywhere below. Then she heard a noise above her. Twisting around, she saw him climb the last few feet before disappearing onto her roof. She listened hard but didn't hear a single footfall.

In the end, she dropped down on her bed, thinking through everything that had just happened. Her body still hummed, her breasts were achingly tight. But more surprising still was the soft smile that curved her lips.

Lips he had kissed. Breasts he had touched. Well, one breast. And how her womb trembled, her private area hot and wet. She remembered this feeling. Remembered, too, what her family would say if they knew what she had been doing and with whom.

It was an exact repeat of how she'd felt when she was sixteen and Nate had taken her into the barn or the forest or up in his favorite tree. She'd spent the last ten years suppressing those memories, telling herself they weren't as wonderful as she remembered or that she'd been wrong to indulge such things.

And now she'd done it again. Was she wrong? Was she wandering down the same disastrous path she'd walked so blithely when she was sixteen? Good God, would she never learn?

Apparently not, because as she climbed into bed, she felt the rasp of fabric against her sensitized skin. She felt his hands on her breast, his mouth on hers, and his tongue thrusting in and out.

Oh God, she didn't regret what had happened this night. She couldn't. Because she desperately wanted to do it again. That and so much more.

Bloody hell.

She needed to get married. She needed to experience these things with her husband in their marriage bed.

It couldn't be with Nate, obviously. Setting aside her family's objection—and they would object loudly—marrying him would mean a life of constant worry. She'd heard from Fletcher how he lived. Feckless, reckless, and not a penny to his name. She'd seen nothing to contradict that, but still, she wondered. She knew Fletcher would paint him in the worst possible light. Could Nate have some secret occupation? The idea was ludicrous. Why would he keep it secret? But he'd had to survive somehow these last ten years. Fashionable clothing didn't come cheap.

Either way, she had no reason to believe he could support her or their children in any substantive way. They could live on her dower property, but would he want to seclude himself in Cornwall for the rest of his life? Would she?

No. Which meant Nate was out. The baron was definitely out. And she…

Well, she'd just have to find someone else who would work. Maybe at tomorrow night's ball.

But first, she needed to rest. And then, first thing tomorrow, she'd head for the lending library.

Chapter Fifteen

AS EXPECTED, NATE'S meeting with Heidi Frid went quickly. She managed to tell him that Madame had no truck with rifles. Indeed, the woman wouldn't be able to tell a rifle from a pistol if they were shoved in her face. Monsieur, on the other hand, had been bragging about a secret business. A new venture with none other than Baron Courbis.

Intriguing, but hardly damning.

He took what time he could questioning Heidi. Nate knew that Madame and Monsieur smuggled goods into England. That was why he'd gone to their party in the first place. Even if Frid hadn't wanted to speak to him, he would have pressed for a meeting with her. She knew everything that Madame did. Unfortunately, she was less well informed on Monsieur's activities.

But she was sure that Baron Courbis was involved. Apparently, he and Monsieur were very friendly now, when previously they'd had very little to do with one another. Indeed, Nate had been surprised to see the baron at the Joguet ball, but had assumed it was for Becca. How intriguing that it was more.

The baron, after all, was on the Board of Ordinance. That was an important government position that gave him access to the Tower of London and all the guns inside. If anyone could get British rifles, it would be him. And if anyone could smuggle those guns out of England, it would be Monsieur.

He'd thanked Heidi, paid her the fifty pound bribe, and then rushed across Mayfair to get to the lending library that was attached to the Minerva Press. He made it there just as Mr. Vawdrey opened the front door.

"Lord Nathaniel!" the man said with a surprised smile. "It's been months since you've visited and never when the doors open."

"True enough," he answered with a yawn. "But sometimes a story grips me, and I must have the next part."

"I completely understand. I'll bring you fresh tea as soon as I can. Will you be in your regular spot?"

"Yes," Nate said as he once again scanned the people who were waiting to enter the large library. Several women, a few with babes, and a couple footmen likely sent to retrieve an order. Becca, however, was nowhere in sight. "Can you bring service for two?"

"Of course, my lord. What name should we wait for?"

Nate chuckled. "She'll ask for me." He had no idea if Becca would come as herself or dressed incognito. Either way, she'd either see him or ask someone. The entire staff knew him here, though most thought he came to read. Those in the peerage thought he had a secret delight in reading scandalous novels—which was true—and would say he was hiding away here to avoid an angry husband. At least that's what he told them.

"Very good, my lord," said the young man.

Nate doffed his hat and headed for the coziest reading corner in the large place. As he passed, several of the employees looked up and smiled. He returned their greeting while sauntering to the back room by the Minerva Press offices. A pair of chairs sat next to a fire, and to one side was a desk set for his exclusive use. He never actually used it except for the locked drawer in which resided several thick journals. He drew out the top one, then sat back with pencil in hand as he began reading.

He did those things by habit, not intention, because he couldn't focus on the words. Not while keeping an eye out for Becca. And not while memories of their last encounter kept spinning through his thoughts. It had been several days now since he'd climbed to her window, but in that time, she'd never been far from his mind.

Becca now was so different than what he'd imagined. She'd always been thoughtful, but now she seemed to triple-think everything. There was anger in her that had never been there before. But damn if she wasn't ten times as sexy. That buttoned-down exterior had come apart the minute he'd kissed her. She'd gripped him whenever he'd tried to draw back. And the moment he'd touched her breasts, she had all but melted.

He hadn't liked the undercurrent of desperation he'd felt, but he wasn't sure that was her. After all, he'd spent the last ten years desperate for her. And once he'd touched her, it had taken everything in him to pull back even after he'd seen her tears.

But why had she been crying?

That was the question that ate at him. She'd been enthusiastic, wildly so. But then why the tears? What had he done wrong?

He was still pondering this when Mr. Vawdrey brought him the tea service. Becca had not arrived, as far as he could tell, so he would let it sit. But then Anthony Newman surprised him by sitting down for tea. The man was the publisher for Minerva Press, and he was the reason Nate had avoided the library of late.

"Good morning, my lord!" Mr. Newman said, his entire demeanor much too enthusiastic for this time of day. "I must say, I was excited to hear you'd come in this morning. Excited and so very pleased."

Nate winced at his overly loud tone. "I do apologize, sir, I cannot make you happy this morning."

The man's face fell even as he served them both their tea. "I had expected you a week or more ago."

"Yes, well, I'm afraid I've run into some difficulty."

Mr. Newman's gaze landed heavily on Nate's face, no doubt seeing the dark circles under his eyes. "A man cannot work while inebriated," he said stiffly.

"Neither can he work when knocked unconscious or half-drowned by thieves."

The man's eyes widened. "What?"

Nate sighed. Clearly, the man did not run in elite circles where the tale of his attack was common knowledge. But rather than argue, he sipped his tea. Might as well drink it before it got cold. "I am behind schedule, not dead. Never fear."

"I wasn't afraid," Mr. Newman rushed to say. "Of course, your health is of utmost concern, but—"

"But I have made promises. I'm aware."

"It's more than a promise, my lord. It's a contract between you and Minerva Press."

Nate winced. "I know…" His voice trailed away. He needed to soothe this particular aspect of his life, but he'd just spotted Becca. She was headed this way, and he didn't want to waste a moment with her. So he pushed to his feet. "I have not forgotten you, sir. But at the moment, I'm afraid I have another commitment."

The man rose to his feet. Slowly. "Perhaps there is some way I could assist you. I have hired an additional clerk—"

"No, Mr. Newman. I'm quite capable of managing myself. Thank you." It was a dismissal, clear as day. But the man would not take it.

"Perhaps I can offer an incentive. What do you say to an advertisement in the paper?"

"I say that you have one planned already. Now if you wouldn't mind—"

"Lord Nathaniel, may I be blunt?"

He wanted to say, no. He wanted to be rid of the man, but in this, he was the one in the wrong. He'd made a promise that he hadn't kept…yet. And so, Nate nodded as regally as he could manage. "What is it?"

"You are three weeks late. This strains the boundaries of our contract. Now, of course, if you have been injured, then I understand the delay. But if—"

Bloody hell! He'd gotten beaten to within an inch of his life, and now he had to prove it to this man? "I honor my commit-ments!" he bellowed at the man. Damn it, he was too tired for this. And worse, Becca was right there. She'd heard every word and would no doubt assume the worst. So he moderated his tone. "You are making things worse for both of us," he finally said.

At last, the man looked around and saw Becca standing there, her expression completely locked down. A statue had more outward feeling.

"Ah, I see you have a visitor," Mr. Newman said. "Perhaps I should bring more tea."

"That would be most welcome," Nate said.

Mr. Newman bowed. He did not, however, pick up the tea service. He snapped his fingers at Mr. Vawdrey who had been loitering nearby. The man rushed forward and grabbed the tea service before backing away. Meanwhile, Mr. Newman couldn't resist one last jab.

"Mine is a noble profession, sir. I print tales that people en-joy." He arched his brows at Nate. "That is noble, my lord. There is nothing wrong with printing joy."

No, there wasn't. And indeed, if not for his work with Mr. Newman, Nate might have gone mad several years earlier. It had been the only way to deal with the pressures of his life. The Minerva Press was his best escape, but he wanted to be the one to choose who knew about it and who did not.

He looked hard at the man. "You think I am wasting my time, sir. You think I have lost days and weeks to idle pleasure. I assure you, I have not."

Mr. Newman bowed. "Of course not, my lord." He said the words, but Nate heard doubt in his tone. Too bad. The man could not print words that were not written. And so, in this, Nate had the upper hand. At least for the moment.

"I need the next installment," Mr. Newman said in an under-tone.

"And you will get it," Nate promised.

And with that, the man had to be satisfied. Fortunately, another patron wandered in, and he went to assist her. Nate didn't care so long as the man departed. Which gave Nate time to focus on Becca.

"I apologize, Lady Rebecca," he said, opting for formal address when in public. "You should not have been witness to that."

Becca inclined her head and took the seat recently abdicated by Mr. Newman. "Are you behind in your accounts here?"

Hardly. At this moment in time, Mr. Newman owed him money. At least that was what he hoped. He hadn't looked at the accounts in ages. He'd been too busy with everything else.

"Not like you think," Nate answered as he glanced at nearby clock. "Did you have trouble getting here? It's not like you to be late."

"Actually, I'm often late. Always have been. It's just that you were even later, and so never knew."

He frowned, thinking back. That couldn't be true, could it? "You always made such a fuss. Said you'd been waiting ages for me!"

Her lips curved and she cast him a mischievous look. "I know," she confessed. "It was awful of me. I kept thinking you'd catch me, but you were always worse."

"Until today," he said with a flash of satisfaction. "And now I shall have no more guilt about tardiness with you."

She chuckled as she stripped off her gloves, then her expression sobered. "What was that gentleman upset about, if it wasn't your account?"

Damn it, this wasn't how he wanted to tell her. He'd meant to confess his trade as a kind of secret triumph. But now that was tainted. She'd see that even in this, his favorite pastime, he was inconsistent. But there was no help for it now. He'd brought her here. And damn it, he wanted to share it with her.

"What do you know of Minerva Press?" he asked. "Do you know what they publish?"

She waved at the large library, her gesture expansive. "These are their books, aren't they?"

He nodded. "Quite innovative of them, I think, to combine press, bookstore, and lending library all together." For customers who could not afford to purchase the books outright, they paid a subscription fee to borrow the tomes. It maximized the number of people who read the books and increased profit for everyone. "What do you think of their catalog?"

She shrugged. "The books are silly, but you know I love them. Have done since I was young, and you gave me a copy of *The Children of the Abbey* for Christmas."

He had given her that. Goodness, he'd forgotten. "Do you have any favorites?"

She flushed. "Several. But you know, it's hard to get them back home, and Fletcher doesn't approve. But Mama likes them, too, so we manage to stock up whenever we're in town."

"Have you read any of the *Wicked Tales* by the Pirate Lucifer?"

"Oh yes!" She smiled as Mr. Vawdrey brought them a new tea service. She waited while he set the small table before them, then bowed himself away.

"Well?" he pressed when she shifted to pour the tea rather than continue what she was saying. "What did you think of it?"

"Well, far be it for me to judge—"

"It's a novel. One to be read and judged by people just like you."

She flushed. "Very well. I think Pirate Lucifer—whomever he is—gets too involved in the wrong details. I don't want to learn how to steer a boat or fight with a sword."

"What do you want to know?"

"If he ever finds Miss Beauty, of course. And will that wretched Governess ever die? I mean honestly, the woman was described as being a wrinkled old hag, and yet she's got eyes good enough to see him on a boat at sea."

He frowned. "Some people see things better when they are far away."

"And some people are just meddling nobodies who need to

get out of the way of true love."

He grinned. "So you think Miss Beauty is Pirate Lucifer's true love?"

"Well, he thinks so. Personally, I'm not so sure."

"Then who do you think would fit him better?"

"Well, he is a wicked pirate. Don't you think a woman with a bit more sass than Miss Beauty would suit him better? All Beauty does is read books and get locked away by her horrid governess. Really, the girl must be in her twenties by now. Who needs a governess at that age?"

He couldn't answer that and so he contented himself with drinking the fresh tea and smiling as he looked at her. This felt so right to him. Sitting with her, drinking tea, and discussing literature. It was just like when they were teenagers, except that they were in public now and she was ten times more intriguing than the girl she'd been.

"Well?" she pressed after a minute or more had passed. "I doubt you brought me here to discuss wicked pirates."

"Actually, I had," he said as he set his teacup down. "You see, I'm the wicked pirate Lucifer." Then he grinned at her, gleefully anticipating her shocked and amazed expression. He wanted her to clap her hands in delight as she had when they were kids. He wanted her pleased with him and his accomplishments.

Except she didn't do that. Indeed, she narrowed her eyes as she seemed to be measuring him from all sides. As if he were a puzzle.

"Didn't you say that Fletcher was Mr. Pickleherring?"

"Yes, but only at the end. He added things to the column after it was sent off."

"And you know this how?"

He huffed out a breath. "Because *I* was Mr. Pickleherring. And damn it, Becca, if anyone found out then I would be ruined!"

"I see," she said in a tone that suggested he was delusional. "You know I asked Fletcher about that."

"I'm sure that went well," he drawled in a tone that implied the exact opposite.

"He called me ten different names that all meant 'idiot.'"

"He's not going to admit—"

"And now you're pretending to be the Pirate Lucifer."

He sighed. "I'm not pretending. I am. That man who was just with me? He's the publisher. I'm late on the next manuscript."

"Really? It has nothing to do with forgetting to pay your subscription fees here? That you're in arrears for tea and sandwiches?" She pointed to the tea service.

"I am not in arrears! They owe me money."

"Oh my," she drawled. "Perhaps we should call over your publisher, then. What was his name?"

"Mr. Newman," he all but growled.

"Yes. If he owes you money, then he ought to pay it, yes?"

"Yes, but I owe him a manuscript, so I'm pretending I haven't noticed."

"Ah. Pretending."

"Becca!"

She looked up, obviously searching for Mr. Newman.

"Stop it!" he hissed. "It won't help. I told him that if anyone were ever to ask, he would have to deny me completely. Make up something else. Do you know how ridiculous I would look to the *ton*? A man who writes silly novels about pirates?"

"I thought you loved them."

"I do!" Why else would he write them?

"Then why—"

"You're being purposely difficult," he huffed.

"And you're lying to me."

There it was, spoken baldly between them. Of all the things that he couldn't tell her, this was his most private. It would be easy to confess being a spy for the Crown, if one ignored the implications for the war effort. But it was hard to tell her that all those ridiculous tales he'd spouted as a teenager had blossomed into real income. In fact, it was thanks to the *Wicked Tales* that he had had any lodging in London at all.

Except, of course, that he was currently living with Ras.

He sighed as he looked down at his hands. "Of all the things…" he said softly.

"What?"

He met her gaze. "Of all the things you've said and believed of me…" He let his gaze roam the bookshelves until he found the shelf that was reserved for his books. It was half empty. He took pride in that. It was half empty because people kept buying or borrowing his words. They liked what he did, even if the *ton* would crucify him for it.

He was a writer. Not of gossip, not of dark things that needed to be exposed to the world. He'd done that as Mr. Pickleherring. But the tales of Pirate Lucifer? He'd done that because he'd loved telling her the stories. Back when they had been nothing more than the wild fantasies of a bored adolescent.

Except he'd matured. He'd written them in his journal when he was sailing back and forth to Spain. He'd lost himself in the tales when the war had gotten too brutal to face. And when he'd come back to London, he'd screwed up his courage and brought them to Mr. Newman.

They'd been published. They'd been loved!

And she didn't believe him.

He sighed as the truth hit him broadside. There was nothing left between him and Becca. Nothing to stand on, if she didn't believe anything he said. And nothing to pine for, if she refused to see him for who he was.

"Thank you for coming, Lady Rebecca," he said. "I won't bother you again."

Then he stood up and walked away. He had a manuscript to finish. And she could go to the devil.

Chapter Sixteen

REBECCA WATCHED NATE leave and her heart sank into her gut. She knew she'd hurt him. Even before he'd walked away, she'd seen the betrayal stark on his face. But the idea that Nate—the boy who couldn't sit still for more than two minutes—could write not just one book, but several? It was ludicrous.

For whatever reason, he felt the need to create dangers all around him. Secrets and lies, dramatics fit for…well, for any of the novels that Minerva Press published.

She frowned, an unwelcome twinge pulsing through her belly.

Nate had fabricated tales as long as she'd known him. Pirates had been his favorite subject, but she remembered a story about a great inventor who created a flying machine. He'd flown over the world, seeing great sights.

Just like in another book. This one titled *Memoirs of a Flying Magician*. She'd loved that one so much, she'd started it over from the beginning as soon as she'd read the last page.

She stood up and searched the shelves for a copy. She found one that was tattered and obviously well-used. Just as she remembered, the author's name was the character's name, Menard da Vinci, the descendant of the great inventor.

As she scanned the shelves, she saw that pennames were common. One of her favorite novels, *Sense and Sensibility*, was written by "a lady." Others listed "a gentleman" or "XYZ" or "author of" an earlier work. Which meant that Nate could be the writer or he could simply be pretending.

She thumbed through the flying magician book, scanning the prose to see if it resembled Pirate Lucifer's book. It did. The style was certainly the same, but the Nate she remembered would not have hidden his authorship. He loved crowing about his accomplishments. She remembered him bragging about the extraordinarily exquisite pig wallow he'd constructed. He'd told everyone!

And, to give him his due, it had been very well done. But it was not something most men would claim as a great accomplishment. Of course, Nate had been seventeen at the time. A boy, really, and boys bragged. Especially to girls who listened.

Setting the book back, Rebecca resolved then and there to figure out the truth of it. She couldn't trust anyone she knew, but she had the means right here. Assuming she could credibly lie to a stranger.

Squaring her shoulders, she walked with determination into the offices of the Minerva Press. She approached the nearest secretary and gave him a winning smile.

"I should like to talk to Mr. Newman, if you please."

The young man frowned at her. "I'm sorry, Miss—"

"You may tell him that Lady Rebecca Pendarves is here. And that I wish to speak to him regarding Lord Nathaniel Killigrew."

The young man gaped for a moment, and she arched her brow in a way that Fletcher and her mother had perfected years ago. This was her first time trying it in public, and it turned out to be surprisingly effective.

"Er, um, yes, my lady. One moment."

She stood waiting, her gaze travelling over the narrow space. Books and papers lay everywhere, and she itched to read them all. She'd never been to a publisher before, and she found the place intriguing. Damn, it was hard to keep her air of aloof aristocracy when surrounded by books in the making!

"Good morning, Lady Rebecca. How may I help you today?"

She turned as Mr. Newman's greeting. "Good morning, sir. Is

there a place we could speak? Someplace private?"

"Yes, right this way."

He led her to his office which was moderately clean compared to everywhere else. Nothing on the floor, a small window, and a very large desk covered in books, though these appeared to be account books.

At Mr. Newman's gesture, she found her seat. He took his, a moment later. "Would you like—"

"Why were you arguing with Lord Nathaniel?" she interrupted.

"Er, I'm afraid I don't know what you mean."

Time to bring out that arch look again. She did so, then abruptly abandoned it. Acting haughty wasn't in her nature. "Let me explain. I have known Lord Nathaniel since we were children. I've stood by his side when our families quarreled." That was an understatement on so many levels. "I have only his best interest at heart."

"I'm sure that's true," he said, clearly confused as to why she was telling him this.

Now it was time for the big lie. "I know all of his secrets," she said. "Or nearly all. And I am in a position to help him over certain difficulties. If, perhaps, he should need the assistance."

He frowned. "I fail to see what help you could provide."

"Are his accounts in arrears?"

The man's eyes widened. "Er, no, my lady."

Oh hell. She was in the wrong then. "Then it is you who are defaulting in payment?" That was what Nate had said, hadn't he?

"Uh, no! Er, I mean, his account… I…" He straightened in his seat. "It is not appropriate for me to discuss these things with a lady."

She nodded. He did have a point. First, women were rarely included in financial matters. Second, she had no claim to Nate's business matters. "Very true," she said. "But you see, I am in a position to help you with what you want."

"You are?"

"A new manuscript, yes?"

Mr. Newman's relief was palpable. "So you do know."

She did now. "I told you as much, didn't I?" And now she owed Nate a huge apology. "Did you think he would give you what you want if you resist paying him what he is owed?"

He man snorted. "The money will be paid when—"

"The money will be paid now." She leaned forward. "I am only middling with accounts, sir. I can add and subtract better than most. Percentages come easily to me. And I am a fair hand at deciphering appalling handwriting."

He frowned at her.

"But my brother, the Earl of Estril, is a veritable genius. He sorts things out for all our friends. It would take him no time at all to figure out what is owed Lord Nathaniel."

"There is no need for that!" the man said stiffly.

"Well, that is excellent news!" she said as she pushed up from her seat. "Once those accounts are settled, then I am sure I can help Lord Nathaniel with his promise to you."

"And what exactly do you do for Lord Nathaniel?" Mr. Newman's tone wasn't exactly insolent, but it did suggest more than a friendly relationship.

"I sometimes act as his secretary when I'm in town. Appalling handwriting, that man." She tsked. "I wonder how you decipher it at all."

He dipped his chin. "It has been a challenge at times."

"I shouldn't wonder. Well, let me see what can be done. There are so many demands on his time, you know. It's—"

"But he's finished his newspaper work! I double-checked to be sure. I assumed that was so he could spend more of his time writing for me."

Newspaper work? Good God, Nate really had been Mr. Pickleherring.

"And how would you know that?" she asked, her voice stiff.

The man folded his arms across his chest. "Do you think I'm completely ignorant? There aren't that many people who write like Lord Nathaniel. I'd recognize his wit if he signed it from the Prince Regent."

"Really? But what about the recent bits? The parts about—"

"Miss Kynthea Petrelli?" The man huffed. "I was surprised by those bits. Not like him at all. I wondered if he'd been struck ill."

Rebecca's hands tightened on her reticule. "Almost as if they were written by someone else?"

He brightened. "That's it exactly! They were written by someone who glories in the petty."

"Someone mean." Like her brother.

"Yes!" He blew out a breath. "Which means I think it appropriate that the column was ended. If Lord Nathaniel hasn't the time for it, then I'm glad he knows we are his first priority. I don't even care which series he continues, so long as I have pages from him on a regular schedule." He gave her a pointed look. "He's one of our slowest writers, you know. He cannot risk the public losing interest in him. Which means he needs to send me pages on a regular, dependable schedule."

Rebecca met his gaze but inside her belly was twisting into knots. The Nate she remembered could never be kept to a dependable schedule. She doubted it was possible now. Either way, she couldn't promise to keep him on track. She couldn't promise he'd even speak to her now. But she could try to keep his publisher from hounding him.

She pulled out her haughty look and prayed that it would work. "Lord Nathaniel has a great many priorities that have nothing to do with you. I shall do my utmost to help him on your behalf," she said, trying to appear gracious, "but neither of us answer to his other obligations."

The man frowned. "What other—"

"Thank you for your time, Mr. Newman. I shall see myself out."

She turned on her heel and walked out with as much dignity as she could muster. Which was all well and good regarding Mr. Newman, but now she had to find a way to apologize to Nate.

That was going to be hard, given that his good-bye had sounded final. As in he never wanted to speak to her again.

She didn't blame him. She knew that Nate prized his honor, and she'd just called him a bold-faced liar. Lord, her brother was right. She had terrible judgment!

And speaking of her brother, there was one more thing she needed to understand. She didn't relish the thought of confronting Fletcher—that never went well. So if she was going to do it, then she had to be absolutely certain of her facts.

But first things first. She grabbed copies of Pirate Lucifer's books. She knew she had a better copy of the magician book already, so she skipped that. She should have found a way to ask Mr. Newman which other series Nate had penned, but these would have to do for now.

She purchased those, then collected her maid from the opposite corner of the library where she was sharing tea and gossip with the other servants gathered there. Normally, Rebecca would disdain such talk, but she was beginning to see that information was vital. Accurate or inaccurate, one had to understand what was said. And out of everyone she knew, her maid Missy was very good at hearing what was said.

"Come along," she said. "I've got one more appointment before we head back home."

"Yes, milady," Missy answered. "Where are we going, if I might ask."

Rebecca waited until they were out of earshot. And then she squared her shoulders and headed in the appropriate direction.

"Milady?"

"We're headed to the newspaper office. I have some things I need to read."

Like every column Mr. Pickleherring had ever written, and in particular, the very last two. And after that, she intended to have a very serious conversation with her middle brother.

Chapter Seventeen

"AND WHERE MIGHT you be going in such a foul temper?"

Nate looked up from the pavement, startled to hear Lord Benedict's cheerful voice in his ear. Damn, he was slipping if he hadn't even noticed the tall man stepping up beside him.

"Sorry, sir. Er, My Lord." Nate closed his eyes and forcibly brought his attention to the present. "I was merely thinking."

"And stomping down the pavement like an angry bull."

Was he? "I'm not used to being up this early." Then he frowned. "What are you doing here? And at this hour?" Benedict was usually up late with various diplomats discussing whatever those drunken diplomats had let slip.

"Haven't been to bed yet. Went for a walk to wake up and saw you stomping down the street."

Nate nodded, delicately trying to find a way to escape his superior. It didn't work. The man was too perceptive.

"My carriage is just ahead. Shall we alight? I'll give you a ride back to your bed. You can tell me all the latest gossip."

"Gossip?" Nate frowned. "I—"

"I hear you gave a hand to poor Baron Courbis. How is the man?"

Oh. That. Was that just last night? The baron would be the center of gossip now for several days, which made Nate a *cause célèbre* because he'd escorted the idiot home. That was usually a favorite situation, as Nate would ride the wave of interest to gain entry to all sorts of gatherings. It was how he stayed on top of society and managed to be friendly with as many souls as possible. One never knew what sort of tidbits were discussed in the darkened corners of ballrooms or in the attached cardrooms.

But at the moment, that seemed like an awful amount of work. He hadn't the heart to for it, and Lord Benedict was too perceptive to miss it.

"Come along, Nate," he said quietly. "Let's have a pint."

"A bit early, isn't it?"

"Not if you've been up all night." Then he shrugged. "Have something else if you want."

He couldn't refuse. And honestly, he didn't want to. He was by nature a social creature and he wanted to talk to someone who knew everything about him. Or cry into his pint with him. Either way, he nodded.

Soon they were in the back corner of a quiet tavern, one favored by Lord Benedict for good food and a discreet owner. Instead of the promised pint, Benedict ordered stew and water, claiming he needed to keep his head clear for the day's work.

Nate felt no such restraint. He also didn't start speaking until Benedict prompted him.

"How are the ribs?"

"Horrid. But healing."

"Hmmm. And I assume you just had a meeting with your publisher?"

Nate's head jerked up. "You know about that?"

"I prefer the flying machine stories to the pirate ones, but I've enjoyed them both."

Oh! He flushed at the compliment. "I had no idea you enjoyed frivolous pastimes."

His superior leaned forward. "I have a confession to make. I began reading your journals in Spain. While you slept."

Nate jolted. "What?"

"I couldn't sleep. I reasoned it was your duty to entertain me. And you did." He took a bite of his stew. "Is Mr. Newman pressuring you for the next installment?"

"No. Well, yes, but I can manage that."

"So what has you so foul a mood?"

"I think it's time for me to travel again." The words surprised him. He hadn't been thinking that at all, but once voiced, he considered it seriously. He had singular focus when he was away from London. Deliver this message, bring back that information. Clearly defined goals with obvious success or failure. And no heartbreak involved.

Better yet, the long nights of travel gave him time to write his stories.

"Have your feet healed?" Benedict asked.

"Well enough." Though they were throbbing right now.

"So you miss working as a sailor, crawling around in ditches, and sleeping in muck."

Nate shot his superior a glare. "I like a clean bed as much as anyone."

"And you're not a young man anymore. Injuries will get worse, recovery takes longer."

Nate stabbed a spoon into his food. "I'm not in my dotage."

"You're past 30. That's ancient in a soldier."

"I'm still useful!" he snapped.

"Yes, you are. But not if you've died in a ditch because you were too slow to run from the guns."

Nate couldn't argue. Even if he hadn't had broken toes, he was noticeably slower than when he'd been a teen. And given his ribs, he wasn't sure he could comfortably run the sails anymore.

"Have you given a thought to marriage?" Benedict asked.

"What?"

The man leaned back in his chair, a thoughtful expression on his lean face. "I'm thinking of it. Got to continue the title and all that. Plus, a wife can always help a man in the diplomatic corps. A smart woman has eyes and ears that can be made useful."

Nate stared at him without speaking. He'd never thought Benedict would marry. He just didn't seem the type. Though such a coldly logical approach to it was entirely in the man's character. Marry because she could be useful as a diplomat's wife? Didn't the man want tender feelings somewhere?

"What happened with Lady Rebecca?"

Nate's eyes widened.

"She's your Miss Beauty, yes?"

Yes. "How'd you know?"

Benedict arched his brows, and Nate looked away. They'd shared the mud in Spain. Benedict—well, mostly his batman Major Vance—had trained them both in that hellhole. The major had practical know-how. Benedict had a keen intellect. And Nate had the charm to make friends out of enemies.

They hadn't only survived in Spain, all three of them had matured. And eventually thrived. Benedict and Major Vance knew more about Nate—and he about them—than even Ras.

Which meant he might as well tell the truth.

"Lady Rebecca was a youthful fantasy," he said, his gaze dropping to his stew. "And as you have so deftly pointed out, I'm no longer young."

"Hmm. Is she going to marry Baron Courbis?"

Nate rolled his eyes. "Not after last night." Assuming, of course, that she could stay strong against Fletcher's pressure.

"Yes, what was that? What I heard didn't sound like a drunk."

"He wasn't drunk. He'd been dosed with a truth serum."

"You don't say!"

Nate explained everything he knew about it and how the baron had come to consume it. Typically, Benedict was fascinated by the concept and pushed for more details than Nate had.

"She said she got it from the same apothecary that sold Ras's fiancée the love potion."

Benedict nodded. "I'll have Major Vance look into it."

"Good—"

"So what have you discovered about the rifles?"

That was Lord Benedict. His mind leaped from one topic to the next faster than lightning. It was up to the rest of the world to keep up.

"Nate?" the man pressed.

"I've barely started investigating. Madame Joguet isn't involved." He'd learned that from Frid this morning. "Something is happening between Monsieur and Baron Courbis, but I don't know what. I have my contact looking in the obvious places, but I'll need to do a thorough search of his office soon. He has that locked drawer in his desk and the hidden safe in the floorboards."

"Do you think it's him?"

"Courbis has easy access to the weapons, but he needs a way to smuggle them out. We know Monsieur has had bad gambling losses lately."

"He has? I haven't heard that."

Nate flashed him a smug look. "That's what I've been doing since the ball. Been compiling a list of people abruptly in difficult financial circumstances." He'd visited nearly gaming hell in town. Fortunately, lounging at a table did not require him to do anything on his feet. Though damn, it had been hell on his ribs.

"Show me," Benedict said.

Nate fished a piece of paper out of his pocket and passed it over. Benedict scanned it, then secreted it away on his own person.

"You never cease to amaze me," Benedict said. "I cannot understand how you get this information."

Nate shrugged. "People like talking to me, and they trust me not to tell." Which, for the most part, was true. He didn't tell anyone but Benedict. And Benedict didn't care...unless the information involved gun running or any other form of treason.

"Very well," Benedict said with a satisfied nod. "You think Baron Courbis and Monsieur Joguet are joining forces."

"It's a possibility. Monsieur needs money, and I don't like Courbis." But that had more to do with the man's interest in Becca than anything else. "Either way, we need to know what Monsieur's new venture is."

Benedict set aside his empty stew bowl. For a man who generally had refined tastes, he did enjoy plain fare sometimes. They both did because they both remembered times when there'd been no food at all.

"When can you search his home?" Benedict asked.

Nate sighed. He needed to rest. He'd been pushing his ribs and feet lately. But he also needed something to occupy him beyond brooding over Becca.

"I'll go tomorrow night," he said.

"And I'll keep a couple people watching the docks. Maybe they'll find something."

"And maybe they'll be knocked on the head and thrown into the Thames."

Benedict shrugged. "They're street boys, Nate. Quick and easily overlooked. Unlike a nob in his thirties loitering where he doesn't belong."

"I wasn't dressed as a nob."

"Either way, you're too valuable to lose because you've caught a chill in the dark. Or had to go swimming in the Thames to save your life."

Nate wanted to object, but he knew Benedict had a point. He'd survived that dockside attack by sheer luck. He could have died in several ways that night. And he was still feeling the effects of it three weeks later. Full health would likely take a month or more.

"Think about marriage, Nate. You could step out of the shadows and into an official position."

"With a wife." It wasn't a question. Benedict had said as much.

"They're useful creatures. For both of us."

Nate shook his head. He'd given up on Becca. She was in his past now. But that didn't mean he was ready to embrace another woman.

"It's a lifetime commitment," he said. "I'm not going to do it just to get a job."

"You've been invaluable to the war effort, but we are going to defeat Napoleon eventually. Sooner or later, we won't need you to skulk about getting us information on troop movements. What will you do then?"

He didn't know, and he didn't like thinking about it. "Napoleon isn't defeated yet," he growled. "I'm still useful."

"Of course you are."

"I'll figure out who's selling those rifles. And then, I'll go wherever you need me." He lifted his chin. "So long as it's not into the parson's trap."

Benedict smiled. "Suit yourself. I suppose a wife would be inconvenient, given where I'd likely send you."

And on that ominous note, the man paid the tab and cheerfully departed. Which left Nate free to get what he needed before burgling the Joguet household.

Even though he had a night to rest, Nate still felt slow when it was time to go. Being quick on his feet had been his best asset when burgling a house. Right now, though, he felt as quick as a sick ox. Normally, he wouldn't risk it, but he was anxious to solve the gun running problem and get out of England. And besides, there might not be another good opportunity for a while.

Madame and Monsieur were attending the theater this night. He went despite his misgivings. Frid let him into the house.

Together they searched Monsieur's known hiding places and found a few new ones.

And then they were found out. Worse, it was Monsieur Joguet who discovered him.

Nate could bribe a servant, but the master of the house was a much bigger problem. Thankfully, he had a backup plan. He'd prepared a cover story and arranged to have a woman substantiate his tale.

Unfortunately, that very same tale would make the rounds of the *ton* by morning.

R EBECCA SPENT THE evening at the theater. Normally, she would enjoy the stage productions, but the London audience was particularly rude this night. It was hard to hear over the noise in the pit, and their seats were not the best, as they were guests of some of Fletcher's friends—two younger sons, both with seats in the House of Commons. And—Fletcher hoped— allies in his bid for a seat of his own.

Neither of her hosts were married, and she could see that Fletcher was watching for any gleam of interest from her. But given what she'd learned in the last twenty-four hours, her opinion of her brother had reached rock bottom.

She believed Nate now. Not just that he was Pirate Lucifer, but also that her brother had been vicious in his attacks on Kynthea. She couldn't definitively say that Fletcher had written those awful paragraphs in Mr. Pickleherring's column, but she did see a marked similarity in style. She'd often been the victim of Fletcher's biting wit. If he knew that Nate was writing the column, her brother could have damaged it out of simple spite.

And damn it, Fletcher had succeeded. The column had been shut down. Whatever income Nate received from that work was gone. It was a miracle that the situation hadn't damaged his relationship with the duke.

Speaking of whom, it appeared the duke and his fiancée were in attendance this night. She could see them in the ducal box, and she was determined to get a word with him. Fortunately, Fletcher was interested in doing the exact same thing. As soon as he noticed the direction of her gaze, he offered to escort her there.

Indeed, all three gentlemen wanted to join her.

She allowed it because she really had no choice in the matter. And as they walked, greeting everyone of a certain status or above, she began to chuckle. Hadn't she once read this in a novel? A heroine escorted by a bevy of gentlemen to speak with a duke! What more could a lady want?

A husband who loved her. Children to nurture. Good work for her mind and body. All of which could be summed up by saying she wanted a life that served her own purposes instead of her brothers'. She included her older brother Henry in this. She'd written the man just this afternoon. She'd voiced her concerned that Fletcher was not who they thought. Indeed, she very much wished Henry would quit his hermit ways and help her manage the family's London affairs.

She did not want to marry the men Fletcher thrust in front of her. And she very much feared that their brother was engaged in unsavory actions. She hadn't been specific about what those actions might be. She wasn't sure herself. But his spiteful personality was becoming clear, especially when she adamantly refused to see the baron this night.

That was, after all, why they were here at the theater and not at another ball. Rebecca had told Fletcher in no uncertain terms that if the baron approached her, she would make a scene out of refusing him. So after ranting for an hour, Fletcher had stormed out. Then a little bit later, he'd sent around a note commanding her to prepare for a night at the theater. She'd agreed because it was an olive branch from Fletcher. A quiet acknowledgement that she was not going to marry the baron.

So here she was approaching a duke's box, just like a heroine in one of Nate's novels. Or not Nate's novels, because those weren't about the women. Those were about a man having exciting adventures while poor Beauty waited in torment at home.

They entered as someone else was leaving, all four of them cramming through the door as if they were entering a spacious ballroom. They were not. The duke's box might be larger than most, but it did not hold enough room for the several people chatting there.

The duke was a popular man. His fiancée, on the other hand, looked like she was tired of all the attention. Indeed, unlike Fletcher's characterization of the woman, she did not seem a social creature. She never came alive when the attention centered on her. Unless, of course, it was the duke's attention. And at the few balls they'd both attended, Kynthea had spent several minutes sitting companionably with the dowagers.

Those were not the actions of a "social climbing hag," as Fletcher had termed her. And here was more proof that her brother was not seeing society with any accuracy.

That was the kindest interpretation Rebecca could give.

Rebecca watched the duke as they stepped into his box. Fletcher and friends were enthusiastic in their greeting. If the duke returned such regard, she couldn't see it. His response was neutral, his expression carefully blanked.

His fiancée, however, wasn't as careful. Her gaze hopped to Rebecca and the two shared a moment of surprised connection. Miss Petrelli seemed startled that Rebecca was open to speaking. And Rebecca was grateful the woman didn't hold her in disdain.

After that, a bit of careful maneuvering—and an ignored scowl from Fletcher—allowed Rebecca to get a quick word with Miss Petrelli. She didn't waste time on pleasantries.

"Miss Petrelli, please, can you get a word to Lord Nathaniel for me?"

"Um, I'm certain I can."

"Please tell him I'm desperately sorry. I was wrong. I believe him." She twisted her gloves as she looked in the lady's eyes. "And I believe you. Please forgive me."

"Oh my. That wasn't at all what I was expecting to hear from you," the lady said. "But I'm pleased."

"That's good," she breathed. "But…" Her gaze shifted to see her brother watching her intently. "I don't really know what more I can do. He's my brother. He controls everything here in London."

"Yes," the lady mused. "That is the unfortunate truth for us women, isn't it?" Then her expression softened. "Would you like to come to tea tomorrow afternoon? Ras will be at the House of Lords, and I should be delighted to share a little conversation with you. My aunt and uncle keep too modest a household, you understand. So it should have to be at the ducal home. If that would be convenient for you?"

"I should be honored to share tea with you." And anyone else who might happen to attend.

Their conversation continued about mundane things. Curiosity pushed Rebecca to ask about reading tastes. Did Miss Petrelli enjoy novels? The answer was a slightly embarrassed, yes, and they began to compare different volumes that they had both consumed. In fact, the future duchess had a particular fondness for *Memoirs of a Flying Magician* which made Rebecca smile in pure delight.

Nate was a talented writer.

Rebecca had no connection to the tales beyond knowing their author, but it still made her flush with pride that Nate had penned something that so many others enjoyed. She was just about to ask about the pirate series, when one of Fletcher's friends made a spectacle of himself.

"I cannot stand it anymore," the man cried. Then he dropped down on one knee before her, grasping her hand while she was still looking at Miss Petrelli. "Lady Rebecca—my love—please say you feel the same about me!"

She turned, no doubt with a look of utter shock on her face. "What?"

"Marry me! I cannot bear to spend one more minute without you!"

Good God, was he serious? She couldn't even remember his

name accurately. Was he Mr. Martin? Marin? And why would he not shut up?

He continued his passionate declarations in the loudest possible voice. Enough that people in the other boxes had quieted to listen as he…oh God, no! He was talking about her bosom! It was all a part of his extolling of her beauty, but sweet heaven.

"Stop it!" she hissed.

He just grew louder. But apparently her refusal was all the duke needed to interfere. He stepped forward, grabbing the man by the arm, but it was Fletcher who shut the man up.

While the duke was saying, "Leave off, man! This is unseemly," Fletcher leaned down and whispered into the man's ear.

Whatever he said, it was effective. The man's eyes bulged, and he stopped mid-word. Then he flushed bright red and ducked his head.

"Mr. Mitchell was overcome," Fletcher said coldly. "He is departing now."

Mitchell! That was his name. And the gentleman in question stumbled to his feet and withdrew with all haste. Meanwhile, Fletcher turned to her.

"It is unfortunate, my dear, that you are so delightful to so many people. You must exercise better discretion."

"Me?" she squeaked. He was Fletcher's friend!

Fletcher turned to the duke. "As you can see, my sister's choices continue to be difficult. For everyone. Please excuse us."

"Fletcher—" Rebecca began, but her brother cut her off.

"We will discuss this later."

And so she was silenced. It wasn't her fault, but to argue now would make even more of a scene. Which was damned infuriating. But it was also a familiar pattern. At least at home, everyone knew who she was. She could roll her eyes at her friends as they left. She could quietly keep her sanity by disappearing to complain to her intimates.

But she had no intimates in London. No one to vent her frustrations to. No one to think that Fletcher was being anything but a careful, reasonable brother.

"Fletcher," she said quietly as he tugged her to the back of the duke's box. "I believe I will let you go with your friend. See that he doesn't harm himself."

"What?"

She looked back to Kynthea. "Miss Petrelli, could I trouble you for a ride home tonight? It appears my brother has other matters to attend, but I should like to stay for the next play."

Fletcher's hand tightened painfully on her arm. "You will come with me," he growled.

"I do love a comedy," she said loudly.

And thankfully, Miss Petrelli caught her cue. "I should love to have your company this evening. We can continue our discussion!"

"Yes," added the duke. "I am quite happy to escort her home."

He reached out his hand, and Rebecca was quick to grasp it. That had her suspended between the duke on one side and her brother on the other, in a kind of tug-of-war. Her brother wasn't one to give up, but then he'd never squared off with the duke before. And she knew for a fact that he wanted to be in the duke's good graces. But did he want that more than he wanted to yell at Rebecca for some imagined mistake?

She didn't know and there was a long, tense moment where quiet fury filled Fletcher's eyes.

"Fletcher," the duke said in a jovial tone. "Pray let her stay as a personal favor to me."

Her brother's expression lightened. "A personal favor? Goodness, Ras, what are you suggesting with my sister?"

Nothing like her brother implied. Nothing salacious. Thankfully, the duke didn't take the bait. Instead, he remained friendly though his eyes seemed cold.

"I should love for my duchess to make a friend in your sister."

"Of course, of course," Fletcher said. "I shouldn't want to stand in the way of that." His gaze turned to Rebecca. "I shall see you when you get home, sister. Don't stay out late."

Ice skated down her spine. Fletcher was furious. She didn't really understand why. None of this was her fault, but that clearly didn't matter. And she briefly thought of giving in. She should go home with him and try to reason—

No. She'd only this morning realized that the things her brother had been telling her about Nate were completely wrong. What else had he told her that was equally off? She needed friends. She needed people who saw things that she could not. And she needed them now.

"Good evening, Fletcher. I do hope you are able to calm *your* friend." She tried to emphasize that Mr. Martin or Mitchell or whomever had nothing to do with her. That little rebellion wasn't lost on her brother either.

"Mr. Mitchell can go to the devil," he said quietly. Then he glanced at the duke. "No man makes my sister uncomfortable."

No man, of course, except him.

God, how had she not seen the extent of her brother's frightening personality? How had all of her family ignored it? And what was she going to do about it now, when he controlled every aspect of her life?

Fletcher bowed to the duke and his fiancée. Then he smiled at her. "I'll see you at home, Rebecca. Good night."

And on that unsettling threat, Rebecca found her seat. The comedy started, but she had no thoughts for it. She fidgeted and twisted in her seat. Enough that Miss Petrelli asked if she was well. And as much as she wanted to spill all her thoughts, she couldn't. The woman was a virtual stranger. Better to wait for a response from Henry.

Sadly, that wouldn't solve what might be waiting for her when she got home.

She was still stewing on her problem when something strange happened. A footman in livery she didn't recognize discreetly entered the box. He bowed to the duke and proffered a note. A moment later, the duke started up from his seat in alarm.

"What is it?" Miss Petrelli asked.

"Nate—" He cut of his words. "My apologies, darling. Do you think you and Lady Rebecca could manage without me tonight? I'll leave the carriage for you."

"Of course," Miss Petrelli responded, but Rebecca was already gathering her things.

"I'm coming," she said firmly.

The duke's brows drew together. He was going to argue, but she would not allow it.

"I have medical training," she said softly. "And knowing him, he probably needs it."

Chapter Nineteen

NATE SAT IN Monsieur Joguet's library, a place that he'd just thoroughly searched to good results. He now knew that the man was indeed trying to join in the illegal trade of guns to France. He found notations about it in the man's dairy, as well as mentions of several meetings with BC, who might or might not be Baron Courbis. But he had no definite proof beyond a desire to join in the smuggling operation.

Which meant he was not the originator of the scheme. Just an opportunist wanting to cash in.

And while Nate kept searching for the identity of BC, he'd tarried too long. Madame and Monsieur had returned home early from the theater and caught him red-handed.

Well, not so much red-handed as hand on bared thigh. Because Madame's maid Frid had been willing to sacrifice her reputation to help the English fight Napoleon. She'd let him in the house and the library so he hadn't had to break in. And she was there when the master and mistress returned home.

If the couple had just gone to bed, Nate could have snuck out. Unfortunately, Monsieur did not. He went straight for his library which meant Nate had to put Frid on the settee and his hands on her body, all while promising to make it worth her while.

Now he sat on that very same settee, his ribs throbbing while the hypocritical ass Monsieur Joguet lectured him on moral rectitude. Frid had been taken away by Madame, no doubt to receive her own lecture and wheedling questions about whether

Nate was useable in her own games.

Thankfully, he knew Frid would remain stalwart. He'd have to make good on his promise to her. He prayed that Foreign Office would help in that regard. They sometimes covered the cost of bribes, especially since he'd gotten good information tonight. All he needed to do now was sit through Monsieur's tirade until he could slink away like a common lecher.

Which was when Monsieur surprised him. Believing that Nate hadn't a feather to fly with, he sent a message to Ras demanding an answer to this terrible situation.

The man must be in desperate straits to be so bold.

So now Ras was further embroiled in Nate's messy life. And Nate was obliged to once again act the part of a feckless womanizing ass. Lord, he was getting tired of this particular role. Maybe it was time to consider Benedict's offer. Or maybe he needed to be done with this half in/half out of society situation for a more direct, concrete role anywhere outside of England. Though, given the way his ribs felt right now, he'd rather not have to crawl through ditches or duck through enemy camps to do it.

Nate sat, his thoughts not on whatever Monsieur was saying, when the knocker sounded. Monsieur immediately opened it, his tone quickly changing from pompous to obsequious. Which meant Ras had arrived. A moment later, the library door opened and…

Oh hell. It wasn't just Ras. He'd brought Kynthea and Becca as well.

He stared at Becca, his mouth slack in shock. She appeared pale but composed. Why the hell was she here?

Anger and embarrassment flooded him, and he shot Ras a furious look. The duke simply shrugged. Apparently, it was his right as a best friend to bring whatever audience he wanted to Nate's humiliation. Good God.

Meanwhile, Becca crossed to him. He knew she was scanning him from head to toe, and he did his best to erase any trace of pain in his expression. Yes, he'd been pushing his ribs. Yes, they ached. But he did not require any medical intervention beyond rest.

"Are you hurt?" she asked in a low voice.

"I'm fine. You don't belong here."

"Neither do you, but here you are."

He couldn't argue that, but he was still angry at her presence. It was humiliating enough without her bearing witness. "Just go. You and Kynthea both. Ras and I can handle it."

"Hmmm," she said, as she abruptly poked his hurt ribs.

"Ouch!" he cried, as he flinched away.

"You should be lying down."

God, how he wished he could. But there were affairs of the nation at stake here.

"Becca, please, just stay out of it."

She looked at him, her gaze heavy, and then she said the strangest thing. "I was an idiot. I believe you." She quickly ran her hand over his. "I'm sorry." Then she turned and backed away, joining Kynthea to stand to the side while Monsieur launched into his performance.

Nate gaped at her. What did she believe? What did she know? There were so many possibilities, not all of them good. But at least she knew something, right? She saw some part of him that was real, maybe?

That shouldn't make him want to launch across the room to take her into his arms. He was still angry at her for dismissing him yesterday. And yet, the more he stared at her, the more he wanted her.

Until Monsieur cut across his field of vision.

"You ladies should not be here. We men must handle this act *horrible!*" He pronounced the last bit in emphatic French.

Ras stepped forward, his tone calm though his gaze seemed troubled. "Just what has occurred here? Does someone need medical attention?"

"No," Nate said on a groan.

"Maybe my lady's maid?" Monsieur stressed. "She was attacked by this vermin!"

"Attacked?" Nate said, his brow arching. "It was her idea." That was the truth, though he knew it sounded like a peevish boy's excuse. He'd wanted to hide in the servants' stairway and take his chances on escape. It probably wouldn't have worked, but he'd been willing to risk it.

"Of course you would say that," Monsieur muttered. He turned to Ras. "And now you and I must figure out what to do about this mess."

Understandably, Ras was completely at a loss. "What to do? Is the woman harmed?"

"No," Nate said.

"Oui! Yes, she is! She is overwrought. She is crying. She is—"

"Where?" interrupted Becca. "Where is the girl? She must say if this was her idea."

Monsieur shook his head with a very loud *tsk, tsk*. "You English think that all foreign girls want your attention. I tell you—"

"I have some experience with distraught girls," Becca interrupted. "I can speak carefully with her."

A girl? Heidi Frid was in her forties and was no wilting child. Of course, an older woman could be overpowered. But in this case, she had been the one who had pulled him on top of her.

"No! No!" Monsieur cried. "My wife takes care of her."

Actually, his wife was probably interrogating Frid to see if there was an opportunity to exploit here. This was a very transactional household from top to bottom. He just hoped that Heidi's loyalties to the cause against Napoleon—and the coin Benedict provided—outweighed whatever Madame was offering.

Meanwhile, Becca folded her hands in front of her skirt. "So this is a liaison, monsieur. Nothing more, nothing less. I fail to see why it is a mess *horrible*." She exactly mimicked his French words.

"What if she is pregnant? What will she do then?"

"She's not," Nate grumbled.

"You do not know that!" Monsieur cried. "Either way, her good name is destroyed. There must be recompense." He looked straight at Becca. "Surely you understand that, mademoiselle. Especially after the baron's actions the other night."

Becca frowned at the man. "Fletcher told me you thought it funny. That you laughed at my outrage because gentlemen in their cups cannot be held accountable for their actions. Did my brother lie?"

There seemed to be an extra amount of tension in her words, but Nate couldn't pursue the topic. Not with Monsieur blustering as he waved his hands about.

"No, no! He exaggerates my words. The baron suffers for his actions, I am sure. The embarrassment is profound, yes?"

She arched her brow. "So we should let Lord Nathaniel's embarrassment be profound, yes?"

Good lord, the woman was brilliant. She was neatly twisting Monsieur's words around to get Nate off the hook. Unfortunately, Nate didn't want to get off the hook just yet. If he did, he would have already sauntered away. He would never have let Monsieur call for Ras. Still, he felt a surge of pride at her defense of him.

But he couldn't let it stand.

"Becca," he said gently. "Please, let it go. Take Kynthea and—"

"Yes, yes," Monsieur agreed. "The ladies should go."

Meanwhile, Ras had crossed to Nate's side. While Monsieur was busy trying to convince the women to depart, the duke spoke in a low whisper.

"What do you want me to do here?"

"He wants to extort money from you."

"I'd guessed as much."

"Let him. But demand to be part of the investment."

That was a big leap, not explained in the short words that Nate whispered. But Ras was a smart man. Hopefully, he would catch on.

Ras started to pull away, but Nate grabbed his arm.

"Find out who BC is," he whispered.

A flicker of understanding, then Ras abruptly straightened.

"Enough," he bellowed, his tone effectively stopping all conversation. The man knew how to use his ducal voice when he wanted. He turned to Monsieur. "What would end this situation quickly?" He lifted his nose as if the room itself smelled. "Quietly."

"Ah well," Monsieur began. "There must be a penalty, otherwise these situations will continue. A forfeit. There are medical expenses. A possible child." He threw up his hands. "Such difficult costs to hide."

Becca sniffed. "I can see to the girl. I can determine if a doctor is needed."

"No, no! We prefer our own doctors," Monsieur declared.

Meanwhile, Ras was folding his arms. "You are squeezing a stone, Monsieur Joguet. Lord Nathaniel hasn't a penny—"

"That is why I called you. You and Lord Nathaniel are the closest of friends, yes? He lives in your house. If your friend is sullied, then you will be covered in mud as well."

Ras sniffed. "You overestimate the level of my friendship with him."

"Do I? Your fiancée might think differently," he said gesturing at Kynthea. "Perhaps she does not want to marry a man covered in mud."

Kynthea rolled her eyes. "Ras knows where my heart lies."

With her fiancé, obviously. And the look that the engaged couple shared sent a twist of envy through Nate's heart. He was happy that Ras had found a perfect love in Kynthea. If only Nate could find such a future as well. But one glance at Becca's irritated expression killed any hope of that.

She might believe him about his novel writing, but that was a far cry from being understanding about him tupping a maid. Even if he hadn't really been doing it.

"You want money," Ras growled. "Bring the maid here and I shall give it directly to her."

"No, no!" monsieur huffed. "I shall take care of her expenses."

"Really?" Ras drawled. "How?"

Monsieur put on a haughty air. "I shall invest it. For her future child."

What a stupid lie. It was simple extortion. Pay Monsieur money to keep silent about this situation, as if anyone would care that Nate had seduced a maid. But Ras was known to be uptight about his reputation, and so the Frenchman was taking the shot. But with the women there, he was trying to be coy about it.

Meanwhile, Ras shifted his expression. Surprise, surprise. The man knew how to look sneaky.

"Invest it how?" he asked.

"What?"

Ras stepped forward, his voice low. "I know you have a scheme, and I'll bet you need more capitol. I have money, but only if I can play as well."

It was a bold move, but a believable one. After all, Ras was quiet about his financial affairs. He was reputed to have money, but no one exactly knew where it came from. Nate knew it was from good management of the ducal estates, but not everyone believed that. And Monsieur likely assumed that everyone was as greedy as he was.

Meanwhile, the Frenchman cut up stiff. "Non! I will not."

Ras nodded. "Then I will not. Nate will have to suffer the consequences of his own stupidity."

Nate winced. Why did his friend have to put it that way? And in front of the women. But Nate was playing the part of an idiot, so he grumbled something incoherent before slumping in his seat.

Ouch. That hurt his ribs. He really needed to get out of here soon.

"Come along, Nate," Ras said as he headed to Nate's side, but he was stopped by Monsieur.

"How much?" the man said under his breath.

Ras paused. "How much do you need?"

"Not so much," Monsieur said. "But the payment is good."

"How good?"

The two men inched to the side of the room closer to Nate, no doubt to hide their transaction from the delicate women. Nate concurred, though not for the reasons they probably thought. He knew from experience that women could be more intelligent and devious than men. There was no need to shield the fairer sex from anything.

But Nate had no desire to embroil the women any more than they already were. Which was when Becca suddenly had enough. After a significant glance at Nate—which he couldn't read—she spun on her heel and walked out of the room. A second later, Kynthea joined her.

That was enough to alarm Ras, who looked up from his discussion with Monsieur, but Nate was already getting to his feet.

"I'll stop them," he said, praying he could. There was no way he would let them wander around this house of vipers alone. God only knew what scheme Madame was cooking up. And what she would do to turn two naïve women into her assets.

Chapter Twenty

REBECCA MOVED QUICKLY upstairs, guessing that the women were closeted up there. She needed to see exactly how hurt this maid was. Or wasn't. She wanted to trust Nate. Indeed, she did trust that what he had done with the girl was consensual. But she still wanted to see the girl with her own eyes.

She crept upstairs, listening for conversation, for sobs or gasps of pain. Miss Petrelli walked beside her, her expression cautious without stopping her.

They heard the voices the minute they topped the stairs. Madame Joguet chattering away in rapid French that was too quick for Rebecca to understand. She glanced at Miss Petrelli who shrugged. She couldn't translate it either. But they both could tell that there was no alarm in the tone. If she had to guess, the lady was in a good mood. Which was greatly reassuring.

Steeling herself to commit a rude intrusion, Rebecca knocked on the door.

The French conversation stopped immediately. A moment later, a woman of middle age opened the door. She looked composed, and though her hair appeared hastily restrained, she smiled respectfully at them.

She was also the maid from the garden. The one at the ball when the baron had taken the truth serum. She'd been hovering in the shadows near Nate during that whole debacle.

Could this be the "girl" whom Nate had debauched? She had to be twenty years his senior.

"Bonsoir, mesdemoiselles!" Madame Joguet called. "Come in! Did you arrive with the handsome duke?"

"Er, yes," Rebecca said. "I apologize for the intrusion. I have some small medical skill. I thought I could help if..." She swallowed. "Well, we don't really know what happened. I thought I—"

"You thought you were needed?" trilled the madame. "You English are so droll. A virgin thinks to teach you, Frid."

The maid in question bowed her head in response, but there was a smirk on her face.

"I would think," Madame continued, "that the future duchess would know more, eh?"

Kynthea blushed, but she held her ground. "From everything your husband was saying, we feared the worst. I take it that Frid here was unharmed?"

"Only by the interruption," Frid said, her tone amused.

Definitely consensual, then. Rebecca's heart squeezed tight at the thought of Nate with another woman. It was illogical. She had long since given him up. Indeed, she'd decided just this morning that she would search for a different husband.

But she couldn't deny a wholly illogical pain at the thought of Nate with somebody—anybody—else.

"You have no need for us, then—" Rebecca said, turning to leave.

"Nonsense," trilled Madame Joguet. "Sit down. Since you have invaded my salon, you must tell me something entertaining, yes? Those are the rules!"

Not any rules that Rebecca honored. Fortunately, a male voice interrupted before she could form a response. It was Nate, his tone cordial if not exactly warm.

"Haven't you gotten enough gossip for one night?"

"And there he is! The culprit himself." Madame twisted so that she could see down the hallway. "Are any more coming?"

"Ras and Claude are negotiating," Nate said. "I am here to..." He turned to Frid. "You are well?"

Frid grinned and sauntered up to Nate. Her strut was suggestive, and her eyes danced with amusement. "I could be better," the woman drawled.

Rebecca didn't think it was possible to see Nate blush. Indeed, if Fletcher were to be believed, Nate spent his days in thievery and his nights in debauchery. So the bright pink color on his cheeks seemed distinctly at odds with his reputation.

"Heidi," he said as he took a step back. "We can discuss this better in private."

Frid turned to her mistress. "You do not need me more this night, madame, do you?"

"Heidi!" Nate exclaimed, his voice strangled.

The mistress and maid both burst out in gleeful laughter until finally Madame waved her hand at Frid.

"Oh, leave the boy alone. You are too much for him."

Nate straightened at the insult. "Not true, madame. I just prefer my affairs more discreet."

Madame unbound her braid and began brushing her hair. "Is that not what Claude is determining now?"

"W-well yes," Nate stammered. "But I know his negotiations have little impact on you."

Now the lady smiled with a cat-in-the-cream-pot grin. "Very true, Lord Nathaniel. Tell me, how shall you buy my silence, while your friend buys Claude's?"

Rebecca felt her insides tighten with shock. She had a great deal of experience with some of the darker sides of life. Healers like Mrs. Chenoweth saw depravity, even in their corner of Cornwall. Especially where horrors could be out in the open and still no one saw.

But she'd never seen such a household before. One where husband and wife turned everything to profit. While Monsieur extorted something from the duke, upstairs Madame laughed at Nate's blushes while simultaneously demanding some sort of coin.

It wasn't exactly depraved, not in the usual sense of the word.

But it was coldly mercenary, and Rebecca wasn't about to allow it continue. That was, if she could figure out a way for Nate to escape.

She needn't have bothered. In this, Nate was clearly an experienced player. Rather than being outraged—as Rebecca was—he relaxed against the doorframe and shot the lady an indulgent look.

"No," he drawled. "I don't think I need your silence. Whatever you say will surely expand my reputation."

"Unless I say that you skittered away from Frid like a boy with his first stiff."

Nate chuckled. "And that would not be believed by anyone."

The lady considered him, then glanced sideways at Rebecca and Miss Petrelli. "No one except these two ladies here. They saw your blush, clear as day." She leaned forward, exposing an expanse of lush decolletage. "Non, Nathaniel." She purred his name. "I require a forfeit."

Nate casually brushed lint off his sleeve. "And what would that be?"

"I should like to know from Lady Rebecca—" Madame pointed her hairbrush straight at her target. "Do you intend to marry the half-dressed baron? Your brother says yes."

"What?" Rebecca squeaked. "He certainly does not."

"He has told me the details of your dowry. A large sum, yes? And a property to make up for your deficiencies."

"My what?" Rebecca's throat had gone tight. Fletcher couldn't possibly have said that. Perhaps to her face, but not to everyone else!

But of course Fletcher would say that to others. It scared away suitors he did not like, leaving her with few options beyond the baron.

"Oh, ma chou," Madame said, her tone half apology, half intrigue. "You are old, that is not news. Madness was hinted at, and I must say, coming to this liaison was not the act of a sane virgin, eh?"

"This lia—No!" Rebecca squared her shoulders. "I am spending the evening with the duke and Miss Petrelli. I had no idea—"

Madame dropped her chin in her hand, her tone gleeful as she bantered back. "You came up here, yes? Uninvited to inspect Frid. What did you think when you saw her? Did you think her too old? I tell you, Frenchwomen of any age make exquisite lovers." And on those last words she blew a kiss to Nate.

He sighed. "She didn't know. Cease teasing her—"

"But she does know, does she not?" Madame's voice had turned cold. "She has seen hurt women before." Madame leaned back in her chair as she fixed Nate with a considering look. "She feared that. From you."

This was getting entirely too personal. And Nate was clearly upset by the thought as he shot her a wounded look. Rebecca shook her head. She hadn't exactly feared that Nate had hurt some poor maid, but she'd needed to be sure.

Either way, she did not like Madame Joguet poking into things that were not her business. And she was about to say exactly that when Kynthea came to her rescue. The woman's voice held the perfect note of sadness and strength.

"We both know," Kynthea said, "what some men do to women. We came to help if needed."

"Because Lord Nathaniel is known to hurt women?"

Only those he'd dallied with as a teenager. And that was as much her fault as his.

"Because," Rebecca said tartly. "I believe nothing from a man's mouth unless I can verify it."

That silenced the room. Indeed, it momentarily shocked Rebecca. Her words had come from a place of dark anger. She hadn't even realized how deeply she felt them until they dropped like stones into the room.

Madame's expression faded, as did Frid's. Nate looked at her with a sadness in his eyes. And maybe guilt. And Rebecca, realizing just how much she had revealed, decided it was time to end this conversation.

"I apologize for interrupting your evening, Madame Joguet. I believe it is time for me to return home."

"Do not apologize," Madame said, her words quiet. "I have very much enjoyed the time."

Of course she had. No doubt she'd blather about the silly English girl for weeks to come. It didn't matter. Rebecca hardly cared what was said about her. The whole exchange had left her with a sour taste in her mouth.

She nodded to them then turned to leave. Kynthea was already ahead of her. But then Nate touched her arm.

"Becca," he said softly. "Not every man lies."

She turned to stare at him, her brow arched. "Really? Do point him out to me, if you can. I should like to meet one." She continued to walk away, and he easily kept pace.

"Didn't you just apologize to me?" he asked, his words still spoken sotto voce. "*I believe you.* Those were your exact words. Along with, *I'm sorry.*" He touched her arm. "I told you the truth."

She heard hurt in his tone and felt a flush of shame. He was right. She had misjudged him this morning. Indeed, she couldn't think of a single time he'd lied to her. It was what everyone else said about him that was the lie. Or more accurately, what Fletcher had said.

But there were secrets about him. This evening's escapade proved it. And, damn it, she was tired of trying to sort through it all.

"I am done trying to figure you out Nate. It is too exhausting."

"Becca, please, let me explain."

She turned to face him. "What is there to explain? You write. You..." She glanced back toward Madame's salon. "You have liaisons. None of it has anything to do with me."

"But it can," he pressed. "I mean, I want it to."

She snorted as they descended the stairs. "I fail to see how."

"Leave that to me," he said. "Let me answer your questions."

They made it to the base of the stairs just as Monsieur and the duke were stepping out. The two were in jovial moods, and Rebecca could smell brandy in the air.

Clearly, they had come to an arrangement. And clearly the duke had been celebrating heavily. As soon as he saw Nate, he threw an arm around the man's shoulders.

"Nate, my old friend."

Were his words slurred?

Nate winced under the sudden weight. No doubt his ribs ached. But he smiled back at the duke.

"Has everything come about all right then?" His tone had the perfect notes of flippancy and shame.

"Yes, my friend," the duke said with a grin. "Your little misstep will make me a small fortune." The duke glanced at his fiancée. "Good thing too, because I have to pay for a damned ducal wedding."

"I'm glad someone is benefiting," Nate grumbled. Then he twisted slightly to stare at the duke. "Any chance that I can join in this good fortune?"

"None!" the duke exclaimed. "You need a feather first before you can fly." He leaned in close to Nate's face. "And you my friend, have nothing to stake."

"But you do?"

The duke snorted. "I have the coin. Monsieur has the connections. And together we shall pay for every hothouse flower at my wedding."

"Enough, enough!" interrupted Monsieur. His cheeks were ruddy, but he was being more discreet than the duke. "This whole affair is done. No one will speak of it again, yes?"

"Yes!" Nate said, his tone clearly aggrieved.

"Your word of honor, Your Grace?"

Ras made a show of straightening himself and setting his clothing to rights. "My word of honor," he said gravely. "No one here will speak of this again." He shot everyone a firm look. "Is that understood?" His tone was hard enough—and sober enough—that Rebecca saw it for the threat that it was.

"Of course not, Ras," Kynthea said quietly.

Rebecca echoed that. "I don't understand what has happened here. I certainly will never speak of it again."

Nate sighed. "I just want this whole night to be over with."

"Excellent," Monsieur cried.

"Yes," the duke said with the precision of a drunkard. "And good night."

Then the four of them scooted outside. The duke straightened, returning to his stiff persona, Nate slumped in the way of a defeated man, and Kynthea shared a troubled look with Rebecca. Clearly the men knew something the women did not, but nothing could be discussed until they were in the privacy of the carriage.

They climbed in quietly, waiting as the duke told his driver to take them home. Then he shut the door, dropped down next to Kynthea, and waited in silence for the carriage to start.

It finally lurched into motion, and everyone released a sigh of relief. Rebecca wasn't even sure why, except that she'd found the experience profoundly disturbing. As if nothing in that place had been what it appeared. And she didn't like being on the outs when everyone else seemed to know what was going on.

Or so she thought, until the duke's cold voice cut through the carriage.

"All right, Nate. Out with it. All of it. Or I swear to go I'll go straight to Castlereagh and damn the consequences."

"Ras—" Nate groaned. "This shouldn't be discussed—"

"In front of the ladies? I don't know about Lady Rebecca, but I'm damn sure that Kynthea has figured out a great deal more than you want her to."

In answer, Kynthea crossed her arms and gave Nate an arch look. Then the duke turned to Rebecca.

"Do you want to return to your home now? Or would you rather—"

"Not home," she rushed to say. "Not yet." She wasn't ready

to confront Fletcher. Not until she understood more of…well, everything. Then she took a deep breath and took a wild stab in the dark.

"Frid is not your mistress. Madame and Monsieur Joguet have a confusing marriage and rival business dealings." She looked hard at Nate. "And you were there to figure out what exactly Monsieur was doing." It had to be Monsieur who was the question because Frid had been much too cozy with Nate. And Frid was Madame's handmaid. "Frid helps you keep tabs on Madame, doesn't she?"

Nate's jaw went slack. "I, um…" He rubbed a hand over his face. "Yes, that's all true," he finally said.

"Well?" Rebecca pressed. "Did you?"

"What?"

"Did you find out whatever it was you needed to know?"

Nate looked to Ras who gave him a curt nod.

"BC stands for Baron Corbis," Ras said.

"I thought so," Nate mumbled. Then he looked back to Rebecca. "Yes, I got the information I needed."

Well, that was something. "So now what?"

Nate sighed. It was a sound that filled the carriage despite the noise of the wheels on cobblestone.

"Now," he said, his attention on Rebecca, "I need you to pretend interest in the baron's suit."

Good Lord. The man had lost his mind.

Chapter Twenty-One

NATE WATCHED REVULSION hit Becca. She did not like the idea of making nice with the baron and he was thrilled that she had such a distaste of the man. But mostly he felt guilt. He did not want her within a thousand yards of the baron, but there was no better way to keep the man occupied than with her.

With her in public, at a ball, where she would be safe.

He'd had to face difficult choices before. Most of his career had been relatively safe for the others around him. He was ferrying messages between Lord Benedict and the Foreign Office. Potentially dangerous for him, not so bad for others.

But there had been times when he'd had to beg for someone to hide him, for a farmer to carry him in his cart, for a soldier to trust him with the truth. That put others in as much danger as him. Sometimes more.

So asking Rebecca to make nice with the man for the evening had been hard, but it was for the war effort and for England. In the grand scheme of things, his request was a small thing. She wasn't risking her life. All she'd lose was a little bit of time.

And yet the request cut at him. Especially since she seemed none too pleased with the idea.

Fortunately, Ras was there to ease the tense silence. "I think we'd best discuss this in private. Once we're at my home."

Nate didn't argue, though his friend was naive to think any place was more private than a moving carriage. Especially if one spoke quietly. But he wanted to be home. He wanted his shoes off. And he wanted to hold Becca's hand as he explained what he had kept so hidden for so long.

She might not accept his touch, but he wanted it nonetheless.

"At home then," he agreed.

Kynthea nodded. "Perhaps Lady Rebecca and I should send messages to our homes. We are spending the night together, two girls getting to know one another." She smiled as she clasped her fiancée's hand. "Ras has enough bedrooms for us all."

"And then some," he grumbled. Then he pulled Kynthea's hand up for a kiss. "I look forward to the day when you sleep beside me every night."

Kynthea flushed pink, visible in the dark carriage more by the way she ducked her head than by the color in her cheeks.

Nate looked to Becca, wondering what she thought of such a display. Did she long for such deep affection? Did she fantasize about the day when she could rest beside her husband, waking in his arms every morning?

He did.

And maybe she did, too, given the quiet way she watched the affianced pair. Was there longing in her gaze? He didn't know, and he couldn't ask. There was too much silence between them for so intimate a question. And so he sat beside her, wishing he could touch her with more than the press of his leg against hers.

And he waited.

Fairly soon, she would know everything about him. And then, perhaps they would find a new way to relate to one another.

When they arrived at the ducal home, the ladies went immediately to a writing desk to pen missives for home. Ras dismissed the staff—he wanted no one about during their discussion—and then belatedly went to look for some food for them to share.

Nate pulled off his stockings and shoes.

His feet were mostly healed. No more infection, only normal swelling after a long day. The cuts were healed, but he knew the bones were still fragile. Still, it felt good to let his toes stretch open and rest without weight.

He left on his other clothing, not because he wanted to but because it hid the wrapping around his ribs. Besides, it was scandalous enough to appear before ladies in bare feet. He couldn't go in his shirtsleeves as well.

And then, they all reconvened in the back parlor. Kynthea set out a plate of fruit and cheese. Ras poured the brandy. And Becca sat quietly on the settee, her gaze troubled.

Nate sat beside her. "You needn't help me," he said quietly. "I am asking a lot."

"I won't help you without a full explanation," she said tartly. "I will accept nothing less."

"I know, but understand," he said as his gaze took in everyone in the room. "I am risking a great deal by telling you this. If someone else finds out, if even a hint—"

"We won't say a word," Kynthea promised.

Ras nodded. But Becca said nothing. And he would not start until she gave her word.

Finally, she nodded. "Very well. I will not speak of this to anyone. No matter what it is."

He could see that she was imaging all sorts of dastardly things. The risk, of course, was that she wouldn't believe him. Once he told her everything, she could laugh it off as imagination. Which was exactly what she'd done this morning.

"Quit stalling," Ras grumbled. "What have you been about?"

Might as well say it boldly. "Starting ten years ago, back when..." He glanced at Becca. "When I left home and did not return to school, I began working for the Crown."

"Working?" Kynthea asked.

"Spying. For the Foreign Office."

Ras blew out a heavy breath. "I thought as much," he said. Of course he did. The man knew him that well. But the ladies looked at each other with confusion. They were not trained in the ways of war, so it was a surprise. Which meant he had to explain.

"In any war," he said, "information is everything. Messages, troop movements, Napoleon's secret plans. If we don't know what he's doing, we can't plan."

"All your trips away," Ras said. "You were going to France?"

"I was going everywhere. I'm a fair sailor. That was the first thing I learned. I worked as a waterman for nearly a year, then I was put on a ship to Spain, where I carried messages back and forth." He shrugged. "That's what I did, but my real skill is in being friendly. People know things. A war isn't something that can be hidden. People hear about troop movements and supply caravans. They see important things, and they like talking about them with their friends."

Becca bit her lip. "And Madame Joguet's maid?"

"Heidi Frid."

"She is one of your friends?"

"She is. She despises Napoleon as deeply as it is possible to hate someone. She lost her husband and two sons to this war."

"But isn't she French?" Kynthea asked.

"She's of German ancestry, but Napoleon is the one she blames. I got her and her daughter to England. She has helped me ever since."

"By spying on Madame and Monsieur?"

"Of course not," he lied. "She is someone who knows my past. We talk when one of us needs a friend." He lifted his chin. "I will not endanger her." And that was the boldest lie he'd ever spoken. Every day she reported on the Joguets was a risk. Though, to be fair, he didn't believe the pair were murderous. If Heidi were discovered, she would be turned out without a reference, and he would help her find a new position.

Meanwhile, Becca spoke quietly, her words cold. "You promised not to lie to us again."

His gaze sharpened on her. "What? I mean, I know."

She held his gaze for a long moment. "There are levels, aren't there? You can tell us about yourself, but not others. You can reveal your own secrets, but not—"

"Becca," he interrupted, stopping her words. He didn't need

her exposing him so clearly. But what could he say? "Life is a great deal more complicated than I ever imagined. Warcraft, even more so."

"And now you want me to help. You want to pull me into a web of lies and deceit."

For the good of England! For the war effort. For all the soldiers fighting on the Continent right now. Not because he wanted to risk her or involve her in any way. But he couldn't hide from telling her the bald truth. Especially when it involved her.

"Yes, I do."

"And you trust me to do that?"

Didn't she hear him before? "I am trusting you with my life right now. If the wrong people learn who I am, a beating by the docks is the least of what will happen to me." He sighed. "I wouldn't bring you into this if I had another option."

"What do you need from us?" Ras asked.

He looked to his best friend. "I believe that the baron is shipping English rifles to Napoleon."

"Bastard!" Ras exclaimed. Then he looked to Nate. "Monsieur Joguet didn't tell me about rifles. He said it was food and simple, healthful things that the French needed. That they would pay handsomely for."

"If Baron Corbis is involved, he's running guns. He's on the Board of Ordinance—"

"He's the damned Storekeeper of the Ordinance!" Ras spat.

Nate nodded. "And he has a half-brother who is a soldier stationed there. Between the two of them, it could be done easily." That had taken him the most time to discover. Fortunately, the baron's nanny was a talkative sort who had no great love for her employer. She did adore the little girl though, and Nate had resolved to make sure she and the child remained safe.

"But he's a military man!" Kynthea exclaimed. "Why would he do that?"

"Money," Ras explained as he dropped back against the settee cushions. "Our rifles are better than any other variety. It's a key advantage for England."

Nate agreed. "Napoleon would pay well to outfit a small force with them."

Becca, however, could not believe it. "The baron does not support Napoleon. The things he said about 'that idiot Corsican'…" Her tone implied she was mimicking the baron's words. "I don't believe it."

"Neither do I," said Nate. "The baron believes in money, pure and simple. He would sell his own mother if he got a good price."

Ras made a disgusted noise. "That's what Monsieur kept saying. That there is profit in war for smart men."

"Fletcher has said that, too," Becca whispered, her face pale. "He admires the baron." Her voice shifted to echo her brother's tones. "The man knows how to make money."

Kynthea shook her head. "But that the problem. He has plenty of money. There's no need to betray his country for coin."

"No need," Nate agreed. "Except—"

"Greed," Becca said. "They are greedy men, pure and simple."

"Yes."

"And you think he and my brother are the same. That Fletcher would betray his country for coin."

Nate twisted awkwardly in his seat. Becca had just made a leap that he couldn't argue. But neither could he agree with it…yet.

"The baron wants money because he likes being rich. He likes the attention it gives him. And he likes the idea of your dowry, especially your dower property. It is right next to the water, isn't it? With a cave that's perfect for smuggling."

Becca swallowed. "Two or three of them have been used for just that purpose in years past." She took a breath. "So that explains the baron's interest in me. And Fletcher wants to trade me for power and respect. He wants the baron to support his bid for a seat in the House of Commons."

Ras snorted. "What power comes from the House of Commons?"

"There's power there," Nate countered. "Especially if it comes with money. Fletcher and the baron could be a powerful alliance." At least Lord Benedict thought so.

Kynthea cleared her throat. "So you're trying to stop the sale of guns to France."

"Yes."

Ras folded his arms. "And I will block Fletcher's bid for a political seat."

Becca winced at that, but she didn't object. It took Kynthea to voice the next obvious question.

"But why does Rebecca have to pretend with the baron?"

"We need to learn the date the exchange will happen—the money for the guns." Nate looked to Ras. "Did you get it?"

"Yes. Next Tuesday."

"Good. I think I can find the location of the exchange."

Ras's brows rose. "Really? How?"

Nate grinned. "I was a waterman, and they know everything about what moves on the Thames. If I know when, I'll find out where."

"And you'll catch them?" Kynthea asked.

It was better than that. Cleaner, assuming his information was correct. "I'll catch the Frenchmen early, before they make the exchange. And then I will impersonate them—"

"And catch the traitorous Englishmen."

"Yes." It was easier to confront each party individually. There was too much risk and it would be too chaotic to do it all at once.

"But that still doesn't explain what Rebecca has to do with the baron," Kynthea pressed.

"The baron knows my face. I'll wear some kind of disguise, but it might not be enough. So he has to be busy. He has to send his second in command."

"But Monsieur Joguet knows you, too."

Ras spoke up then. "Monsieur isn't part of the operation yet. He spoke of larger shipments, bigger supplies that have to be purchased then smuggled out—"

"Through my dower property," Becca said. She lifted her chin. "If I keep the baron busy that night, who will he send instead?"

"His half-brother, most likely," Nate said. "I'm not sure. I just have to keep the baron away while we catch his accomplice. And once we have him, we'll be able to implicate the baron."

Kynthea still didn't see the sense in it. "But anyone could distract the baron. He will attend parties. He enjoys the social rounds."

"He can't," Becca answered, catching on faster than her friend. "He's a pariah right now. No one will accept him back into society, not unless I entertain his suit. If I show him all is forgiven, if he thinks I will accept him, then he will come."

Nate nodded. "He wants your dower property, and for that he has to marry you." He waited while she absorbed everything he'd said. Kynthea still looked confused. Ras was angry, but completely on board with the plan. But it all hinged on Becca, and she was clearly thinking the whole situation through, silently examining it from all different angles.

In this, she reminded him of Lord Benedict. Silently considering all the options before making the right decision.

"So I am the baron's way back into society. He'll come to the ball, and then what? Do I get him to talk somehow?"

God, no! "That would be too dangerous. Can you let people know that you'll dance with him at the Penrose ball? That's next Tuesday. I can get him an invitation, especially if you indicate that you'd be open to forgiving him."

She nodded slowly. "And after that?"

He shrugged. "Then you charm him. You dance with him and talk with him. But do not under any circumstances go outside with him. You must stay inside the ballroom, where there are lots of people." He glanced at Ras and Kynthea. "I will count on you to make sure she's safe."

"Of course—" Kynthea said, but she was interrupted by Ras.

"Absolutely not. If you are risking your life impersonating French smugglers, I shall be there to help you. I'm a good man in a fight, if you recall."

"That was when we were twelve," Nate said. "I have everything in hand." That was a lie, but he would not risk his friend.

Ras shook his head. "It's too dangerous."

Nate felt a rush of gratitude for this man. A duke who would risk his own life just on Nate's word. "Thank you," he whispered. "But no. You are not trained."

He refused to budge on this point, and eventually Ras was made to see reason. But of course, everything hinged upon Becca. He strongly believed the baron would refuse any other lure, so it had to be her.

She'd been noticeably silent while he argued with Ras. And her body had gone so still, she looked as if she'd been turned to stone. So when bit by bit all three of them turned to her, she looked away, the confusion and anxiety stark on her face.

"I cannot understand how this is real," she said. Then her gaze slowly lifted to his. "But if any of it could be, it would be you. I see that now. You were never going to be a quiet man of the land like Henry. Always, you had to be spectacular."

His lips curved in a slight smile. "You'd be surprised how wearisome 'spectacular' can be. I am only trying to serve my country."

"And I can do no less?" she challenged.

"That's not what I meant."

"I know," she said. "I'm just afraid."

"Of what?"

"Of another disaster."

He knew what she meant. The last time he had drawn her into something, her father had died from the shock of discovering them. This wasn't the same thing, of course. That had been youthful indiscretion. This was something entirely different. But he could read the fear on her face, and the memory of her father's heart attack was stark in both their memories.

"I am not a boy anymore," he said as he reached for her cold hands. "And you are not a green girl. I am only asking you to dance with a man who wants to marry you."

"A man who is a traitor to England."

True.

"But I've already sworn to Fletcher that I won't consider him."

"If you don't want to do this Becca, I'll find another way."

"Oh stop!" she huffed as he pulled her hands away from him. "You know I will. I have never refused one of your schemes before. I just have to work myself into believing you."

That hurt. Did she think he'd made all this up? That he was a man of elaborate fantasies?

"What can I say to convince you of the truth?"

She looked to Ras. "You believe him?"

The duke's answer came swiftly. "Absolutely. I've suspected something for a while, but when Lord Benedict visited his sickroom, I was sure." He shrugged. "I also listened at the door, so that helped."

She nodded. "Very well." Her tone was decisive, and Nate knew she wouldn't waver from that decision. "But I must ask something from you in return."

"Anything," he answered.

"After this is done, you must help me escape my family."

She was looking at Nate, but Kynthea was the one who spoke first.

"Escape? And do what?"

Becca smiled. "Whatever I want." Her gaze locked with Nate's. "You must help me get my dowry—the money and the property. I can sell the land for more money, and then I will live by myself as far away from Fletcher as it is possible to get."

"By yourself?" Nate asked. He wanted her far away from Fletcher, too. But without anyone? "Won't you be lonely?"

"Never."

Whether true or not, she believed it. And her vehemence told him clearer than anything that she needed to be free. Of everyone and everything.

"Done," Nate said. And for him, it was as firm a commitment as a vow before God. Even if it meant he never saw her again.

Chapter Twenty-Two

Becca tried to force herself to relax. The decisions were made, the details were important but not significant. So she listened and even asked a few more questions. Nothing worthwhile came of it except for the frustration of hearing Nate say, "I cannot answer that."

At least he wasn't trying to lie anymore. But that didn't make him any less mysterious. She'd never really believed all the horrible things Fletcher had said about him, but was being a "spy" any more rational than a Lothario? She'd never heard of being a spy. The word wasn't even in his books. And, honestly, couldn't a man who wrote such fantastical tales create an elaborate fantasy like spying for the crown?

Of course he could. But she didn't think so.

Which meant, as fantastical as it all sounded, she believed him. And she believed *in him*. So she would do what he asked. For England. For the war effort. And for him.

Mostly for him. Because she wanted to believe everything he said, even when her rational mind thought the whole thing silly. Why would any man raised in England sell out his country for more money? Especially when he already had plenty?

She sighed as she looked out the window at the dark night. These were all hypothetical questions, mind candy that distracted from the real problem. Even the temptation, the hope that Nate and the duke could get her dowry free for her was nothing more than a someday dream.

The real problem came in the morning when she had to go home.

She had defied Fletcher tonight. That was not something he was going to forgive. But how far would he go to punish her? Would he be satisfied when she agreed to meet with the baron at the Penrose ball? She hoped so. But more likely, he was right now devising a truly cruel punishment for her.

Fletcher was sneaky. And half his punishment was in making her wait, belly tight and mind spinning, for a cruelty she didn't see coming. His revenges had been petty when he was a boy. He'd broken her dolls or framed her for eating forbidden sweets. But he was her brother, and she'd been told that she had to forgive him. Little boys acted out. He'd just needed more attention, more love, more sweets.

And that had been assuming anyone believed her in the first place. Hell, she'd barely believed it herself. He couldn't possibly have been devious enough or cruel enough to maim her favorite mare. Or get Nanny fired for stealing.

His rages, those violent tempers where he'd destroyed everything in reach, were simply a product of adolescence. Every boy had them, though Henry never had. But then Henry had been a hermit, who spent his adolescence holed up in his room or working the fields alongside their tenants.

So how would Fletcher punish her for tonight's disobedience? And was there any way for her to mollify his behavior?

She found no answers as their group headed for bed, each to their own bedrooms. Kynthea acted as her maid, helping her out of her gown before disappearing down the hall. Which left Rebecca to sit in her shift as she brushed out her hair.

She wasn't surprised when a knock sounded at her door. She guessed who it was and sat in indecision. Could she speak with him while sitting in her shift? Could she look at him and not remember how it felt to have his hands on her body?

Could she refuse to answer the door?

No. She wanted to see him, if only to remind herself that he had set her aside. That the last time he had touched her in her bedroom, he had stopped. As he had always stopped, even when they were teenagers.

This time, it would be her who said no. This time, she would not humiliate herself by asking for more.

She opened the door and Nate stepped in. He closed the door quietly behind him, then looked at her face—just looked at her—for a very long moment.

"Nate?"

"How bad is it?"

"What?"

"When Fletcher gets angry, what does he do? How bad it is?"

She turned away. This wasn't something people shared. It wasn't spoken of, even among her own family. No one discussed Fletcher at all.

"I can handle my brother," she said. And inside, she prayed she wasn't lying.

He touched her arm, gently pulling her around to face him. "I can tell when you're lying. Just like you always know when I'm hiding something." He stroked his thumb across her cheek, and she felt the heat of it in her whole body. "Please, Becca, trust me. I can help. I got Frid out of France. I found jobs for her and her daughter. I can—"

"What will you do? Hurt him? Kill him? He's my brother."

"I will keep you safe."

A beautiful thought, but he couldn't get her dowry out of Henry by tomorrow. And tomorrow was when she'd have to face Fletcher.

"It's Fletcher's job to keep me safe. And Henry's. And maybe my mother's."

"They aren't doing it."

She gave him a sad smile. "I've learned to be sneaky. I'm here tonight. I'll figure something out tomorrow."

"You used to say that when we were younger." He sat down heavily on her bed, one hand pressed against his side. "Just how long have you been afraid of Fletcher?"

She didn't answer, mostly because she couldn't. Fletcher had always been volatile, even as a little boy. Thankfully, he'd been gone most of the time at school. It was only when he was home that she'd learned to hide from him.

Rather than say that, she focused on Nate. "You should be resting. How painful are your ribs? Are they hot to the touch?" That would indicate infection.

"They're healing," he said. "No infection. And I'm not leaving until I know you're safe."

"I am fine tonight," she reassured him. "Go rest."

He shook his head. "Tomorrow has other tasks. I want to talk about this now, Becca, away from everyone else. So you can tell me the truth." Then he gingerly reached behind him as he stretched out on her bed. "But I will lie down, if you don't mind. My ribs do ache."

She watched him settle back, his bare feet lifting onto the counterpane as he sighed in relief. She remembered his feet from years ago when they'd gone swimming in the creek. Large, masculine feet. Hers had been tiny beside his, but now she realized how unformed they'd both been. Stupid to see so much in feet, but she did. He had calluses now that had never been there before. And could feet show weight? If so, his had been softer then. Now they were narrowed with hard sinew.

"Have you gone barefoot often?" she wondered aloud.

"Hmmm? We never wore shoes aboard ship."

She saw the fine ridges of cuts along his soles. She saw now that it was his calluses that had saved his life. If he hadn't had all that protection, the wounds on his feet would have gone deeper, bringing infection to his blood.

Her gaze returned to his face, seeing anew that he was a man now and not the boy she remembered. And the man was so much more impressive.

"I'm so proud of you, Nate," she whispered. "You are so much more than I ever thought you could be."

His eyes widened and a slight pink crept into his cheeks. "You believe me now."

"I have since the bookstore. It just took some time for the truth to get past Fletcher's lies."

She'd always known Fletcher shaded the truth for his own agenda. She just hadn't wanted to believe he would outright lie. Or that he would trade her away to a traitor—a man who sold guns to Napoleon—as if she were no more important than a bale of hay.

"Becca, how dangerous is Fletcher?"

She shook her head, but before she could form words, he gripped her hand.

"Do not try to pass me off. It is not a problem for tomorrow. It will not go away, and neither will I." He reeled her closer to him until her leg bumped up against the bed. "You would always brush things off when you were younger. You'd say, 'It's fine. It's not a problem now.' And I let you."

"It *was* fine."

"You had bruises. I remember them now. We would be... I would touch..."

"When we were kissing," she said.

"Yes. You flinched every now and then. There were bruises on your ribs. Sometimes your legs."

She swallowed. "They weren't from Fletcher, if that's what you're thinking."

"Then who?"

Her father. It had been part of life. This was how men interacted with women in their families, or so she had been taught.

His eyes darkened the longer he looked at her. "Who hasn't hit you?" he wondered aloud.

Nate. Henry. Well, not exactly Henry. He'd taught her how to fight back. He'd shown her how to defend herself, and they'd occasionally sparred so she could learn. That had been done in secret, far away from anyone.

"I know how to protect myself from serious damage," she

said. "And I know how to hide."

"I will kill him." The strength and power of his vow startled her.

She sighed. "He is my brother."

"And he is supposed to protect you! Good God, when did this begin? Your father? Your grandfather?"

She looked away. "It wasn't so bad. They never—"

He squeezed her hand. Abruptly. Not enough to hurt, but it surprised her. She jolted back to look at him, and he immediately dropped her hand, his face ashen.

"Sorry. So sorry. I didn't mean to hurt you."

She gaped at him. "You didn't." Did he think she was as delicate as that? "It was a squeeze."

"You cannot accept anything like that. Not the tiniest pinch. Not the smallest slap."

"I won't break. I haven't."

"Becca," he said softly. "God, I am so sorry."

"For what?"

"I didn't know. For not knowing." He touched her face, his hand cupping her cheek. "No more. You will not be frightened anymore."

"Really?" she drawled. "The world is frightening. Walking down the street can be frightening. How can you protect anyone from that?"

He didn't have an answer. At least she thought he didn't. Until his eyes grew moist. He drew her hand to his lips and pressed a kiss to her fingers.

"You will always be safe with me. I can promise that. Here, in my presence, in my arms. You will always be safe."

She didn't think that was a big promise. Honestly, she'd heard it lots of times. *Don't worry. I'll make sure you're safe.* In fact, Fletcher often said it.

But Nate meant it. Nate had never hurt her. He'd gone ashen when he'd just squeezed her hand. She really would always be safe with him.

The moment she understood that, everything inside her crumpled. All of her reserve, all of her doubts, and all of her strength… disappeared. They fell into him, or around him, or somewhere she couldn't name. In that moment, he became part of her. *He* became *we*. For better or worse, richer or poorer, for the rest of her life.

She was now a *we*. With him. And it felt so right.

She kissed him. She pressed her lips to his, opening his mouth and pushing her tongue in. She felt his reaction, the surprise and the welcome. And then, he met her and dueled with her.

And typical to the annoying man, he gently gripped her arms and pushed her back.

"Becca. I am not here for that."

Frustrating man. She was beginning to think he didn't want her.

"Do you know," she said, "I have done all that I was told for the last ten years. I have kept my brother's house, been hand-maiden and doctor to my mother, and served my village as the face of my family. Tonight, before I return to appeasing Fletcher, I would like to have one thing for myself. One night. With you."

His eyes looked anguished as need gripped him.

"Don't go back tomorrow. Stay safe. Ras will protect you."

"And then who will distract the baron?"

He looked tortured by the question. He had no clear answer. She saw that in his face, and she smiled.

"I am my own woman," she said. "I make my own choices. And tonight, you are my choice."

He swallowed. "I won't take your virginity. I won't take away your ability to marry."

He already had. How could she marry anyone else but him, now that they were one? But she didn't say that. Instead, she leaned in for another kiss.

"Becca," he whispered. "Are you sure?"

She'd never been so sure of anything in her life. At sixteen, she had questioned, even as she said yes. Tonight, she wanted to feel safe. And she wanted to feel alive.

"Yes," she said as she pulled apart the ribbon that tied her shift. Then she kissed him again. He supported her weight, his hands on her shoulders, both keeping her close and keeping her from descending further into his kiss. And when she lifted away from him, she smiled.

"Yes," she repeated. Then she stood up. With a simple shrug of her shoulders, she let her shift slip off her body. It clung for a moment, hanging on her breasts. She inhaled, lifting it higher, then let it slip down with her next exhale.

His gaze tracked it. His eyes were hot as they watched the fabric pause on her hips, then fall all the way down to pool at her feet. She stood naked before him, and the flare of heat in his eyes kept her from feeling anything but desired.

Right now with him, she felt beautiful, seductive, and oh, so alive. It was as if the blanket of the last ten years had been pulled away. Or perhaps it was a protective coat that she stepped out of. Only one thought made her pause.

"Your ribs," she said. "Will they—"

"They are nothing compared to my desire for you," he said as he pulled her forward. "God, let me look at you."

His gaze traced her curves, his hands skimmed over her collarbone and breasts. And his body grew taut. She knew enough of men to see the lift in his pants. He wanted her. And she wanted to see him. She wanted to know his possession. She wanted to touch him the way he once touched her.

"Take off your clothes," she said.

He swallowed even as he levered himself upright. "Not everything off. Becca, I have wanted this for so long, I don't trust myself."

She stretched up her arms, lifting her breasts and breathing deeply for the first time in ages. It was so freeing to be naked. To be so before him, seeing the way his hungry gaze followed her every movement—it made her feel precious.

"Stay like that," he said.

"What?"

He reached up and wrapped her left hand around one of the posts of the canopy. Then he tugged her other hand forward, setting it on the headboard. That made her lean down, her breasts dangling so delightfully in front of him.

He skimmed his hands down her arms then, around her breasts, to settle on her hips.

"Such a sight," he murmured.

"Nate—"

"Don't move."

He cupped her breasts then. First one, then both. He drew them up, squeezing them, pinching her nipples, one after the other.

She gasped as sensation shot through her body. Her back arched and her spine lengthened. Everything in her was stretching for him, but her hands and her legs kept her back. All while he touched her everywhere.

He focused on her breasts, kneading them while she murmured in delight. Then he set his mouth to them. And as his tongue teased her nipples, she shivered. Her womb tightened reflexively, and she gasped when he began to suckle. One hand squeezed while his mouth pulled.

Fire rolled through her, up and down from her nipples to her womb, then flashing outward. Her breath came in gasps and her weight shifted on her feet. She didn't want to be standing. She wanted more. She wanted…

He fell back on the bed, his one hand on her breast continuing to work. But the other hand slipped down her belly.

"Can you stay standing?" he asked. "Can you keep from crying out?"

She nodded not because it was a coherent answer but because she did not want him to stop what he was doing. She would say yes to everything—anything—so long as he continued. He must have understood because his free hand slipped lower. It pushed into her curls and slid between her thighs.

She bucked at the feel of something touching her there. Her legs spread without her willing it. Her body knew what he was doing, though her mind was whited out with sensation. His finger pushed between her folds. His fingers on her nipple pinched in a pulse that throbbed in every part of her body.

"Let me move," she whispered. "Let me feel—"

His fingers curled and he thrust one inside her. She cried out, her mouth pressed against her arm to muffle the sound.

"Just feel," he whispered.

She could do nothing else. His one finger thrusting in her, then pulling out. Then thrusting in again. In and out, first one finger, then more. Two fingers. In and out.

Her back arched, her mouth opened on a silent gasp.

In and out. He stretched her.

"More," she said, her voice a hoarse rasp.

This time when he pulled out, he slid his fingers upward. He rolled through her folds, and then there was the rough brush of his callused finger across her... Across...

Lightning flashed behind her eyes.

Her body bucked.

And suddenly he stilled. "Have you felt this before?" he asked.

"What?"

"Do you know what this is?"

"What?" She had no mind to understand him. All she knew was that it was wonderful. It was all-consuming. "Nate" she gasped. "Please."

"Don't scream," he said. And then he began to stroke her.

Deep inside, then the slow withdrawal. It was that part she relished as he moved over her most sensitive place.

In and out, then the deep slide.

He kept going, never long enough, never hard enough. Until she began to bear down.

She arched against him, and he didn't pull away.

She ground down as he moved.

She thrust her hips up and down.

She took what she wanted as tension built. Pleasure built. *Everything* built.

Until it exploded.

A burst of ecstasy. Light flashing outward behind her eyes. Pulsing again and again.

It was wonderful.

She rode the waves with abandon. No thought, no question, just a rolling float of *yes*.

And when it was done, she sighed happily against his chest.

His chest? Good lord, she had collapsed on top of him. Well, that was a nice place to land.

"That was wonderful," she whispered as she pressed a kiss to his skin.

"Never had a quickening before?"

"Never. Why didn't you show me that when I was sixteen?"

He snorted. "Because I was nearly as ignorant as you."

"Well," she said slowly. "I'm glad you learned."

"I'm glad you let me show you."

"Does that happen every time?"

"It should."

She smiled. "Hmmm. I like that."

He grinned.

"But what of you?" she asked. Her gaze slid down to where his organ was a clear bulge in his clothing.

"What do you know of men?"

"I've tended to sick men before. I know what it looks like on the old and very young."

He touched her chin, bringing her gaze back up to his. "I am neither."

"And so, I am curious."

He chuckled. "You were always curious."

"Will you teach me?"

His gaze grew fond, his expression hot. But in the end, he looked away.

"I fear I am teaching you too much."

She thumped his chest in annoyance. "You will not choose what I learn," she said. "I have always found a way to learn what I want. My parents could not stop me. Fletcher has never stopped me. And you will not either."

His expression tightened. "Are you saying you will learn this from another man?"

No. She wouldn't. But she let the suggestion stand.

"You will not!" he growled. Then he caught her chin and pulled her in for a kiss. It was deep and possessive. And she loved it.

Then when she pulled back, she arched her brows at him. "Show me, Nate. Please."

And so he did. He unfastened his pants and his falls. He opened up his body to her gaze, and he waited in taut patience as she looked.

As she touched.

As she explored.

"God, you're going to kill me," he groaned as she continued to caress him. Her touch was light, her explorations gentle, but still, his breath tightened as if in pain.

"You want something different?" she asked, knowing he was holding back for her sake.

He didn't answer except to guide her hand. He showed her how to hold him, how tight to squeeze. And when he began to thrust into her hand, she gloried in the way he watched her, as she watched him, eye to eye while pleasure suffused his expression.

His breath shortened. His mouth pulled tight as he thrust into her hand. But always, his eyes held hers with such intensity that she felt as if she were his whole world.

She knew it was the reality of the moment. But it still locked inside her heart. It made what they were doing something shared. As if she were integral to his pleasure and not just any willing woman.

She was part of his *we*, and that made her exquisitely willing.

His pleasure built quickly. His thrusts were powerful, and she struggled to restrain his movements. She needn't have worried. Soon, he threw back his head as he climaxed.

She watched in fascination, seeing the pulse of his seed and remembering her own contractions. So that was how it was meant to be. His thrust matching her contraction. And if they pulsed as one, their bodies would bring seed and womb together.

"Amazing," she whispered.

He laughed. It was a kind sound, filled with humor and sweetness as he caressed her cheek.

"From now on, I will never stop you from learning. Anything you want. Any time you want."

She grinned. "I shall hold you to that."

He chuckled. "I'm sure you will."

"Right now."

He lifted his head. "What?"

"I have more questions. And you shall answer."

He blinked. "What?"

She squeezed his organ as a pretend threat. She would never hurt him, but it was enough to get his attention.

"Becca!" he cried.

She eased her grip. "I want to know everything."

"What?"

"What you have been really doing for the last ten years. More than you told us all tonight."

"Becca, I cannot tell you everything."

"I will not press for details, but you will explain."

He nodded slowly. Then he gently pulled her hand off his organ. Fortunately, he had a handkerchief available to clean himself. She helped. There was water and cloth nearby. But when it was done, she sat on the bed beside him.

"Tell me everything," she said. "Please."

"On the condition that you do the same. You must tell me what happened to you. What have you done since I left."

"Agreed."

And so their bargain was struck. And hours flew by as they talked.

They should have been more careful. They should have known they hadn't all the time in the world. But just like when she was sixteen, she lost track of everything but him. And so when morning came, it was a shock to them both.

Especially when the maid walked in to find her asleep in his arms.

NATE HEARD THE gasp and was out of bed in a second, already reaching for the knife that was always strapped to his thigh. His pants had a special flap to allow him to draw it quickly and now was no exception.

He stood at the ready, knife drawn and Becca at his back before he remembered where he was, who he was with…and that he was looking at Ras's maid—what was her name?—and Kynthea, standing behind her.

Both women's eyes were wide, and a tray of morning chocolate trembled in the girl's hands.

"Ah, good morning," Becca said behind him. "Is that chocolate? We never have it in the country. Lord Nathaniel, do put a shirt on. Trousers are not enough."

He turned to look at her, stunned by the calm he heard in her voice. If it weren't for the bright pink of her cheeks, he would think being woken with a man in her bed was an everyday occurrence for her.

"Um, of course." Sometime in the night, he had stripped off his shirt, but the bandages remained tight around his ribs. It was the work of a moment to pull on his shirt. And also sheathe his blade.

Meanwhile, Kynthea took over, gesturing to a side table. "Set the chocolate right there, Dorothy. Thank you. Lord Nathaniel, would you like a cup? Dorothy can go for another glass while we all talk."

There was a note of steel in her voice that matched the hardness in her eyes. She might have spent last night in Ras's bed—he knew that for a fact—but they were engaged. Right now, Kynthea was being protective of Becca's reputation, and he appreciated that.

"Oh my," Becca interrupted as she grabbed the counterpane and wrapped it around her shoulders. "Dorothy, is it?"

The girl curtsied after she set down the tray. "Yes, milady."

"Lord Nathaniel needed some help with his bandages last night. And then we got to talking and well…" She shrugged. "I'm afraid I fell asleep." Her gaze steadied. "Are you interested in advancing in your position? I need a lady's maid in London. Missy, my regular maid, misses Cornwall so much. Would you be interested?"

The girl's eyes widened and no wonder. Becca was handling the situation like a seasoned conspirator. The girl had seen something best kept secret, and so Becca was giving her something she wanted in return for loyalty.

Well done.

"You understand," continued Becca, "my brother's staff is rather, um, nosy regarding my life. I should like an ally in that house. And I can pay handsomely for your help with that."

"Oh milady, I should like that very much."

"Excellent! Assuming, of course, the duke doesn't mind."

"He won't mind," Kynthea said. "But I should still like to discuss—"

Nate took a breath, deciding to get the most significant information out there. "Nothing happened, Kynthea. We talked most of the night through. That's all."

That was a lie. An obvious one, given how little Becca was wearing. At least she'd pulled on her shift during the night. But they had definitely done some things.

Still, Kynthea seemed to accept it. What other choice did she have?

Her brow arched. "I suggest you go get dressed, Lord Nathaniel. I'd like to have a nice chat with Becca alone, and then we'll talk altogether downstairs."

He nodded but didn't leave just yet. Instead, he turned to Becca. "You know I've wanted to marry you since I was seventeen. That hasn't changed."

"And now," interrupted Kynthea, "she will have a private moment to consider your proposal."

He had no choice but to leave. He bowed as formally as one could when in shirtsleeves and left for his bedroom. He tried to focus on the mundane tasks of the morning. Washing, cleaning, changing without aggravating his ribs or his feet. But his mind would not focus on that. Nor could he ponder how he was going to manage getting Baron Courbis an invitation to Lord and lady Penrose's ball. Especially if word got out that he had just compromised Becca.

Hopefully the ladies had that well in hand, but there were so many other logistics to manage. But all he could think about was his night with Becca. The sexual exploration had been wonderful, but he kept returning to the things she had said, the secrets she had revealed.

She was more than marginally acquainted with medical matters. The woman had as great an education as many doctors he knew. For ten years, she had been tending the sick in Cornwall alongside the witchwoman and any visiting surgeon. She'd helped birth cows and sheep, not to mention a few horses. She'd stitched up cuts and set broken bones.

All while tending to her family and *not* accepting any of the suitors that had come to court. That was the most fascinating aspect of her story. There *had* been suitors. People Fletcher or Henry had brought home specifically to interest her.

She'd rebuffed them all. Her exact words were, "I was content with what I was learning. They only wanted to give me more work. I was to manage their houses, tend to their needs, and bear their children. Not a one seemed interested in me except at the most superficial level. And so I sent them on their way."

What strength of character! He knew no young woman who was so assured in her interests that she would refuse the life of leisure that could be had as the wife of a nobleman, even a selfish one.

Or perhaps, Becca was just a good judge of character. He knew all the men who had come courting, by reputation if not personally. None were worth a penny to her.

And so he had said. And so she had rewarded him with a kiss. Which led to more. Which led to an extra delight.

But now it was morning, and he needed to know if she regretted what they had done. More important, did she classify him with all the other men who had come calling? Was he simply adding to her plate without giving her anything in return?

After all, he'd asked for her help in distracting the baron while he ended a traitorous gun-running scheme. That was work with little reward beyond a thanks from himself and Lord Benedict. He didn't count his promise of getting her access to her dowry. That wouldn't be too hard, he suspected. She'd told him last night that Henry had always acted as her protector, as long as something was brought to his attention. So he doubted Henry would be an obstacle. It was the bankers who would cut up stiff. Ladies weren't allowed to manage their own accounts, but there were workarounds if one knew where to apply pressure.

In any event, he couldn't progress with any of his questions while alone in his bedroom. He dressed with as much speed as possible and headed down to breakfast to find Ras already there, perusing his correspondence.

The look he threw Nate was disapproving, which was rich considering what the duke had been doing with Kynthea last night. The difference, of course, was that Ras and Kynthea were engaged. In fact, it looked like the mail that day was filled with bills for their upcoming wedding. There were no such promises between himself and Becca. Indeed, there had been a great many refusals.

"Don't judge me," Nate grumbled as he took his seat. "She is still pure."

"Pure has many levels, as you well know."

He did.

Ras shot him a look. "If you did it to force her hand—"

"I didn't!" The very idea was insulting.

"I won't force her," Ras continued. "She is under my roof and therefore my protection. I will not force her where she does not choose."

Nate was getting very tired of defending his intentions. "I want her to choose me," he said firmly. "I always have."

"But you are not above influencing the decision." The way he said "influencing" implied a great many salacious things.

Nate shot him a glare. "You don't know me as well as you think."

Ras's brows shot up. "That was exactly what I was thinking yesterday. And last night. And this morning."

Hurt sliced through him even though it was deserved. Ras and Becca were his closest friends. The way they constantly questioned him and his motives cut deeply.

He knew that was the life of a spy. Indeed, Lord Benedict had often warned him of such. But now he felt the ache of it as he never had before. Now he wanted true friendship and real love.

But that required honestly, and he was the one who had broken that trust, not them.

"Lord Benedict made me an offer," he abruptly said. "A diplomatic post."

Ras looked up, his gaze alight with surprise and hope. Then behind him, he heard Becca gasp as well. He knew the sound of even that small noise.

She came into the room wearing one of Kynthea's gowns, though it was tight on her in several delightful places. And, it appeared a bit too long.

He didn't care. She looked beautiful to him. He rose, as did Ras. And he moved to take her hand, completely ignoring where Kynthea stood. Let Ras take care of his fiancée. Nate would speak with Becca.

"How are you this morning?"

"Resolved," she said.

That was an ominous answer.

"To what?"

She glanced significantly around the room, her gaze lingering on Ras's butler who stood discreetly in the corner. Then she shrugged.

"To entertaining Baron Courbis's suit."

She was playing the part he'd assigned her. She was pretending in front of the servants as all good spies did. Even friendly servants. And yet, her words still cut deep into his gut. He didn't want her near that bastard, much less dangling herself in front of him.

"Maybe you shouldn't—"

"Your Grace," Becca interrupted as she turned to Ras. "Dorothy—one of your maids—has graciously accepted an offer to become my maid. I hope you don't mind."

Ras was holding Kynthea's seat out for her. He looked up and shook his head. "No, no. I'm happy for her. There isn't much room for advancement here. I'm pleased she can be promoted, and I hope she serves you well."

"Thank you, Your Grace."

"Good God, please call me Ras." Then he looked to his fiancée. "How did your chocolate discussion go? Did you resolve everything?"

Kynthea nodded. "I'm very pleased to say that Lady Rebecca has agreed to be a bridesmaid for me. We will go to the modiste together this afternoon."

"Excellent!" Ras said, his expression equally bright. And as Nate watched, Becca too smiled warmly.

"I'm pleased," he said softly. "I glad you two are good friends." Indeed, if she tossed him aside tomorrow—or more likely today—then he would still be reassured that she had trustworthy people in her life.

She smiled at him, her expression reassuring. He saw no

hatred or distrust there. Only the same sweet look of affection he'd seen last night when they'd talked.

"What do you plan for today?" she asked.

So many things. None of which could be detailed to her now. "I must speak with Lord and Lady Penrose," he said. He had to get the baron an invitation to their ball or none of this would work. Then Lord Benedict. Then some of the watermen he knew who would help him watch the docks. And… and…

The list of things he had to do was daunting. And that didn't even include what he'd promised to his publisher.

She must have seen the anxiety on his face because her expression grew gentle.

"Poor Nate," she said without irony. "I just have to go shopping with Kynthea."

"And establish Dorothy in your household," he reminded her. He would need to have a word with Dorothy, making sure the maid understood that she stood to gain a great deal by being protective of Becca, and ensuring that she would get a message to him if either of them were in any danger.

"Did you know that Dorothy has older brothers?" he quipped. "Grew up learning how to fight from them."

Everyone's eyes widened in surprise, and it took him a moment to realize what he had revealed. He was friendly with Dorothy, enough to know her particulars. And that was rare for a man in another man's household.

"How the devil do you know that?" Ras asked.

"I've been living here for a while. How did you *not* know?"

"I—" Ras frowned. He was a duke. It wasn't typical for him to know the details of his female staff unless something nefarious was going on. "I leave that to my butler."

Nate nodded. "We chatted when she was setting the fire in my room." Then he glanced at Becca, seeing her study him closely. "Becca—" he began, but she cut him off.

"Lord Nathaniel has never stood on ceremony."

Which was a nice way of saying Nate talked with everyone. A

charitable man would say that he was approachable. Lord Benedict said that made him the perfect spy. He was not aloof, and servants knew everything.

"Does that bother you?" Nate asked. He knew that it was a lot harder for her to make friends. She'd always been shy.

"No," she said. "I admire that."

Good. But as he watched her, doubt kept creeping into his thoughts. Was she really as comfortable as she seemed? Was she saying that just to appease him? He'd learned last night how capable she was at telling Fletcher exactly what he wanted to hear while secretly doing exactly as she wished.

Which put Nate in the unaccustomed position of wondering what she was thinking. He'd built an entire career on his ability to read other people. And if that failed, he usually had access to their servants. Separate ways of learning whatever needed to be known.

And yet, with Becca, he didn't know if she was appeasing him or meant what she said.

"Becca—" he began again but was forestalled as she turned to Kynthea.

"Now, I must know everything you plan for your wedding. I've never gotten to attend a society wedding. Is it as overwhelming as it seems? Or do you have everything in hand?"

"I have absolutely nothing in hand," Kynthea laughed. "And I would welcome your assistance."

And so the conversation went for the rest of the meal. And given everything the women had planned, he would get no more time with Becca this day. Just as well, he thought with a sigh. He had things to do too.

But soon, he would put his heart on the line with her. As soon as everything else was resolved, he would get her to say "yes" to their marriage. Or he would kiss her goodbye before he disappeared back into the war.

Chapter Twenty-Four

REBECCA HAD TO face Fletcher at some point. Though she dreaded it, she knew it was inevitable. So she packed up Dorothy and accepted the burly footman that Ras insisted on sending with them "to help carry Dorothy's valise."

Dorothy had a small carpetbag, easily carried by any of them, but Rebecca accepted the help anyway. It soothed the duke and reassured Kynthea. It was an illusion. If Fletcher wanted to hurt her, he would find a way that no footman or maid could help her.

So she pressed a kiss to Kynthea's cheeks, swore she looked forward to their afternoon at the modiste (which was very true), and looked long and hard at Nate.

She believed him now. Everything, without reservation. Their night's conversation filled her mind with all the wonderful and scary things he had told her. Months and months of hardship, scary midnight rendezvous, and the occasional stretches of safety. All through it, he'd written his stories as a way to keep sane. And she marveled at all he had accomplished when all she'd done was wait on her family and serve her village.

His world was huge compared to hers.

And yet underneath it all, she sensed a growing weariness in him. Or perhaps she sensed her own. They were both due for a change. But what that might look like was anybody's guess.

They'd fallen asleep on that question. And this morning had offered no time for further examination. And now she was headed home to face Fletcher with no clarity and no way to sort through the knot of her feelings. Did she love Nate? Did she want to marry him? Or did she want to wash her hands of the whole thing and go back to the life she'd built in Cornwall?

Not that. Of course, not that! But something similar. Money of her own. A home where she could do what she wanted without worrying about anyone else. But why did that life seem so small compared to what Nate's had been?

She had no answer as the carriage pulled up in front of their London home. She disembarked, watching as the footman carried Dorothy's carpetbag and a small valise that held her ballgown from the night before. As she walked, she tried not to tremble as she approached the front door.

It was opened by their butler, a man who had a disapproving look for everyone, herself included. When she entered the house, her mother cast her an imperious sniff before turning her back on her.

Oh dear.

"Mama," she called. "I have some wonderful news. I spent the evening with the duke's fiancée, and she has asked me to be one of her bridesmaids! That means you shall have a prime seat at the duke's wedding. Isn't that wonderful?"

Her mother paused on the stairsteps, turning around slowly as she appeared to consider the news. Mama was making a show of it, but Rebecca knew that the prospect of a ducal wedding was enough to occupy the woman for weeks to come.

"We'll need to discuss your dress—" Rebecca began, but she was forestalled by Fletcher's interruption. He stood to her left, having just stepped out of the library which was his exclusive domain.

"A bridesmaid," he drawled slowly. "You were supposed to become friends with Ras, not that woman." He sneered that last word.

Rebecca sighed. "I do not know what you hoped to accomplish with that. The duke is deeply enamored of Miss Petrelli. It does no good to disdain her if you want to maintain a relationship with him."

He took a hard step forward, his manner calm, but his eyes glittering with fury. "Do not seek to school me on relationships."

She lifted her chin. "I wouldn't dare," she drawled. "You obviously know everything about everyone."

Never before had she used such sarcasm with him or anyone. But her night with Nate had emboldened her. She knew Fletcher's "guidance" was nothing more than his pride dressed up as social machinations. He might be better at it than their mother, but they were machinations nonetheless and she was weary of it.

"Now if you'll excuse me—" she said.

"Who are these people?" he interrupted.

Ah yes. She needed to make the introductions. "This is Miss Dorothy Shaw, my new maid. I thought Missy could use a holiday. She's been working so hard."

"Missy has been dismissed."

She blinked. "What?"

"She was impertinent. She has been sacked."

"Without discussing it with me? She's my maid!"

Fletcher's brows rose. "She is my servant. I pay her salary. I decide whether she stays or goes."

"Henry pays her wages!"

"Then she can apply to him if she wants to return, but I will not have her in my house."

Rebecca stared at her brother. She didn't bother arguing that Henry paid him an allowance for everything in their London home as well. Fortunately, she knew that Missy was indeed missing Cornwall and had enough money to pay for passage home. Rebecca would write to Henry to make sure he made good on her wages. And she would write a reference as well, trusting to Henry to see it delivered.

"Well then," Rebecca finally said. "I am pleased that I found a replacement so quickly."

"And this man?" Fletcher asked.

The footman bowed. "I'm here to help move their things, sir.

Then I'll be on my way."

Fletcher snorted. "Have you hired a woman so frail that she can't carry her own valise?"

"No sir," Dorothy said as she took hold of the carpetbag. "If you'll just show me to your room, milady, I'll start my duties right away. Your gown needs airing, and maybe you could do with a lie-down while I refresh—"

"My sister is occupied," Fletcher snapped. "Rebecca, join me in the library." It was a command, not a request. "I should love to hear everything that transpired last night. It seems you had quite the adventure."

A shiver of fear slid down her spine. One on one chats—behind closed doors—were her father's favorite method of discipline. He didn't even have to hit them. Just the moments of terror in his library were often enough of a deterrent. Unless, of course, he did hit her. That was always worse.

Tactic one—delay. "I should be happy to, Fletcher, but I'm afraid I need to bathe before this afternoon's visit to the modiste."

"It will take a while for the water to be prepared," Fletcher countered. "In the meantime—"

"Honestly, I cannot—"

"You can and you will. Now."

Tactic one failed. Very well. Next step: partial compliance.

"Very well, but do have tea brought in. I'm parched."

This might keep the doors open and the servants coming in and out.

"Of course." He looked at their butler. "See the new woman installed and the other," he waved at the footman, "may go."

"Right away, my lord."

So much for the dubious protection of her burly footman. But she'd already known that he wouldn't be much help. She handed off her hat and gloves and then proceeded into the library.

To her surprise, tea was already prepared. "Go ahead," Fletcher said as he shut the doors behind him. "I knew you'd need refreshment. You should drink it while it's still hot."

Oh. She sat down in front of the teatray. "But there's only one cup. Let me send for—"

"I'm awash in tea this morning. That pot is for you."

She could have refused it. Indeed, it was her instinct to do so, merely because Fletcher wanted her to drink. But that was childish. Besides, she'd already claimed to be parched, so she had to stick to her story.

With a bland smile, she poured herself a cup, sniffing at the strange odor. It wasn't their usual blend.

"What—"

"I'm experimenting," he said. "You often tout the benefits of new draughts and medicines. I thought to try a new blend of tea. This is called gunpowder green tea."

"What an ominous name," she said.

"I like it."

"Very well," she said as she poured then sipped. The taste was strange. Bitter, even, but a dash of sugar helped.

"Good?" he asked as he stretched out next to her.

"Not so bad with the sugar."

"Then by all means, have some more."

He refilled her cup, but she did not drink it. Instead, she folded her hands in her lap. "Fletcher, perhaps you could tell me about your friend. Why did he propose so impetuously?"

Her brother stretched back in his seat, letting his legs extend before him. "Mitchell has never minded his tongue as he ought." He arched a brow at her. "Do you say you have no interest in him at all?"

"I didn't even remember his name!"

Fletcher nodded. "Well, let me tell you about him. About both of them."

"But—"

"Listen!"

She bit her lip. Clearly he was in the mood to expound. Her best strategy was to let him. Perhaps lecturing her would put him in a better frame of mind.

"Very well, tell me about them. I shall endeavor to listen with an open mind."

And so he did. He spoke at length about the dubious virtues of both men, where they had first met Fletcher, and the extent of their impressive tailoring. After twenty minutes of this, she began to believe the only reason Fletcher liked them was because of the condition of their boots and the cut of their clothing.

They had other attributes as well. Their ancestry was blue, their pockets full, and both seemed to be especially malleable to Fletcher's ideas. And if that didn't put her off them, nothing else could.

Eventually she got tired of the discourse. "Fletcher," she interrupted, "what is all this about? And why did you really fire Missy? She wasn't impertinent." Indeed, the woman was fawning to the extreme.

"She was to me," he countered. "Now tell me what happened last night."

She arched her brows, taking a drink of tea to delay her answer. "Well," she finally said, "there isn't much to say. I was having such an excellent time with Miss Petrelli that when she offered to continue our evening, I happily agreed. Honestly, Fletcher, I've needed some female companionship. It was nothing more than two girls getting to know one another."

"And yet you left early from the comedy. The one you expressly said you wanted to see."

She chuckled. "You caught my fib. What I wanted was to spend more time with Miss Petrelli." She flashed him a mischievous look. "And it worked! I'm to be her bridesmaid, so our family shall be further entwined with the duke's household. That's what you wanted, isn't it?"

"Do not think to mollify me with your ridiculous conclusions. I told you to get close to the duke."

She sighed. "There is only so much I can do if the man is besotted with his fiancée." She took another long pull of the tea.

"And really, so much can be learned from women's talk, don't you think?"

She was trying to do exactly what he thought: mollify him by showing him what other advantages she could offer. Women's talk, however, did not appear to interest him.

"If you lack for women's chatter, spend more time with Mama."

"You know what I mean, Fletcher. Mama has her cronies, and I need mine."

"Then I shall draw up a list of women who are appropriate companions to you."

"Ack," she cried, startled that such a sound came from her mouth. "Don't bother. I can make my own friends."

His eyes narrowed as he watched her, his expression growing more intense. "And yet your discernment is sorely lacking."

She bristled at that. She always bristled at that, but this time she chose to speak. "Fletcher, you're my brother and I love you, but really, it's time to retire that accusation. I'm seven and twenty now. I can make my own friends without my brother telling me how to do it."

Far from being annoyed, his expression cleared, and he slowly leaned closer to her. Part of her tightened at his proximity. He'd never liked being so close to her or anyone. And yet, here he was leaning forward as if to sniff her.

"Fletcher, what are you doing?"

"Rebecca," he said slowly, "how do you feel?"

"Like I am done with this conversation. Really, I don't understand what you want from me. I am here to find a husband. I am done with catering to everyone else. It is time I established my own household, my own family."

"And yet, you will always be part of ours."

That was true. But... "Are you sniffing me?"

He was, but at her words, he drew back. Then he pressed her abandoned teacup into her hands. "You must drink up. You said you were parched."

She pressed it back on him. "Well, I'm not now."

He shook his head, his expression growing gleeful. "I think you are. You said you were, don't you remember? Come come, you were parched. Was that a lie?"

"Yuh...uh—" She cut off the word 'yes' with a truly awful gag. Lord, her head was getting fuzzy. "I think I shall go now, Fletcher. The late night is getting the better of me. Perhaps a lie-down—"

"Finish the drink!" Fletcher commanded and she jolted as she stared at him.

"No." Then she looked down at the cup, remembering the strange taste. Had he dosed her? "What did you do?"

"Finish your tea, and I'll tell you." He held the drink to her lips, trying to force it down her throat.

She reacted as anyone would. She twisted away, and when he grew more forceful, she jerked out of his hold—Henry had taught her how to do that—and knocked the teacup away.

She'd surprised him, that was clear. But she also surprised herself as a wave of dizziness swept over her.

"What is in that?" she asked.

"Truth serum," he said. "The exact same thing that you dosed the baron with, so don't pretend to be high and mighty with me."

"I asked him!" she shot back, steadying herself on the armrest of the settee. "He took it. I didn't give it to him unawares!"

"A meaningless difference," Fletcher said with a wave of his fingers. "The point is that he drank it, and now you have as well. So sit down and we shall talk."

He grabbed her arm and hauled her back into her seat. She tried to evade him. Indeed, she'd seen his hand move, but she was not as quick as usual and her head was spinning.

She landed with a thump, and she pressed her hand to her head to steady it. Good God, just how much of the stuff had he given her? The baron had drank the whole bottle, but he was several stone heavier than she was. Dosages were tricky things. What was safe for one could be lethal for another.

"Why would you do this to me?"

"Why did you do it to him?"

Wasn't it obvious? "He was pressuring me to marry him. You both were. I wanted to know why."

"And did he tell you?"

She snorted. "My breasts. And my dowry."

"Did he say anything else?"

She frowned. "Not really. He was very focused on my breasts."

Fletcher snorted. "Then this potion is as useless as you are," he snapped. "Or perhaps you just don't know how to question a man."

That was certainly true. At the time, she'd been more interested in keeping the baron dressed than on pressing her questions. She wished she'd known to ask if he was selling English rifles to Napoleon.

Meanwhile, Fletcher's gaze narrowed. "What secrets have you been keeping from me?"

So many. Too many to recount, though the urge to speak nearly choked her. Instead, she went on the attack, at least verbally.

"What secrets have you kept from me? Why is the baron so important that I must marry him?"

"I have no secrets sister dear. I am only looking out for your welfare."

A lie. She felt its falseness in the air between them, heard it in the tenor of his voice.

She frowned. "You are only looking out for me?" To her shame, her voice came out weak with confusion.

"Of course! You are my precious sister, and I want the best for you."

Another lie.

The falseness in his words shook her. Her brother was difficult, sneaky, and occasionally violent, but he was still her brother. She loved him despite his shortcomings. After all, she had several faults in her personality, too, or so he often reminded her. She'd always thought he felt the same about her. He was often frustrated by her and misguided in his attempts to manage her, but deep down, he still loved her as a brother ought.

But his words rang so false that she knew she'd been wrong. He didn't love her. And he certainly wasn't looking out for her.

"Fletcher," she whispered, grief filling her.

"Rebecca, let me take care of you."

No, no, no!

"I can manage my own life," she said.

He exhaled a long-suffering sigh. "I know you believe that—"

Truth.

"—but I know what is best for you. I know *who* is best for you."

Lie.

"Who?" she asked, the pain in her heart keeping her words short.

"The baron."

"No—" The denial came up swiftly.

"Yes, my dear. I know now why he acted so strangely. It was you. You dosed him." He tapped a finger on her nose. "Don't try to deny it. He told me all about it. And Missy told me where she'd bought it."

All of that rang true.

"The baron wants you. He loves you."

Truth. That startled her. The baron didn't know her well enough to love her.

"Is it hot in here?" she asked, waving a hand in front of her face.

"You must allow the baron to make things up to you. You must let him show his love."

Truth again.

It took her some time to realize that it was Fletcher's truth. He believed the baron loved her.

"You don't understand love, do you?" she said. "Love is wanting the best for someone."

"He does!"

Lie.

"Fletcher why are you like this? Why do you want me to marry the baron. The truth this time."

"He is the best for you."

She really focused on his words. She opened herself up to the serum, understanding now that it showed her the truth or lie in other people's words. Which meant that Fletcher believed the words he was saying.

"You mean," she said slowly, "that he is the best for you." Not her. For Fletcher. "He has offered the best inducement to you. What is it?"

"Oh, you know," her brother said. "He will help the family."

Lie.

"He will help you, you mean. But how?" she pressed.

"Am I not your family? Don't I deserve something too?"

And that was when she heard it. A petulant child beneath all his bluster and demands. A little boy who wanted so much.

"What do you want?" she asked.

"A seat in the House of Commons. He'll help me with that, you know."

"No, no," she said, waving a hand in front of her face. It was so hot. Her clothing was so tight. And Fletcher's answer hadn't been the little boy's answer. "Is it money?" she asked. She knew Henry had put limits on Fletcher's funds. "How will my marrying the baron get you money?"

"He has a business that he will share with me," Fletcher said. "Business that is very profitable."

Oh dear. Didn't he see the contradiction? "No man shares what he doesn't have to. Not even with his wife."

Fletcher touched her cheek, pulling it toward him. Had her head been lolling to the side? She blinked, trying to get her eyes to focus. It was a struggle. Everything seemed to be in multiple layers. And at the deepest layer of Fletcher was an unhappy child.

If she squinted, she could almost see it.

"Don't you think I know?" Fletcher asked.

"What?"

"I know how clever you are. I know all your secret tricks."

Rebecca blinked. "You do?"

"I do," he crowed. "That is how I know you will make him help me. Just by being your difficult, devious self."

"I don't understand."

"He will not get your beautiful breasts unless he shares with me. I will make sure of it." He grinned. "It is part of the marriage contract."

Truth. And the coldness of his statement shook her.

"But I do not want him," she whispered. She swallowed down any words about who she did want.

"You do," Fletcher said. "You must."

Lie.

"No," she said.

His grip on her chin tightened painfully. "You will obey," he commanded.

She flinched, not from the pain but from the memory of those words. The harshest beating she'd ever had followed those words. Her father had told her to obey. She'd said, no.

That was her first and only time she'd experienced cracked ribs. At least her own. Because after that, she never openly defied her father again. And in her confusion, in her dosed state, she said the words she'd meant to ask her father.

"Why? Why don't you love me?"

"I do love you!" he said.

Lie.

"Fletcher, I protected you. Henry and I both did. We stood between you and our father."

"You kept him from me," he rasped.

Truth. At least as far as Fletcher understood it. But maybe it was true from her own perspective. Each of them had worked to stay in their father's good graces one way or another. And when

Father was being kind, she certainly hadn't wanted her moody brother around.

"Yes," she whispered. "I suppose I did want him all to myself."

"You bitch!" he rasped, jerking her head around again. "You bloody bitch!"

"Fletcher!"

"You wanted his love for yourself. You poisoned him against me!"

What? "No!"

"And then you killed him!"

Truth.

"No! That's a lie."

"It is not!"

Truth. At least her brother believed it.

Rebecca's head was reeling, her body felt on fire, and her clothes itched. She longed to take off her stockings, to feel the cool air on her thighs. But mostly, she wanted to be away from her brother. All she felt from him was a noxious cloud of hate. It was so thick and dark, she felt like she was choking on it.

But she couldn't stand without reeling and her vision was distorted. Plus, he was still gripping her arm, leaning over her as he tried to press his words bodily into her. He was ranting, spewing words at her as he let his darkness out.

He wasn't yelling. No, that might bring the servants. Instead, he was whispering such hateful things into her ears that she couldn't process it. Neither could she block it. But if she squinted her eyes, if she looked deep into him, she could still see that little boy. The angry, furious little boy throwing a tantrum.

A justifiable tantrum, maybe. He seemed to want his father. But the loving father he wanted never existed.

"Why are you doing this?" she croaked. "Father wasn't a good man. Not always. Don't you remember?"

"Lies! All of it lies."

She swallowed, gathering her resources to fight back. "You dosed me. I can't lie," she lied. It was hard to do, but it was possible. The serum made it so she could hear his lies. And so she pressed him again.

"What do you gain if I marry the baron?"

Pleasure flooded his system as a slight smile curved his lips. "His money for us," he said. Meaning money for Fletcher.

"What makes you think he'll share?"

"He wants your dower property. He has to share with me to get it."

"How?" she pressed. "How does it work?"

"Doesn't matter," he shot back. "Just see that you marry him."

She shook her head. She knew Nate wanted her to pretend, but she couldn't promise this. Not marriage. But she could give in a little.

"I will talk to him," she said. "I'll see him at the Penrose ball." She closed her eyes against a wave of dizziness. "He can have a dance."

"That's days away."

"We have to wait until his scandal dies down. The Penrose ball should be far enough away. He can probably get an invitation."

Fletcher seemed to consider it. He knew as well as she did that a few days would quiet the scandal, then everything would go smoother. "Very well. You'll give him three dances," he declared.

"Two." She was growing exhausted. He was wearing her down.

"And a walk outside."

"I can't go outside with him." She had to stay in the ballroom. Nate said so.

"Outside." Fletcher grabbed her chin. "He needs a kiss."

Nausea pushed into her throat. "No!"

His fingers tightened on her chin and his other hand, on her arm. Tight fingers, boring in. But they were nothing compared to his anger. And when she opened her eyes, she didn't see him. She saw a little boy breaking all his toys.

And she was one of his toys.

"You will do this," he whispered into her ear. "Or I will serve you up to him without benefit of a ring. I will put you in his bed and let him do to you what he did to his first wife."

She didn't know what that meant, but she could feel it in him as surely as she felt the clothes on her back. It was dark, malevolent, and it gloried in her fear.

She tried to say something back to him. She tried to reach the angry child inside. She knew that he wanted love but could not find a way to receive it. She knew these things, but she couldn't voice them.

She was too afraid. And he was too filled with hate.

So she said nothing. And in her silence, he said one last thing.

"And if he doesn't, I will find someone else to do the deed. Someone much worse."

She cried out in horror. He wouldn't. He couldn't.

"You are nothing more than a cunny for sale, sister. If you do not do as I will, then I will break you, and you will do what I want anyway." Then he tossed her aside and walked out.

She collapsed, her entire body shaking. Tears streamed down her cheeks, but she didn't care. Her brother was a monster. A cruel, angry monster who'd once been a frightened, lonely little boy. The two images collided against each other. How could a lonely boy act so heinous? How could a monster be a child at heart?

She closed her eyes. She stayed where she was, and she felt herself drop into darkness. It was a spinning, rolling, nauseating vortex of darkness, but it was easier than when he'd been in the room with her. And in time—she had no idea how long—Dorothy found her. She gently eased her to her feet. She helped her walk and climb the stairs. Eventually, Rebecca slid into a hot bath.

Then Dorothy brought her some food. Little bits of fruit and a few biscuits.

That eased the nausea. It grounded her more in the present reality, though her vision was still blurry. Then, when Rebecca felt she could, she called for pen and paper.

She had letters to write.

Chapter Twenty-Five

NATE SPENT MOST of the morning meeting with Lord Benedict. His plan was complicated, required attention to detail, and needed him to personally speak with the people involved. That last bit was the frustrating part. He couldn't shake his worry for Becca. She was going home to face Fletcher, and though she'd reassured him over and over that she could handle her brother, Nate was not so confident.

Fletcher was playing in deep waters. That often pushed a man farther than he ever meant to go. And it was usually his family who suffered the most.

So Nate fretted, even as he did what he needed to do for the war effort. But the moment he was free, he went searching for her. Fortunately, he knew she planned to go to the modiste with Kynthea.

He headed there as fast as he could reasonably move while still appearing casual. And when he arrived, he did so with an air of genial nonchalance. Lord Nathaniel was a useless fribble who didn't have a care in the world.

That lasted for ten seconds. He sauntered into the modiste's, smiled warmly at the girl who was not used to gentlemen entering their establishment, then leaped into motion when he heard Kynthea's exclamation.

"Rebecca! Oh my God!"

He didn't wait. He leapt past the girl to the back rooms. She must have cried out, but he didn't hear it. Instead, he was completely focused on finding Becca. And find her, he did.

There she was standing in front of a mirror with a dreamy expression on her face. Her hair was pinned up loosely and a few curls had tumbled down. The dress she wore was exquisite. The color was a brilliant jewel tone of sapphire blue that brought out her eyes, and it curved perfectly to emphasize her full breasts.

But what struck him the most was the way she seemed to float as she looked at herself in the mirror. Her arms were slightly lifted and her hands moved in exaggerated ways, both expansive and slow. And while he stood there scanning her, he realized she was wavering on her feet...which was made worse when she turned at the sight of him.

"Nate—oh!" She had to reach out—too slowly—to catch herself. Fortunately, Kynthea was there with a stabilizing arm.

"Lord Nathaniel!" Kynthea exclaimed. "What are you doing here?"

All his made-up reasons for being there flew out of his mind. Instead, he watched as Becca wavered on her feet, her happy expression making her more beautiful than he'd seen her in a long while. She was relaxed, her face seemed soft, and her smile was so genuine it made his heart ache. Especially since her expression was trained on him.

"I—I was worried about her," he finally admitted. "Becca, are you well?"

"Look at this dress!" Becca said as she turned—slowly—back to the mirror. "Kynthea has excellent taste, don't you think?"

"Yes, she does," he said, the words automatic. Then he stepped forward to help steady her on the opposite side. "How are you feeling?"

"Hmmm? Oh, I'm quite lovely."

"Yes," he said softly. "You are." Because at this moment she looked positively radiant.

She turned to look at him, her expression beaming. "That was the truth!" she said. "I can hear it in your voice."

He opened his mouth to answer, but no words came to mind.

Her expression was one he'd never seen on her before, not even when she was sixteen. She was open and happy, and looking at him like he was completely new. As if she'd never truly seen him before and was fascinated by the sight.

"Say something else," she urged.

Was she drunk? He couldn't smell any alcohol on her, but there was definitely something different.

"I'm here because I was worried about you. Did you have any problems with Fletcher?"

She grinned. "You really were worried!"

He frowned. "Becca—"

Kynthea interrupted, her voice loud. "This gown will be perfect," she said. "Do you think we can have it altered in time?"

"Yes, Your Grace," said the modiste with a deep curtsey.

"I'm not 'Your Grace' yet," Kynthea murmured. "And perhaps you have a private room where we could have a spot of tea? Just so Lady Rebecca can sit for a moment and have refreshments?"

"Right back here," the modiste answered with a gesture. "No one will hear. I'll make sure of it." Then she looked at Nate. "If my lord would sit back there, I can get the tea prepared—"

"While I help Rebecca change," Kynthea finished. "Yes, that will work." She looked at Nate. "We'll just be a moment."

Clearly there was something wrong, but he knew better than to push. Not with servants hovering nearby. And yet, his worry for Becca kept him in place. "What happened?" he pressed, sotto voice.

"Fletcher dosed her," Kynthea answered, her voice equally low. "She's fine. Just a little fuzzy."

Fury rolled through him, smashing past a dozen mental barriers that usually kept his thoughts to himself. His hands tightened, and it took him a moment to control them enough to help Becca walk behind a screen. When he could finally speak, he pushed out three words.

"Dosed. With. What?"

Becca turned, proving that there was nothing wrong with her hearing. "A truth serum," she said, her expression shifting back and forth between happiness and a frown. "It was wrong of him, but I don't mind anymore. It was awful for a bit, but Kynthea's here and now you are, too. I'm happy. And this dress feels so good." Then she ran her hands down the silk gown. It was clearly meant for her experience, but the gesture started at her chest and ran over her breasts. Her nipples pebbled as her body arched.

Oh good God. Now his body was thickening when he really needed a calm head. Because if he gave into emotions now, he'd likely go beat Fletcher to a bloody pulp.

"I'm so glad you like it," Kynthea said, her tone light. "Now let's get you out of it so madame can work on it."

"But it's perfect!"

"Not with all those pins in it. Come on. Raise up your arms."

Meanwhile, Nate sat down in the secluded alcove. He needed to make some quick decisions. First off, Becca was not going to be alone with Fletcher ever again. That meant she needed another place to live. Back home in Cornwall? She'd probably be safe there, though it ached to think of sending her away.

He could marry her, of course. Right now. But where would she live? Until this current situation was resolved, he was holed up in Ras's guest bedroom. Hardly an appropriate place to take a new wife. But it was still a possibility.

He was mulling over options—each one more ridiculous than the last—when Kynthea and Becca joined him. Becca moved in that same floaty way. And when she sat, she kept trying to remain upright only to slowly sink into a half sprawl. It would be adorable, if he weren't worried for her safety.

"When did this happen?" he asked, his voice low.

Becca appeared fascinated by the design painted on the wall, so Kynthea answered as she poured the tea.

"I think soon after she returned to her home. Fletcher was waiting for her. I didn't get there until several hours later. By that time she was much better—"

"This is better?" he said watching Becca trace a painted swirl with her finger.

"Oh yes," Kynthea said. "Though I think that was more emotional upset. She insisted on coming here. And I thought she was safer with me here than there."

Damned right. "Emotional?"

Becca was still running her finger along the wall design, this time outlining the edges of a flower. But when she spoke, her words were clear. "Fletcher's an angry and lost little boy. Henry and I weren't good siblings to him. I see that now."

"Fletcher's an adult. Don't romanticize—"

Becca gripped Nate's hand with surprising strength. "You don't understand," she huffed.

"What don't I understand?"

"The serum," she said. "It doesn't mean I tell the truth. It means I *see* the truth. And hear it." Then she pursed her lips. "And it's really hard to lie, too. But I rarely lie, so that isn't a problem for me."

Nate gaped at her, trying to adjust his thinking. Just to test it, he frowned at her and lied. "That's the silliest thing I ever heard."

She turned to him, her expression a tight frown. "You've heard a lot sillier things, haven't you?"

He chuckled. "Yes, I have." Then he pressed the teacup into her hand. "Drink up. Maybe it'll help."

She pushed it away. "I don't want help," she said. "I'm trying to hold onto it, but it's fading. And soon I'll have to go home again, and—"

"No. You're not going back," he said. "It's too dangerous."

She snorted. It wasn't a delicate lady-like sound. It was a full snort. "You're worried for me."

"Of course, I am. Kynthea—"

"No, no," Becca interrupted. "Don't talk to her. Listen Nate. Fletcher's angry and petulant. Oh, how that boy loves to sulk. But I've always been able to reach him before."

He shook his head. "This is different."

"And so am I," she said, her voice more confident than he'd ever heard it. "I know how to reach him."

"He dosed you. What else is he willing to do?"

She shrugged. "I'm doing what he wants. I'm going to give the baron a chance."

He didn't like it. He didn't want to risk her in any way, but he didn't see a better option. Worse, he wasn't sure he could stop her.

"We could marry right now. You and me."

Becca burst out with another full-throated laugh. "Wouldn't that shock everyone?" she cried.

"I don't care about anyone else. I'm worried about you."

Rather than answer, she abruptly surged forward, pressing her mouth to his with too much speed. They banged together while he caught her elbows. Then he steadied her, all without breaking the kiss.

God, she was amazing right now. All enthusiasm and need. She thrust her tongue at him, and he dueled back. Trading thrusts like this made his blood surge. This was not a timid woman, uncertain of her path. This was Becca, bold and assured.

And she was kissing him in a way he'd longed to feel from her. He did not want it to end. But Kynthea was right here. And though he distantly heard her clearing her throat, it was the way she firmly pried his fingers off Becca that finally caught his attention.

"Stop it," she was saying. "Good God, you two are incorrigible."

He pulled back, his heart racing and his body urging him back to Becca.

"Nate, really! You know better."

Did he? Yes, he supposed he did.

"You're one to talk," he muttered. He'd been witness to a few of her and Ras's kisses. They were no better. But of course, they were engaged. And he was…he had no idea what with Becca. But he wanted it all.

Kynthea's cheeks colored pink, but Becca looked lush. Her eyes were heavy lidded, her lips swollen, and if they were in private, he knew he could not have held back. But Kynthea put a hand out to stop him.

"Did you make the arrangements for the Penrose ball?"

He nodded, doing his best to wrench his thoughts away from Becca.

"I did, but…" God, he hated sending Becca back home.

Then the woman stopped his thoughts. Becca took hold of his face with both hands. She didn't even have to apply pressure for him to turn to her. He would always turn to her.

"Trust me," she said. "I have been managing my family since before we met. I will be safe."

Belief echoed in her words. Whatever the truth, she was confident in her abilities. And damn it, he had no other choice.

"Very well," he said. Then he looked at Kynthea. "But you and Ras will be by her side throughout the ball. And do you think you could stay with her until then? Wedding preparations or something like that?"

Becca immediately brightened. "Oh, I should love that above all things! I like you so much. Even in Cornwall, there's no one whom I like quite so much as you."

Kynthea smiled. "I think I like this potion," she said to Kynthea, her voice a bare whisper. "Since I feel exactly the same about you."

And so it was done. Nate spent the rest of the afternoon with them. As more time passed, Becca was steadier on her feet and absolutely delighted with the idea of shopping. Since Kynthea had a million shops to visit in preparation for her wedding, they fell into step with one another. Nate carried the packages and spoke entertaining nonsense. And he gloried in seeing Becca blossom at the happy tasks.

By the time it was all over, she and Kynthea had cemented their friendship. But what would become of him? As delighted as Becca seemed, she had not expressed interest in marrying him.

Indeed, she had laughed straight in his face at the very idea.

Desperate for one last moment with her, he touched her elbow before she climbed into the carriage with Kynthea. "Go to the Carre ball tonight," he pressed. They had a couple days yet before the Penrose ball. He would use that time before he put her life at risk.

She frowned at him. "Tonight? Why?"

"I want to dance with you. A waltz." He couldn't ask for more without tipping his hand or further upsetting Fletcher. But one dance could be easily explained away as being polite. One dance when he could hold her in public and he could court her as he'd always longed to do.

"One waltz," she said. "I'd like that."

Then his expression fell as his logical side reasserted itself. "Actually, I should ask, and you should refuse me. That would reassure Fletcher."

"But I wouldn't!"

He grinned. "Or we could make a scene."

He heard a very loud groan from inside the carriage. It was Kynthea as she grabbed hold of Becca and dragged her inside.

"Stop it," she hissed in an undertone. "There will be no scene tonight, and no more looking at each other like that in public. Not until all is resolved." Then she very pointedly glared at Nate and said, "Go away!"

His eyes widened at how angry she sounded. It was forceful enough that he backed up a step. And then his peripheral vision showed him exactly what Kynthea must have noticed. Several members of the *ton* were nearby. Several who would now take tales of a loud altercation rather than a heartfelt goodbye.

Very well, he could play the part.

"You are becoming quite shrewish, Miss Petrelli," he retorted. "I believe Lady Rebecca is having a terrible influence upon your nature."

And with that, he spun on his heel and left. While inside, he mourned. He couldn't dance with her now. Not after that display.

Unless he thought of something very clever.

Chapter Twenty-Six

B Y THE TIME Rebecca made it home, Fletcher was waiting. He was furious she had spent the day shopping, but he could hardly lambast her when Kynthea stood beside her gleefully talking about what a marvelous time they'd had and how she'd love to have Rebecca and her mother over after the wedding.

Fletcher barely hid his distaste of Kynthea, so that was no inducement. Rebecca's mother, however, was delighted at the idea of befriending a duchess. As were several of the ladies sitting in Mama's afternoon salon. So Fletcher would appear churlish if he openly scoffed at the idea. And though their mother usually bowed to Fletcher's tantrums, he knew that even she would stand up to him at the prospect of entering the intimate circle of a duchess.

That was when Kynthea repeated the wonderful news that Rebecca would be one of her bridesmaids. Goodness, that set all the women into cries of delight. Which exactly echoed Rebecca's feelings.

Fletcher was none too pleased. She knew his moods and could see the underlying fury beneath his genial smile. She didn't bend, though. And with every other woman in the room delighted, he had no choice but to pretend to approve.

Then he got in his blow.

"Such a delightful celebration," he said. "But I know you weren't feeling well this morning. I think it would be best if you stayed home tonight to recover. Can't have you looking peaked during the festivities, can we?"

"But I feel fine!" Rebecca said.

"Nevertheless, sister, I insist. Your health is of paramount importance."

Such a petty revenge, she realized, taking away her treat just because he was ill-tempered. A week ago, she might have passed that off as misguided worry for her health. But the scales had fallen from her eyes, and she clearly saw the petulant child in him crying for attention in all the wrong ways.

Perhaps she could help him then. If he wanted attention, she would give it to him. "Very well, Fletcher," she said. "I have been meaning to spend some more time with you anyway. A quiet evening of discussion with my brother sounds like just the thing."

"Discussion?" he scoffed. "Whatever about?"

"Your negotiations regarding my dowry, for one," she returned. "You should know that I wrote Henry this morning suggesting he sell my dower land. I should like to purchase something closer to London." She glanced at Kynthea. "I have made friends here and would like to visit them more often. Cornwall is so far away."

He straightened off the wall. "This is why women are not allowed into business affairs!" he snapped. "Selling that property is the height of idiocy!"

Perhaps. But it was also the best way to keep her brother from getting embroiled in the baron's gun-running business. Without that land in her dowry, she strongly suspected the baron's interest in her would disappear. Especially since plenty of other less difficult women had large breasts.

She squared off with Fletcher, her chin lifted and her eyes steady. And he matched her, though his hands were clenched into fists and his glare seemed to burn across the room.

"You will not do it!" he growled.

"Of course not," she returned blithely. "Henry will. And as the head of our family—"

He jerked forward, as close to hitting her as he had ever been.

Especially in public. But when their mother gasped—not to mention some of the other ladies—he abruptly stopped.

"Rebecca," he growled, "you are meddling in things you do not understand."

She swallowed. If anyone were to reach Fletcher, it would have to be her. Mama was not up to the task and Henry wasn't here. And so she smiled at her brother. "Then please, Fletcher, will you not stay with me this evening and explain it?"

"Do not question me!" he roared.

"I am merely trying to help," she said. "We were once great friends, you and I. Could we not spend an evening together talking? I should like to hear all your wonderful plans."

Her tone was gentle, her expression warm. She called on all the ways she had reached him as a boy. She hadn't been the best sister. He was two years older than her and had his own pursuits. But there had been good times between them.

Did he remember them?

She saw his gaze flicker. Was there a flash of yearning? A moment's wavering to show that she had reached him?

Maybe. But a moment later, he locked it all down.

"Your judgement has always been lacking," he drawled. "I see no cause to think otherwise now." And on that, he spun on his heel and stomped out of the room.

Rebecca watched him go, her heart squeezing tight. She hadn't expected him to open up to her, but she'd hoped for more than a flicker in his eyes. Still, that little waver gave her hope. She could still reach her brother before things got too ugly. Indeed, if she could delay things just a little bit, then Nate would capture the baron and all of this traitorous business would be done.

She just had to hold on a little longer.

Meanwhile, Kynthea and the parlor full of ladies were reacting to what they'd just witnessed. And Mama launched in with her usual admonishment.

"Really, Rebecca, must you antagonize him so?"

"Really Mama," she countered, "can you not see that he is a

man grown who should learn how to handle disagreements without stomping about?"

"But that is what men do!" another lady exclaimed. "It is up to us to soothe them."

And that perhaps was the root of the problem. When would men grow up? Why was it up to women to coddle and manage their emotions? She looked at Kynthea for support and found a wealth of understanding in her eyes. God, it was good to have a friend.

"Let's go unpack our purchases," the future duchess said. Then she glanced back at the ladies. "Would anyone else like to come see?"

Some of the ladies did, though most took their leave, no doubt to spread the gossip of Kynthea's newest bridesmaid. Mama had likely told everyone already, but now they had seen the proof of it in Kynthea's enthusiasm.

Everyone seemed to accept that men were moody creatures who must be managed, if not indulged. Indeed, that had been Rebecca's opinion up until very recently. And here she was, once again struck by how badly she had misjudged Nate. He wasn't a feckless boy who was as childish as her brother. He was a man who took responsibility for his actions, who was striving for the safety of England, and who truly worried about her without suffocating her.

How could she not love him?

But that was a thought for later. A feeling to examine when all this turmoil was over. And so she smiled at the bevy of women who chattered away as they headed up the stairs to her bedroom. Unfortunately, the noise was too much for Fletcher who came stomping back out of his library.

"Cease prattling!" he bellowed. "Can a man not get a moment's peace in his own home?"

A little boy, still demanding attention. Even Mama saw it this time.

"We are a trial to you, aren't we?" she said. "Why don't you go to your club now and enjoy yourself? Perhaps it's time for you to find a wife, hmmm? Someone who could smooth your troubled brow."

Fletcher stiffened. "Do not instruct me about my affairs!" he growled.

"Fletcher," Rebecca said gently, "she's trying to express her love to you. She wants you to be happy."

"By foisting a woman on me?"

"By encouraging you to find your own, whomever you want."

"I am not a child to be a coddled! I swear, the two of you need to be told where to go and what to do." He pointed his finger at her. "You will stay home and rest. You must look gorgeous for the baron. And Mama, you need to remember that all those women who prattle at you are merely trying to get close to me." He lifted his chin. "This is the way it is in London, and you had best learn that now. Or I'll send you both back home!"

After that, he headed for the door, stopping only to stare straight at Kynthea. She stared back, and for a moment Rebecca feared something ugly, though she had no idea what. To her shock, Fletcher softened, his expression becoming cordial.

"I am sorry you had to witness that, Miss Petrelli. I admire you, you know. You've played the game well and have nabbed a duke. Congratulations."

He was quick as he caught her hand and drew it up for a slow kiss. Kynthea allowed it, though her wary look quickly smoothed down into a placid expression.

"I have been very lucky," she said politely.

"Yes, you have. And maybe you and I can find a way to extend that luck."

"Oh?"

"Yes." Fletcher straightened to his full height. "But not if you lead my sister astray. She may be of age, but she is naïve in the ways of London. You must encourage her to take the guidance of her family who loves her."

Kynthea's brows arched. "You don't think you're being over-protective?"

Fletcher appeared to consider the thought. "Maybe, but I doubt it. My sister can be surprisingly willful at times. She knows the country, of course. She has managed well there for years. But here? No, I am a better judge of what is acceptable here." He looked back fondly at Rebecca. "And she knows I have her best interests at heart. Don't you, my dear?"

Rebecca knew the exact opposite was true, thanks to her dose of truth serum. Worse, she saw now that it was too late to reach the little boy inside him. There was too much anger in him, and she felt too betrayed to maintain this charade. "I know you think you do," she said. "But I am my own person."

His brows rose. "No, Rebecca. You are a woman."

She knew he meant it as an insult. As a woman she had no power in the world or against him. And perhaps, on one level, that was true. But she had never looked to him for her self-worth. She was not about to start now.

Still, she swallowed down her response. He needed the last word to feel like he'd won. And so she lowered her gaze as if she were cowed. He snorted as if to cement his victory. Then he strode for the front door, slowing long enough to grab his hat before departing.

She stared after him, her thoughts quietly churning. The gloves were off between them now. He'd never spoken so cruelly to her. Not in front of others. No doubt, he was feeling the pressure of his plans. She would have to hold out, though. If Nate had the timing right, she need only delay a few more days and this would all be over. The baron would be arrested for treason, and whatever schemes Fletcher had with the man would be gone.

But she would have to be doubly careful around him until then.

Kynthea reached out and squeezed her hand. "Let's look at what we bought today, yes?"

She nodded. "Yes."

Mama, on the other hand, pressed a hand to her forehead. "I believe I shall go lie down. I need to rest before tonight's party. Pity you won't be able to come tonight, Rebecca, but your health comes first."

"Yes, Mama," she said meekly.

Two hours later, she was dressed and ready to go to the Carre ball. The other ladies had departed, leaving just her and Kynthea. They had to go by her home, as she also needed to dress. And when Mama came out of her bedroom to wonder at the noise, Rebecca merely laughed.

"I feel so much better now, Mama! See you at the ball."

Then she and Kynthea rushed out of the house, giggling like two young girls as they escaped. Now this was being childish. But it felt so good that Rebecca refused to feel bad about it.

Indeed, she was filled with delight well into the evening. She adored Kynthea. And thanks to her proximity to a future duchess, her dance card was abruptly full. Every dance, that is, except for one waltz.

Several men asked for it. Several men saw the waltz held and tried to find out which lucky gentleman would get the dance. And several women commented as well, but she never told. Kynthea knew, though, and she didn't hold back her opinion.

"You cannot," the woman muttered when she saw the empty space. "Everyone is watching."

What she meant—as she'd said over and over in the carriage—was that anyone looking at her and Nate would see the growing relationship. Whatever their plans were in the future, she had to pretend to be interested in the baron next Tuesday. So she couldn't be seen making eyes at Nate.

It was logical, and Kynthea likely had the right of it. It was just one dance but given the amount of speculation surrounding her single blank line, she knew that everyone was watching for who she was saving it for. Everyone would know and gossip about it. And if she danced with Nate, then everyone would know he was special to her.

She couldn't pass it off as just a dance to be polite.

So when Nate finally arrived, looking so handsome she wanted to swoon, she had to keep her face cold. She had to allow him to bow over her hand, to stroke her palm with his fingers, and she had to sternly pull her dance card back.

"My card is full," she said loud enough for everyone to hear.

"Full?" he asked, his expression wounded. "But there's a—"

"Full," she repeated. And then she turned away.

A cut direct.

She had to. She had to. She had to.

She heard his breath catch. She heard the whispers around her. And she saw Kynthea's small nod of approval. It was for show, she knew. Kynthea didn't like hurting Nate any more than Rebecca did. But it had to be done.

A few minutes later, Lord Nathanial left the ball.

And in the morning, things got worse.

A new gossip column began with the words, "Has Lord Nathaniel overstayed his welcome? The future duchess of Harle certainly thinks so and her attitude is catching. Lord Nathaniel's star grows dim."

Oh hell. All she'd wanted was a dance with him, and now she'd just ruined him in society. Few people ever recovered after printed gossip like that. Whether or not his star had been dimming, it certainly would now. And she had no idea how important it was to him.

Fletcher looked over her shoulder to read the column. His laugh was loud and cruel.

"Couldn't happen to a more deserving bloke," he chortled.

She had to press her lips together to keep her harsh retort inside, though she felt like she was choking on it. Fletcher noticed. Of course he did. She wasn't as good at keeping her emotions hidden as she'd once been.

"You care, don't you? You don't want his star to dim." He settled down in the chair nearest her while he studied her face. "Why?"

She didn't like him this close. Yesterday, his hatred had been palpable. Now he seemed congenial, almost kind. Nevertheless, she had to answer.

"Because gossip is cruel and always unfair."

"You once said you were in love with him," Fletcher continued. "Are you still?"

"I never said that," she stated flatly. Because she'd been sixteen and her father had just had a heart attack from discovering them. She couldn't claim love then. Not with the feud between their families re-ignited.

"You felt it. You cried—"

"For Father."

"So he was an itch to scratch? Is that what you are? A whore to spread your legs—"

"Enough, Fletcher!" She pushed back from the breakfast table. "I am your sister, someone who loves you. But that does not give you the right to speak to me like that."

He was silent for a long moment, then he nodded. "Of course. My apologies. But Rebecca, tell me the truth. Do you love him?"

"No."

Lie.

"Then you'll have no trouble with me increasing the speed of his fall." A statement, not a question.

"What are you going to do?"

He shrugged. "The ground is fertile now for all sorts of tales. Perhaps I'll start with the one about how he killed our father."

"You will not dredge that up! It will hurt me as much as him."

"True," her brother mused. "I suppose I'll just have to hold that back for now."

"For now? Fletcher, why do you insist on threatening me?" She looked at him. She hated this. He was her brother. She ought to feel better about him. They ought not be at war.

Meanwhile, he gave her a slow, deliberate smile. And with the way the sunlight was hitting his face, she was struck by how handsome he was. Curly brown hair with golden highlights. A sweet smile and earnest eyes. And words that sounded so nice and yet still managed to give her chills.

"Rebecca. You're my sister. Why would I want to hurt you?"

"I don't know." That was the truth.

"I love you, and I'm just looking out for you."

How easily he said the word "love."

"I don't need—"

He banged his hand down on the table hard enough to make her jump. "That's where you're wrong, Rebecca." He spit out her name like bad meat. "This is a delicate time for you. You will heed my advice or I will send you back home. Immediately."

And there again was the real threat. He would send her home. But that wasn't as terrible a fate anymore. Back home, she could convince Henry that she was a spinster who wanted to live on her dower property, in quiet contemplation. But that wasn't true. She wanted more out of her life than the hermit existence that he had. But she could convince her oldest brother of that and move on from there.

But what would Nate do? He'd be left without anyone to distract the baron, and Fletcher would get trapped in whatever nefarious activities the blasted man had going. She couldn't do that for either man.

And so she bowed her head. She gave in to Fletcher because she only needed a few more days. Just until Tuesday's ball. Then everything would look a lot different.

Seeing her diminished attitude, Fletcher straightened up from the table. "Have we reached an understanding?" he asked.

Delay. Delay. Delay. "Yes," she said.

"Good. I have spoken with the baron. He's received an invitation for the Penrose ball."

She looked up. Nate worked fast.

"He's very excited to put that unpleasantness behind you both. Especially since it wasn't really his fault, now, was it?"

"No, I suppose not." She couldn't blame him for how he'd

acted under the influence of the truth serum. Just for the things he'd said.

"Excellent. Wear a dress he'll like."

"I can pick my own clothes, Fletcher."

"Now don't get tetchy with me. I'm only trying to help." He smiled indulgently down at her. "I am to see him this afternoon to work out the details. He'll want the first dance with you. And then three waltzes."

Three! That would be tantamount to an engagement.

"I cannot promise that."

Fletcher sighed as if she were growing tiresome. "You always have to do things your way. Very well. Two waltzes, but mind that he has the first dance. And make sure they are the last two waltzes. It's best if you keep him dangling after you all night."

"Why?"

"Because he must work for what he wants."

Yes, she supposed that was true. And it helped that it was exactly what Nate wanted as well. "And what will you do?"

Fletcher grinned. "I will be securing my position in this little dance." He was smiling as he gave her a slight bow. Was he mocking her? It was hard to tell. "I won't be around the next few days. Mother will have to escort you. Pray don't create a scandal while I'm gone."

"Where are you going?"

"Back to Cornwall with the baron. He wants to see your property."

"But—"

"I've written Henry. Told him that selling the property would be a huge mistake. You were having a lover's tiff with the baron, and he should disregard anything you've written."

She stared at him. Henry would see the truth, wouldn't he? That Fletcher wasn't speaking truthfully. Of course, now that she was thinking of a vastly different future, she didn't want her brother to sell the property either.

Good God, Fletcher had done her a favor.

"I'll write to Henry as well, tell him not to sell." Her oldest brother would think she had taken leave of her senses. Two contradictory instructions in so short a time.

"Good—"

"But why must you go to Cornwall with him?" She didn't want her brother anywhere near the baron. The more distance she could put between them the better. "Let him see the property on his own. You should stay in London—"

"I cannot remain here, waiting upon you hand and foot."

"But—"

"Enough. Your task is to remember how good the baron will be for you. Be prepared to accept him when we return." He grinned as he adjusted his waistcoat. "Everything is finally going the way it ought. Do not overturn the applecart now. Good day."

She watched him leave, a spring in his step like she'd rarely seen on him. Why did the sight make her heart sink? Was it because her brother was up to something? Ridiculous question. Fletcher was *always* up to something, and she rarely cared what.

Or was it because she'd just lied to her brother with such certainty that she wondered at her own feelings. She'd said she didn't love Nate and never had.

But she did.

She loved him. She wanted to marry him.

But how exactly was she going to accomplish that when she'd just destroyed him in society and her family was dead set against him? She didn't really care about her family. She'd like Henry to give her away, but even that wasn't really important.

The problem was Nate's diplomatic career. He'd told her about Lord Benedict's offer. That he didn't have to run around being a spy anymore. He could take a respectable diplomatic post.

But would that still be possible if he was ruined socially? If she only brought him scandal and difficult in-laws? She didn't know. And she couldn't get an answer until after Tuesday. Everything hinged on that.

Chapter Twenty-Seven

NATE STARED INTO his ale and tried to calm his racing thoughts. This was the time he'd usually pull out a pencil and paper and write his next chapter in an exciting pirate adventure. Living as his main character, he'd cut the evil doers to shreds, rescue the fair maiden, and ride off into the sunset.

But he had no heart to write such lies tonight. His fair maiden had ripped his heart apart, and he was tired of feeling alone.

The irony was that he knew why she had done it. She *had* to refuse him. There'd been an apology in her eyes and misery in her body language even as she gave him the cut direct. So he knew she was lying but was forced to do so for his sake.

All so she could pretend to be interested in the baron tonight. So he could be the spy his country needed and put an end to the rifles going to Napoleon. So he had brought her, an innocent girl from the country, into his double life. And it was making her miserable. Which made him miserable.

"You're not writing," Lord Benedict said as he settled onto the bench across from him. The man looked completely different from the urbane gentleman he usually seemed. Rough clothing, unshaven face, and a slump to his shoulders made him look—to the casual observer—like nearly every man who frequented the docks.

But Nate could see the difference. It was subtle. Something about Benedict's innate arrogance always showed through. The man was an aristocrat and wickedly smart, so playing someone abused by the world was difficult for him. Not so much for Nate. He often felt knocked about by life.

Lord Benedict gestured for an ale as he leaned carefully on the filthy tavern table. "Why aren't you writing?"

"Don't have the words," Nate answered.

"You always have words. I never worry when you have words. It's when you're stopped up like a buggered sheep that I rethink things."

Nate winced at the crude words. It wasn't like Benedict to be so graphic. And he certainly never betrayed anger in his tone. But it was there, vibrating underneath everything.

"What's got into you?" Nate asked.

"English selling guns to the French, that's what." Benedict clenched his jaw shut as the barmaid brought his drink, but the moment the woman turned her back, he was speaking again. "How does a man betray his own people? Our boys are dying, and this arse is selling guns to the French."

Nate nodded. He felt the same. Indeed, if he had his way, the perpetrator would be hung, drawn, and quartered for every single life his rifles had taken. Over and over until the debt was paid. If ever such a thing could be paid.

The two of them shared an angry glare meant not for each other but for whomever they were about to catch. Ultimately, it would be the baron, of course, but first, they had to get the underlings.

Benedict took another pull from his drink. He didn't even grimace at the taste, which Nate thought was very well done of him. This swill was awful, and Benedict liked good wine.

"I see you've neatly extricated yourself from society," Benedict said after he swallowed. "Nobody will think twice if you disappear for a time now."

"I didn't do it. She did."

His superior's brows rose. "Hates you that much, does she?"

"No. She did it for me."

It didn't take Benedict long to understand. "You've told her who you are."

Nate nodded. This was a dicey thing, and something he should rightly have discussed with Benedict first. But he hadn't, and now was the moment he would have to pay the piper.

"She's clever, then," Benedict said. "Able to do what's necessary even when it hurts?"

Again, Nate nodded.

"Can we use her?"

"No!" Nate slammed his hand down for emphasis. His voice was hard, his volume unrestrained. Fortunately, it was part of his persona here. A cantankerous sailor perpetually on the outs with somebody, somewhere. The action fit. It was also something he'd never done around Benedict. Until today.

The man straightened, leveling him with a hard stare. "So it's love then? Real, true love?"

Yes. Damn it, yes! Which made it horrendous.

"I'll not pull Becca into this life," Nate said. It was too dangerous, too painful. One could never really be honest with family or friends, and that was a damned sight harder than he'd ever expected.

"That's a problem for you then. Even if you pull out of this work…" A quick gesture indicated his spy work on the docks. "There's more of it as a diplomat. It's more open, of course, but there are always secrets, always problems. And that can be dangerous."

"I know," Nate growled.

"What are you to do then?"

It was probably a rhetorical question. Either way, Nate treated it as such and refused to answer.

"Find a home in the country?" Benedict mused. "Pen your fun stories while remembering the dangers you'd once faced?"

"Everyone gets old. Everyone wants a warm fire and a cozy bed."

"And that's what you think of that life. It's something for an old man with a gray beard and a dog at his feet."

Nate shuddered at the thought, mostly because it was true. He hadn't expected to retire to a fire and his bed until he was nearly in his dotage. He was still a young, vital man. And he was good at this work. He was a good spy and could be a great diplomat. But to come out of the cold, he'd need a wife on his arm. Diplomatic circles needed a woman who was equally savvy, equally dangerous in her own way.

It was a world where women could be more vicious than the men. And he had no desire to put Becca in such a situation.

But the other option was to walk away completely. To disappear back into the French countryside, waiting in taverns there, sleeping in hay fields and drinking from horse troughs. He could do it. He had done it. But damn, he was already tired of it.

"Have you asked her?" Benedict pressed.

He nodded. "She laughed in my face."

Benedict winced in sympathy.

"She was…drunk." Actually, she'd been under the influence of that damned truth serum, but he didn't want to explain that to Benedict.

"So that's your answer then."

Yes. She didn't want to marry him. Except…

"We spent a night together."

Benedict's brows rose.

"Not that way. Well, yes, but not *completely* like that."

"Oh."

Nate rubbed a hand over his face. Why the hell was he talking like this? Normally he kept these thoughts to himself. But this was too big for him to keep inside. It hurt too much. And he loved her too much.

"I… She…" God, what did he want to say? "We work well together." No that wasn't exactly right. "She makes me feel better." He didn't need to explain to Benedict how important that was. They'd both done things that haunted them. They'd both faced choices that destroyed moral men. To find someone— anyone—who eased that pain, who saw them for who they were and still loved them… Well, that person was worth her weight in gold.

"And you think you'll make her life worse?"

He swallowed. "This life is complicated, and she's got enough to handle."

"You want to protect her?"

"Yes."

"Then you're a bloody idiot."

Nate's eyes widened in shock. "You know how difficult this life is."

"Of course I do. And I know that some women aren't suited for it. But that's not your problem."

"What?"

Benedict reached forward and tapped the blank page in Nate's journal. "You've always put her on a pedestal. She's been your lost princess to rescue, the sweet damsel who needs your help. But now, you see that she doesn't need rescuing. That she might like the work as much as you do."

"No—"

"Yes. Suddenly she's not this ideal woman, and you don't like it."

"What?"

Nate pulled back, but Benedict grabbed his arm, roughly pulling him forward. It was part display for the tavern, part truth, and they both treated it as such.

"Talk to her," Benedict growled, too quiet for anyone else to hear. "Find out what she wants."

Nate swallowed but was unable to move the lump in his throat.

"Or maybe," Benedict mused a little cruelly. "Maybe I'll talk to her myself. I could find work for a clever girl, especially since you're on the outs with society now."

"No!" Nate cried, ripping his arm out from his superior's. But he couldn't go far. They were supposed to capture the French half of the smugglers this afternoon. That was why he'd been sitting here waiting for Benedict. And so, there was no way he could stomp off, and Benedict knew it.

The man slowly straightened from his seat. "Come along, boy," he drawled loud enough for everyone to hear. "You're going to pay me one way or another, and now's the night for it."

It was all pretense, and it wasn't. Anyone watching them would think he was off to do something illegal, forced by someone bigger and badder than him. That worked perfectly to keep his image of a down-on-his-luck sailor who had contacts and skills useful for exploitation. It was how he'd learned half the dirt he did, just hanging out at various taverns. He was a morally grey petty criminal, perfect to exploit by other criminals. Or those higher up on the food chain.

He'd never resented it—or Lord Benedict—more. And yet, such was the game he played.

"It won't be so bad," Benedict teased. "And you'll gain a useful skill in the process." Then he threw some coins on the table and started walking toward the door.

Nate had no choice but to follow. He slumped as he walked, always keeping a step behind Benedict. Master and servant. For the moment.

If they continued as usual, he'd reappear next week all smiles and with coins, bragging about something he'd learned how to do. Maybe he had a way to get some goods from them Frenchies. And of course, movement of goods one way meant that an enterprising Englishman could send information the other way. If he was of a treasonous bent.

Nate called it dangling bait. Sometimes they caught nothing. Sometimes they caught an Englishman smuggling rifles to the French. It all depended on luck.

And today's luck was that he knew when the French buyers were coming in. He knew what boat and what coin. He just had to catch them before they met up with the English traitors.

Once out of the tavern, Nate took control. He might look like a paid lackey slinking along behind Benedict, but he whispered instructions ahead, and Benedict followed them to the letter. They wove in and out of the docks, mixing with various groups and even ducking into a place he knew where they could change clothes. Different hat and coat, difference gait, and most important, different shoes. Benedict liked his well-made pair that made little sound and conformed to his feet. But it was a dead giveaway to anyone who knew how to look.

Major Vance joined them. He was Benedict's batman from Spain and the most loyal servant a man could ask for. He was smart and quiet, savvy in a way that he'd had to teach the two aristocrats. But thanks to their time in Spain together, all three worked well together, even in cheap shoes.

They made good time to the stairs along the Thames. It was a simple nab, assuming everything went well.

As soon as they arrived, Nate peeled off to talk to the watermen. They were the army of boatmen who ferried passengers or cargo from the ships that anchored mid-river in the Legal Quays. Those surly men had tipped Nate off to the Frenchmen after the Frog's last visit months ago. It had been too late to catch the enemy then, but not this time.

It was pure speculation that these men were the ones buying the English rifles, but the timing worked out. And either way, they needed to be caught. So Nate returned to Lord Benedict and Major Vance with a cocky grin and quirk of his finger.

"They're on Vidone's wherrie." He described the waterman because he was easier to pick out among the mass of boats. "Black cap, thick mustache, and fists like hams."

Benedict nodded. He'd met Vidone before. But it was Major Vance who caught the important information.

"They?"

"Yes. Two Frogs." It was supposed to be one Frenchman, but this time, there were two. And neither of them were small men.

"We'll do it," the major said as he squared his shoulders.

Yes, they would.

They waited in the shadows. There were always people coming and going on the stairs, and a steady choke of people clogging the area. Most waited for cargo or passengers, many waited to board outgoing vessels. Hackneys sat nearby, and pickpockets loitered. But Nate was well known to the watermen, and they all knew he was here to grab some Frenchies.

Lots of people turned a blind eye to smuggled goods, but selling English guns to Napoleon was different. The watermen couldn't fight in France, but they'd been happy to help Nate catch a couple Frenchies on English soil.

Vidone saw Nate as he guided the boat to the rail. They exchanged a couple quick hand signals, and Nate relayed the information to Benedict and Major Vance. The two Frenchmen sat at the back of the boat and would be easily caught when they disembarked.

It worked like a charm.

Major Vance caught the smaller one with a single kidney punch as Benedict crowded the area to box the Frenchman in. Nate used his height to wrap an arm around the other man's neck. From a distance it could look like a friendly hug.

It wasn't.

And after a very annoying struggle, the bastard went slack and the purse that was meant to pay for the rifles landed square in Benedict's hand.

"Well done," Benedict said as they headed for his carriage.

"It's only step one," Major Vance said in an undertone, as he effortlessly propelled his culprit forward.

Nate didn't say anything. He already knew that capturing these guys was only the beginning. Next, he had to impersonate them in order to catch the men selling the rifles. That would be the hard part.

What he should have realized, of course, was that strong-arming a conscious man into a carriage was much easier than lifting an unconscious one. And damn it, his man was bloody heavy.

"I'll help in a moment," said the major. "Then I suppose we'll both have to turn ourselves into Frogs."

Because there were two men here. Which meant Nate couldn't hide in the background. He would have to impersonate one of the French buyers along with the major. And didn't that just make his insides twitch? His face was well known, even under make-up and a French cap.

But there was no help for it now. And all the reason in the world to get it done tonight. He would not risk Becca again.

Chapter Twenty-Eight

T HE BARON WAS in a jovial mood. Rebecca could tell he was working to appear somber. He needed to come across as contrite as he made his way back into society. And since Fletcher insisted Rebecca publicly apologize to the baron for dosing him—an irony if there ever was one—the man had reason to expect full exoneration.

So he was grinning as he bowed over her hand that evening. She'd already marked the dances she would give him. The first dance and the last two waltzes. His smile was triumphant as he took out a pencil and made to scrawl his name on a third waltz, but she abruptly pulled her hand back.

"Baron, what a pleasure to see you this evening. I do want to apologize again for what happened the other night. I had no idea my cough medicine would affect you so dramatically. I should never have given it to you."

"Don't fret, my dear," he said as he made to retrieve her dance card. "One doesn't expect women to understand the intricacies of medicines."

She kept her arm back as she continued, her voice tart despite her intention to remain cordial. "I understand them very well," she said, but then honesty forced her to confess the truth. "But I'm afraid I was not experienced with this particular one. And I didn't expect you to—"

"Never mind, my dear. Look! I see your brother over near the lemonade."

Fletcher was nearer to the bottles of spirits, but it wasn't polite to mention that. "Do go see him, Baron. I'm afraid I've promised to stay with Miss Petrelli for a while. Did you hear the news that I am to be one of her bridesmaids?"

"Yes, yes! Wonderful! But I'm sure she can spare you for a few minutes. I want to show you off. Nothing compares to having a beautiful woman on one's arm."

"But—"

"I insist."

Well, he clearly already considered them married. The high-handed way he ordered her around set her teeth on edge. But tonight she had to keep him dangling beside her, so she cast Kynthea an apologetic look.

Thankfully, Kynthea understood. She glanced significantly at the duke who stood nearby. He was surrounded by people who wanted to talk with him, but Rebecca was confident that he would come to her aid, should she need it.

"We'll just take a turn around the ballroom," Rebecca said. "Then I'll be right back."

"Oh, I should love some lemonade as well," Kynthea said with a smile.

"Excellent," the baron cried as he offered his arm to the future duchess.

Rebecca hated giving him so much consequence. His social standing rose every second he had her and a future duchess beside him. But it was a small price to pay to keep Nate safe.

As expected, the man took his time wandering across the room. He clearly wanted to maximize this return to society, so he greeted everyone there, making sure to crow about having two such highly prized woman with him.

Fletcher watched them traverse the room, his expression smug. But by the time they finally made it to him, he became more conciliatory. He greeted them warmly, he kissed Kynthea's hand, and offered to get the baron a glass of something more sporting than lemonade.

Rebecca tried to take that opportunity to escape the man. "Kynthea, let's get the lemonade—"

"No, no, stay with us," the baron interrupted. "After all, we'll be family soon. Even you Miss Petrelli! Fletcher says he and the duke are old school chums."

"Yes," Kynthea said with a tight smile. "So he mentioned."

Fletcher grinned. "Do allow me a waltz, Miss Petrelli. We must get to know one another better."

"I'm so sorry," Kynthea said. "I'm afraid the duke has captured all of those."

"Ah then, at least a quadrille."

And so the conversation went. Polite discussion, all smiles, and every time Rebecca tried to escape the men, one of them firmly pulled her back to the baron's side. And because Kynthea was showing herself to be a loyal friend, the future duchess remained nearby, even when other people tried to gain her attention.

Rebecca couldn't have been more pleased when the dancing finally began. Since this was a come-out ball, the young lady and her father had the opening dance. After that, everyone could join, and Rebecca dutifully allowed the baron to take her hand.

"I'm very pleased that your brother and I could come to an understanding," he said as they stepped into position. "He compromised on the last point and is anxious to see our two families united." The baron waggled his eyebrows. "He spoke of a special license so we can wed immediately."

She arched a brow. "Immediately?" No doubt to finalize that before the sale of her dower property. "And what exactly is this understanding?"

"That you and I shall live happily ever after together." He leaned forward and winked. "Your dowry shall see to that. I saw everything I wanted during my visit there. Excellent piece of land."

Oh really? She bit her tongue rather than speak her true thoughts aloud. "And what shall I get from this?"

"Ecstasy in the bedchamber."

Her eyes widened. That was a bold thing to say straight to her face.

"Don't blush! Fletcher tells me you're well-versed in these things. The benefits of a country education, I suppose."

"And what does Fletcher get out of this situation?" She wanted to hear the words straight from the baron's mouth.

"The opportunity to work with me!" He turned and gave a broad wink to her brother who was joining the dance line with his own partner. He stood right next to the baron as he addressed Rebecca.

"Don't worry, my dear," he said loud enough for everyone to hear. "Everything is working out splendidly." Then he grinned at his partner as they prepared to dance.

She gave her brother a wan smile. Both men were in the happiest of moods. Well, let them enjoy their crowing. So long as she kept the baron engaged—without becoming *too engaged*—then everything would work out all right.

But she couldn't exactly roll over for him, either.

"Do not be so sure of me yet, sir," she said archly. "You wouldn't respect me if I tumbled too easily."

The baron snorted. "You must learn when to resist and when to submit. But never fear. I will give clear instructions when necessary."

A shiver ran down her spine at those words. The man didn't like her challenging him, especially in public. Well, he would learn—after tonight—that she was not a woman who allowed others to make her decisions. But for right now, her task was to dance a quadrille.

So she did.

She smiled, she danced, and she even enjoyed some conversation with others at the ball. Thankfully—or miserably, she wasn't sure which—the baron stayed nearby. He had his own dance partners, of course, and times when he stood along the wall drinking whatever liquor he fancied. But he never let her out of his sight and so she was easily able to keep track of him.

If she were brutally honest, he wasn't much different than other men she'd met. The attitude that her marriage could be decided by her brother was a typical belief. The fact that he never talked about his daughter was also normal. And his general attitude that he would teach her to obey, well that was a common as bread. Her brother couldn't understand why she was upset about it.

And she was. Because she was the unusual one here. The one who had secretly learned medicine in defiance of her family. The one who blithely said yes to her brothers, then went off and did whatever she chose without guilt. Or without much guilt.

And now, she was the one who had an acute distaste of the baron because she'd spent the night with a man who appreciated her tales as much as she enjoyed his. She'd told him about sneaking out of the house just so she could tend to a set of sick twins. He told her about tending ill sailors and the horror of drunks trying to manage the sails.

She doubted that the baron would enjoy her stories nearly so much. Nor would he touch her the way Nate had—with reverence and an innate glee at watching her discover pleasure. She had enjoyed many more peaks that night than he did, and he didn't seem to care. Or count!

Every man she knew measured every aspect of his life in gains and losses. Every man except Nate. What they had shared was love. It was as pure as it had been ten years ago, but with the added perspective of maturity.

She just had to get through tonight. Then she'd—

Where was Fletcher going?

She'd been getting some lemonade because she was parched. Dancing took a lot of work. Then she'd looked for the baron, only to find him with Fletcher. The two shook hands, the baron clapped her brother on the back, and then Fletcher departed.

Not to the card table.

Not to the garden to get some air.

He'd left the ball and Rebecca wanted to know why. He was her escort as Mama had elected to go to a different fete tonight. He wasn't supposed to abandon her in the middle of a ball. She could go home with Kynthea and the duke, but that wasn't what was important. Why would he leave?

She made her way to the baron, careful to keep her expression neutral. He was in the middle of speaking effusively with an MP in the House of Lords. She waited, listening with interest to his political views. They were measured, thoughtful, and very typical when speaking with a conservative member of the Tory party. But she'd also heard him expound on the exact opposite views when speaking with a Whig.

She stifled an internal sigh. She already knew she couldn't point out his double-dealing. Ladies weren't supposed to weigh in on political matters. So she waited as every good maiden must, and then when he finally turned to her, he had something else entirely on his mind.

"Is it time for our waltz already? Goodness, don't say I've forgotten the time!"

"No, no! But...I just saw Fletcher leave. Do you know where he's going?"

"Oh that. Don't worry. He shall be back in time to escort you home. And if not, then I shall be happy to—"

"That's not appropriate yet, sir," she said, feigning an embarrassed giggle. She'd learned that he loved it when she played the coquette, but damn it turned her stomach. "He didn't say anything to me about leaving."

"Nonsense. He's merely doing me a favor. Won't take long." He turned away from her, smiling at another MP who loitered near the liquor. "You go on and enjoy yourself," he added over his shoulder. "The next set is about to begin." Then he seemed to remember he was supposed to be courting her, so he turned back and gave her an elaborate bow. "Don't concern yourself with men's matters. He's only doing a quick errand for me at the docks. Then he'll be right back. Has his eye on a young lady and he won't miss his chance with her, I assure you."

She knew how he expected her to answer. He thought she would pursue the identity of whatever woman had caught Fletcher's eye. She couldn't care less, but she used the excuse to peruse the ballroom floor looking for Kynthea or the duke.

"Oh," she said in a sweet voice. "Which girl?"

Damn it, both the duke and his fiancée were caught in discussions. It wasn't surprising. People were always trying to sidle into their orbit. They were, after all, duke and future duchess. But that didn't help her any.

"Why don't you see if you can guess?"

She gave the baron a vacuous smile. "What a fun game," she drawled. "All right. I will." Then she gave him an outrageous wink. "You think you have outwitted me, but I am smarter than that. I don't think the lady is out here at all. I believe she is in the ladies' retiring room, and that's where I shall be quizzing all the girls about my brother."

The baron grinned. "Clever girl."

She all but danced away as if to show her delight. In truth, she needed to be out of his sight. And out of Kynthea and Ras's as well. Because she very much feared exactly what errand her brother was doing.

He had to be handling the gun exchange for the baron. After all, it couldn't be trusted to any underling. And what better way to inextricably tie her family to the baron's except by a shared crime?

The very idea made her sick. Her brother was many things, but she'd never believe he'd turn traitor.

And now she had a difficult problem. If it truly was her brother who was going to sell the baron's rifles, then he would recognize Nate and know it was a trap. But even more important, Nate would recognize Fletcher, and her brother would be caught as a traitor.

He would be drawn and quartered for that.

She wanted her brother stopped, not killed. Which meant she

had to halt the exchange. They would just have to catch the baron some other way. She could not have her brother hung nor Nate's secrets exposed.

She ought to grab the duke or Kynthea. They would help her get to the docks, but they would also turn Fletcher in. They had no family loyalty to her difficult brother. So she had to go alone. And she had to go now.

She slipped out through a side door, mentally calculating the time. The front lane was clogged with carriages. It wasn't a simple thing to leave a ball and climb into one's carriage. The driver needed to be notified, and a carriage brought round. And her brother did like travelling in comfort. There wasn't any crest on his carriage, but it was well appointed and very comfortable inside. Plus, he and his driver were thick as thieves. She'd noted it on several occasions.

Which meant her brother would not have bothered with a hackney but would take his own carriage to the docks. In fact, there it was! It was hard to be sure in the dark, but it was the best guess she had.

Making some quick calculations, she ran past the line of carriages, ducked through an alleyway to the next road, and hailed the first hackney she found, directing it to the docks. Then she settled against the squabs and tried to calm her racing heart.

She'd almost managed it. She was nearly calm when the carriage abruptly stopped, and the door opened.

"What—"

"Going somewhere, my dear?" the baron asked.

Chapter Twenty-Nine

"**W**HAT ARE YOU doing?" Rebecca cried. "Go away!"

Far from being concerned, the baron climbed into the carriage and firmly shut the door. He was grinning as he eased back in his seat. "Where are you going, my dear?"

"That's none of your affair!" she snapped. "Good God, you're going to ruin my reputation!"

"Nonsense. It's perfectly normally for an affianced couple to disappear together for a little bit. Not exactly approved, but common enough."

Ice slid down her veins. He was right. "We are not affianced."

He chuckled. "We are now. You left first, my dear. And I might have noted that fact to a few people as I ran after you."

Cold fury replaced the ice in her blood, and she knew she had to fight or end up married to this man. But how? She thought of Nate and how he'd lived this life of spies and lies, but she was nowhere near as clever as he was. She could stay with her ruse of being a complete idiot girl, but she was tired of pretending to be stupid. And so she went with simple bluntness.

"What do you want from me?" she asked.

His brows rose. "Don't worry, my dear. I've already gotten it, thanks to your impetuous departure from the ball."

"Marriage, obviously. You do know that Henry has sold my dower property, don't you?" It was a lie, and the baron knew as much.

"You mean you've directed him to sell it. But it's already in the contract, my dear. And Fletcher and I have both signed, so you're stuck."

"He can't sign. It must be Henry."

"But Henry gave Fletcher his proxy."

Ice slid into her veins. She hoped that wasn't true, but what did she know about proxies or marriage contracts? Nothing. What happened if the lady refused? Either way, she had a more pressing question.

"What is Fletcher doing for you now?"

"He's going to prove to me his abilities." The baron waggled his brows. "As beautiful as your breasts are, I want to expand my business. And to do that, I need someone like your brother. Someone capable, who is tied inextricably to me."

In selling rifles to France.

"And if he refuses?"

The man's laugh was cold. "Your brother is very eager to please me. He will not refuse."

Was it true? Could her brother be so easily turned traitor?

She shuddered. "What, exactly, has he promised you?"

The baron had the audacity to pat her knee, as if the action didn't make her skin crawl. "Don't worry. You'll see him in action very soon."

"Where are we going?" she asked, working hard to keep the panic out of her voice. She knew she should have asked the question earlier, but there were so many things colliding in her thoughts.

"Your brother claims to be an excellent negotiator. And he was clever when discussing our marriage."

Of course he was.

"But disposing of a sister is different from what he will be doing now."

"Which is what, exactly?"

"Which is what I want from him. Exactly."

And that was all he said. And she was at a loss what to do about it.

She looked out the window, her eyes picking up details here and there. They were nearing summer, so it was still light out, even this late. But even if she couldn't see much, she could smell the Thames.

"We're heading for the docks. Is my brother buying something for you?" She looked at him, her expression as open as she could make it, but inside she was praying he said yes. Purchasing smuggled goods wasn't nearly as terrible a crime.

"With what money? Henry keeps Fletcher's purse very lean."

"With your money, I assume."

"I do not make a habit of allowing someone else to carry my purse."

"So he's selling."

The baron gave a quick nod. "He and my brother."

She frowned. Nate had said something about that, hadn't he? "Your brother?"

"Half-brother. My father's bastard. Works at the Tower of London with me." He grinned. "He gets the rifles out but is a damned coward when meeting the French. Runs at the first sign of trouble. I've lost good money because he turned tail."

"So you sell them—"

"Me? Goodness no. All that skulking about on the docks? A man could get his head bashed in for that."

There was something in his tone of voice, something in the way he said those words that made her look at him sharply. "Get his head bashed in," she echoed slowly. Just as Nate had before. "You did it?" she asked quietly. "You've bashed someone's head in, just for being at the docks?"

He patted her hand. "There's a time and place for everything, my dear. If someone pokes his nose into my business, I poke back." Then he squeezed her hand with increasing strength, harder and harder until she tried to jerk it away. She couldn't. He was too strong, and pain began to radiate up her arm. If he kept it up, he was going to break her bones.

"Stop it!"

He abruptly let her go, and she pulled her throbbing hand back to her chest. "Why would you do that to me?" she whispered.

"I want you to understand. I can be very generous, but I also must be obeyed."

The threat was obvious. Indeed, she might think him an overblown villain in a novel, except that he was right here with her. He was telling her everything as if she…as if she could do nothing about it. As if he could not conceive that she would ever betray him.

"We're not married," she said. "I will tell—"

"And see your brother hanged? Drawn and quartered for treason?"

"You're the one—"

"No, my dear, he is. And we are going now to watch him, you and me, so that you will know what we are a part of."

"But I'm not!"

"But you are, because you are his sister. And I am on the Board of Ordinance. It makes perfect sense that I would make friends with your brother just so I could expose him as a thief and a traitor."

"What?"

"I see you begin to understand but let me make things clear. Fletcher is about to turn traitor to England. He is selling rifles to Fance. And if you say anything about it, I will claim that I was investigating you both, with my brother's help, of course. And then you will hang right beside him."

He could do it. He could spin a tale that sent both her and Fletcher to the gallows. And to make everything worse, she knew that Nate was there, with officers from the War Office. They would capture Fletcher, and the baron would take great glee in letting her brother hang for his crime.

She had to stop this. For her brother's sake. For her own sake. For the nation's sake, she had to stop the baron.

But how? What would Nate do?

She had no idea, except for what she'd read in his novels. What did his characters do to outwit the villain? They pretended to go along until they had an opportunity to destroy everything.

Very well. She squared her shoulders and faced him with her most arrogant stare.

"So I am to be your wife. I am to go along with your scheme." She swallowed. "I will, but I have a condition."

He snorted. "You have no bargaining room here. Consider yourself lucky. You get to stand at my side, clothed in riches, as you care for my sons."

His sons. Of course. Nothing about his poor daughter. Which, naturally, gave her an insight into what he did want.

"Did you know that there are ways to prevent pregnancy? That no matter how much you do your, um, manly duty, I can prevent any son from growing in my womb." She leaned forward. "That is why you want a wife, yes? So you can have an heir? Someone to carry on your glorious name."

He stared at her, completely dumbfounded. Clearly, he'd never heard of such a thing. "Nothing can prevent me from planting my son in your womb."

"Oh sir, you are misinformed." He opened his mouth to counter her, but she raised a single finger. "And before you toss me aside, let me warn you that I will tell any woman you marry exactly how to do it."

"Then I shall kill you this night and be done with you."

He said it so swiftly that she was inclined to doubt him. It was one of those throw-away phrases that never usually came to pass. *I'll kill you. I'll beat her. I'll wring his neck.* Except she knew of too many cases where it had happened. The threats were real. And perhaps a man who could blithely betray his country for coin could just as easily kill her tonight.

But she couldn't cave now or she'd never have any footing with the man. So again, she tried to echo what Nate—or at least, the hero in one of his books—had said and forced her lips into a casual smile.

"You can try," she said. "But we girls in the country learn how to defend ourselves against man and beast alike."

"I have three stone weight on you. There's nothing you can—"

She punched him. She'd never done it before except in practice with her older brother. Henry knew she tended to the ill in her village, often at all hours of the night. He taught her this punch—made her practice it over and over—as the quickest way to shock and disable an opponent. Or kill them.

She jabbed him straight in the throat.

Or she tried to. She missed, but she gave him a glancing blow enough that he choked out of reflex. And she followed up quickly with the lie that she'd meant to miss.

"If I'd hit that a little harder, you'd be dying right now," she said. "Even a glancing blow will kill. Remember that next time you think I don't know how to hurt a man."

Henry's plan for that punch was so she could jab then run. Unfortunately, she was in a moving carriage. She could jump out and run, but to where? She needed to stop Fletcher, and the baron knew where the meeting would take place.

So she sat and waited while he recovered his breath. And she tensed for the backlash to come. He was not a man who could be struck without fighting back.

It came as she expected it to—a backhand hard enough to shatter her cheek. She blocked it as much as she was able. It softened the blow to a glancing bruise, but the pain of it radiated through her body.

Didn't matter. She didn't change her tone of voice.

"Are we to trade blows then like children?" she taunted. "Or do you want to learn what I require to be your willing partner, rather than your pawn?"

"You're a woman!" he growled.

"And women can get things, go places, and manage people you cannot. Do you think you could get an audience with the Queen?" she pressed.

"And you can?" he scoffed.

Absolutely not. "You have no idea what I can and cannot do."

She left it there. It was a threat she'd read in Nate's books often enough, but it was a shock to use it in real life. Perhaps his tales weren't as far-fetched as she thought. Meanwhile, the baron proved that he wasn't an idiot by dropping back in his seat and staring at her for a very long time.

Good God, he'd obviously never considered that a women could think. But he was certainly considering the possibility now.

"What do you want?" he finally asked.

"Leave my brother out of everything. He isn't who you need."

"And you are?" The man scoffed, and she had to agree. After all, she had no intention of helping him. So when she remained silent, he folded his arms across his chest. "Fletcher and I have made our arrangement. I'm a man of my word, so think of something else."

He was not a man of his word, but she wasn't going to quibble about stupidities. Instead, she nodded. "Tell me everything about how you make your money. I will show you how a woman can help you."

It took him a minute to accept that. But then he started talking. He began with the smallest of his ventures—a simple bribery scheme wherein soldiers paid him for a position at the Tower of London, something he could influence, given his position on the Board of the Ordinance. "What," he challenged, "could a woman do to benefit me in that?"

She rolled her eyes. "You accept money? That's it? That's the smallest thing people have to offer, especially poor soldiers."

He frowned. "What are you talking about. What else could I want?"

"Do you not think these men have wives? Mothers or sisters? They have things to offer that are much more valuable than a few coins. If nothing else, they can sew your attire for free. But they also listen in important households, they clean important places."

She folded her arms in a mimicry of him. "You cannot talk to those people as I can. They will tell me which woman is desperate to sell her jewelry, who sleeps with whom, and much more. And you cannot tell a well-made coat from a poorly made one. That much is certain."

"What?"

"Your seams are crooked and the thread weak." It wasn't more crooked than most gentlemen's attire, but she knew he had never thought to look at the seams of his coat much less the threads before. "You could benefit from a woman's eye."

He frowned as he tried to see his seams. He couldn't, not inside the carriage, but it was enough to make him think.

"Go on," she prodded. "Challenge me to see where else I can help you."

And so he did, speaking slowly and carefully as he revealed his schemes, one by one. Thank God the trip was taking so long. She would have a wealth of schemes to expose to Nate and the authorities.

Eventually, they arrived at the docks, the carriage stopped, and he pulled her out. The sun was setting, so it was hard to see, but it wasn't long until he drew her into the back of a dark building.

"What is this place?" she asked.

"Shhh!" he snapped. And lest she try to delay by dragging her feet, he jerked her forward.

Fortunately, it didn't take long for her eyes to adjust to the darkness. They were in a large building with crates and boxes. A warehouse, obviously, but not a large one. He made her crouch behind a stack of carefully arranged boxes while he peered over it at...nothing as far as she could tell.

Instead, she fingered a pile of fabric bolts. Silk, she believed, and of decent quality.

"Are these smuggled?" she whispered.

"Of course not," he said as he turned back to her. "Merely an extra tip, so to speak, from the ships that store their goods with me."

"Do they know they're tipping you?" she drawled.

"What they do or do not know isn't my business," he said with a grin. Then he looked at the silk. "Do you know who best to sell that to?"

She nodded. She could think of several modistes who would jump at this fabric. "You need to sell it soon before the rats get to it."

He nodded. "That shall be your first task, then."

"So we are partners now?"

"You and your brother," he said as he jerked his head to a side door where her brother was just now entering with another man.

"Is that your brother?" she asked, seeing a vague similarity between the baron and Fletcher's companion.

"*Bastard* brother."

As if that made a difference when they were both betraying their country. "What are they carrying?" They set down two large crates, clearly heavy, between them.

"Shut up and watch," he growled.

He wasn't going to tolerate any more questions. And he wasn't going to let her escape either, given the grip he had on her arm. So she remained quiet, listening as Fletcher and the baron's brother traded small talk. It was mostly grumbles about the weight of the boxes and the weather. And how the Frenchies were late.

If she had any doubt before that her brother was involved, it disappeared now. It was Fletcher, dressed in his ballroom finery. He'd pulled on an overcoat, but she recognized it. His voice and the condescension in his words were typical Fletcher. He had no respect for his co-conspirator but was excited to get good money out of the French.

Worse, he knew the box contained rifles. Good English guns that were better than anything else on the continent. And he didn't care that they would likely kill English boys. It was all about the coin and how often this exchange happened.

A traitor. Her brother.

Or rather, a would-be traitor because it was clear from his conversation that this was his first time making an exchange. She looked at the baron.

"Who handles this when my brother isn't here?"

"My brother. And he's terrible at it." He flashed her his teeth. She wasn't sure if it was a grin or an implied threat. "Though I'm always here watching."

He'd directed the hackney to wait nearby in case he needed to depart quickly. Just in case this was a trap, which it most definitely was.

Damn it, she couldn't let this go on. She couldn't let her brother sell rifles to the Friench. And she couldn't let him be arrested and hung. He was an awful brother, but that didn't mean she wanted him dead. There were precious few options here, and time was ticking away.

And while she sat there, everything got worse. The baron pushed her down onto the floor. She might have been able to break his hold, but she saw no reason to fight him yet. So she ended up with her bottom on the floor in her ballgown while he...

He pulled out a pistol and aimed it at her brother.

"What are you doing?" she hissed.

"Just in case of trouble."

She looked at him. She looked at her brother. And then she watched as the door opened again and the two Frenchman walked it. She didn't recognize one of them. He was a broad man with sturdy legs who looked like he could single-handedly carry the box of rifles. And the other Frenchman? It was clearly Nate. Dressed differently and with a beard, but she would know the shape of his body anywhere. Even when he slumped and shuffled his feet.

And so the negotiations began. Fletcher had made some small effort to lower his voice before, but he wasn't now. And so she made her choice.

Given no other options, she went with the only action that might save her brother.

She screamed.

Chapter Thirty

THE EASIEST THING Nate had to do all day was transform into a Frenchman. He donned a hat, rubbed dirt on his face, then adopted a hunching gait and a scowl.

He'd feared that the Frenchmen wouldn't give up the meeting location, but a stroke of luck made that easy. They'd written it out on a crude map, complete with the time and amount of money. Indeed, it was so lucky that Major Vance began to grumble. He distrusted easy things. Nate, however, never questioned luck. He just thanked it with all his heart.

Very soon, the two of them headed to the meeting place. Nate let the major lead, doing his best to hide in the background in case Becca couldn't keep the baron occupied at the ball. Lord Benedict stayed even further behind, waiting in the shadows because he was a good shot, but a bad brawler.

Normally, Nate would have arrived early. He would have liked to scout the area, but there wasn't time. Indeed, they were very nearly late by the time everything was sorted. And so he went in with as many knives as he could hide on his body. Guns were too uncertain in close quarters.

They entered the warehouse, swaggering with confidence that was a complete lie, only to have all of it dissolve the moment he saw the English traitors.

The baron's half-brother was no surprise. They'd already put together the connection to Corporal Skewes, but it was nice to have the guess confirmed. It was seeing Fletcher that set Nate back on his heels. Nate had assumed Fletcher wasn't deeply involved yet, but obviously he was wrong. He wasn't completely surprised, but he knew this would destroy Becca. For all his faults, Fletcher was still her brother, and she loved him.

Nevertheless, Nate's job was to stop England's traitors. Brother or not, Fletcher was going to be arrested.

The major began the exchange, only for everyone to realize that Fletcher was brand new at this kind of thing. Or he was trying to show off for someone's benefit. Either way, there was way too much posturing.

Fletcher crowed as he opened the first crate, talking about how superior the English rifles were to anything else the French had. Then he asked for the money, and the major tossed him the purse.

Fletcher made a show of looking at it, then he rocked back on his heels. "This'll get you one crate," he said, shoving the first crate forward. "The second will cost you."

"That wasn't the agreement," the major growled.

"It is now," Fletcher said, as he dropped his boot on top of the other crate. "You've got more on you. You Frenchies always do."

Good God, how stupid could he be? Napoleon didn't go about handing large purses to his smugglers, and no one shoved a box full of rifles forward then demanded more money. That was handing over weapons that could be turned against him.

The major shot Nate a look. It was the signal to end this farce. Between the two of them, they should be able to take down Fletcher and the Corporal. But then the unthinkable happened.

A woman's scream split the air.

Becca!

He knew her voice immediately, even distorted in this warehouse. And then she bellowed, "Run!" before a sickening sound cut her off.

Chaos erupted. Corporal Skewes took off with the major sprinting right after him.

"Stop!" the major bellowed, just as a shot rang out in the

warehouse.

It was Lord Benedict shooting from his hiding place, and the corporal let out a high-pitched scream. Nate didn't bother to watch. He was already running straight for Becca. He had to skirt around crates, listening for the sound of her—any sound—but there was too much chaos for him to hear anything else. And too much stuff in the way for him to find her.

"Becca!" he called, only to hear her cry out in pain.

Where was she? And what the hell was she doing here?

So many thoughts crowded in. He couldn't fight them all as he searched for her. She couldn't be involved, could she? He couldn't believe it. But her brother was here. Had Fletcher dragged her in? But… No… And…

Damn it all to hell! Where was she?

He heard a muffled sound from his left. It was a heavy thud and a scramble as someone large ran away. The baron? Could be. It could also be Prinny, for all he could tell. Either way, he jumped over several bolts of fabric only to see the one thing he feared.

Becca. Crumpled to the floor, surrounded by blood.

Chapter Thirty-One

BECCA WOKE WITH a pounding headache. She felt strong arms around her and heard…chaos. Men's voices. Grunting sounds. And Nate murmuring in her ear.

"Wake up, sweetheart. You're safe. Wake up."

She felt such joy at hearing him. Such wonder to feel his arms around her. He was safe. She was safe. They were together.

She pressed her face into his chest and breathed deeply.

Then a flash of pain had her stiffening.

"Ow," she said.

"You've hit your head," he said. "Go slow. Does anything else hurt?"

Anything else? Everything else! But nothing so specific as the pounding in her head.

Damn it, she was going to have straighten up out of his arms. She didn't want to, but the sounds around them were getting clearer. A man's voice issuing commands. And Fletcher complaining.

Oh hell. Fletcher.

She remembered everything now. The baron. Her idiot brother. And her choice to scream. She should have done it at the beginning. Then Fletcher would have had the chance to run, but she'd been looking for a better option and waited too long. As it was, she'd struggled with the baron, trying to hold him here so Nate could arrest the real culprit. Then…

He must have hit her.

"Becca," Nate said against her ear. "Why were you here?"

"To stop Fletcher."

He grunted.

"Where's the baron?" she asked.

"Was he the one who hit you?" There was a hard growl in his voice that Rebecca appreciated. She'd like to do the man more violence as well. But at the moment, all she really wanted was to stay in Nate's arms.

Unfortunately, she heard footsteps approaching as another man called out.

"Nate? Where are you?"

"Over here," he answered. Then he spoke low into her ear. "Don't say anything. Let me explain."

How she wanted to do exactly as he ordered. She could just close her eyes and let Nate handle everything. Especially when he started to shrug out of his jacket as he whispered, "I'm going to try to hide your face. Maybe we can—"

"No."

Hiding was the reaction of a child, and she needed to take responsibility for what she'd done. And though she hated the necessity, she had to take responsibility for her brother, too. Because she'd already made the decision that she couldn't bear to see him hang.

Damned arrogant idiot.

"They're going to think you are working with your brother. You'll hang too!"

She swallowed. Up until this moment, that hadn't even occurred to her. But she'd screamed to warn her brother. Of course, they would think her in league with him.

"I won't hide what I've done," she said.

He touched her cheek, his expression tight. "I can't protect you," he whispered. She heard true anguish in his tone, and she gave him a wan smile. He'd always wanted to protect her, but he couldn't. And he needed to know that was all right.

"I made my choices, Nate. I always have. You're not responsible for this."

He winced. "I knew you'd say that. But Becca—"

"You are not responsible for my choices. You never have been."

She saw her meaning hit him. He knew she was talking about her father's heart attack, the separation between their two families, and even his lies. He was only guilty of his own actions, and she her own. There was no more blame between them.

"Becca," he said, his voice breaking. And then they were out of time.

Lord Benedict appeared in front of them, his expression tightening as he looked down at her.

"A family affair then," he said, and it wasn't a question.

"No," said Nate.

"Not like you think," she said. Then she smoothed out her skirt, wincing as blood smeared down her dress from her hands. She hadn't realized they were scraped until this moment. Well, she didn't want to wear this gown again anyway. "Is there someplace we could talk?"

"You mean gaol? Because that's where you're both going."

She winced as she watched the other pretend Frenchman pull her brother around the crate of silks. Fletcher was in handcuffs, and he was sputtering all sorts of stupidities. He was innocent. He was trying to capture French spies. This wasn't what it looked like.

"Shut up Fletcher!" she snapped. "It was exactly what it looked like. You were trying to sell rifles to the French. You betrayed yourself, your family, and your country." She grimaced as she struggled to gain her feet, thanks to Nate's support.

Damn her head hurt. She pressed a hand to temple. It came away bloody, but not overly so. And though she hissed as she explored the wound, she already knew it wasn't deep enough to threaten her life. Indeed, the more she thought about it, she realized her jaw hurt like the devil. The baron must have punched her, and she'd fallen on the other crate.

She was lucky she'd only lost consciousness for a moment. She could have broken her neck.

"Shut up, you stupid bitch!" her brother bellowed.

Nate punched him. Straight in the jaw, hard enough to snap his head around, but not so hard as to shut him up. Her brother howled in response, and it took Lord Benedict to silence him.

The aristocrat got eye to eye with him and said with silky ease, "Be quiet or I shall authorize the hangman's noose for you right now. You will not be the first person the major and I have dispatched. Nor will you be the last."

The man restraining Fletcher—the major, if she guessed correctly—glanced out the door. "The Thames is right there. I gather he's the one who flung Nate in it a month ago. Would be a fitting punishment. We can see if he can swim as well."

"We'd have to break his ribs first," Nate growled.

"It wasn't Fletcher. It was the baron's men," Rebecca said, her tone weary. "My brother only watched."

Nate grumbled something incoherent, then shook his head. "Just keep him quiet."

"I'm sorry they didn't kill you," Fletcher growled.

She sighed. Her brother really was the sorest loser. What was it in him that kept him from accepting his mistakes? Whatever it was, she couldn't let him hang.

She straightened and addressed Lord Benedict, as he seemed to be the man in charge. "Fletcher wasn't the one in charge of this disaster. Even I could see that he was miserably bad at it." She looked at her brother. "You've never been in charge of such an exchange before, have you?"

His jaw firmed, refusing to answer. He would rather hang than admit he was bad at something.

"Doesn't matter," Lord Benedict said. "Once is all it takes."

"But wouldn't you rather have the baron? And not just him, but all of the people involved in his schemes?"

The major's eyes narrowed. "Do they all involve trading with the French?"

"Not all. But Corporal Skewes is not his only stooge working in the Tower. He has two more."

Fletcher's eyes widened at that, and his weren't the only ones. Corporal Skewes was tying a bandage around a shallow wound in his arm, but he managed to throw her a hateful glare. "An' how would you know that?"

Because the baron had told her. Then she'd told him how to expand his business with the use of women. It was only luck of the moment—with Nate as inspiration—that had pushed her to getting that information.

"I'll tell you everything." She looked straight at Lord Benedict. "But only if you let my brother go."

Lord Benedict didn't say anything. He left it to the major to question her.

"How do you know?" he pressed. "And how will we know it's true?"

She shrugged. "Some men are idiots around women. Others—" Her glance flicked to her brother. "Are just idiotic. Henry's due in town tomorrow. He'll see that Fletcher doesn't sin again."

"Not good enough," the major snapped. "He would have gleefully sold guns to the French. He's a traitor."

Becca winced, but she'd been prepared for this. "What if you transport him," she said. "He can't help the French while in the colonies."

"You can't! I'm the son of an earl!" Fletcher cried, but no one paid the least attention to him.

Then Nate spoke, his soft words were almost kind. "He was terrible at it. Without the baron, I doubt he could cause more trouble."

"It was treason!" the major growled.

"He failed at it."

Benedict stepped forward. "He'll cause more problems. Wherever he is, he'll try something again."

Nate nodded. "But it will hurt her if you kill him. I can't... I can't agree to that."

Rebecca felt a flush of heat roll over her skin. If anyone should be out for Fletcher's blood, it should be Nate. But he was pleading for Fletcher's life—for her sake.

"Thank you," she whispered to him.

His gaze turned to her but steadily hardened as he looked at her head wound. "You need a doctor," he said.

"No," she said, as she gingerly tried to wipe the blood off her temple. "A surgeon will do. But someone should come with me. I need to tell you everything while it's still fresh in my memory."

"I'm not leaving your side," Nate said.

She smiled. "What about Fletcher?"

"Gaol," Lord Benedict said. "Until we know that he will bring no harm to anyone else."

Until he was sure that her information was good.

Fletcher objected, of course. It made no difference. The major took control of him and the corporal. Rebecca heard him say something about arranging for the baron's arrest as well.

She left that to them. Her head was swimming, and exhaustion was beginning to pull at her. Nate supported her, guiding her gently to a waiting carriage. But they were not left alone. Within seconds of heading to a carriage, Benedict grabbed Nate's elbow. The two stepped aside for a few whispered words, and then Benedict left to help the major.

"What was that about?" she asked Nate.

"Just making sure that my head's on straight."

She frowned at him. "Is it?"

"I honestly don't know. We can transport Fletcher, but he can just as easily board a ship back."

True. But that wasn't tomorrow's problem. Right now, she was grateful to climb into the carriage and rest her head back on the squabs.

"I hope I don't get blood on everything."

"If you're worried, lean on me."

"Then I'll get blood all over you."

"I've suffered worse from your family."

She shot him a worried look, but his lips were quirked into a smile.

"You're making fun!" she realized. "My head is pounding, and you're making fun."

"It made you smile."

Had it? Yes, she supposed it had. "I'm sorry about Fletcher," she said. "About everything."

"It's not your fault."

"It's not yours either."

His lips curled as he pulled her close. "I love you," he whispered. She heard it clearly, even though his words were barely audible. She tensed, wanting to straighten up to face him, but he didn't let her. Especially when his tone turned angry. "And what the devil were you doing there? I told you to stay at the ball!"

Ah yes. Well, that would take some explanation. Fortunately, there wasn't time as Lord Benedict climbed into the carriage.

"We're going to the best surgeon I know," he said as he shut the carriage door. "Better even than Nate at stitching up a head wound."

Her eyes widened. Nate knew how to sew up wounds?

"He's joking," Nate said in an undertone. "The major has the best stitches in the field. But we'll go to a surgeon who has ten times the experience of either of us. You might not have a scar."

"Of course I will." She'd be lucky if she didn't have a long, big bare streak of a scar through her hair.

"Hush," he said, squeezing her shoulders.

"Speak," Lord Benedict contradicted. "Tell me everything, and don't try to soften it. I still think you should be hung right alongside your brother."

"No!" Nate cried, but she stopped him by squeezing his hand.

"I'll tell him." And so she did. But even as she recounted everything the baron had said, her mind was on something else entirely.

Nate loved her. And she had yet to tell him how she felt.

Of course, none of that would matter if she was hung for treason.

Chapter Thirty-Two

BECCA WASN'T HUNG for treason, though it took all of Nate and Lord Benedict's combined influence to keep her from prosecution. Keeping her out of the scandal was impossible, and Nate quietly seethed every time he heard a whisper of gossip about her.

Everyone knew she'd been courted by the baron. And everyone guessed that she'd disappeared from the Penrose ball with him. No one could know what she'd risked to expose the bastard. Whenever Nate thought about that, his blood ran cold. She could have died so easily! And every time he thought of losing her, he dreamed about running the man through.

Fortunately, justice for the baron came swiftly. He was drawn and quartered under great public spectacle. His daughter was swept away to live with her maternal grandparents, which was a relief to everyone. Nate managed to send her nurse along as well, since the woman would never get a position in London. And the scandal died down with relative speed as other things took precedence.

Like a ducal wedding.

Ras and Kynthea were married with all the pomp appropriate to the situation. And that was a much-needed boost to Nate and Rebecca. Being the best man to a duke was a feather in his cap, but he cared much more that as a bridesmaid to Kynthea, Becca was finally given some grace among the *haut ton*.

Even her older brother Henry seemed pleased. And nobody

remarked on Fletcher's absence. It was well known that he had departed for the colonies. Indeed, he'd made quite a show of investigating "exciting opportunities," promising to write to those who wanted to invest. Nate and Lord Benedict were on hand to watch him board the ship, and they both breathed a sigh of relief when the boat finally left port.

But this moment was about the official end to the season. Kynthea and Ras were married and waved off on their bridal trip after hosting a wedding breakfast for nearly a hundred people. Nate was left to manage Ras's correspondence for the summer, and Becca was given leave to remain in her family's London house with control of her dowry.

That had been the biggest shock. She and Henry had closeted themselves together for a full day after Fletcher departed. They'd come to an arrangement that allowed her to be independent for the summer as a test. It helped that Henry had friends who would keep an eye on her. Gentlemen friends, it turned out, that Nate then spent a week investigating.

They were acceptable, and Becca was in alt at being in near complete control of her life. Especially after she trimmed the staff to its bare minimum and replaced all her brother's servants with ones of her own choice.

If only the two of them could find some time alone together. Between the wedding and mopping up the fallout from the baron's arrest, neither of them had had any time. He'd managed to dance with her at various balls, but it was never private and never enough.

Worse, after everything, they seemed awkward with one another. Now that all the traitorous drama was over, they ought to be able to speak openly with one another. Instead, their lives were consumed with the wedding and deporting her brother. But all of that finished after the wedding breakfast. Once the happy couple was sent away, the servants began cleaning the elaborate affair, and they were finally able to catch a moment alone.

Nate waited until Becca finished giving instructions about the flowers and the leftover food. He was happy to rest while she finished. He'd been on his feet, directing the parade of the carriages as they departed from the banquet hall. Everyone wanted a last word with him, not because he was important but because they hoped for a last bit of gossip about the duke. He'd obliged, of course, with something innocuous. That was Lord Nathaniel's specialty, after all, and he had to maintain the persona. At least until he was private with Becca again. Which came a few minutes later when she collapsed into a chair beside him.

"The duke has an amazing staff," she said with a sigh, "but there's still so much to do."

"What happened to Zoe?" She was Kynthea's cousin and her maid of honor. Normally, supervising the cleanup would be her task.

"She left for her horses during the breakfast. She loves Kynthea, but she's got a bet with Prinny she intends to win."

"So she left all the tasks to you," he said as he took hold of her hand.

Becca smiled at him. He was watching closely, waiting for the tension to appear between her brows. It came in slowly but was undeniable once her gaze slid from his.

"Becca," he said, opting for a bluntness that hadn't been possible in the middle of a ball. "What has happened between us? Why won't you look me in the eye?"

Her gaze jumped to his, disproving his question. But then her cheeks flushed pink, and he knew something was up.

"Becca," he said, "we have been through too much together for you to run scared now."

She swallowed. "Lord Benedict has spoken with me."

Fear sparked hot and bright inside him. He didn't want her to risk herself in any way ever again. But Benedict had seen how calmly she managed the baron, how well she remembered every detail of what she'd gotten him to say. She would be an asset to the country, and Lord Benedict knew it. More importantly, she would enjoy a life beyond the restriction of a country wife and mother.

But the danger was real.

"Do you know what he wants?" he asked carefully.

"I believe so."

"And do you want to work for him?"

"I think so."

He swallowed. His own training had taken years, but he'd been sent into a war. She would most likely have a part to play in society. "You would need to get married. Debutantes are too restricted, and even ladies with their own fortunes need masculine help."

"I know."

He paused, then he squeezed her hands. "Does that mean you are reconsidering my marriage proposal?"

She snorted. "I never *stopped* considering it."

That was heartening.

"Henry made me promise not to make any significant decisions until after the summer. He believes there have been too many changes, and I need to understand what it is like being on the shelf before I consider anything else."

Nate chuckled. "Henry loves taking a great deal of time to decide everything. Even down to the color of his waistcoat."

"Oh," she said blithely, "that takes no time at all. He chooses black. Always black because it can be used for every event from a funeral to a wedding."

Yes, the man had been wearing black this morning. But at least he had managed a white cravat. "Becca—"

"I do not know if you still want me," she finally blurted out. "My brother is a traitor!"

He sighed. "Of course, I—"

"Don't say, 'Of course!'" she snapped. "I came to London an aging debutante. Now I am an independent woman, after a fashion, and Henry is right. I don't know who I am now, but I know you are in love with a sixteen-year-old me who hasn't existed for a very long time."

"That's not true." And when she cast him a doubtful look, he lifted his chin. "I still love her, yes, but you are so much better than her." Then he leaned back in the chair. "Or perhaps you are delaying because you do not know me now. After all my deceptions, that is not surprising."

She opened her mouth to deny it but stopped at his arch look.

"It is only natural to be unsure of me," he said.

"Natural or not," she said, her voice prim, "I have a solution." Then she flashed him an uncertain smile. "Or at least an experiment."

His brows rose. "Yes?"

"Would you like to try the truth serum with me?"

It took a moment before he could process what she said. And he was still confused. "What?"

"We'd take it at the same time. We can ask questions of one another and hear the truth in each answer."

"It's not dangerous?"

She shook her head. "I don't think so. But I don't have much experience with it. It would be a risk."

One he was very open to taking. Especially since Lord Benedict had expressed interest in the brew as well. "The only way to get more experience is to experiment," he said.

"I agree."

"When should we do it?"

She grinned as she looked around the rapidly clearing hall. "No one expects us to do anything after today. Weddings are exhausting affairs."

"You should rest. We have the whole summer." Assuming he wasn't sent off to France on another mission.

"I will rest," she said firmly. "This afternoon." Then she leaned close. "Come to the back entrance of my house tonight."

"Are you sure—"

She pressed a finger to his lips. "I am sure. But you must be certain as well."

He'd never been more certain of anything in his life.

Chapter Thirty-Three

WHAT A WONDERFUL thing to be mistress of one's own home! No more placating Mother, no more trying to get Henry to wash the mud off before meals, and most especially no more tiptoeing around Fletcher's moods. She was alone in her own home, and she could give the servants the night off whenever she wanted.

And tonight, she wanted.

She knew where tonight might end. She'd already spent a night in his bed. But she also knew that Henry was right. Everything had changed for her in a very short amount of time. How could she possibly know what she wanted now? It was too soon to decide anything.

But Henry never decided anything that he could avoid or put off, so his opinion wasn't worth much.

Either way, she prepared for the evening by first going to the apothecary and learning everything she could possibly learn about the creation, storage, and uses of the truth serum. It didn't take long. She was given the recipe and told that no one had ever come back to describe their experiences. And that Rebecca was the only soul who had asked for a second dose.

Then she dressed casually, ate dinner, and sent her servants away. Tonight, she would be alone, she declared. And then she sat by the servants' entrance and pretended to read a book. Nate's most recent book, actually, and her pretense fairly quickly turned into reality.

He entered well after dark while she was curled around a candelabra trying to make out the next page and the next and the next. He opened the door quietly, saw what she was doing, and grinned as if she had gifted him with the stars themselves.

"Oh good God," she moaned as she set aside the book. "Tell me the villain doesn't fall for that stupid a trick."

"Which one? No wait. Don't tell me. You'll just have to read it to find out."

"Oh never mind," she huffed. "Besides, I'm sure he doesn't. Your villains are always smarter than I expect." She dropped her chin on her hand. "Just like you." It was his heroines who needed work.

"I, smarter than you expect? Or extra villainous?"

She grinned. "I won't tell you. You'll just have to guess."

He smiled back and then took her face in his hands. The motion was quick, but his touch was gentle. And then he pressed his mouth to hers. After the awkwardness between them, this was like a balm to her heart. He still wanted her. He still cherished her. And he kissed like a dream come true, all sweet gentleness but with increasing hunger. She felt it in the pressure against her lips, in the thrust of his tongue, and…

And the way he pulled back when she wanted to arch into him.

"We said we were going to talk." He flashed her a rueful expression. "I don't mind waiting, but…"

"We need to be sure of one another first."

He shrugged. "I'm sure."

She was, too. She wouldn't have invited him here if she wasn't. But prudence dictated that she at least pretend to consider her options. And besides, she had something important to discuss with him. Something in which he was the only one who could properly advise her.

"Have you eaten?" she asked. "Cook has been trying to learn a Cornish pasty. She has a long way to go before making it perfectly, but it is—"

"Truly?" he cried. "Oh, how I have missed those!"

She laughed and unfolded herself from her seat. "Then we shall—"

"No," he interrupted. "Not yet. Let us do what we came here for first. I confess, having never been dosed with a truth serum, I am anxious about its effects."

She nodded. "Of course." To be honest, she was nervous as well, but that had nothing to do with the serum. It was all about what she had to share. "I've got it set up in the upstairs parlor."

His brows rose. "Upstairs? Isn't that—"

"No one is home. I have sent them all away on holiday for the rest of the week."

"The week!"

"Yes. I told them I needed quiet."

"But a week without servants," he said slowly. "Are you sure—"

She lifted her chin. "Do you imagine that I cannot dress and cook for myself until Monday? How long have you gone without a servant?"

"For most of several years, but—"

"But I am a lady of leisure? Do you forget that I have tended the sick, managed a household, and often done so without benefit of help?"

He flushed at her arch tone. "Yes, I suppose I had."

And right there was the crux of why she was afraid of leaping ahead with him. "You still think me a pampered child of sixteen. Even though I was never all that pampered."

"Not a sixteen-year-old," he said. "More a..." He glanced down at the book she'd been reading.

She guessed what he was thinking without him saying the words. "I am the heroine of your books, aren't I?" It wasn't conceit. She'd already seen similarities between herself and the women in his books.

"That's not how I see you."

She arched her brows.

"It's not how I see you now."

She wanted to believe it. She wanted to believe that he understood she was a lot more capable than anyone had ever given her credit for. But she was so used to being under-appreciated that she doubted anyone could see her true self. And as her husband, he needed to see her.

"Let's go upstairs," she finally said. "I want to know what you really think."

He swallowed but held out his arm for her to show the way. "You think this will tell you?"

"Yes," she said. Then she hedged. "Maybe. We will have to try it to find out."

He agreed, and very soon they were seated in two cozy chairs by an unlit fireplace. She poured the appropriate amount in two glasses of wine. They clinked, then drank, watching each other's eyes over the rims.

And when they were done, Nate set his glass down and pulled off his cravat. "How long will it take to go into effect?"

"Fifteen minutes or so. Not long."

"Hmmm." His gaze held hers for a long moment before looking away.

"Lord Benedict visited this afternoon," she abruptly said. "We spoke for nearly an hour."

"Today! That was fast."

She nodded. "He doesn't seem to be a man who waits, once he's made up his mind."

"No, he isn't. What did he want?"

"He wants me to assist the Foreign Office. Nothing fancy, he said. Little stuff to see how I adjust and learn."

"Is that all?"

"No. He mentioned that he is interested in finding a political wife. According to him, gentlemen with talented wives are the most valuable diplomats."

Nate's expression tightened. "You are not a political woman. You have never been involved in such things."

"I haven't," she said, feeling a twinge of guilt that she was enjoying Nate's discomfort. "But a smart woman can learn, can't she? And I—"

"You are teasing me," he said. "You have never expressed interest in marrying Lord Benedict."

She cast him a coy glance. "That wouldn't be the polite thing, would it? To speak of one suitor with another."

He leaned forward, capturing her hands. "I thought we were beyond such games. You do not need to tease me to make me jealous of all the men who prance after you."

There hadn't been that many men, but it was nice to feel noticed. And since he was being so earnest—and honest—she twisted her hands until they were palm to palm. "I'm not trying to make you jealous, Nate. I want to know what you think. You know better than anyone what work with Lord Benedict would entail. How dangerous is it?"

He struggled with his answer. His mouth twisted and his jaw flexed. But in the end, his words were exactly what she'd feared. "A little dangerous sometimes, a lot dangerous sometimes, and everything in between." He pulled her hands to his mouth, pressing a kiss to her fingers. "I want to marry you, Rebecca. I want you to have my children. And I want to be with you as they grow, writing my books in the country and—"

"You would give up your work? The work with Lord Benedict?"

He paused before giving her a careful answer. "I am too old to keep working as I have been. But…" He shrugged. "Benedict thinks I could come out of the shadows. That I could be helpful when this war has ended."

"He said as much to me. That the work for women is vital, especially during peace negotiations."

Nate tightened his grip before releasing her. Then he stood up and began to pace about the room. She watched his slow movements, seeing in him a suppressed fear. One that she could not name but knew would come out before the night was over.

And indeed, he began the tale by abruptly turning to her. "So Benedict has offered us both a position. As a couple, we could work with him and Lord Castlereagh. We could help shape the world after Napoleon's defeat."

She nodded. That appeared to be exactly what Benedict was offering. And she was intrigued. For a woman who had been locked up for most of her life in Cornwall, the idea of participating on the world stage was extraordinarily appealing. Assuming, of course, she had someone beside her to teach her how to go on, to show her how to be both safe and effective.

Someone like Nate. But only if he wanted to.

She looked at him, trying to feel what he wanted. What she wanted. "Do you truly want to sit by a fire in Cornwall and watch our babies grow?" she asked.

"Yes," he said. "I don't want to put you in danger."

"I think you would be bored."

"I think you would be, too." There was defeat in his tone. They had a way forward, it seemed. Marriage and work with Lords Benedict and Castlereagh. Except he didn't seem to want it.

"You must be honest with me, Nate. As you have never been before." She stood up and felt the world wobble a bit as she did. The truth serum was taking effect. She welcomed the experience even as she crossed the room to look in Nate's eyes. "What are you afraid of?"

Her eyes widened as she spoke. She hadn't meant to ask that. She'd meant to ask him what he wanted. But instead, those words came out. And once uttered, she did not take them back. She knew he wanted her. He'd said as much from the beginning. But now she had to know what kept them apart. And that rested upon his fears. And hers.

"You are unsteady," he said. "How do you feel?"

She heard the concern in his voice. And she *felt* it, too. He was genuinely concerned about her.

"I am fine. You?"

He swallowed. "So I will not be able to lie to you now?"

"Try it."

"I have danced naked in African ceremonies covered only in white paint."

She blinked, startled by his words. Worse, she couldn't tell the truth or the lie of it. All she felt was his humor.

"Have you done that?"

"Not at all." He dropped his head forward until it touched hers. "But I have spoken with those who have."

"And I have sewn purple dresses to be worn by the King of England." She wrinkled her nose. "But I wore it first."

He laughed at that, the humor seeming to sparkle around them in tiny flashes of joy.

"I should love to see you in a gown of purple velvet."

She smiled, feeling as if they were starting to meet each other in this strange place of truth. It wasn't so much that they couldn't lie to one another, but that they were feeling each other more. Their emotions were clearly communicated to one another. A lie would require a separation between them that would be noticeable.

He touched her cheek. "So this is the truth serum?"

She nodded, feeling the arousal that came with his touch and the desire that vibrated between them. But she needed some answers before she surrendered to it. Before she gave herself completely to him.

So she stepped back. "What is your fear, Nate?"

"I have many of them," he said. "But you can guess them all. I fear that you will be hurt. I fear that you don't love me. I fear that just when everything is perfect, it will be ripped away."

She felt the truth in his words. Indeed, it was as though she could see him opening to her gaze. It was the bravest thing she'd ever seen. And then he said the cruelest thing she'd ever heard.

"But it is not my fears that are keeping us apart. It is yours."

She frowned. "I have no fears. Only excitement at the possibilities ahead. I have my own money and establishment now. At least for the summer. I have work ahead if I want it." She touched his arm. "I have a man who says he will marry me."

"All true. And yet, here we are, still talking, still discussing when we should be acting."

"I am not the reason we are apart," she said. And even she could hear the discordance in her words. From the moment she had arrived in London, he had stated his desire. He wanted to be with her. And she was the one who distrusted him.

She felt her face flush. They both knew she'd lied.

"How many of my books have you read?" he asked.

She blinked. "All of them." Those she had missed before, she'd greedily read after she'd learned he was the author.

"And what did you think of them?"

"I loved them, of course." It was true.

He smiled, and this time his fingers stroked down her arms. "What a pair we are. I wrote stories glorifying my love for you, but I never went home to find you. And you read those stories about you, but you never stepped off the page to find me."

"I didn't know!" she said. "No one knows you wrote them."

He nodded. "And you have believed all the lies you were told about me."

She frowned.

"You are no damsel in distress, Becca. You are not my princess to rescue nor the trapped girl in Cornwall who could never escape. You were just told that, and you believed it."

She frowned at him. "And where could I have gone?"

"Exactly where you wanted to go. You went to Mrs. Chenoweth and trained with her. You wandered throughout the county—"

"I didn't wander! I was treating people. Helping and learning."

He nodded. "Exactly. You did as you wanted." He smiled. "And I admire you for it. So now, you are being invited to help your country. It is something you say you want. Why are you hesitating?"

"I'm not. I'm thinking about it."

He arched a brow. "What are you thinking?"

"That… That…" She had no words, and that wasn't like her. But fear echoed in the air between them, which is when she realized he was right. It wasn't his fear that was stopping them. It was hers.

"Don't think," he urged. "Just tell me what you're feeling."

Which would work if she had the words. Instead, she crumpled forward. She knew he'd catch her. And indeed, in a moment, she felt his arms around her. She felt his lips press into her forehead. And then she felt nothing else. Just him. His love. And his patience.

Then words spilled from her lips.

"I don't want to do it alone."

"You won't. You never have to be alone if you don't want to be." He gently guided her to the settee. "If not me, then Lord Benedict and Major Vance will see you safe."

"Benedict said I should be married."

"There are things unmarried women can do. Becca, you are an independent woman now."

"Only for three months!"

"Tell me you can't convince Henry to make it permanent. You have been managing the household money since you were a teenager. The real question is how Henry will manage without you."

Well, that was true.

"You are free, Becca. You can be alone if you want to be. Or not."

She lifted her face to his. "Not."

"But you are afraid." It wasn't a question.

She nodded.

"Because you don't know if you can trust me. After all, you trusted Henry and your mother, and neither one paid any attention to what you wanted. You trusted Fletcher and discovered a million lies."

Perhaps not a million, but close.

"And even I left you when you were sixteen. We were caught—"

"Papa died, and you disappeared." She squeezed his arm. "That wasn't your fault."

"No, but the truth doesn't change. I left."

"So I went my own way, however I could."

"So you have been betrayed by everyone. I suspect trusting me now would be hard."

"But I do trust you!" she cried. And though part of her knew it was the truth, there was a small part who still wondered. Who feared.

He stroked her chin, pulling her gaze up to his. They stayed there, eye to eye for a long moment. Neither said a word, but she felt so many things.

She felt his arms around her as he supported her.

She felt safe here and cherished as she had never been.

She felt his desire for her, slowly climbing as was her own.

And she felt her defenses crack. Bits of the wall she'd built between them—between her and any man—began to break.

"I'm sorry," she whispered. "I guess I don't completely trust you."

He accepted it without complaint. Indeed, he didn't seem surprised. "How can I prove myself to you? What do you need from me?"

Love.

The word reverberated in the air between them. She hadn't asked for it or even said the word out loud. Perhaps he was just offering it. Either way, she felt tentative as she reached for it. Nothing was said, but she felt the decision nonetheless.

Imagine having to choose to accept love. Shouldn't that be easy?

It wasn't. And yet, he was worth it.

So she let her defenses crumble. She allowed her heart and mind to open to his love. She felt it slip in quietly through the cracks. And then it became everything. It filled her. It warmed her. It was…

Perfect.

"No more lies," she said, meaning she would not lie to herself anymore. Of all the people in her life, he had been the most consistent. He'd tried to protect her. He'd given her his trust. And even if he hadn't shown her everything he was, she knew enough. And there would be time to learn everything else.

"No more lies," he echoed. Then he waited until he had her full attention. She gave it to him. Indeed, she couldn't look away if she tried.

"I love you Becca. I always will. Which means I shall do everything I can to protect you, even if you want to become a spy." He leaned forward. "I've never wanted to clip your wings, but you can't fault me for wanting to catch you, should you fall."

"I want you to catch me," she said.

"Anything else?"

She smiled. "I want to marry you. I love you, too."

There it was. They'd both said it and the truth of it reverberated in the room around them. And once said, once expressed in the most honest and open way possible, she decided to express it other ways.

She pressed her mouth to his, kissing him with all the heat and the love she felt inside. He returned it a thousand-fold, not just with his lips and tongue but with the truth swirling around them.

He loved her, and she opened herself up to him completely.

He was slow to undress her. She let him take his time because every touch of his fingers, every brush of fabric against her skin was like a further unfolding. She felt like she was shedding not just her clothes, but the restraint of every lie she had been told about what she could and could not do.

And the biggest lie of all was that she was a poor judge of character. She was an excellent judge! It was only that she had thought the others could see what she saw. In herself. In Nate. In the world.

"I love you," she whispered to him as she at last stepped out of her chemise. "I love every part of you. Even the parts that I am only just learning."

She took her time pulling his clothing away. He appeared equally sensitized. His breath caught every time they touched skin to skin. And when he could caress her, he did so with reverence as awe trembled between them.

"I love you," he said as he drew her naked breast into his mouth.

She arched into him as he teased her nipple with his tongue. And when he began to suck, her knees lost their strength.

He carried her to her bed then. It was an impressive feat given that they were in the parlor and he had quite a few steps to take. But he seemed effortlessly strong to her. And she relaxed into his power, his strength, and the absolute love she saw in his eyes.

"I love you," she whispered as he set her on the bed.

"I love every part of you," he answered as he began to kiss her ribs, her belly, her mons.

She let him spread her legs, opening herself up to his fingers as they thrust inside her. And she grinned when he let her explore his cock as he had never allowed before.

Odd how she felt his every gasp as if it were her own. Glorious that he seemed to revel in her responses. Amazing that they could feel each other this way and know it was the truth.

"Ask me again," she whispered when he settled between her thighs.

"Will you marry me?"

"Yes. A thousand times yes."

"Are you sure about this?" he asked as he pressed his tip at her entrance. "Once we do this, I will not be stopped. Not now, and not tomorrow when I drag you to church."

"Not now, not tomorrow, not ever."

Then she surged upward, using his shoulders for leverage. She arched as she did so, and with her legs wrapped around his thighs, she pulled him inside.

A single quick thrust, and it was done.

She was his. And he was hers.

"I love you," he said as he began to move.

"I love you," she echoed as her body paced itself to him.

And then there was no more talking. Only feeling. Bodies moving, tension mounting. And love. It echoed around them, through them, within them.

When climax hit, it felt like the smallest piece of this glorious experience.

Physical ecstasy.

Soul to soul connection.

Love.

In the morning, when the serum had worn off, and they were face to face with each other, they did it all again.

Then, to her surprised delight, he did indeed take her to the nearest church. He had the special license in his pocket. He'd gotten it a week before and had been waiting on her.

They were married that afternoon.

It took them another week, though, before they met with Lord Benedict to map out their very exciting future.

About the Author

Flirty, dirty and fun! That's how Katherine Lyons likes her love stories. One would think that would lead her to contemporary romance, but she's always loved the witty dialogue and hot, sexy humor of regency romance. She's a big fan of *The Bridgertons, Big Bang Theory* (even though it's over), and her favorite movie is *The Avengers* because she loves the MCU. Stop by her website to sign up for her newsletter, special contests, and geeky giveaways!

www.katherine-lyons.com